Holly Miller grew up in Bedfordshire. Since
university she has worked as a marketer,
editor and copywriter. Holly currently
lives in Norfolk with her husband.

Also by Holly Miller

The Sight of You
What Might Have Been

The Spark

HOLLY MILLER

**HODDER &
STOUGHTON**

First published in Great Britain in 2024 by Hodder & Stoughton
An Hachette UK company
This paperback edition published in 2024

3

A CIP catalogue record for this title is available from the British Library

Paperback 978 1 399 70088 7
ebook ISBN 978 1 399 70089 4

Typeset in Plantin Light by Hewer Text UK Ltd, Edinburgh
Printed and bound in Great Britain by Clays Ltd, Elcograf S.p.A.

Hodder & Stoughton policy is to use papers that are natural, renewable
and recyclable products and made from wood grown in sustainable
forests. The logging and manufacturing processes are expected to
conform to the environmental regulations of the country of origin.

Hodder & Stoughton Ltd
Carmelite House
50 Victoria Embankment
London EC4Y 0DZ

www.hodder.co.uk

The Spark

1

Then

He felt as strongly as I did. Looking back, that was always the best part. With Jamie, it was never one-sided. He loved me in a way that felt like we'd been matched by the universe, the chemistry from colliding stars.

We'd met at high school. A spark straight away, even though we weren't yet teenagers. We lived two streets apart, though we may as well have been under one roof. We walked to school side by side, pretended to study together at night, learnt to love music in his bedroom, one earphone each. He taught me how to play cards and flirt. I liked to make him laugh till he had to leave the room. We were each other's oxygen, inseparable to the point that teachers commented. His parents thought it was adorable. My mother declared us insufferable.

We kissed for the first time on my fifteenth birthday – back row of the cinema, mouths hot and hesitant and shy. Exactly two years after that, we slept together – though everyone already assumed we'd long since done the deed. That had made it even better, because the holding out was a secret we shared. Twenty-four months of snatched glances and sweet anticipation, squeezed hands and whispered compliments.

The moment itself, in the firm familiarity of Jamie's bed and his arms, was exactly how I'd imagined. The months of longing made everything magical. Meaningful and assured, my heart turning to helium.

In our sixth-form yearbook, we were named *Couple most likely to get married.* We got a lot of stick for that, but we didn't care.

The day of our A-level results, Jamie, Lara and I took a bottle of cava to the riverside in the shadows of the Tudor buildings backing onto Elm Hill.

Finding a sun-worn patch of grass, we lifted our faces to the hot blue sky. Above our heads, doves sailed serenely between the pantiled roofs. Down on the river, people were messing about in hired punts. We could hear the splash of struck water, the occasional blurt of a disgruntled goose.

Next to me, Jamie reached for my hand. My mind galloped, the stress of results day finally starting to ebb away. Our future was a gift I'd been waiting for for years, and now it was here, moments from being unwrapped.

Lara popped the cava cork. My best friend, my fiercest ally. I'd known her since day one of primary school. 'Freedom,' she declared, then passed the bottle to me.

'Freedom.' I drank, the bubbles tart on my tongue, before handing it to Jamie.

'Four A-stars.' Lara looked at Jamie. 'Cheers for showing us all up.'

He snapped the head off a daisy and flicked it at her.

Lara had spent the past few years rebelling hard and barely studying. But she'd done better than me and only marginally worse than Jamie. She was just naturally bright like that.

'Your mum and dad will be so proud,' I said to Jamie.

Jamie could have done anything, gone anywhere. We all knew it. He'd wanted to be an architect since he was old enough to ask where buildings came from.

He groaned. 'They still want to take me out for dinner tonight.'

'Just you?' Lara said. 'Not Neve too?'

I shot Lara a look. 'You should go,' I told him.

He shook his head, lay back on the grass. 'They'll only lecture me.'

About how you're ruining your life, staying here with me.

Jamie's father had made his fortune in real estate six years earlier, and now he had money to lavish on his sons, and grand ambitions for Jamie, his youngest. Russell Group university, exotic travel, well-connected friends and acquaintances, members' clubs. First-class and five-star everything. Essentially, Jamie was destined to become a clone of Harry, his older brother.

'I'm not going to dinner with them,' Jamie said, rolling towards me, fixing me with his lodestone eyes. No-one could spellbind me with their gaze the way Jamie could.

Lara tilted her head. 'I think you're the only person I know who's more stubborn than me.'

I wasn't sure I agreed. Jamie was principled, not stubborn

– though I knew Lara would say there wasn't a difference.

We passed the cava bottle between us, getting steadily tipsier as the grass drank in damp and the sky grew dark. We made the short walk into the city centre, dumping the empty bottle in a bin. I wished, afterwards, that we hadn't thrown it away.

The three of us stayed out till the early hours, moving from bar to bar. Jamie's hand was around my waist the whole night. Our phones ran out of battery. Lara left us to go to a party with a boy she'd just met. Eventually, as dawn spilled like milk over the church spires and rooftops, Jamie and I found ourselves kissing against the bowed wall of an alleyway. The prospect of our future burned in my mind like the rising sun. We stumbled the two miles back to his mum and dad's house, anaesthetised by booze.

We wobbled upstairs to his bedroom. Shared a pint of water, kissed, had sex with our clothes still on. We gasped each other's names again and again as the bed rocked and squeaked beneath us.

Twice, I saw the light go on in the hallway. Heard the creak of a floorboard, then muffled voices.

It was only later that I realised how loud we'd been. How disrespectful. That I'd given his parents another reason to loathe me, if they didn't have enough already.

I woke late and alone. Sitting up, head thrumming, I could hear voices again. Only this time, they weren't muffled.

Sunlight was pouring like warm water through a gap in

the curtains. I craved fresh air. Jamie's room was stacked high with half-packed cardboard boxes, the precursor to his parents' forthcoming move to Putney. Jamie's grandfather had died that spring, after years of needing constant care, so now his parents were fulfilling a long-held ambition to move to London.

·They had wanted Jamie to move there too. But Jamie knew I couldn't afford to go to uni in London. So he'd told his parents he wanted to study architecture in Norwich, and move into a house with me. We'd been together three years by then – but what they'd once thought adorable had turned into a cause for concern. They kept sitting him down, asking if he was sure. Chris, his dad, even took him out for beers and reminded him there were 'lots of women' out there. He asked Harry to talk sense into him.

I'd never asked Jamie to stay. I wouldn't have. I wanted the best for him, too.

They had taken all his posters down. The walls were now scarred with smudges of Blu Tack. I felt a twinge of sadness that I would probably never see this room again. The room where we'd fallen in love. Where we'd spent so many hours laughing, touching, kissing. Planning all the ways in which we'd stay together for ever.

Eventually, the door opened and Jamie walked in, carrying something under his arm. He set it down, then sat heavily on the edge of the bed. I could see the back of his neck had flushed red, the way it did whenever he was upset.

I leaned over to see what it was. A painting – though I didn't recognise it. It looked American, depicted four people in a diner after dark. It had a desolate, almost eerie

5

aura, and I loved it instantly, even though I didn't understand it.

'They all waited for me at the restaurant last night,' Jamie said eventually, flatly. His light brown hair was damp, indicating he'd already showered. He smelt of Lynx and toothpaste. 'My grandma was there. She'd been wanting to give me this, to say congratulations.' He gestured to the painting. 'It was my grandad's. He knew how much I loved it.'

I realised how it must have looked: that I'd encouraged him to stay out drinking last night. *Sod your parents, scrap your plans, you only live once.* Not only that, but they'd had to listen to us too, when we finally stumbled home. We'd been so thoughtless.

But the truth was, I loved Jamie's family. I envied them. I enjoyed feeling, even for just a few snatched moments every now and then, that I was somehow a part of what they had.

'Guess what Dad just told me,' Jamie said.

An impossible challenge. I waited.

'He bought a flat, a couple of months ago. In London. Soho. For me to live in.'

I didn't say anything, though I felt ribbons of disquiet kinking through me.

'Kind of like . . . a leg-up,' he said.

Not to me. A leg-up was Lara being awarded money from a hardship fund so she could go to uni. Being bought a flat was . . . a lottery win.

They'd done the same for his brother Harry, helped him out with an apartment in Zurich, where he now lived and worked as a banker. He was ten years older than Jamie, and

I'd only met him once, a few years earlier. I could only remember that he smelt very strongly of tobacco.

Still. His parents having money wasn't Jamie's fault. I'd known him when they were struggling financially, too.

'A flat in Soho sounds . . . pretty amazing.' I reached out and stroked the back of his neck. His skin was warm and smooth as a pebble on a beach. He arched against me slightly, the tension sinking from his shoulders.

'Money's not everything, Neve.'

I was pretty sure only people with money said stuff like that. But I let it slide.

'I mean, yeah. London could be good. But they're missing one massive thing.'

'What?' I whispered.

'I wouldn't have you.'

This could only mean that me living in that flat with him was explicitly Not An Option. Or possibly conditional of the whole arrangement.

'I want to be with you,' he said. 'Let's build a life here.'

'Don't sacrifice anything for me.'

'I won't. I'm not. I love you.'

I leaned forward and kissed him, felt him shiver. 'What does it mean?'

'What?'

'The painting.'

'Grandad said . . . it was about loneliness. Or maybe fear. It was painted during the war.'

I kissed him again. 'Your parents think I'm holding you back.'

'I don't care. I love you. I love you, Neve.'

I slid my hand inside his dressing gown and felt him inhale, breath sharp with pleasure as my fingers skated over his skin. I couldn't help myself. I wanted to show him, again, just how much I loved him.

People kept telling me it was impossible that, aged eighteen, I'd found the person I wanted to spend my life with.

And yet, here we were.

'It's you and me, Neve, for ever.' The words slid from his mouth into mine. They tasted so good, exactly what I wanted to hear.

'For ever,' I breathed back.

2.

Now

My screen is now the only light in the deserted office. It glows bright as a fish tank in the gloom. I check the time, stretch my arms above my head. Ten o'clock. Another hour should do it, then I can hit *save* on this pitch pack before my final read-through tomorrow.

My phone rings. Its vibrato makes me jump in the library-like hush of empty open-plan.

It is, surprisingly, my ex-boyfriend Leo.

'Hey,' he says languidly, like it's this time last year and he's asking me what type of beer he should pick up for tea.

'I'm working,' I say politely, not at all keen on encouraging any misplaced nostalgia. 'What's up?'

'*Plus ça change.*'

'I don't know what that means.' (Neither does he.) 'Can I help?'

He exhales. I hear the click of a lighter. Within the space of ten seconds, I've been reacquainted with the key traits of Leo's that used to wind me up the most. I just need him to call me *babe* and start talking about cryptocurrency, and he'll have covered at least the top five.

'Babe, I thought you should hear it from me first.'

I keep my eyes on my screen, delete a rogue apostrophe, add in a couple of commas. Is the font too small?

'I'm getting married.'

'Oh. Really?' A beat. 'Congratulations.'

His girlfriend – now fiancée, I guess – is an ex-colleague. They met while Leo and I were still together. The jury's out on whether things overlapped. But the truth is, in my heart, I'm not sure I care that much.

'You should come.'

'To the wedding?'

'Well, yeah.'

This baffles me. I've had maybe three conversations with Leo since I ended it, zero with her. He's the only person I know who would issue an invite to a wedding more casually than he would one to dinner at Nando's.

I sigh, scan my screen again. The presentation is a pitch for new business that I'm handling alone, the conversion of a Grade I listed mansion close to the North Norfolk coast. Winning the work would be another huge tick on my path to promotion.

'I don't think that would be appropriate,' I say, eventually. 'But . . . I sincerely wish you all the best, Leo.'

For a couple of moments, he doesn't respond, just fiddles with his lighter. *Click, click.*

'Can I offer you some advice, Neve? As a friend?'

I bristle at both suggestions. 'Sure. Why not?'

'You work too hard.'

'That's not advice.'

'Okay. Well, call it . . . a well-intentioned observation.'

I consider reminding him that if I were prone to needing life tips, the last person I would take them from is a man who's been fired from three jobs in the past four years. But instead, I draw a breath and smile, the way I do whenever a client is losing their cool. 'Is that everything?'

Click, click. 'Yeah, I guess.'

'Good luck, Leo.'

At this, he just laughs, then rings off.

I block his number, and return to my screen.

I walk home along deserted streets blanched with moonlight. I answer a message from my colleague Parveen, who's up with her young son but still finding time to worry about my work ethic. She mentions high blood pressure. I assure her I've left for the night, then stop off at the shop just before it closes to buy a bottle of wine.

Back home, I kick off my shoes, ditch my bag, stick the white wine in the freezer.

I have spent the last few years lovingly renovating my tiny terraced house, saving hard for quality pieces from designers I adore, scouring junkyards at weekends for reclaimed fireplaces and doors with stained-glass panels, and wooden shutters for my windows. I can't imagine ever leaving this place, now. Leo once asked if I fancied getting a flat together and I reacted like he'd suggested we take up organised crime for a hobby.

I can hear my neighbours arguing. Nothing new there. Something to do with him not making an effort on the night out they've just got home from. I switch on the TV, turn up the volume. I sit in front of it for about five minutes, failing to observe a single thing, then decide I may as well tick a few items off my to-do list while I'm waiting for the wine to chill.

Leo asked me to marry him, once. The context was inexplicable. We were in a bar in Greece. Both drunk in an unstable way, being passive-aggressive about money. Thankfully, I had the presence of mind to turn him down. I knew in my heart – maybe I'd always known – that he wasn't my person.

He did have some attractive qualities. He was very good at making me laugh, and tended not to sweat the small stuff, which offset my inclination to do the opposite. He was also infuriatingly handsome, which probably kept the spark alive well past the point at which we should have jointly snuffed it out. But ultimately, I knew I didn't want to open my eyes when I was eighty, and see Leo lying next to me. For me, the decision was that simple.

I slip on a pair of rubber gloves and set to in my bathroom with steaming water and spray cleaner. I mop the kitchen floor. I run the dishwater on empty with half a lemon stuffed into the top rack, fold linen, apply a hair mask. I steam the creases from my bedsheets.

It's two in the morning by the time I turn out the light. My neighbours have swapped the fight for a session of agonisingly vocal sex. I shut my eyes against the migrainous thump of it, fumble for some headphones so I don't have to hear the things they're taking it in turns to say. I try not to think about my last time, with Leo. And though I do manage that, I don't succeed in stemming the spate of thoughts that follows.

Which is how I find myself downstairs, cross-legged in my pyjamas at three thirty in the morning, trying to meditate my way to relaxation. I fail quite quickly. I never did get the hang of meditating. I just don't have the right wiring for it.

Eventually, I give up on sleep and all efforts to empty my head and make my way into my tiny back garden. Drawing a breath of early-morning air into my chest, I think – as I often do – of Jamie, and of Lara.

I stay out on the patio till I'm shivering, then remember with a jolt something I forgot to do.

Which is how my Friday begins: with the hazardous extraction of glass shards from the white wine explosion inside my freezer. Well, it saved me the hangover, at least.

3.

At lunchtime, Parveen returns from a meeting at a local architect's firm.

She is humming.

Parveen never hums. In fact, none of us do. This isn't that kind of office.

Don't get me wrong – it's a happy place to work. But it's the opposite of leisurely. We are never carefree enough to hum. Some days, we barely have time to caffeinate.

'What's got into you?' I ask her with a smile, as she slides into the chair next to mine.

'Just had a great meeting. At Crave & Co.'

'Oh, for the Millbrook thing? How's it all looking?'

Kelley Lane Interiors, the interior designers where Parveen and I work, has won the interiors contract for the Millbrook Retirement Complex, a purpose-built facility currently under construction to the east of Norwich.

Parveen fans her face with an elevation plan. 'Don't know if I'm just hormonal, but the architect on it is *hot*.'

I laugh.

'Seriously. What's wrong with me? I couldn't stop thinking about having his babies.'

'You've already had babies with someone else, remember?' (Twins, with her lawyer husband, Maz, whom she loves to bits.)

'Oh yeah,' she says, mock-dolefully. 'Still. A girl can dream.'

I've known Parveen for eight years. We started work at KLI during the same summer, and I couldn't imagine being deskmates with anyone else. She's super smart, fiercely quick-witted, and – entertainingly – also the clumsiest person I've ever met, to the point where she now refuses to participate in office coffee runs due to a credible risk of inflicting third-degree burns.

'Tell me about the project.' I love the early stages of a new contract – the meetings and information-gathering, the glow of possibility and potential.

She smiles. 'His name's Ash Heartwell.'

I smile back. 'Genuinely just interested in the project.'

I know Crave & Co. architects – we work with them all the time – and I know *of* Ash Heartwell, but I've never actually met him.

An email pings into my inbox. From Parveen. A link to Ash Heartwell's profile on the Crave & Co. website.

'Er, I'm not going to stalk him. Do you need to borrow my fan, or something?'

'Just have a sneak peek,' she pleads. 'His profile picture looks like an aftershave advert. You can practically smell the Paco Rabanne.'

Reluctantly, I click on the link. It's true – the black-and-white portrait does remind me of something you'd see on the inside front page of *GQ*.

I scan his bio.

Ash joined us after training at the Bartlett School of Architecture. He turned to architecture following an accident in his twenties, which made him reconsider his chosen career path. Having won multiple awards throughout his period of study, Ash is currently assisting on a number of projects.

'You know who he is, don't you?'

'Hmm?' I say, clicking out of the page and back into the fly-through on my screen.

'He's the one who got struck by lightning.'

I feel my mouth turn chalky. I reach for the glass of water on my desk and take a swig.

'Don't you remember? It was a few years ago now. It was in all the papers.'

I do remember the man who got hit by lightning. But I didn't pay attention to it at the time. Because it happened on the same night as something else, something catastrophic that split my world – and my heart – in two.

'. . . Neve?'

I blink away the threat of a flashback. 'Sorry, what?'

'I was asking if you could do me a favour later.'

I shake off my disquiet. 'Yep, sure.' This is easy: Parveen is one of those rare and gorgeous people who never asks awful things of her colleagues because she can't be arsed to do them herself.

'You don't know what it is yet. And actually . . . it is your least favourite thing to do.'

Okay, I take it back. I groan and lower my head to my keyboard. 'Please no more Year 11s.'

KLI does a lot of careers outreach locally, going into schools, sixth forms, and universities. We take interns at degree level, and work with degree providers across various projects. None of which I mind doing – in fact I quite enjoy it – but the last group of Year 11s I spoke to were brutal. I got laughed at, then heckled, and the teacher who assured me I'd gone down a storm had been typing on her phone the whole way through the session.

Heckling I can deal with. Having my time wasted, I can't.

Parveen slides a cardboard invitation across the desk to me. 'I'm supposed to be going to this private view tonight at this art gallery on Magdalen Street but I totally forgot, and Maz is leading this big mediation at work that might go into the night so I absolutely *have* to be home for the twins.'

I loathe talking to people about art, as Parveen well knows. She is KLI's resident art expert, usually liaising with dealers on behalf of our clients, because she studied art history at uni and genuinely can't get enough of the stuff.

It's not that I can't do it: I can turn my mind to pretty much anything if I have enough reading time. It's more that I have a very low pompousness threshold. Leo used to love going to art galleries and talking nonsense to show off. He knew absolutely nothing, but his ego was rooted in pretending the opposite. It was the same with wine, literature, and – this was always the worst one, especially at dinner parties – international politics.

Parveen makes a pleading face. 'Half an hour, tops, just so I can say the company showed its face. All you need to do is drink the free wine and mill a bit, and then you can leave.'

'Drink, mill, and leave?'

'Promise.'

'I suppose I can stretch to that,' I say, returning my attention to the Art Deco kitchen I'm working on. 'But you're doing the next load of Year 11s.'

'Deal,' she says brightly. 'And hey, you never know – you might end up talking to someone really interesting.'

I think of Leo and raise an eyebrow. 'Appreciate your optimism, Parv, but let's not get carried away.'

4.

I arrive a little late, having lost track of time on revisions for the fit-out of a two-storey barn conversion that dropped into my inbox last-minute from the developer, asking for a tight turnaround.

The gallery is quiet. The artist is talking. I slip in at the back and take a warm white wine from the table next to me. The exhibition in question is oil on canvas, each piece a mass of muted colours, their subjects obscure.

It's then that I see him. On the other side of the room, also cradling a glass of white wine. He's listening intently, but for some reason, as I'm looking at him, he turns his head.

Our eyes lock. The world takes a breath. I feel the heat of his gaze lick through me like a flame.

My whole life, there's only been one other person who's looked at me like that.

I realise it is the lightning-strike guy. Parveen's new work crush. He's semi-famous locally, in the same way as you might be if you'd survived a shark attack, or a rhino charge. But I don't know the details. If I were to search for the events of that night, I know I'd stumble across the other accident that happened mere moments away, just one street across. And I don't ever want to look at any of those news reports again.

The artist stops talking. There's a polite smattering of applause, which gives way to a thick hum of conversation.

Across the room, I watch Ash start to move past the paintings, pausing by each one, giving them time and consideration. He cuts a solitary, thoughtful figure among the buzz of bodies. I find myself tracking him around the space, my eyes only on him. I am so absorbed, I don't even register him getting closer until he literally comes to a pause by my side.

And then. It barrels into me like a train: the scent of Tom Ford Noir. It is unmistakeable. I'd know it anywhere.

I try to collect myself. He's tall, I realise, even taller than me. He looks like he's just left off work too, in a pair of dark jeans and pressed shirt.

I decide to introduce myself, since I'm starting to suspect he's the one who gave Parveen the invite.

'Hello,' I say brightly, switching into work mode. 'I'm Neve Lambourne. From Kelley Lane Interiors.'

His expression lifts. He turns to face me. 'Oh. Hi. Parveen said you might drop by.'

I smile to myself. *Did she, now.*

He puts out a hand. 'Ash Heartwell.'

We shake. His grip is firm and warm. Somehow, it hits every touchpoint in my stomach.

He nods at the painting in front of us, perhaps to

avoid the risk of an awkward pause. 'What do you think?'

The space is small and hot, and packed with bodies. Every surface is floodlight-bright. I feel a prickle of sweat against my back, the sensation of being assessed.

'Very . . . visceral,' I say, firmly. (This is my go-to adjective for describing abstract art. It usually buys me enough seconds to pivot topics, or failing that, segue to a respectable exit.)

'Visceral,' he repeats, nodding. Then, 'For me, it's all about the colour palette. The way it connects to both light and dark, you know?'

This is why I am allergic to art galleries. People expect articulate analysis. The truth is, I'd much rather be back at the office right now, working on that barn conversion.

'Mmm,' I say, nodding and wishing I'd at least found the time to read the catalogue before I clocked off earlier.

Ash dips his head towards mine. 'Just joking. I know zero about art.'

I laugh with relief, take in his bright, steady eyes, his firm jaw. The trace of laughter lines. The faintest hint of mischief in his smile.

He sips his wine. 'So, if you don't mind me asking, what are you doing here? If you're such an art-phobe, I mean.'

'It's not like that. It's just that I feel quite . . . neutral about most of it.'

'Everyone has at least one artist that does it for them.'

I feel his eyes on me. He's right, of course – there is one artist who does it for me. Whose paintings make me feel close to Jamie again somehow. Who always has. 'Well,' I concede, 'I guess . . . Edward Hopper. There's this one painting of his—'

'*Nighthawks*,' he says, without missing a beat.

I stare at him. My breath is a storm cloud suspended in my throat.

'I actually have that painting in my apartment. Well, a print of it, obviously.'

'Me too. I have one at home.'

As I take him in again, inhaling the Tom Ford, a woman wearing a tweed suit that might be Chanel approaches us. I know her via Kelley; she's a property developer and director of a local arts charity. 'Hello, Neve,' she says warmly, air-kissing me. 'How are you, my darling? Can I be terribly rude and borrow you for a moment? There's someone I'd like you to meet.'

I glance at Ash and smile apologetically. 'Excuse me.'

'Of course,' he says, and then I am swept away.

After Kelley's contact introduces me to her friend, I start working the room, making introductions of my own. KLI is high-profile locally, and I know virtually everyone here, even if only indirectly.

Occasionally, I sense Ash watching me. I haven't fully recovered from our interaction earlier, or managed to work out why it didn't quite make sense.

An hour or so later, he catches me by the door.

'I've got to go now, but . . . this is me.' He hands me a business card.

Despite my faint unease, I smile. 'You want to . . . continue our discussion about art?'

He laughs, softly. 'Yeah. Exactly that.'

I catch his eye. 'It was nice to meet you.'

'Likewise.'

5.

Then

The three of us moved into a two-bedroomed terraced house on Edinburgh Road. Jamie and I had the biggest room, agreeing to pay an extra twenty-five quid a week for the pleasure.

Technically, both Lara and I could have continued to live at home – mine was less than half a mile down the road, and Lara's family was just five miles door to door. But neither of us were keen. We wanted to at least pretend we'd flown the nest. Lara's parents were sweet, but her recent rebellious phase was proof that she was ready to go. She needed to be free.

Jamie and I moved in on a Sunday night in early September. Lara wasn't there yet. His mother dropped us off, her awkwardly parked SUV taking up nearly the entire pavement as we ferried boxes from it to the house.

She'd insisted on taking him out to buy piles of things I was sure we wouldn't need. John Lewis bed sheets and potted plants, cushions that would have looked more at home in her Regency-style living room in Putney. Cookbooks – Delia and *Good Housekeeping*, and something from the

River Cafe, to which Jamie had been twice. An actual coffee machine, the kind that came with pods. And a whole two buckets' worth of cleaning stuff.

When I'd said goodbye to my own mother earlier in the day, she'd slipped me twenty quid and a packet of cigarettes.

'Er, I don't smoke?'

She patted my arm. 'They might come in handy. Just in case.'

'In case of what?'

'Everyone else is doing it?'

'Okay. Thanks. Top-quality parenting there, Mum.' Was it really too much to ask for a sensible going-away present, like a bottle of wine, or some new pyjamas?

'Well,' she said, 'they do count as currency, you know. You can always swap them for something you really want.'

'I'm going to uni, not prison,' I said.

As we were arranging our things, Jamie discovered a picture hook on the wall, opposite our bed. He removed the *Nighthawks* painting from the towel he'd wrapped it in, and set it in place.

'It looks beautiful.' I slipped an arm around his waist as we stood back to admire it, like we were seeing the real thing in a gallery for the first time. My eyes strayed to the bronze alphabet bookends now propping up the tiny library we'd brought with us. An N and a J. He'd given them to me the previous night, encased in primrose-yellow tissue paper.

'Something to mark our first ever home together,' he said. 'So wherever our next bookshelf ends up being, we'll always remember our first.'

I surveyed the books now. His dog-eared copy of *A Place of My Own: The Architecture of Daydreams*; *Analysing Architecture*; and *Art and Illusion*, all arranged together in order of height. My half included an illustrated history of *Vogue* magazine, a coffee-table book of dream houses that was a little too square for the shape of the shelf, and two Nick Hornby novels that my mother had once brought home from a charity shop, never read and wouldn't miss.

Jamie's mum came into the room then, ripping the rubber gloves from her hands. She'd been executing what she called a 'decontamination', even though to me, the house already seemed pretty clean.

She stopped when she saw the painting. 'No, Jamie.'

We both looked at her.

'You can't keep that here. It might get stolen.'

'It's only a print,' Jamie said. 'It's not valuable.'

'Value and sentiment are not the same thing, darling. Let me take it home. I'll keep it in your bedroom for you, until you find somewhere nice to live.'

I knew she hadn't meant it like that. But the comment still stung. The house was fine. We were in a good area. The street was one of the better ones on the list we'd been given.

'We'll take care of it,' I said to her.

She looked at me then, which was something she rarely did. Whenever the three of us were together, she mostly addressed Jamie, save the occasional glance in my direction.

'Please do,' was all she said, her voice cracking slightly. I knew then that she was asking me to take care of Jamie, too.

★   ★   ★

'Oh, Debbie, you beauty,' Lara said, peering into the fridge an hour or so later at the four bottles of champagne resting inside. She looked over at Jamie. 'Am I right?'

She knew his mum's name was Debra, that no-one ever dared to call her Debbie.

Jamie nodded. I think he secretly enjoyed Lara's boldness. 'Housewarming gift.'

'Obviously.' Lara rubbed her hands together. 'Well, what are you waiting for, posh boy? Crack it open and let's get this party started.'

We drank champagne in the living room as the light shrank from the sky, playing cards and listening to Muse. Debra had – of course – given Jamie a box of crystal glasses to go with the Moët, but Lara pointed out that drinking champagne from flutes on the first day of uni would be the most tragic thing ever. We agreed, so we poured it into the mugs her mum had given her instead, which bore natty slogans like *LIFE BEGINS AFTER COFFEE* and *CUP OF POSITIVI-TEA*.

'Were these . . . a joke?' Jamie said, examining his mug with a kind of appalled fascination.

'Sadly, no. And Mum knows there's nothing I hate more than a vapid little soundbite. I'd rather have had the cash.' She looked at me. 'I bet your mum just slipped you twenty quid and a packet of cigarettes, didn't she?'

Lara and I had been friends for fourteen years at that point. There was nothing we didn't know about each other.

I had seen her drunk, high, ravaged by despair, and hyperactive with joy.

What I loved most about her was that she was tender beneath her toughness. She was the kind of person who'd be first to fetch a plaster if you'd cut your finger. Who would make sure you'd drunk a full pint of water and popped two Nurofen before bed after a heavy night.

When I first fell in love with Jamie, I had no idea what to do about Lara. Because there were suddenly things I wanted to do alone with Jamie – trips to the cinema, listening to music in my bedroom, walks around town and dinners in Pizza Hut. But Lara never bitched, or made things awkward. Instead, she simply slotted in beside us when it felt right, and stepped back when it didn't. We never talked about it, because it never seemed like we needed to.

She must have known, I guess, that he was a boy worth loving.

But I still needed her. So when she decided to stay in Norwich, and even share a house with us, I was almost euphoric with relief.

She made other friends instantly. She found it easy, always had. By the following night, a lad had already invited her to a house party on Angel Road, and she insisted Jamie and I go too.

She disappeared the moment we got there, swept up into a crowd of new acquaintances. Jamie and I sat on a sofa together. There was house music playing, a relentless, drilling beat.

After an hour or so, I disappeared to fetch more drinks. When I returned, I paused in the doorway. Jamie was talking to a girl – blonde, smoky eyes, endless legs emerging from a pair of tiny black shorts.

Jamie was drunk, by then. He could no longer detect when he was being flirted with. His face was flushed, hair flopping over his eyes.

I stood where I was, listening. The girl hadn't seen me, was focused wholly on Jamie. She seemed to be asking him a series of questions.

'All right then. Secret skill?'

He considered this. 'Poker.'

'Favourite thing to do on a Saturday night?'

'Pub, pool, kebab.'

'Favourite film?'

'Anything with subtitles.' (Jamie liked to think of himself as something of a world cinema expert. It came from his brother, I think, who was always referring offhandedly to things like Taiwanese New Wave, or Italian Neorealism.)

'Do you cook?'

'Yep.' (Another truth. His mum had taught him well: he was much better than me.)

'Best way to spend a Sunday?'

A beat. 'Go to the beach, then . . . come home and drink whisky and talk crap and make out and forget what the time is, you know?'

At this, she appeared so enchanted, she set a hand on his leg, which meant I was going to have to step in.

'Okay, last question. This is the most important one. Are you ready?'

'I'm ready.'

'Cats, or dogs?'

'Dogs, obviously.'

She squealed with delight. I noticed her grip tighten.

I leaned down to pass Jamie his refill.

She looked up at me, and blinked twice, like, *Can we help you?*

'Here you go,' I said.

'Hey, this is Neve. Neve, meet . . .' He trailed off, then shrugged.

'*Claire*,' she said, with a look that could have curdled milk.

I did feel a bit sorry for her, as she walked away. She'd brought her A-game and worn her smallest pair of shorts, and Jamie hadn't so much as clocked her name.

6.

Now

Not long after I get home from the art gallery, my phone rings. I have just sorted through today's post and put a wash on, and now I'm tidying crockery from the draining board.

I've been unsettled since meeting Ash earlier. Not necessarily in a negative way – but enough to make me feel that sitting still is not an option.

I take a tentative look at the screen, praying it's not the barn conversion guy trying to advance his deadlines. I'm not averse to working weekends, but the last few days have been hectic and I'd been planning on being lazy for the next forty-eight hours, pottering around the house.

Jamie would have loved this place. I bought it partly because it reminded me so much of the house we shared for two years at uni. Sometimes, I take a detour along Edinburgh Road just so I can look at it again, feel the memories reel through me.

It's Parveen. I put her on speaker.

'How was the private view?'

'Yeah, yeah. Nice try, Parv.'

I can tell she's smiling before she even replies. 'Oh, come on. A man that gorgeous cannot go to waste. If I can't have him, someone needs to, and that someone should be you.'

'I already told you, I'm not looking.'

'Remind me why again?'

'I'm busy. And I don't have the energy to date. They all want to have sex in cars.'

'That was one time, one guy, Neve.'

'Anyway – how do you even know Ash is single? He might be married with three kids and one on the way.'

'I asked one of his colleagues, after my meeting this morning. Told her I knew someone who'd be his dream match.'

'Please tell me you're joking.'

We both know she isn't.

'Anyway, come on. Why aren't you and Ash getting wasted in a pub together right now? I *need* some salacious gossip in my life. I'm currently wiping shepherd's pie off a wall.'

I pause, looking down at the cloth in my hand. 'Sometimes I think you don't know me at all.'

'I do know there is zero shepherd's pie on your walls. You have no excuse.'

'The private view wasn't that kind of vibe.'

'It was free wine on a Friday night.'

I give my draining board one last buff.

'Please, Neve. What have you got to lose?'

'My sanity. Good night, Parv.'

★   ★   ★

But a few minutes later, despite everything I've said and feel, I find myself fishing his card from my wallet.

As I turn it over between my fingers, the scent of Tom Ford Noir rushes back to me. The eye contact. The lightning strike. *Nighthawks*.

Maybe Parveen is right. Maybe I don't have anything to lose. Ash seemed genuinely nice, and anyway – there is something about him that makes me intensely curious.

Which is how I find myself doing something I haven't done in a very long time.

> Hi, Ash. It's Neve from the gallery/KLI
>
> It was nice to meet you earlier
>
> Do you have plans this weekend? Wondering if you fancied a drink?

I hold my breath as I watch the ticks turn blue, then the dots start to bounce.

> Hey. It was nice to meet you too.
>
> A drink sounds great.

Straight away, my mind begins to rattle with questions and emotions. Fear and fascination, but also, an urge to see him again that I know is to do with Jamie, my boyfriend of nearly a decade ago. A spark that is unmistakeably excitement. Excitement it makes no sense for me to feel.

7.

We live in adjacent postcodes, so I suggest the Ribs of Beef, a pub which is halfway between us.

I get there early, because I always do. But Ash is already waiting at a table inside.

My solar plexus sees him first. His sharp profile and blue shirt, sleeves rolled to the elbows. I try not to think too hard about how attractive he is, about the girls on the next table who eye me up as I arrive and share a disappointed laugh.

As I sit down, I catch it again: Tom Ford Noir. It air-kisses me briefly, like a long-lost friend, then recedes, leaving me reeling.

'All the tables were full outside, sorry.' He smiles and slides a glass of wine across the table. It's rosé, looks dry, my favourite. 'Hope I guessed okay. I did message to see what you wanted, but . . . there was pressure at the bar.'

My phone's deep in my bag. I thank him with a smile. A dry rosé is my summer drink of choice – which means either he just made a very good guess, or he has inside information on me.

I shed my jacket and adjust the neckline of my dress, feeling suddenly apprehensive in a way I haven't in months.

I've been on just three dates in the year since Leo. The first arrived late and left early, the second thought he could be condescending about my job (because he was a molecular biologist), and the third I shared quite a nice kiss with and thought I might see again until he breathily suggested we do it in the back seat of his car.

Ash raises his pint of Guinness to my wine glass. 'Nice to see you again.'

'And you. Sorry we didn't get to chat much last night.'

'Not at all. It looked like you were in demand.'

'I was sort of there as a favour to Parveen.'

He smiles. 'Yeah, she mentioned that.'

I meet his eye and smile back. 'Can I ask you something?'

'Of course.'

'Were you the one—'

'—who got struck by lightning?' He nods, but reluctantly.

I wince. 'Sorry. You must get that a lot.'

I usually stay far away from topics that bring to mind the worst night of my life. But there's something about Ash that reminds me so strongly of Jamie. Though I can't quite work out why, I feel impelled to find out more about him.

'It is kind of a weird thing to be known for,' he says, sipping his pint. 'I don't feel the novelty factor in quite the same way as other people.'

'I get that,' I say, wishing now I'd not brought it up. 'My mum knows a guy that got attacked by a crocodile. He's pretty much known for having a massive bite mark on his arse.'

Ash smiles. 'Is that supposed to make me feel better?'

I shut my eyes briefly. 'No. Sorry. Absolutely making it worse.'

Beneath the table, I feel his knee nudge mine. There's no way of telling whether it's accidental.

'So, how is it, working for Kelley?' he asks. 'She's got a pretty fierce reputation.'

'Actually, I love it. She's basically my idol. Though she would frown on this.'

'Us . . . having a drink? Why?'

'She'd say it was unprofessional.'

He raises an eyebrow. 'So why did you suggest it?'

I meet his gaze across the table. His eyes are inky blue, the colour of the sky at night. 'I was curious,' I admit. 'You remind me of someone.'

He waits, presumably for me to elaborate.

'Someone I knew . . . a long time ago.'

He looks intrigued. Maybe he suspects I'm referring to an ex. 'You're going to have to give me a bit more than that.'

I glance briefly out of the window. The setting sun is scorching the rooftops. The horizon is burned red.

'What made you want to become an architect?' I'm pretending to change the subject – though of course, I'm not really, because Jamie was an architect too.

Ash tips his head back and forth almost imperceptibly. 'Well, after my accident, I wanted a change of direction. I was training to be a doctor before. I guess I just . . . didn't want to waste any more time on things I had no passion for.'

'Had you always been into it? Architecture?'

He smiles. 'No, and . . . this might sound a bit . . . But it just kind of hit me while I was in hospital, that architecture was what I really wanted to do. Something inside me sort of clicked, out of nowhere. It was weird, but it was also the best decision I ever made. Maybe it was divine intervention, or something.'

I stare at him, my heart a series of misfired beats. 'Who's your favourite? Architect, I mean.'

'I'd probably have to say Norman Foster. You've got to love the Gherkin.'

'Got to,' I say faintly.

'Anyway. Enough about work. I would ask what you do for fun, but that is officially the world's worst small-talk question.'

I smile. 'Yep. Hate that too.'

'Right? If someone says "fun" that's supposed to mean bungee jumping, or skydiving, or go-karting, or waking up naked on the ferry halfway to Rotterdam.' He laughs. 'Actually, I was that guy, back in the day. Before my accident. I was all about the fun. Call Ash if you want a fun time. Everyone used to call me a "livewire" but I really think that was just a polite word for twat.'

'You felt different, then? After the accident.'

He nods.

I sip my wine, slowly, carefully. 'In what way?'

He takes a moment to answer. 'I don't know why exactly, but suddenly I just . . . wanted to stop all the craziness and climbing up lampposts and getting arrested for breaching the peace. No more wild nights out ending with me waking up in ditches or train depots. Much to the disappointment of my friends. They all thought I'd been taken over by aliens.'

'So, you had a near-death experience and then . . .?'

'Well, exactly. It changed me.'

'Just like that?'

He nods softly. 'It was a wake-up call.'

Something about this doesn't feel quite as straightforward as he makes it sound, but I decide not to push it. 'So, what do you do for fun these days?'

'I thought we'd agreed not to ask that question.'

'Pleasure, then. What do you like to do for pleasure?'

Our gazes grip tight for just a moment. 'That's better.'

'Go on.'

He groans.

'Okay, I'll make it easier. Let's see . . . Secret skill?'

'I'm actually a demon at poker.'

I swallow. 'For money?'

'Sometimes.'

'Standard lads' night out?'

'Pub, pool, kebab.'

'Odeon or . . . arthouse?'

'Arthouse.'

'Cook, or order in?'

'I cook, actually. Promise I'm not just saying that.'

My heart rate picks up. I have overheard a version of this conversation before, many years ago. And all the answers are the same.

'Beach, or city?'

'God, beach.'

'Cats, or dogs?'

'Does anyone ever say cats?'

'Idea of a great date?'

His gaze fuses with mine. 'Let's see. Maybe just . . . one of those long nights drinking and talking crap and forgetting what the time is.'

'Best hangover cure?'

He starts to speak, then changes his mind. 'Ah, I can't tell you that.'

'Go on.' The way Jamie and I always solved hangovers was with sex and coffee, lots of both.

He hesitates, then, 'Strong coffee and . . . you know. Good company.'

I feel tears in my throat.

'Sorry. That was a bit TMI.' He examines his glass. 'Am I drunk?'

Despite myself, a laugh slips free. 'Let's hope so.'

I get another round in. Ash asks more about what I do and where I live, and I tell him about renovating my house, how much love I've poured into every last brick of it. But then, as he starts to describe his place – even though I think I know what he's about to say – disbelief blows through me.

'It's nice. It's on the river, actually. High up, really great views.'

I grip my glass, worried that if I don't hold on to something, I might start to shake.

Top floor, middle four windows.

'Is it one of the . . . converted factories?'

He nods. 'The Old Yarn Mill. Do you know it?'

In my mind, I journey back to Boxing Day nearly ten years ago, when Jamie and I stood on the riverbank, staring up at the Old Yarn Mill. *If someone told you they'd just bought an apartment in that building, and they wanted you to design the space and make it beautiful, how would you feel?*

'I do,' I say softly. 'I bet it's gorgeous.'

'Well, it could be. Though, it turns out I can do space planning and compliance and lighting and joinery, but when it comes to furnishing, I have a bit of a blind spot. I struggle when it comes to colour and fabric palettes and styling and stuff.'

I observe him for a couple of moments. His hair is definitively dark, where Jamie's was lighter, closer to bronze. Jamie's eyes were brown, but Ash's are the deep, rich blue of open oceans. Ash is taller, I think, and I'm guessing he might have an athletic physique, where Jamie was always quite soft around the edges.

Still. He resembles Jamie so closely. In every way but looks, he could almost *be* him. The things he said about his personality changing after his accident niggle at me too, but I can't quite figure out why.

'Neve?' Ash says gently.

I snap back to the conversation. 'I could help, if you like. Give you some design pointers.'

'Serious?'

'Yes, I'd love to.'

'That'd be great. I'd pay, obviously. I wouldn't expect you to do it for free.'

'No need. I'd love to. Whenever you like.'

40

'I'm away next weekend, but . . . the Saturday after, if you fancy it?'

I exhale. A fortnight for me to figure out how I feel about this guy, who resembles the love of my life in a labyrinth of ways. Tonight has been like going back nearly a decade in time and sitting in the pub with Jamie again.

'Great,' I say.

He extends his almost-empty pint glass for me to clink. 'Looking forward to it.'

We part ways on Fye Bridge with a hug and a peck on the cheek. But on the way home, I feel a clot of fear forming in my chest. The similarities between Jamie and Ash are . . . so, so bizarre. No, more than bizarre. Does he know about Jamie, somehow? Is he trying to impersonate him? Is he an old friend, or enemy, or even some kind of troll – has he looked him up online?

I message him as I walk home.

> Meant to ask . . . have you ever known someone called Jamie?

> I know two actually (and a half)

My heart somersaults. What is the *half* code for?

> ???

Half = ex-work colleague who I never see. Surname?

Fraser

His reply is instant.

Nope. Should I?

This is too messed up. I should just cut off all contact with Ash and forget I ever met him.

And yet.

No worries, mix up.

8.

On Wednesday lunchtime, I call in to Mum's. It's only a fifteen-minute walk from the KLI offices, so I try to pop round a couple of times a week.

Even people who aren't fussed about house porn struggle not to be impressed by my mother's sprawling, four-storey Edwardian end terrace. It makes her seem wealthier than she is, and might also explain why property developers keep asking her out.

She and Dad panic-bought the house nearly three decades ago, when the Golden Triangle was still affordable, and Dad had just received a never-to-be-repeated pay rise and bonus. The place is undeniably gorgeous – red-bricked with high ceilings, brimming with features and character detailing, like stained glass and ceiling roses, cornicing and cast-iron fireplaces, and stunning original tiles in the hallway. But Mum has never bothered to maintain it, and over the years, the place has slid into disrepair.

A small part of me has always hoped that one day, she and I might restore the house together, return it to its former glory. She has a modest pot of savings, earmarked for a future renovation – I just need her to give me the green light and I'll be ready to sand surfaces and fill cracks and call in the damp-proofing people, get the roof fixed. But every time I bring it up, she changes the subject. I guess she's got used to the patchy paint and brown blooms of moisture, leaks in strange places and rotting timbers. It's mostly sound, if she treads carefully and doesn't try to peel back any carpets or wallpaper, and there's always something more pressing she can spend the money on, I guess. But to me, a house as beautiful as this deserves to be cared for, cherished, loved.

'Is that you, Neve?'

'Yep.'

'Phew. Thought you were Ralph.' Mum comes bustling downstairs in a silk kimono, cigarette in hand, then kisses me on both cheeks. It makes me cringe, this pretentious imitation she's always trying to do of a glamourpuss. I inherited the slight build of my father, but Mum is full-figured, all curves and proportions. She has a dramatic head of thick, dark curls that tumble past her face and bounce around her shoulders. The silk kimono exposes her cleavage.

'Why don't you want to see Ralph?' I ask her suspiciously. Whenever my mother has a new love interest, she gets bristly with Ralph, the sweet, gentle man who I suspect has been faithfully in love with her for nearly fifteen years. She reckons they're just friends, but he's always here, and I see how he looks at her.

'Oh, you know,' she says, waving a hand through the air, drawing on her cigarette and wafting past me.

'No?' I follow her through to the kitchen.

'Sometimes I just need a bit of *space*,' she says. 'You know?'

I roll my eyes, not bothering to remind her how many times Ralph has picked her up off the floor over the years, literally and figuratively.

'Tea?' she says. 'You'll have to have it black, though. No milk.'

'Fine,' I say, pulling up a chair at the farmhouse-style table at the far end of the kitchen.

Mum fills the ancient kettle and plonks it on top of the equally ancient Aga. The table is crammed with dirty glasses and bowls doubling as ashtrays, *Guardian* newspapers so old they've turned crispy – all of them undoubtedly unread. There are empty wine bottles and half-punched pill packets, and . . . There it is. An elaborate bouquet of flowers, their effect slightly diminished by the rinsed-out coffee jar they've been stuffed into.

I resist the urge to get up and tidy, wipe surfaces, take the bins out. I have done, in the past, before realising that attempting to tame the disorder in my mother's house is a bit like trying to hold back an avalanche using only my hands.

'Who're the flowers from?'

'Hmm?' She's playing for time.

I speak slowly and loudly, as if there's a language barrier. 'Who are the flowers from?'

'Just a friend.'

'Ralph?'

She snorts. 'Don't be ridiculous.'

'Who, then?'

'Oh Neve! Just a fan, okay?'

Mum's not famous, but she is a singer, mostly of power ballads and love songs. It's how she makes her living, through a combination of regular gigs and one-off bookings like weddings. It's the only job she's ever had, and I'd be devastated if she tried to do anything else. I'm still not fully sure how she never hit the big time. Might be because she's easily distracted, I suppose, not to mention vehemently determined to keep smoking. Still. Whenever I see her sing, it does something unexpected to my heart. It dismantles, temporarily, all the barriers between us. It frees me, watching her sing.

The downside, however, is her 'fans'. By which she means 'flings'. Because that's all they ever turn out to be. She always falls hard, at the start. Give her a pricey bunch of flowers, and she's anyone's.

Ralph tolerates it because it's not his right to do otherwise, since he and my mother are officially just good friends. But I see it in his eyes whenever someone new crash-lands into her life. I imagine how it must feel – a kick to the chest, the kind of rejection that leaves you struggling for breath.

'Who is he, then? This fan.' I only just resist the urge to use air quotes.

Mum brings the tea over and pulls up a chair. Sunlight slices through the floor-to-ceiling windows and onto the table, helpfully bleaching out all the red wine rings and grease stains.

She smiles, already giddy as a schoolgirl. I've seen that look so many times before. 'Oh, it's early days.'

I sip my tea. It tastes terrible without milk, and is weak and bitter. I set the mug back down. 'Does he have a name, at least?'

'Actually, I'm not sure.' She frowns. 'They just call him "The Duke", at the pub.'

'What is he, a mob boss?'

She looks at me blankly. 'Why would you say that?'

'Because he sounds like a cut-price Godfather.'

She waves this suggestion away as if it is more ridiculous than him being called The Duke. 'His family must have been something to do with landed gentry, I suppose, back in the day. He shares a flat with his brother now, though. They fight like cat and dog, apparently.'

'Sounds a bit chaotic.'

She shrugs. 'Anyway, I just call him Duke.'

'Any gigs this week?'

'Three. The pub, a wedding anniversary and an actual wedding.'

Mum always looks sensational when she's gigging. She takes it seriously – spends hours on her hair and make-up, and wears gorgeously lavish dresses. She sings under her maiden name – Daniela DiMarco – and to look at her, you'd think she lived a life of non-stop continental glamour. But most people never see the side of her that gets up at midday and drinks too much and smokes instead of eats and seeks out unsuitable men to help her forget her pain.

'You'll never guess who I saw in town yesterday,' she says, tapping her cigarette over a cereal bowl, releasing a grey worm of ash.

'Who?'

'Lara.'

My stomach brakes hard against my ribcage. 'What?'

'Yes, with a man.'

'Did you speak to her?'

'Well, no. I didn't know what reaction I might get. It's such a shame you two fell out. She was always so lovely.'

'Did the guy . . . look like her boyfriend? You're sure it wasn't her dad?'

'He was rather handsome, actually. Impeccably dressed and *very* tall. They were holding hands, so yes – I assume he was her boyfriend.'

I feel my heart start to pound. The impulse to flee becomes urgent. 'Just need to pop to the loo.' I stand up and move past her, out of the kitchen and into the hallway.

'Use the one upstairs,' she calls. 'Duke dislodged the seat off the downstairs loo.'

I shake my head, trying not to imagine how in the hell he'd managed that.

Upstairs, I sit on the edge of my childhood bed. Mum hasn't touched this room since I went to uni. Same books and Justin Timberlake posters, same photos of Lara and me tacked up all over the place. Some have fluttered to the floor now, leaving hardened wads of Blu Tack in their place.

The room always feels stale whenever I walk into it. Unloved and unattended to, like it's one more job Mum can't be arsed to tick off her to-do list. Not that she's ever had one.

The room needs airing and polishing, a good vacuum, a lick of paint.

I get up and wrench open the sash window, swollen now from years of damp and inattention. The trill of birdsong drifts through the gap, along with the screech of a van accelerating up the road. Fresh air floods the room. I inhale it, briefly shutting my eyes.

Lara.

Lara can't be back. Can she?

I run a hand over my stripped mattress. It held Jamie's body long ago, his form warm and firm against mine. Long kisses and fevered touches, stifled giggles whenever my mother wafted past the locked door, singing. Sometimes, she would rap on it, to make us both jump.

Mum never warmed to Jamie. She would always change in his company, becoming mute and watchful. They didn't bond. Never so much as shared a joke. After their first few meetings, I avoided bringing him round here as much as I could, because the reception he got was always tepid at best.

Whenever I asked Mum about this, she flat-out denied there was a problem. So I had to conclude she was being awkward for the sake of it. Or that maybe a tiny part of her was jealous. After all, it hadn't worked out too well for her, meeting the love of her life when she was only in her teens.

She never got over my dad leaving. Even though their relationship had been turbulent, I truly believe he was the only man she had ever really loved.

The affair, apparently, had been going on for two years.

Bev was younger than Dad, but that was where the cliché ended. She was Dad's boss at the logistics company where they both worked. She spoke four languages and didn't stand for anyone's crap. She was far from the empty-headed bimbo my mum made her out to be.

Bev didn't need my dad, not one bit. She *wanted* him.

Mum had suspected for a while, and so had I. Dad would whistle his way to the office, and was working increasingly long hours without complaint, taking extra pride in his appearance. I suppose he was good-looking, if you can say that about your own father. Dark and trim-figured, with a twinkle in his eye and a wicked sense of humour. He was the kind of person people always wanted to sit next to at the pub.

The day Mum discovered the texts, I came home from school to find Dad with blood all over his face, storming between the various floors of the house, gathering belongings. Mum was nowhere to be seen.

'What happened?' I asked, although I could guess, of course.

Dad didn't respond. He just flung his things into a suitcase then left, not even bothering to shut the front door behind him.

I scrambled to the window of the living room.

A BMW was parked on the other side of the road beneath a street light, engine purring. I watched Bev take in my dad's bloodied appearance as he climbed into the car before shaking her head, just once, then pressing her foot to the floor. Bev was better than all this drama, I could see that, even at the age of twelve. She wouldn't indulge such histrionics. She was wearing sunglasses and a leather jacket. Her dark hair was bobbed and glossy. To me, she looked like a movie star. In some messed-up way, I felt in that moment that Bev was my idol.

I found Mum in the first-floor bathroom, sitting on the closed lid of the toilet. Some of Dad's things were in the bath. Work shirts and trousers. A pile of photographs. Vinyl records. Slippers. A dressing gown. Boxer shorts. The stuff, I assumed, he didn't want Bev judging him by.

I smelt bourbon, too. The expensive bottle Dad never let anyone touch, not even Mum. Well, she was touching it now, tipping it liberally over all the items in the bath, in between taking giant swigs. In her lap was a box of matches.

'Mum!' I exclaimed. 'Don't!'

She turned to stare at me. Her demeanour was wild, but she wasn't out of control. I could see that instantly. This was vindication, I realised, after months – years – of being gaslit. Her fury had a place at last. Her anger was justified. She was now unstoppable. 'Why the hell wouldn't I?'

She struck the first match. I left the room and went to sit on the landing while she turned Dad's possessions into ash.

'Did you hurt him?' I asked her after a while, through the bathroom door. I couldn't stop thinking about his face covered in blood.

There was a long silence. I'd almost given up waiting for an answer when her voice cut through the smoke of the fire she'd made, brittle and bitter.

'Not like he hurt me,' was all she said.

9.

Then

That first term at uni felt like letting out a breath I'd been holding for years. I had finally escaped: Jamie's parents' disapproval, my mother's baggage and weird manfriends. The permanent sense I had at home of being in a car driven by someone who could lose control at any moment and steer us both into a ditch.

I loved meeting so many different people, learning new stuff, that all the usual rules had been vaporised. If we wanted to breakfast on leftover Thai takeaway, or sleep till midday, or get in at three a.m., not one person in the world was going to stop us. Our lives were up to us now.

Most mornings, Lara would come into our room first thing and flop onto the mattress, sunglasses on, giant carton of apple juice in hand. Jamie would tut and ask if it was beyond her to use a glass, and she would tell him she drank the last of ten tequila shots less than four hours ago, so yes, it was beyond her. Then when Jamie got up to make coffee, she'd tell me about her night. (Always booze and boys, lots of both.) Invariably, she'd fall asleep as she was talking, but I'd stay there next to her until she woke again, just to be sure she was okay.

Whenever we were all at home, we'd listen to London Grammar on loop, sipping cheap whisky, playing cards and taking it in turns to be profound. Jamie liked to cook, too, from the books his mum had given him. He was never short of money to buy whatever he needed, items that seemed exotic to me and Lara, like artichokes and crabmeat and ricotta and miso, which only gave Lara another thing to tease him about.

There was always a scrappy kind of energy between the two of them. Lara would rib Jamie for being posh, for his naivety and privilege. He would challenge her on her stubbornness and socialist ideals, her (as he saw it) needless cynicism. She had a habit of sitting in the dark, smoking or drinking, and making him jump when he walked into the room. (I never did. I had animal instinct when it came to her, always able to sense when she was nearby.) She would bring people we didn't know back to the house, then turn up the music until the early hours. I never cared, but Jamie always felt obliged to apologise to our (tolerant working professional) neighbours the next morning.

Lara would answer the door to charity people, then chat to them for hours as Jamie fumed from the upstairs window about why they were targeting students. Sometimes, I thought she did it just to wind him up. Our bathroom had a dodgy lock, and we'd all agreed to knock first, but Lara always forgot, and on more than one occasion had caught Jamie half naked. Once, she claimed she'd caught him 'giving himself a treat', something he furiously denied as he got pinker and pinker. And while I found it genuinely hilarious, I never did get out of her – or him – whether she'd been joking.

I guess I sat somewhere in the middle of the two of them, personality-wise. They say you're shaped by the people around you, and I'd spent more time with Jamie and Lara than anyone else in my life. Probably even more than my own parents.

Jamie's mum still messaged him several times a day. I got the feeling this was about asserting her presence from afar, but could I really resent her for that? She missed her son, and loved him, her youngest child. Hardly a crime.

To be honest, I envied how much she doted on him.

Lara and I spent Christmas together that year, as we always did. Jamie was at his grandma's, and I'd been invited to join his family on Boxing Day. For the first time, he was cooking lunch on Christmas Day for all of them.

I didn't exactly blame him for the day itself being off-limits: the Frasers' Christmases were always weirdly sacred close-family-only affairs. Despite the fact that Harry – the prodigal son – wasn't even going to be there.

My mum usually had a gig on Christmas Day, so each year, I would head to Lara's parents' house, for endless food and bottomless drinks and a torrent of festive television and Christmas tunes. Lara's mum, Corinne, would save like a demon for the occasion, pooling her money with the rest of the family to make everything stretch further.

I'd seen photos of the perfect silver-and-white-themed decorations at Jamie's parents' house. But to me, it always looked cold, like Christmas inside an ice palace. Nothing was ever like that at Corinne's – each year, the house throbbed with laughter and warmth, everything a garish multi-coloured tangle of lights and tinsel and baubles.

And I loved it.

The few months at uni had begun to heal whatever adolescent rifts had sprung up between Lara and her parents, so that year, Christmas felt harmonious again. After lunch, Lara and I went upstairs to her bedroom to watch *Skyfall*. She was studying illustration, and had ambitions to work in film or television, designing sets, and she loved that film for how evocatively it depicted Shanghai, subterranean London, Macau, the Scottish wilderness. 'This,' she said dreamily, as she lay back and peeled her fourth clementine, 'is what I want to do with my life.'

Downstairs, someone turned the music up, and for a few moments, we were watching James Bond coming back from the dead while Wizzard played in the background. Then there was whooping, a crash, and hysterical laughter – definite indications that a conga was taking place. I thought of what I'd be doing at home, alone, and felt a rush of gratitude. Christmas just wasn't Christmas without Lara.

'I got you something,' I said, turning towards her on the bed.

She was still wearing her paper hat. Her eyes were glazed with laughter and Baileys and her passion for cinema.

I passed her the parcel. She sat up and tore the paper off, then stared at me, blinking in disbelief.

I'd tracked down a jumper she'd lost – baby pink cashmere. It had been a gift from her aunt, shortly before she died. But Lara had left it at a boy's house a couple of months ago, couldn't remember his name. She'd thought it was gone for ever. But I'd scoured eBay for weeks, eventually hitting upon the exact same jumper. (Whistles, cost a fortune.)

'Neve.' Her eyes filled with tears. 'Where—'

'On eBay. And hey, you never know – it might even be the same one.'

'Where was the seller?'

'Glasgow.'

We both knew she'd been nowhere near Glasgow, but she was happy to pretend. 'God, yeah. Maybe it is.' She shook her head. 'I can't believe you did this.'

'Well. I know how much you loved it. And I wanted you to know . . .' I began, but then trailed off. Why was it so hard to put into words what she meant to me?

Because it was beyond words, I think. How lost I knew I would be without her.

She just pulled me into a hug. 'I know,' she whispered. 'I know.' Then she moved back and smiled. 'Hey, I got you something too.'

She left the room for a couple of minutes, before returning with a gift bag. 'Sorry, but life's too short to arse about with wrapping paper.'

I lifted out the book inside. *On Decorating* by Mark Hampton.

'I know you're studying textiles and you have no idea what you want to do with your life, but . . . here's what I think you should do.'

At that point, my career was the only part of my future that still seemed fuzzy to me, a picture not quite yet in focus. Jamie was going to be an architect, Lara was putting out feelers for internships in film and TV, and I . . . still hadn't found my passion. I wasn't interested enough in the fashion industry to want to work in it, and I felt no pull towards retail or merchandising. I was enjoying my textiles course but it didn't set my heart on fire. Not the way Jamie's did for him.

'Decorating?' I said, flipping the cover cautiously, but liking what I saw.

'Well, interior design. You're a natural, always have been. You have the *eye* for it. Look at what you've done with our place.'

I'd done what I could with our tiny rental. Sourced a beautiful oak coffee table on eBay. Softened the sofa and armchairs with velvety blankets. Angled lamps into dark corners. Filled the house with potted plants and gorgeous cut-price crockery, again from eBay. I'd even asked our landlord if I could uncover the original oak floorboards in the upstairs bedrooms. They'd needed sanding and waxing, but other than that, they were perfect. I did the work myself, then found some rugs to complement them, at a huge discount in a closing-down sale.

Maybe Lara was right. I did have an eye for pattern and colour – just not when it came to clothing. I definitely had an instinctive leaning towards interiors and furnishing, things like wallpaper and upholstery.

'But interior design isn't just decor,' I said doubtfully. 'There's quite a bit of crossover with architecture. And I'm really not technically minded.'

'Pity you don't know any architects, then, isn't it?' Lara said, laughing as she topped up our Baileys. Then she pulled on the pink jumper, lay back with her head in my lap, and we returned our attention to the film.

The next morning, Jamie and I took a walk along the north bank of the Wensum before heading to his grandmother's house for lunch. The air was astringent with cold, the sky plate steel. There wasn't much traffic, or many people around. Just us and the geese in the silvery hush of a frost-kissed Boxing Day.

I still look occasionally at the selfies we took that morning. At Jamie, handsome in jeans and a collared jumper beneath a thick woollen coat. He was wearing a burgundy-coloured scarf, too, a gift from his grandmother the previous day.

And he smelt amazing. Harry had FedExed him a bottle of Tom Ford Noir.

'Lara thinks I should become an interior designer,' I said, as we walked.

'Great idea. You've got a real flair for that stuff.'

'You think I could do it? All those technical drawings you do look horrible, if I'm honest. And I'm literally allergic to maths. Anything remotely scientific makes me sweat.'

'Yeah, but plans are just a means to an end. They're not the essence of the job.'

We reached the area of the river where the new residential conversions were lined up along the far bank. Old mustard factories and woollen mills, now with views of the football ground and retail park. History made immortal. I thought of how many decades had passed since their bricks were laid, the scale of transformation that must have been witnessed through those windows.

'Hey,' he said then. 'If someone told you they'd just bought an apartment in that building, and they wanted you to design the space and make it beautiful, how would you feel?'

I followed his gaze over to the Old Yarn Mill. Its façade was just visible through the mist – the vast, industrial windows and long roof, that timeless red brickwork emerging out of the chilly water, the charm of the project-ing gantry detail on the building's facing wall.

'I'd be ridiculously excited, obviously.'

'You'd have ideas?'

'Are you joking? Millions.' I'd never set foot in the place, but already my imagination was stirring with images of huge, high-ceilinged spaces and expansive floors, of uncovered brickwork, brushed-steel lighting, looming concrete beams.

'Okay. Then I'll tell you what. Once I qualify, I'm going to buy us an apartment in that building.'

I smiled. 'Jamie.'

'And you're going to make it look amazing. When you're not too busy being a hot-shot interior designer, that is.'

He turned to kiss me then, setting off fireworks inside me as ever, even though his lips were cold and damp from the wintry air. I could never understand it when people said the spark faded, once you'd been with someone a long time. Because for me, it had only ever got more intense.

'Want to know what my favourite part is?' he asked, as we drew apart.

'I can guess.'

He raised an eyebrow and smiled, that way he had of challenging me.

'Obviously the windows.'

'Yep.' He laughed. 'Is it weird that I have a window fetish?'

'Well, I have a floorboard fetish, so let's call it even.'

'So, which one do you like best?' He stepped behind me, looped his arms around my shoulders.

I pressed my back against his chest, the wall of him barricading me from the cold. 'Any. You pick. I'd love them all.'

'Okay. Let's see.' He pointed a gloved finger towards the building. 'Well, how about . . . that one? Top floor, middle four windows.'

'How are we ever going to afford something like that?'

'Mortgage ourselves up to the eyeballs and die broke and in debt, obviously.'

I knew that would never happen. His dad was too rich. I guessed that was how he could joke about it, dabble in the notion that being poor was somehow romantic. 'But we'll be happy.'

He kissed the top of my head. 'We will. The happiest.'

10.

Now

A fortnight after our drinks at the Ribs, I meet Ash at his place for coffee on Saturday morning.

Top-floor apartment, middle four windows.

Before pressing the buzzer, I pause on the pavement, my mind electric with emotion. I picture Jamie and me coming to view this place together, if things had been different. Agreeing a price. Moving in. Might it be us living here now, in another life?

I shake it off as Ash buzzes me up. When I walk out of the lift, he's right there waiting for me, barefoot in jeans and a dark-blue sweater. He's got a couple of days' worth of stubble on his face, and it looks pretty good.

As he leans forward to kiss me hello, I know from the way my stomach flexes that I'm attracted to him. I've been thinking about him a lot, much more than I usually would after a couple of weeks and zero official dates. But whether that's down to how similar he is to Jamie, it's hard to know.

Inside, Ash shows me into the main living area. The space is vast, and crisp with the lemony light of early summer. Exposed brickwork spans the room, along with runs of steel pipework, plus two enormous central steel columns. It smells ever so faintly industrial, of bricks and concrete and past lives.

I walk over to the windows, from which I can see the spot where I stood in the mist that Boxing Day with Jamie. It all looks so different today in the sunlight, beneath an unflinching blue sky.

I follow Ash around the rest of the space. It's double-height and super airy, with heritage windows, double-stacked of course, and concrete ceiling beams. Even the floors are stunning – polished concrete in submarine grey. The lighting and electricals zone everything subtly, playing off the building's heritage.

We return to the view. I reach out and touch one of the windows with my fingertips. The frame feels fridge-cold against my skin.

Ash is at my shoulder. 'Incredible, aren't they?'

'They look original.'

He nods. 'Just with some secondary glazing inserted behind. I grilled the agent on every last detail about the place. I've got . . . a bit of a window fetish, I'm afraid.'

I turn to him. 'Sorry?'

He half smiles. 'Figuratively speaking. Not an *actual* fetish.'

I laugh this off with a lightness I don't feel. Am I being played here? Is the joke on me?

Are you doing this on purpose? And if so, how?

Because the man Ash so closely resembles – my ex-boyfriend Jamie – is dead. He was killed nearly a decade ago, aged just twenty, in a car accident less than two miles from where we lived. There was a vicious thunderstorm that night, and even now, I feel snakes in my stomach every time it rains.

And now – unbelievably – here is someone who is, in every conceivable way, the man Jamie was destined to become.

I turn back to the room. The space is undeniably stunning, but it is virtually devoid of any personal touches, save for a single framed picture on the far wall, above the sofa.

And it's a painting I'd recognise anywhere. One I've pored over and admired for more hours than I care to remember.

I go over to it. Take a breath.

Nighthawks. Edward Hopper.

'Coffee?' Ash asks, as I'm staring at the painting and trying to right my breathing.

'Please.'

While he's making it, I turn away from the Hopper and walk over to his bookcase. I can't help myself. I need to check if they're there. The shelving itself is laminate – an actual crime, in an apartment like this – but I can't pay attention to that now. There's only one thing I'm looking for.

The collection is sparse – probably no more than ten or fifteen books in total, which makes it easy to spot them. *A Place of My Own: The Architecture of Daydreams. Analysing Architecture. Art and Illusion.* All arranged together, in order of height.

'Sorry,' Ash says, from the kitchen area. 'It's not the sexiest book collection you'll ever see.'

For so long, my only wish in the world has been to have just one more conversation with Jamie. To tell him how much I still love him. To show him everything that's changed since I last saw him. To hold him and kiss him again, tell him I would have waited ten more lifetimes for another chance to see him smile.

The coffee's ready. Mind spinning, I perch on a stool at the enormous hulk of a kitchen island, which is about the size of a ten-seater dining table. I can see the river from here, framed by the windows like a polyptych artwork.

Jamie would have *loved* this place.

'So, what's the verdict?' Ash passes me a coffee in a satin-black mug.

'He'd have loved it.'

'Sorry?'

A kick of panic in my chest. I stare at him for a couple of moments.

Ash smiles, like he thinks there's a joke he's not getting. 'Who would have loved it?'

A beat passes. 'No-one. Sorry. Misheard you.'

He appears to shake it off, then tries again. 'Verdict on the décor?'

My eyes alight on a copy of the *River Cafe Cook Book*. I blink back memories of Jamie's copy, sauce-splattered and dog-eared, back at Edinburgh Road.

Come on, Neve. Pull yourself together.

'Well, that depends,' I say, sipping my coffee, which is just how I like it, strong and smooth. 'How much are you looking to spend?'

He grimaces. 'Not a fortune, sadly. I spent enough buying it in the first place.'

How are we ever going to afford something like that?

Mortgage ourselves up to the eyeballs and die broke and in debt, obviously.

But we'll be happy.

Ash misinterprets my expression. 'I inherited some money from my grandmother. Could never have afforded it otherwise. As it is, I'm mortgaged up to the eyeballs.'

I open my mouth to tell him I wasn't making assumptions about his finances, but he's already moved on.

'It all depends on what you'd suggest.'

'Well, we're definitely not talking about spending a fortune. First, I'd say you need to energise the space with some colour.' I get up with my coffee and cross the room towards the sofa – a blank block of charcoal grey, no cushions, no pattern. 'But you don't want to overcrowd it, or complicate it. You just need a few well-judged additions.'

'Such as?'

'Well, most people would be tempted to buy everything vintage, but you need to work some modern pieces in too or it will end up looking . . . too theme-y.'

'Theme-y. Exactly. I was worried about that.'

'But you can nod to it. Don't be *afraid* of vintage, but don't flood the place with it either, you know? You could go for some reworked industrial pieces, which will give you enough of a modern twist.'

He is frowning, nodding. 'Reworked pieces. Yes.'

I press my palm against a warm patch of sunlit brickwork. 'And brick's a gift, actually. It can carry bright colours really well, so don't be afraid to be bold. It's all quite monochrome in here. Plus, brass and steel always make a good textural contrast to brickwork, which you could achieve with lamps or picture frames.' I glance at him, and he's smiling. 'What?' I say, smiling uncertainly back at him.

'No, it's . . .' He shakes his head. 'I love how passionate you are. Carry on.'

'Well, I always advise clients to experiment with texture – if you use different materials, it can help the place to feel cosy, even though it's a big space.' I spin round, taking in the scale of the room again. 'So, you could use curtains in here, instead of blinds, for example. Oh, and you need a few lamps, to create a softer ambiance . . . and you could actually ask Parveen for ideas about art. She's kind of our in-house expert.'

'I could just buy more Hopper.'

I smile. 'Definitely not. That much I do know. You need to mix it up.'

Ash walks over to the pendant lampshades suspended over the table and kitchen area. They're a strange shade of bottle green that's far too heavy for the airy space. 'What about these?'

'I'd actually recommend glass.'

'The filament-style ones? I quite like those.'

I shake my head. 'Too much. I'll find you some good ones.'

He tops up our coffees and we go outside onto the balcony. The punchy scent of river water is drifting up towards us, mingled with the fragrance of blossom.

'So, where did you live before this?' I ask.

'Actually, for a while ... Airbnbs. Friends' sofas. My parents' place, for a few months.' He lets out a breath. 'My girlfriend and I were sharing a place together, but ...'

I wait for the pause to unfold.

'I found out ... she'd been seeing someone else.'

'I'm sorry. How long had you been—'

'Two years. Missed all the signs.' He shakes his head, sips his coffee. 'How about you? Do you ... live with anyone?'

'No. I've ... been focusing on work recently, really. I broke up with someone last year.' I throw him a look of solidarity. 'He was seeing a friend of mine, I think. They're getting married now. He rang me a couple of weeks back, to tell me.'

Ash looks appalled. 'God. That's brutal. At least Tabitha had the decency to slink off and never contact me again.'

'It's fine,' I assure him, with a smile. 'I don't think by the end I was really in love with him anyway.'

And then – maybe it is something about the way Ash returns my smile, that kilowatt gaze of his, that makes my mind pivot back to Jamie. I still can't work out why Ash resembles him so closely. Is it linked to the accident, his lightning strike? I don't see how it can be, and I have no idea yet how the dots join up. But something about it all is nagging at me. The personality change he says he went through.

'Can I ask you something? If you don't mind talking about it.'

'Sure.'

I try not to picture Jamie, his twisted body in the road, being pummelled by falling rain. 'What . . . happened on the night of your accident?'

He sips his coffee, takes a few moments to answer. 'I don't have massively clear memories of it, actually. But from what I can remember, and the stuff I've been told, it was this insane weather, like . . . the most apocalyptic storm you've ever seen. And I was at a mate's flat, and he had this little balcony, and being the idiot I was, I thought I'd go outside and—' He breaks off, shakes his head. 'Actually, I honestly don't know what I was doing. Squaring up to the lightning, or something.'

Despite myself, I smile. 'Wow. Picking a fight with a thunderstorm?'

'Like I said. I was an idiot back then. Anyway, that was when . . . I was hit.'

'What did it feel like?'

'No idea, thankfully. I can't remember.'

'And afterwards?'

'I was in hospital for a week.'

'Were you injured? Physically, I mean.'

'Some burns. And broken ribs from the CPR.'

'CPR? You mean—'

He nods. 'Yeah. My heart did actually stop beating. They had to bring me back.'

'That's crazy,' I say quietly.

'Yeah. I'm . . . insanely lucky.' He lets out a breath. 'What else? I have some scars on my chest.'

'From the lightning?'

He nods. 'I'm like, a much cooler Harry Potter.'

'Is that how you introduce yourself to girls in bars?'

'Oh, so *that's* where I've been going wrong.'

I smile. Then I take a breath, start to probe again in a way I know I probably shouldn't. But I feel a deep, elemental need to know. 'And mentally . . . you said you felt different too? Like you'd had a personality change?'

'Well, the best way to describe it is as though I'd had this bolt of clarity. Like I'd been sleepwalking up till that point. That was when I quit medicine, moved to London to train as an architect. Everyone around me thought I'd lost my mind, obviously. They all thought I had a brain injury or something.'

'And . . . did you?' I ask, as delicately as possible.

'Did I what?'

'Have a brain injury.'

He shakes his head. 'Thankfully, no. Given that most people in my position – they wouldn't have survived. Or they'd have had severe brain damage, or been in a coma, or had long-term neurological issues. I mean, I do get occasional nerve pain, but nothing like what I could be living with. That's why I find the whole "lightning strike" thing a bit frustrating. The novelty factor. Because actually, it can destroy lives. *Has* destroyed lives.'

'And your family and friends,' I press. 'You said they think you're like a different person?'

He nods. 'Yeah. I guess because after it happened, I seemed to have this sudden sense of . . . disconnect from them. Like the people and things I'd known my whole life felt . . . I don't know. Alien. Like they were nothing to do with me. And my memories from before the accident became patchy. I could only seem to remember stuff when people prompted me. I had this very definite sense of ... being dropped into a life I didn't recognise. And that was upsetting for everyone.'

'But for you?'

He takes a couple of moments to consider this, as though it's the first time anyone has asked. 'Not ... so much. People kept telling me I'd changed, and I knew it objectively, but I couldn't *feel* it, you know? And the thing is, leaving my old life behind actually felt good. Because people change all the time, right? They grow, become better versions of themselves.'

I nod. *They do, but* ... 'Didn't you ever think it was strange, though? Didn't you want an explanation?'

He shrugs. 'No, because it wasn't medical. Looking back, it was more like ... a life stage. A wake-up call.'

'But your family never accepted it.'

'No. And it is hard for me to think they still pine for the loud-mouthed idiot I was back then. But it's been nearly nine years. I guess as time moves on, I'm hoping they might forget who was I before and concentrate on who I am now.'

He tells me about his twin sister, an anaesthetist who lives in Norwich. But he says they don't hang out much.

'We don't have ... loads in common any more. She's still a bit of a wild child, I guess you could say.' He shakes his head. 'I know I'm *supposed* to miss Gabi, and the bond we used to have, but ... I guess I've just moved on.'

'Sorry. Feel like I'm grilling you a bit.'

He smiles. 'I do normally have to be a couple of whiskies down before I get into stuff like this, but with you . . . I guess not.' He tips his coffee cup to me in a kind of toast as I feel his ankle find mine.

11.

I first see Lara again on Sunday morning as I'm heading home from a spin class. She is walking towards me along London Street with a man, her hand wound into his. She's wearing a long blue-and-white dress that billows around her ankles. Her blonde curls are cropped shorter now, and she's thinner than she used to be. But it is her smile I recognise first. Like sunshine slicing through cloud.

We've not spoken since that night. For years I pictured seeing her again, coming face to face. I practised what I would say. I wondered if anger would overwhelm me, if I might reach out and slap her, or throw a drink at her, if I had one to hand.

She glances up now, sees me. Stops walking. Our eyes meet.

I watch as her boyfriend (or maybe it's her husband) follows her gaze. As he looks at me, I know he knows. She's told him everything.

She swallows, takes another couple of steps forward. I do the same.

I can recall very little about our conversation, the last time we spoke. Though I do remember knowing that I never wanted to see her again.

The sky today is surly and grey, the air heavy with humidity. It keeps threatening to rain, a few errant spots landing here and there. It suddenly seems fitting, somehow, as for me, rain is the weather of loss and heartbreak.

Despite everything, her face reflects none of my trepidation. Her eyes glow warm and bright. 'Neve. Hi. How are you?'

It's an almost unfathomable question, but Lara always did have a habit of launching into huge, unassailable topics, no matter the context. (As we were getting ready to go out: *How many different kinds of love do you reckon there are?* Over dinner: *Do you think addiction is nature or nurture?* While we were watching TV: *Would you say cancer's mostly genetic or environmental?*)

It was one of the things I loved most about her. How deeply she made me think.

'You're back,' is all I manage, one of the million things I could say.

'Temporarily. Family stuff.' She glances up at the man by her side. 'This is Felix. Felix, meet Neve.'

He puts out his free hand and grips mine, looks me right in the eyes. His demeanour is gentle and warm, and he is very tall, just as my mother said. Six foot three at least, possibly taller. 'Pleasure to meet you.'

Is it? I think, the cordiality catching me off guard. *You must know our history.* And then, *You're American.*

'Felix is my—'

Don't say husband. Please don't say husband. I'm not sure I can face hearing about Lara getting married without me.

73

Even though I uninvited her to my own life many years ago.

'—boyfriend.'

I nod, then can't come up with anything else to say. Even though there is so much. Too much.

'You know what,' Felix says. His voice is very soothing, a deep river of charm. 'I have some things I need to catch up on, so why don't you go ahead and grab a coffee? I can see you back at the house.'

What house? I think, wildly, and then, *Who are you to suggest we go for coffee?*

Lara looks at me. 'Do you have some time?'

Even just a couple of weeks ago, I'm sure I would have shaken my head and walked away. But everything has changed since then. I have met Ash, who reminds me so much of Jamie, I've been pulled unexpectedly back into my life of nearly a decade ago, of which Lara was a huge, unalterable part.

'Okay,' I say.

Felix puts an arm around Lara's shoulders and squeezes her, then pecks her tenderly on the head. 'You going to be okay?'

She nods meekly, and straight away I marvel at how much she has changed, that when I last knew her, she would have baulked at such over-protectiveness. She might even have shoved an elbow into his ribs.

But she doesn't do that. And I don't even comment with my eyes, as I would have done once, because it is no longer my place to.

★   ★   ★

Lara suggests a cafe we both used to love, and though it feels all wrong to go there – to time-travel back to the days when she was my closest friend – I agree.

Back then, I wouldn't have known how to survive nine days without her, let alone nine years. But after the accident, my anger became like a creature living inside me. Over the years that followed, I missed her so badly the pain of it felt physical sometimes. But I simply couldn't picture her face without picturing what she'd done too.

She tried hard to make contact at first, sending post-cards and letters and emails, leaving messages. She even dropped in on my mum a couple of times. But I never responded. A few years passed, then she sent me an email from a work account, a couple of WhatsApps. But I deleted them unread. It made me angry, the idea of her thinking the years would have smoothed away the sharpness of what had happened.

She stopped trying after that.

'You look great, Neve,' she says now, as we regard each other across the table.

She looks mostly the same as she did back then. Her teeth are a little straighter and whiter, maybe. Her skin carries a few new creases. Her face has lost its adolescent plumpness, which makes her blue eyes seem even more striking, somehow. Freckles pepper her cheeks and nose. She always got them in summer, would try to cover them with concealer, until I persuaded her not to.

My heart is a starfish in my chest. My oldest friend is right in front of me. *Right here.*

Our server comes to take our order. Lara asks for black decaf. I go for espresso, maybe to indicate I don't plan on staying long.

'Neve. There are some things I need to say to you.'

I shake my head. 'Not now. I can't do that . . . now.'

Her expression recalibrates slightly. Perhaps she had a speech prepared. Maybe, like me, she's stood in front of myriad mirrors over the years, mouthing the words she imagines it will make her feel better to say.

'Tell me about Felix,' I say instead. Because, despite everything, I know I'm happy for her. I guess some instincts you can't overturn.

She smiles, and it glitters. Love has blazed its trail across her face. 'He's from California. Well, he was born in Chicago, but he moved to Santa Cruz a few years ago.'

'How did you meet?'

'I beat him at pool, at a house party in St John's Wood. He used to be a professional tennis player, so he was used to winning everything. Anyway, he found me later and challenged me to a rematch, obviously, but I was enjoying this amazing view out on the balcony, overlooking the cricket ground. The sun was coming up, so we just stayed out there talking. And he ended up trying to explain cricket to me, which was hilarious, because it was obvious he didn't have a clue, so I just waited for him to finish like I didn't either, then I told him he'd got practically *all* of it wrong. And when I started explaining what *actually* happens when one side declares, I don't think his ego could quite handle it, so to shut me up he kissed me, and . . . Well. Here we are.'

I smile, because I can just imagine her calculating exactly the right moment at which to take him down. 'Whose place was it?' I ask, wondering exactly how much a balcony flat overlooking Lord's sets a person back these days.

'The director of a film I was working on. I'm ... a production designer now.'

I know this, of course, because I stalk her online from time to time, checking her IMDb and Wikipedia like she's an ex I can't get over. She started out in the theatre before moving into TV and film, recently working on a BAFTA-winning series set in the 1800s and even an Oscar-nominated film, a science-fiction love story.

Before I can stop it, I feel second-hand pride bloom in my belly.

'So are you ... Will you move to America? To be with Felix? Is it better for work out there?'

She hesitates. 'I think ... I'll probably move in with him at some point, yeah.'

The server returns and sets down our drinks.

'Is he retired?'

Lara laughs. 'Ha. No. He's in tech. He co-founded a robotics company.'

'Tennis to robotics? That's ...'

'I know. He's one of those infuriating people with the Midas touch. And he's insanely intelligent. Honestly, Neve, sometimes he starts talking and I just have to stop him and say, *I literally have no idea what you're on about.*' She laughs. 'And we go to these dinner parties, and ... they're on another level, some of the people he hangs out with. Seriously. So clever. All these investors and tech people and serial entrepreneurs.'

I think about how protective Felix seemed just now. I picture him lecturing her about cricket or robotics or the Nasdaq, and I wonder if it's possible Lara can have become a completely different person in the years since I last saw her. 'You're intelligent,' I remind her, in case she's somehow forgotten how she barely needed to study for those A-stars in her exams.

She meets my eye and smiles. 'Bad choice of word. I guess I meant we're from very different worlds. But I love him to bits, Neve. From that first night, I was just . . . blindsided by him. Like, I knew he was my person, you know? I'd never felt that way about anyone before.'

I think of Jamie, and swallow.

'And actually, I have you to thank.'

'Me?'

'Yeah. Remember that night you came to get me? After—'

'Yes,' I say, because I'll never forget that night. How it sat in my stomach for weeks afterwards, the way close calls usually do.

'Well, you told me that night that I deserved better, that I deserved someone who knew my worth, and . . . I never forgot it, Neve. I thought about it for years afterwards, and . . . Felix was the first guy I met who truly fitted that description. So.' She holds my gaze for a couple of moments, and I am taken right back to that horrible night, the way she cried and doubted herself, and the fury that flared inside me on her behalf.

'And you?' she says. 'Are you seeing anyone? What about work? I want to know everything.'

I tell her about my job, that I'm hoping to be promoted, that I'm probably borderline workaholic but wouldn't have it any other way. I describe my house, all the work I've put into renovating it over the years.

'Oh,' she says, her eyes lighting up. 'You'd *love* Felix's place. It's a designer's dream, honestly. It overlooks Monterey Bay. It's completely insane.'

She gets out her phone to show me, and as I look through images of the panoramic views and pool, of the walk-in wardrobes and floating staircases, of the wine cellar and movie room – the calibre of interiors, frankly, I could only dream of having the budget to execute – I realise this man is rich. Like, off-the-charts wealthy.

'Lara,' I say, looking at her.

She makes a face. 'I know. Sorry. I'm honestly not trying to brag. I had no idea when I met him.' She puts her phone away. 'Anyway. You never answered my question.'

'What question?' I say, though of course I know.

'Are you seeing anyone?' She speaks tactfully, like an addiction counsellor trying to discern whether or not I've fallen off the wagon.

I swallow. 'There's someone . . . I like. Through work. But it's not . . . turned into anything yet.' I don't mention, of course, how much this person resembles Jamie. That there are so many similarities between them, it's starting to feel weird.

She smiles, says something about a boy from school I don't quite catch because I keep getting distracted by the fact that we're sitting in this cafe, chatting as if we're spin class buddies, as if we have no history, as if we don't know the meaning of tragedy. Fear keeps rising inside me in waves: did I make a mistake by cutting her out of my life? Was I too stubborn, too unreasonable? But then I remind myself of what happened that night, and the queasiness of doubt subsides.

If I'd known talking to Lara would feel this physical, I'd have forgone the espresso.

'So tell me about this guy,' she says, but suddenly it's too much, this muddle in my head of Ash and Jamie and now Lara being back . . . and I have no idea how to feel about any of it.

'Actually,' I say, checking a watch that isn't on my wrist, 'I really have to go.'

'Please give me your number,' she says, like she's been fully expecting me to try to leg it. Across the table, she covers my hand with hers, and it feels nice and absurd all at once, a bit like it does when my mum tries to touch me. 'I really want to see you again, Neve. It's been way too long. Please.'

I hesitate, then make the mistake of looking right into her eyes. They are the beautiful, depthless blue of Californian skies, and I have missed them. 'Okay,' I say.

She passes me her phone, and I tap in my number, then pass it back to her. Straight away, I hear my own phone buzz.

She meets my eye and smiles. 'Just wanted to make sure.'

I nod, and pull on my jacket, grab my bag.

'This was nice,' she says.

At this, finally, it ignites inside me: the anger and indignation, a white-hot flare of fury. *Do you think because we've had coffee, all is forgotten? Do you really think this is all it takes?*

'I know you don't want to talk about that night,' Lara says, 'but I have to say this to you, before you go. I'm so sorry, Neve. I'm so sorry about what happened.'

I just stare at her. She's told me this before, of course, but maybe this time – maybe – I am finally ready to hear it.

12.

Late morning on Monday, Parveen returns from an on-site meeting at Millbrook and strides straight over to my desk.

'I need to brief you on something.'

I'm absorbed in adding notes to a presentation for the design of a wellness spa in the basement of a house in Cambridge. It's one of those dream projects that gives you rare licence to really indulge (hello infrared sauna, sun tunnels and Roman bathhouse tiling) because the owners have a ridiculously roomy budget and want high-end everything, no expense spared.

'Now?' I ask her, suspecting this might be to do with Ash.

'Now.'

You can overhear pretty much everything in our open-plan office, so I'm relieved to follow Parveen into one of the glass-walled meeting rooms.

The Kelley Lane offices made me melt, the first time I walked into them. They're on the ground floor of a converted Edwardian house on Newmarket Road, open-plan and high-ceilinged, with walls the colour of rock salt and floors of pristinely weathered oak. Our desks sit on vintage-style pastel rugs – all cabling discreetly disguised, of course – and the space is finished with potted plants and Parveen-recommended artwork. There is a space-age coffee machine and a handful of bladeless fans, but we keep the ugly office printer out of sight in a cupboard. The air is fragranced with Jo Malone, and whenever we meet in here with clients or contractors, they always seem inclined to linger. I've sometimes wondered if it's all just Kelley's way of making us willing to work longer hours.

After the accident, driven by grief and anger and a thunderbolt of momentum that took even my own breath away, I started working so hard that my final-year projects and grades turned to solid gold. By the time I applied for the post at Kelley's, I'd already interned for her three times. I'll for ever be indebted to her for hiring me permanently, because it allowed me to fulfil the potential that Jamie so often insisted I had.

Parveen shuts the door behind us, crosses her arms. She hasn't even removed her jacket. 'Exactly what have you done to Mr Heartwell?'

A tiny glitter canon goes off in my stomach. 'Er, I'm not sure?'

'Well, he wouldn't shut up about you the whole time I was on site today. He kept raving about how talented you are, and how much you've got in common, and how easy you are to talk to.'

I try and fail to hold back a smile. I messaged Parveen as soon as I left Ash's apartment on Saturday – after a second coffee and a peck on the cheek goodbye – to let her know that yes, it had gone well, but no, we didn't kiss.

'God, Parveen, you'd have *loved* his apartment. It's one of the old mills on the river, and the conversion is completely—'

Parveen raises a hand. 'I'll Google it later. What I want to know is, did you honestly not make a move?'

'No!' I say, laughing. 'We just had coffee. It was all very platonic.'

And though technically this is true, it's about a million miles away from how I really feel.

'Well, that's the opposite of what he's thinking, believe me. He could not stop talking about you.'

In lots of ways, Parveen has come to replace Lara in my life. Or, not replace – but fill part of the gap she left, maybe. Other acquaintances feel more casual – spin class buddies, ex-colleagues. The kind of people you meet for coffee rather than confide in. But Parveen has become the latter.

I think I probably told her about what happened to Jamie within a week of meeting her. She knows he's the only man I've ever loved; that I've been semi-serious about just three people in the nine years since he died. She's aware of what happened with Leo, of how cynical I've become about love, how laser-focused on work. Sometimes, when she's describing something nice she's done with Maz and the twins, I get the impression she's trying to remind me that there is still magic to be found in long-term relationships.

Parveen taps a manicured fingernail against the table. She takes her nails very seriously. I don't think I've ever seen her without French tips. 'So. Are you going to see him again?'

'I want to, but . . .' *He's so much like my dead boyfriend, I can't breathe, sometimes.* 'I'm busy, and after what went on with Leo . . .'

She rolls her eyes. 'Two terrible reasons. You know as well as I do that Ash is a catch-with-a-capital-C. Trust me, if I wasn't with Maz, I'd be fighting you for him.'

'You don't fight over boys,' I say, with a smile.

'Actually, I threw a pint of lemonade over someone once, when I thought she was coming on to Maz. Guess who it turned out to be?'

'I couldn't possibly.'

'His *sister*. I'd never met her before. I wanted to die. Lucky for me, his family are a *very* discreet bunch. In that it's been brought up at every single family occasion since. If I never see another bottle of R.White's in my life it'll be too soon.'

Kelley floats past the glass doors in a fitted floral dress, presumably back from a meeting somewhere. Automatically, we both get to our feet.

'You never told me that before,' I say to Parveen, with a smile.

She pauses with her hand on the door. 'That's because I wanted you to think I'm way too well adjusted for cat-fighting in bars, obviously. Anyway. Are we decided? You're going for it, with Ash?'

I wish it could be that simple. But the truth is, I've been trying to find Jamie again ever since he died. Which I know to be about as healthy and rational as my mother fantasising that my dad might one day come home.

And Ash is so much Jamie, I can't imagine that getting into something with him is going to solve my problem.

13.

Then

For Christmas that first year of uni, Jamie's parents bought us tickets to see London Grammar the following spring. Since the gig was in London, the weekend of Jamie's birthday, they were also treating us to a night in a posh hotel – a gesture that made me wonder if they were finally on the way to accepting me – and had booked a table for the four of us in some trendy Mayfair restaurant. I was excited to spend a weekend doing things we'd never normally have been able to afford. Or that I wouldn't, anyway.

Work at uni had ramped up that spring. Not for me so much – having spent most of my contact time that year in the print and dye workshop, my main focus now was on writing a research essay on the role of smart materials in textile design, the pace of which was fairly relaxed. Jamie, on the other hand, had been frantically juggling essays, drawings, models and presentations, in between site visits and workshops, in preparation for assessment at the end of the year.

He had military focus. We didn't go out much. He'd take his laptop to bed, then get up early to flip through library books on land law, and health and safety, and building regulations. He said working hard was how his brother Harry had got to where he was, and how his dad had made his fortune. He carried around notes on topics far beyond my sphere of curiosity, like ideological positions in architecture, and the impact of green buildings on sustainable development. I'd watch him sketching plans of every kind of structure from cinemas to cricket pavilions as he drank his morning coffee. I knew he was driven primarily by ambition – he wanted to have his name on something iconic, to be known for a famous building. Something world-class, he told me, like a concert hall, or a museum, or a city skyline landmark. He always said he wanted to be the next Norman Foster. 'I'm going to design the next Gherkin,' he would say. And I didn't doubt for a moment that one day, he would.

I envied his drive, sometimes. I was still toying with the idea of working in interior design, so had been paying more attention to the relevant parts of my course, like workshops on how to use CAD, and the employer engagement project briefing us to produce six different designs of curtain. I started buying interiors magazines, and creating scrapbooks and mood boards of rooms that inspired me. I followed interior designers on Instagram. I let the thought of it percolate. I went to bed dreaming of warehouse conversions, and the apartment Jamie and I were going to live in one day.

The arrangement for the gig was that Jamie would go to London a night early, to catch up with his parents and attend some architectural function with his dad. He would meet me off the train at Liverpool Street the next day.

Jamie had visited London a handful of times that year, to see his parents. I'd gone with him twice. His dad had ended up renting out the Soho flat, so when we visited, we stayed with them in Putney.

From the outside, the Putney house was Edwardian period perfection: red brick, with a wooden-framed porch and mock-Tudor cladding and timbers on the front apex. But inside, it felt like exposure therapy for migraine sufferers. It had been stripped of any residual character – whether by Jamie's parents or the previous owners, I wasn't sure and couldn't ask – resulting in a mish-mash of laminate flooring, a series of increasingly bizarre lamp-shades, fireplaces painted in garish colours and a jumble of furniture spanning several architectural periods. The only bit I liked was the garden – long and wild and unkempt, it was somewhere I felt I could sneak away to, and there were always a couple of deckchairs handily propped up near the shed at the bottom, well out of view of the house.

Less than an hour before I was due to catch my train to London for the gig, Jamie reappeared without warning back at Edinburgh Road.

Lara and I were lying on my bed, looking over some screen-printed cushion covers I'd made earlier in the week. We were trying to decide if the pattern on them more closely resembled amoebae, or neurons. My tutors

always seemed to want us to come up with profound inter-
pretations of the stuff we created.

'Amoebae can eat your brain,' Lara was saying, reading
from her laptop. 'Better call them neurons.'

It was then that Jamie appeared in the doorway, hands in
pockets, making us both jump.

After a second or two, Lara said, 'Well, that Pukka Pie
isn't going to microwave itself,' before vanishing, heading
downstairs to the kitchen.

'What's wrong?' I said, scrambling into a sitting position.
'What are you doing here? Are you okay?'

He slung down his bag. 'The gig's off. I can't do it. I'm
sorry.'

'What? Why?' We'd been looking forward to this for
months, ever since Christmas.

'Had a massive row with my dad.'

'About what?'

He shook his head and came to sit down next to me.
Then he let out a breath so long and heavy I wondered if
he'd been holding it in for hours. He pushed the hair back
from his face. It had grown longer since we'd been at uni,
and I knew it annoyed his dad (which was possibly why I
liked it so much).

'He's still on about the flat, in Soho. He wants me to
move there in September, and finish my degree in
London.' He drew a hand down his face, seemingly
exhausted. 'He's obsessed, honestly. Anyway, I told him
where to shove it. Which didn't go down well. He even
ended up getting Harry on the phone, to try to "talk
sense" into me.'

My heart stung with the knowledge that Jamie's dad had effectively asked him to dump me and move to London alone.

Jamie took my hand. 'He's just ... worried about us committing too soon. You know.'

I swallowed. 'Jamie. Is there any part of you ... that agrees with your dad? Because if there is, I don't want to be the one who—'

'Not a single, tiny part, okay?' He took my face between his palms and kissed me. 'His dreams ... they're not my dreams. I'm happy, why can't he see that?'

'Maybe he can. Maybe that's what frightens him.'

He pulled away slightly. 'How do you mean?'

'Well, if you're happy, and content, you don't need him any more, do you? And maybe that scares him.' I didn't add that I thought his dad was egotistical in the extreme, that he lived for constant capitulation to his views.

We sat there for a few moments, not speaking, just holding hands. Then Jamie got up, and said, 'Wait there.'

He left the room, and I heard him jog downstairs.

I drew my knees into my chest. Secretly, I'd always hoped that one day, Jamie's parents would warm to me. That eventually, I might become part of his family. A family who never forgot birthdays, who celebrated Christmases together. Who could name each other's favourite TV shows and music and preferred flavour of ice cream.

I knew Jamie's brother Harry had a girlfriend in Zurich. But I had no idea whether it had been an uphill battle for her too, with his family, at the start. Whether it still was.

After a few minutes, Jamie returned. He was holding Lara's plastic beer cups from last year's Glastonbury, each one filled to the brim.

Passing me a cup, Jamie extended a hand. 'I guess we're just going to have our own private gig right here.'

I smiled as he pulled me to my feet.

'I have glow sticks and everything.'

'Lara's saving those for Latitude.'

'I won't tell if you won't.'

Music kicked in on his phone: 'Hey Now'. He grabbed me around the waist, pulling me into him for a kiss. 'Neve, you need to know . . . I don't care what my dad says, okay? I don't care what anyone says. You and me – we're meant for each other.'

'I know. I love you. I know.'

'I want to be with you for ever. I don't care if we're young. I can't imagine my life with anyone else.'

We talked as the music became water around us. We dreamed out loud about the home we'd share one day, the jobs we'd have, the new friends we'd make. The holidays, the gigs, our adventures-to-be. The memories-in-waiting. And then he dipped his mouth to my collarbone, and I let my head roll back as a shiver of pleasure ran through me.

We played the album six times that night, warm as nesting animals in each other's arms, the glow sticks like beacons as dusk descended. The darkness became our intimacy, our permission to say anything.

So in the end, Jamie's dad's attempt at driving us apart had had the exact opposite effect. Because after that night, I knew we were closer than ever.

14.

Now

A colleague recommends a Chinese film playing at the Picturehouse, and I message Ash to ask if he fancies it.

The film turns out to be a powerful love story about two thirty-something aspiring artists. My colleague had very much emphasised the art and skipped over the part about it being an epic and highly-charged romance.

Inside the darkened cinema, all my senses seem heightened. I am very aware of Ash's warm proximity, how good he smells, how he has angled his knee into my space, and how I'm enjoying it. I know, already, that I'd love to reach out and feel for his hand. That in my head, I'm mere moments from kissing him.

Maybe it's partly the film that is stirring me up like this. Romance isn't usually my preferred genre, but I'm surprised to realise it has overridden much of my cynicism. And aside from mild embarrassment at having been the one to suggest it, I'm actually enjoying all the things it's making me feel.

'Love this building,' Ash says afterwards, as we make our way back towards the main doors.

I nod. 'It's so beautiful.' The cinema is sited in a Grade I listed part-medieval merchant's house, its oldest sections dating back to the fourteenth century. Now, it's a sympathetic blend of old and new, a perfect synthesis of flint, glass and low-hanging beams.

On the steps outside, I turn to him. 'Did you like the film?'

'Loved it.'

'Really?'

'Didn't you?'

'Yes, but I wasn't expecting it to be so—' I break off, fumbling for the right word.

'Romantic?'

'I was going to say sentimental.'

He smiles. 'Ah, I'm not averse to some good old-fashioned sentiment.' Reaching out, he runs a hand down my arm, slow and tender in a way that makes me shiver. 'Do you . . . fancy a nightcap?'

'Yes,' I say, although I already know that heading back to his place will surely only supercharge everything I am starting to feel.

Back at the apartment, he takes my jacket. I privately hope he likes the dress I'm wearing. My hair is tied back in a long plait that falls between my shoulder blades.

Ash is wearing jeans and a soft grey sweater, understated in a way that makes me smile inside. I bet he'd be genuinely surprised – and probably mortified – if he knew just how many people in my office have a fairly major crush on him.

He pours two glasses of wine and dips the overhead lights. We sit down together on the sofa. Music floods the room.

At the sound of London Grammar's first album, my heart lurches.

'Apologies for the glasses,' he says, passing me one. 'They're only Habitat, I'm afraid.'

I twirl the glass round by its stem, grateful for the distraction. 'Do you think I'm a snob?'

He smiles a *no*. 'I guess I just presumed . . . you import yours from Italy, or something.'

I smile back at him. 'Actually, if I did, they'd be from Austria, but that would be a step too far even for me. Anyway, there's a difference between what I might advise my clients to do, and what I do myself.'

'Ah, I know that feeling. "Do I agree that your Grade II listed manor-house is crying out for a swimming pool with neon-purple uplighting in the orangery? Absolutely."'

I sip my wine. I want to get to know him better, and I'm curious about his ex. 'Tell me about Tabitha,' I say cautiously, hoping I'm not being too personal.

He doesn't seem fazed. 'Well, she was . . . quite hard to work out, sometimes. Our relationship wasn't particularly easy.'

'In what way?'

'I had trouble pinning down . . . who she really was. She's one of those people who thinks that if it's not online, it didn't happen. And I guess that all came with a bit of self-absorption. She didn't really have that much time for me, or my world.' He smiles faintly. 'She used to hate it when I talked about work. Which was kind of a problem in the end, because I think about work a *lot*. I'm not sure we ever really had that much in common, if I'm honest. I kept having to hide more and more of myself from her, just to keep things harmonious, and in the end . . . I think we were just dating each other's shadow. Which is why it made it so easy for her to cheat, I guess.'

'I'm sorry. That all sounds quite stressful.'

'Ah, don't get me wrong. There was good stuff too. I was pretty infatuated, at the start. But I guess after we broke up . . . I knew I wanted to find . . .'

I wait, breath stalled in my throat.

'. . . something real.'

He shifts his position, lets his knee fall against mine. The room suddenly seems bigger, almost cavernous. My heart goes into freefall. I am insanely attracted to him – more than I've dared to admit to myself until this moment. He is handsome, of course, but I also feel a connection to him I haven't experienced since Jamie. Mind-altering chemistry, the kind that comes with side effects, withdrawals.

Several simmering, spellbound seconds. One of us has to make the first move.

The music segues into 'If You Wait'. I lean over and put my lips to his. He responds instantly. And the kiss isn't shy or tentative, but assured and intense, as if it's been on both our minds for hours, days, weeks. Ash kisses like there's something at stake. I haven't had a kiss like this since Jamie, with a heat that lights up every cell in my body.

After a minute or so, we pull apart. He exhales heavily, keeps his hand at the back of my neck. I take in the bloom of pleasure on his face, the dimples and laughter lines that spring to his skin as he smiles.

I move towards him again, but as I do, I feel something crunch beneath me, and realise I am sitting on a piece of paper.

I pull it out from under me and hand it to him with an apologetic smile, resisting the urge to read what's on it. 'Sorry. Hope it's not important.'

He laughs, then passes it back to me. 'Actually, I was making a list. Of stuff I should buy for this place.'

I stare down at it, and as I do, the writing starts to blur.

This is Jamie's handwriting. I'd know it anywhere.

I blink once, twice. The words seem to shuffle and sharpen again.

The handwriting of someone you love . . . it's something you'd recognise for ever. You never forget it.

'You okay?' Ash asks, reaching out to touch my leg.

I stare down at his hand on the bare skin of my thigh.

How are you doing this?

I swallow, attempt to refocus. 'Yes. Yes.'

A moment passes. 'Are you sure? Is this . . .? I don't want to make you feel—'

But before he can finish, I drop the paper and move towards him again. I want to push Jamie from my mind. I don't want to put the brakes on this, because it really is so good.

I feel Ash smile as our lips meet.

Think about this instead, I tell myself. *About the man who's right here, in front of you.*

15.

B ut I don't stay. As soon as the kiss becomes so good that I don't want it to stop, I make an effort to peel away from him, and whisper, 'I should go.'

I've never been one to rush in. And even though every last atom of me wants to take things further, I imagine waking up tomorrow and worrying that it had just been a little too much, too soon.

Plus, the thought of Jamie is still nagging at me. It's an uncertainty I can't quite place or discern, like the sense of being followed in the dark. My brain keeps about-turning, trying to alight on what it is that's disturbing me, but much like peripheral vision, it remains frustratingly foggy.

I decide to walk – despite Ash's pleas for me to take a cab – as the night seems warm and still, and I fancy the fresh air. Halfway home, however, the skies deliver a sluice of early summer rain and I get back to the house soaked through.

I strip off and rub my hair with a towel, then find a T-shirt and tracksuit bottoms, pulling on an old hoodie and socks in an effort to warm up. I scrape my hair into a topknot, then sit on the sofa without even turning on the light, or drawing the curtains.

Reflexively, I check my phone for work emails, missed calls, but there is nothing. Just a message from Ash.

> Thanks for an amazing evening
>
> Let me know you got home safe
>
> I think you're great, Neve x

I smile, then sit very still for a moment, my mind whirling, my insides still rocking from the pleasure of kissing him.

I think about what I would do at work, in this situation.

Start at the beginning, then break it down.

So I open the notes app on my phone, then start to make a list of all the ways in which Ash reminds me of Jamie.

Architect

Lives in the Old Yarn Mill – in 'our' apartment

Same books

Same handwriting

Same likes and dislikes

Tom Ford Noir

Nighthawks

Window fetish

London Grammar

Norman Foster + Gherkin

Had an accident on the SAME NIGHT as J. Less than
    100 yds away.

I pause to review the list. It's already so long. How can this many similarities possibly be coincidence?

My mind pumps. What next?

A little desk research, Neve.

I tap into my browser, then enter the most ridiculous search term I think I've ever typed.

When a person dies . . .
. . . can someone else take over their body?

The results load. I start tapping in and out of entries, one after the other. I search again. I read whole pages. News article after news article. I make leap after leap, searching and searching until my eyes start to burn, with exhaustion or tears or both.

Do YOU believe in walk-ins?
Wandering spirit 'walked in' to my husband's body
My best friend never truly died
DEAD woman's soul is INSIDE my niece!

Reams of articles – some of them obviously clickbait – describing a phenomenon I'd never heard of until now. The idea that a soul can 'walk in' to another body during a moment of trauma – or death. Could it be possible that when Ash's heart stopped beating that night – at the moment he 'died' – Jamie's soul moved in and somehow . . . took over?

Might Jamie not have been quite ready to leave this world – or me?

Ash checks off most of the supposed symptoms of being a walk-in. Major accident or life event. Disconnect from family and friends. Patchy memories of life before. Total personality change.

By now my mind is a blizzard. But not the type that looks pretty at Christmas – more like the kind of hazardous mess that causes pile-ups on the motorway.

I dive deeper, reading articles and blogs, watching videos and clips from podcasts.

Am I going crazy? Is this what madness feels like?

Outside, the rain is making steel drums of the window panes. To anyone else, the sound might sound meditative – beautiful, even. But to me, its relentless clatter only precipitates a rising panic inside me. It just reminds me of that night. Of the shining wet horror of the accident.

For the first time in a long while, I have the strangest urge to call Lara. She would know what to say, what I should do. She always did. Having Lara in my life was like being insured against adversity. Whatever happened, she would help me get through it – and vice versa.

I hover over Parveen's number for a few moments. But I can't do it. She's at home with Maz and the kids, and – much as I usually feel I can confide in her – this isn't the sort of thing I can offload to a work colleague. She can't do her job if she no longer respects me.

I turn back to the last web page.

Could Jamie have come back? Could his soul have walked into Ash's body? Might Ash actually *be* Jamie?

Perhaps this explains Ash's personality change. Maybe he was not taken over by aliens, in fact – but by Jamie himself, when he died.

No, my rational mind says. *The idea is completely preposterous.*

My thoughts are actually starting to scare me now. Maybe I need some time off. I haven't had any for months.

The last time I had a holiday was that ill-fated trip to Greece with Leo, well over a year ago. I've sold back annual leave to Kelley on more occasions than I can count.

Or maybe all this is simply confirmation that I'm just not ready to start seeing someone new. My mind clearly isn't in the right place.

I tap out of Safari and into my photo roll, seeking comfort, the balm of distraction.

Jamie and me at the beach, my bronzed face tipped up to his. Jamie amusingly off his tits at some gig or other. Him walking in front of me, along a tree-lined footpath. Smoking a bong. Scrawling his signature on my school shirt, the last day of exams. Dancing to ABBA on New Year's Eve. Sprawled out by the river on A-level results day.

Uncertainty resurfaces. Maybe he's returned to continue the love story we never got to finish. To become who he was always meant to be.

But . . . what the hell would that mean for me? I never thought I'd have the chance to finish what Jamie and I started, yet now . . .

I can't cope with this. I'm used to being in control of my emotions, my relationships, the world around me.

I stand up. I need to do something. Something that keeps me busy and unthinking, that occupies my hands. I head into the kitchen, grab a bottle and a cloth, then start to wipe down all my inside window frames with a spray that smells of clementines.

It's hard to know when the stress-cleaning kicked in. I definitely wasn't this way before Jamie's accident. But in the aftermath, I think I used it as a way to distract myself from the pain of losing him.

After a couple of hours, I crawl back onto the sofa, exhausted. Just as I used to do round Mum's, when Jamie first died. Even though they'd never really bonded, she was there for me then. For once, she was quiet and calm, her presence placid as snowfall.

I suffered with insomnia, right after it happened. It was vigilance, I see that now, stemming from the idea that Jamie's dying was a mistake. That his vanishing was only temporary. That he would come back to get me somehow.

And now – impossibly – maybe he has.

The next thing I know, the room is billowing with morning light. I start my Saturday with a shiver, incredulous and unnerved.

16.

L ater that afternoon, I call in at Mum's.

Ralph is in the kitchen, heating soup on the Aga. He doesn't have a family of his own. He does have a cat called Maisie, and a small group of acquaintances. But no kids, or spouse, or even ex-spouse, as far as I know.

'Hello,' I say. I always make the effort to be pleasant to Ralph, because he is only occasionally afforded the same courtesy from my mother. 'Where's Mum?'

'A little worse for wear,' he says, enunciating delicately, as if he's the one with the hangover. He tilts his head towards the ceiling. 'Having a lie-down.'

'Pub?'

He shakes his head. 'Wedding. Open bar.'

'Ah.' Mum always gets emotional at weddings, I assume because her own marriage didn't work out. 'Hence the soup?'

'Oh, no, this is for me. Late lunch. She still can't keep anything down, bless her.'

I wonder why Ralph's treating Mum like she's been struck down with norovirus, rather than a hangover that's entirely self-inflicted.

He decants the soup into a chipped bowl and takes it to the table, sits down and begins to eat. He's a creature of habit, Ralph. I'd wager he's had soup for lunch every Saturday of his life.

I survey the kitchen. It looks like it's lived in by students who've already written off their deposit. The tap drips non-stop. Empty bottles, plastic cartons and ashtrays litter every surface. One pane of the sash window has been replaced by cardboard, and I know for a fact that none of these lightbulbs are working. There are three dead plants by the sideboard, their leaves virtually dust. A few floor tiles are cracked, too – no doubt from when Mum's been drunk and dropped or dislodged something – and are patched together with duct tape. I know Ralph would sort it all out if he could, but Mum gets snippy with him whenever he tries to help.

There is a small bunch of wild flowers stuffed into a jam jar in the middle of the table. My mum doesn't do things like pick her own sweet peas from the jungle that is her back garden, so either they've been thoughtfully collected by Ralph, or Duke's reduced his budget for bouquets since I was last here.

I take a seat at the table opposite Ralph, rubbing at an old red wine stain in the woodgrain with my thumb. 'Can I ask you something?'

I've been thinking all morning about sharing what I know – or think I know – about Ash. My first inclination, still, is to call Lara, because she had that gift of making even my most outrageous confessions seem tame. With her, the lack of judgement always felt permissive and comforting.

I sometimes wonder who relies on her friendship these days, who enjoys the pleasure of simply knowing she's in the world. But Lara's not my wing-woman any more, and she won't ever be again. Some clocks you can't turn back.

There's no point talking to my mother about the idea of walk-ins – I'd probably get more sense out of that murdered cheese plant than I would from her – but Ralph has always been a good listener, thoughtful, and pragmatic. He is a tug boat of a man, always trying to guide everyone around him to where they need to be.

It does feel slightly strange, to be about to confide something so objectively odd. But if I can trust anyone not to laugh, or ridicule me, or be dismissive, it is Ralph.

And maybe a tiny part of me is testing the water, too. Seeing how my fledgling theory sounds, once it's out of my brain, and into open air.

'Of course.' Ralph nods, sets down his spoon and wipes his mouth. He is slight, with greying hair and kind, steady eyes. Looks-wise, I suppose he is fairly unremarkable. So different to my father, who is the kind of guy women would stare at when he walked into a room.

'I . . . I've started seeing someone,' I begin.

'Ah. Well, good for you.'

Ralph met Jamie a couple of times. He knows the basics of what happened to him, courtesy of my mum. But we've never directly discussed him, just the two of us.

'The thing is . . . I can't help wondering if . . . Jamie's come back.'

Ralph blinks twice, then reaches for his soup spoon again. 'Come back?'

'I know it sounds weird, but . . . This guy I've met. It's like he's Jamie, nine years on. It's almost as though . . . he's the person Jamie never got to be. If that makes sense.'

Ralph swallows his mouthful with a gulp that makes him sound almost comically alarmed. He pushes his glasses back up the bridge of his nose. 'It doesn't entirely, no. I'm sorry, Neve. Can you explain what you mean?'

From upstairs, I hear the creak of floorboards. My mother moving around. I think guiltily that it might be nice if she stayed in bed just a little while longer so I can try to soak up some of Ralph's soothing energy before the court-jesting starts.

The next thing I know, I am telling him everything. In fact, I give the poor man the whole damn lot. I fill him in on the architecture and the apartment and the books and London Grammar and *Nighthawks* and Ash's accident and . . . well, everything. I explain what I found online, how terrifyingly plausible it seemed, how the whole idea made a warped kind of sense. Like taking a telescope to the night sky and unmuddling the stars.

'Do you think I'm mad?' I say, when I eventually finish, my voice small.

'No,' he says, firmly. 'Not at all.'

'Do you believe in . . . any of that stuff? You know, souls and the afterlife and things like that.'

'I think . . . your mind can convince you of anything, if it serves what you're looking for in that moment.'

'Then you do think I'm mad.'

He frowns and shakes his head. 'Do you want to know why I spend so much time here with your mother, Neve?'

He doesn't need to tell me. It's because he loves her. And I do get why: my mother is charming and beautiful in a way I can imagine makes her infuriatingly easy to adore. 'You love her.'

He nods. 'Yes. But it's also because I believe Daniela – your mother – loves me.'

'Mmm,' I say, after a couple of moments, trying not to sound dubious.

He smiles, a little sadly. 'I have no idea if that's true. But I do know it's what I *want* to believe. Neve, life is . . . well, it's wonderful, of course. Like living inside a magic show, sometimes. But the trick is to be aware of what you're seeing. It may not be real, even though you can't work out how it's done. An illusion. No matter how plausible it feels. It's how the world keeps us on our toes.'

'Then how do you ever know what's real?'

'You don't. You just have to trust, and hope, and follow your heart. That's what love is, after all, isn't it? Faith, and blind optimism.'

'God. That's depressing.'

His eyes crinkle with a smile. 'No, it's the opposite. Isn't that the beauty of loving another person? How dull would life be if we knew every outcome? Part of the joy lies in the risk.'

At this point, with all the grace and timing of a debt collector, my mother appears in the doorway. She looks pale and unsteady, like she's just spent the last twenty-four hours at sea. A powerful hit of perfume wafts into the room with her, no doubt freshly sprayed to disguise the various seeping toxins of her hangover.

'Christ, Ralph. What is that *smell*?'

'You?' I suggest, sweetly.

'Country vegetable soup,' says Ralph.

A cloud crosses her face. 'Oh, hello Neve.'

'How's the hangover?'

She groans. 'Bloody weddings.' She wobbles to the sink, grabs a mug from the draining board and holds it under the tap. She rummages inside the only functioning drawer (the rest are stuck fast at awkward angles) for a couple of moments before turning and saying, 'Ralph, be an angel and pop out for some ibuprofen, will you?'

'Mum,' I say sharply. 'Ralph's eating.'

He shakes his head and gets up. 'Just finished.'

'Mum,' I admonish her again, once he's disappeared and the front door has shut behind him. 'You could have got that yourself.'

She switches on her infuriating megawatt smile. 'Just here for a social visit, were you, darling?'

The answer's no, of course, but I still can't talk to her about Ash. Mum doesn't believe other people have problems, in much the same way that she doubts the existence of God.

'Sounds like you socialised enough for us both last night.'

'Well, you know. My vice always has been an open bar.'

'The bar isn't the vice, Mum.'

At this, she winces like I've turned on the radio and cranked it up to top volume. 'I really don't have the brain-power to argue semantics with you today, Neve.'

'Have you thought any more about . . . doing this place up?' I ask her, tentatively, surveying the neglected kitchen again. I've long dreamed of the day when she'll say, *Yes, come on, what are your ideas? Let's work on it together. It'll be our project. You and me.*

Before her rebellious phase, Lara and her mum used to decorate their family home together. They'd pore over colours and wallpaper patterns, scour shops for discounts on light fittings and curtains, rearrange furniture and teach themselves how to fit laminate flooring, tile walls, re-grout the bathroom. Corinne rarely had the money for holidays, and I sometimes thought that decorating was their substitute: time spent together as they created something beautiful, made memories. I always secretly envied them for it.

'I've still got those paint samples we could try if you like,' I say. 'And . . . I can call a handyman. Get someone to sort the washing machine and fix the floor tiles and the tap and—'

She cuts me off with a raised palm. 'Oof. Some other time, yes? Think I'm going to pop off back to bed.'

'How's it going with Duke?' I ask, as she's turning to head back upstairs.

She smiles, gives a coquettish little shrug. 'Fine, thanks. He's in Mallorca at the moment. He goes every year for two weeks. Fishing, with friends.'

I feel grimly convinced that this is why Ralph's here. 'But you're still together?'

'I told you, Neve. We're not "together".'

God, I think. These are the kind of meagre scraps of denial she probably tosses Ralph's way for him to cling to, and still he maintains the whole situation is magic.

'The flowers weren't from Duke, then,' I say, nodding at the jar.

'No,' she says vaguely, and not at all appreciatively. 'Ralph picked them.'

'They're lovely.'

'Duke does miss me, though. He's called twice today already.'

I feel a flash of anger on Ralph's behalf. I picture him sitting here, arranging the flowers while Mum phone-flirts with her new boyfriend in between chucking up last night's open bar.

'Have you made it up with Lara yet?' Mum asks.

'No,' I say, defensively.

She makes an annoying, puppy-dog face. 'Lovely Lara. Why not?'

At this, I feel my patience get up and leave the room. 'Oh, I don't know – maybe for the same reason that you haven't made it up with Dad?'

I hadn't planned to say it, and the unnecessary venom clearly throws her.

'Sorry, Mum.' I stand and go over to her, slip my arms around her. But she remains stiff and unresponsive.

After Dad left, Mum called him so many times she had to buy burner phones just so he'd pick up. She went to his new house, too, the one he moved into with Bev. The police kept finding her there in the small hours, banging on the front door and yelling expletives at darkened windows.

But Dad no longer wanted her. He loved Bev.

Dad knew getting Mum out of his life for good meant cutting off contact with me too. And for a long time, I blamed her for that. For behaving so crazily that she destroyed any hopes I had of retaining a father.

But when I lost Jamie, I finally understood the intensity of her pain. That animal urge to do anything – *anything* – for the chance to be with a person again, just one last time.

17.

Then

The summer of our first year, Jamie's dad arranged work experience for him. It was in London, a top architectural firm, his contact a friend-of-a-friend. Jamie would stay in the Soho flat. The lodger had just moved out, so it was free for the summer (and also, I suspected, indefinitely).

I knew I couldn't go with him. Mostly because of Jamie's dad, but also because I had to earn some money. I already had a part-time job at a pub down the road – the decent one that had recently gone gastro – and my big plan for the summer was simply to increase my hours.

'What are you going to do?' Lara asked me one night. We were in her bedroom, listening to Bombay Bicycle Club, and she was French-plaiting my hair, because I could never do it neatly myself.

'About what?'

'Your career. Your future. What are you doing with your summer?'

'I'm working at the pub.'

'You should get proper work experience. Something you actually want to do. What about that company you designed those curtains for?'

Kelley Lane Interiors. Kelley had given us the brief herself, singling me out for praise after our final presentation, complimenting my creative use of pattern and texture. Her company's Instagram was job porn for students, popping with pictures of incredible projects – swish hotel lobbies and Georgian manor-house kitchens and bathrooms-to-die-for in new-builds with panoramic coastal views. I salivated over photos of their offices, too – the manicured hands clutching coffee cups, the flatlays of fabric palettes, the swish 3D renderings on giant computer screens.

But I still wavered, overwhelmed by imposter syndrome. Jamie had always been my benchmark for ambition and drive, and whenever I compared myself to him, I felt as though I fell way short.

'The pub's easy money,' I told Lara.

'Neve. I'm going to say something to you now, and I need you to listen. Sit up.'

My plait was only half finished, but I sat up.

'Easy money doesn't exist. Not in the real world. Not after we graduate and our loans are gone. Are you going to work at the pub your whole life? How will you make ends meet?'

'I'll have Jamie.'

Her eyes widened. 'You did not just say that.'

'Not like *that*. I just mean, everything's cheaper if there's two of you.'

'What if Jamie got run over by a bus tomorrow?'

I blinked at her. 'Lara.'

'I'm serious. You've got to look after yourself. You need to start thinking about how you're going to make money and have a fulfilling life and dreams and ambitions of your *own*.' She looked at me. I'd never seen her so stern the whole time I'd known her. 'Your life can't just be about Jamie. You know that, don't you?'

It was the first time anyone had really said it to me. Not once had I wanted to picture my life without Jamie in it – partly because he'd always felt like family to me. The family I'd never had.

'You don't want to turn into your mum, do you?'

'What? No. What?'

'I mean, you don't want a life that revolves around a man.'

I thought about my dad, who for the past few weeks had been in receipt of a series of increasingly hostile phone calls from my mother, each made from a different phone like she was a drugs baron on the run.

I felt a tingle of indignation. 'I'm nothing like my mum.'

'Then create your own life and your own dreams. A career you're proud of. A home of your own. Don't rely on Jamie for *anything*.'

I swallowed. 'All right. I know. I won't. You don't need to tell me all this.'

'Yes, I do. Do you want to know why?'

'Go on,' I said cautiously.

'Because . . . you're brilliant, Neve, and you deserve for the world to realise it, okay?' She gestured for me to lie back down. 'I just wish you would realise it too.'

I stretched out next to her so she could finish my hair, trying not to think about how hard my mother would scoff if she had overheard this conversation. I decided to change the subject, because for the time being at least, I knew Lara's life plans were far more interesting than my own. 'What about you? Any luck with the work experience?' She had been trying for weeks to arrange shadowing or even just a coffee with someone in TV set design, and had so far got nowhere.

She started combing the other side of my head for the second braid. I liked having my hair done by Lara. Her touch was gentle, so unlike my mother's, who – on the rare occasions she'd done my hair as a child – would yank forcefully through my dark waves with a comb as though her intention was to render me completely bald.

'Actually, yeah. I got a call today from a production designer who does heaps of stuff for the BBC. We're having coffee tomorrow.'

'Lar, that's amazing.' I twisted my head to face her. 'God, I can't wait to see you on TV.'

'I won't actually be on TV.'

'Your name, then. On the credits.'

She paused. 'But I want to see your name up in lights, too, Neve. Not just mine, or Jamie's. Yours too. Right up there. Okay?'

'Okay,' I said. 'Okay.'

I'd been feeling a cold drip of apprehension as Jamie's leaving date approached. At night, I would lie awake, picturing him meeting some fellow aspiring architect with a shiny ponytail called Ginny, who'd probably gone to private school and spent her free time fine-dining and influencing from Dubai. Temptation was everywhere, I knew that. Soho was cool, and London was overrun with Ginnys.

But at the same time, Lara's words had struck a tiny tuning fork somewhere inside me. Maybe an enforced break from Jamie was my chance to make something happen for myself. That way, I wouldn't spend the summer missing him, but doing something positive with my life instead.

On Jamie's last morning in Norfolk, we went to the beach. We'd stayed up late the previous night, watching a Swiss film Harry had recommended, and I felt tired and sluggish, craving fresh air.

The beach was swarming with kids dressed in expensive clothes and wellies, their parents laden down with cool boxes and beach bags and windbreaks. The sky flared with sunshine, the view an artist's tableau of flying kites and scampering dogs and picnickers.

I could see this for me and Jamie, one day: living in North Norfolk, maybe buying one of those beautiful flint-walled coastal houses, having children, a dog.

'What happened to your aunt's beach hut?' Jamie asked, as we passed the row of pastel-coloured huts nestling in the shadow of the pine trees.

I looked at him, impressed. I'd mentioned it maybe once

in passing, years ago. 'She sold it. I think she needed to buy a car, or something.'

'Shame. Be worth a fortune now.'

It occurred to me then, that with his confident stride and hundred-pound wellies, discussing beach huts like they were legal tender, that Jamie really fitted in here. He could have been any one of these people, who all seemed to have money and the world at their feet.

I imagined Lara admonishing me for this. *You don't have to be a certain sort of person to fit in outdoors, idiot.*

Just as we were finding a place to sit, on the sand just north of the beach huts, a loud noise made us both start. It filled the air, disquieting and mournful, like the wail of an old air-raid siren.

'Are we about to be bombed, or something?' I was only half joking. What the hell *was* it?

Jamie laughed. 'It's the high-tide warning. They sound it when the tide turns. To let you know to get to dry ground, or you might be swept out to sea.'

Even though I could feel the blaze of the sun on my face, I shivered. I couldn't imagine a much worse way to go than being swept out to sea.

Jamie laughed and slung his arm across my shoulders. 'Don't worry. I wouldn't let you get swept off anywhere.'

'What about you?' *You're getting swept away to London tomorrow.*

'Well, if I did . . . I'd just have to come back and haunt you.'

'What?' I laughed.

'Yeah. I've fully got plans to haunt you, if I go first.' He turned to face me, dipped his mouth to mine and kissed me. I can still remember that kiss, even now. Salty and sun-soaked and wholehearted, like we were moments before the credits rolled in a film. I could practically hear the orchestra.

'Just so you know,' I said, as we drew apart, 'I'm really not a fan of ghosts.'

'I'd be a friendly ghost. We could have fun.' He waggled his eyebrows, brown eyes dancing with laughter.

I tilted my head, tasting sea salt on my tongue. 'It sounds like you're saying we could have ghost sex, which is . . . just about the creepiest thing anyone has ever said to me.'

'Come on. Ghost sex with me would still be better than sex with anyone else. Right?'

Well, I wasn't going to argue with that. It was impossible to imagine anyone being better at sex than Jamie. But still. 'Stop saying ghost sex.'

'Not until you agree that if I die, ghost sex with me will top any other sex you have.'

'If I do, can we please stop talking about you being a ghost?'

'Only if you say it.'

'All right. Ghost sex with you, Jamie, will always be the best.'

'Promise? No-one else will come close?'

'I promise.'

He laughed, and kissed me, and we carried on walking.

18.

Now

The idea of Lara has been shimmering at the back of my mind since our coffee last week. I can't relax, knowing she's just down the road. Over the years, there's always been an outside chance of bumping into her without warning, given her parents still live in the area. But that risk has been minute, the odds reassuringly low. Not enough to keep me awake at night.

But now she's back, and the unsettling thought keeps coming to me – *I want to see her again.* For so long, I've felt so angry with her, so certain I wanted her out of my life for good.

So when she messages to suggest we get together, just the two of us, the feeling is both wrong and right. It's something I half want, but know I should probably steer clear of.

We meet at the picnic meadow at Whitlingham Country Park. Lara brings a hamper packed with M&S goodies, and glass bottles of rose lemonade.

'This is all very Famous Five,' I say.

'I know. Never thought I'd be a picnic meadow kind of girl.'

'I never thought we'd be nearly thirty.'

We spread a rug across the grass. Above our heads, the sun burns a perfect circle in a sky the colour of cornflowers.

I ask Lara where she and Felix are staying at the moment. I'm assuming they're crashing with her parents, that Felix hasn't flexed his wallet on some city centre penthouse since they got here.

Lara stretches out next to me, propped up on one elbow. She has shades on, so I can't quite read her expression, but when her lips tighten slightly, I know it's bad news.

'With Mum,' is all she says.

That can only mean one thing. 'Oh, Lara.'

'Dad died. Five years ago.'

I feel the shock as keenly as I would have back then. *No. Not Billy.*

My mind becomes a squall of dismay and sadness. Billy – who'd always welcomed me into his home as though I were his second daughter, giver of unlimited hugs, who filled the gap my own father had left in so many ways – is dead.

I think of Corinne, of how deeply she loved him. Life wasn't always easy for Lara's parents, but they were each other's North Star. Once, staying over, I came downstairs for a glass of water in the middle of the night and found them dancing together in the kitchen, turning slowly to the Etta James version of 'At Last', eyes shut, heads resting on each other's shoulders. I remember just staring at them, cemented to the spot, thinking, *Oh. So this is how love looks.*

It's not about PDAs at weddings or parties. It's dancing together in a cold, dark kitchen when you think no-one is watching.

I slip my hand across the picnic rug and into Lara's slender fingers, because it is the only thing I can do. 'God, Lar. I'm so sorry.' Offering my condolences feels a little off-key, given everything that's happened between us. But I knew and loved Billy before all of that.

Still. I know words are inadequate. That they can't so much as touch the edges of how Lara must feel, what she must have been through. Words could never soothe the anguish of losing smiling, full-of-love Billy.

'What happened?' I ask.

'Lung cancer,' she says softly. 'It was pretty grim.'

'I'm so sorry.'

There is a pause. 'We did have . . . a bit of quality time together, at the end. Well, not quality. It was hideous, frankly, with the chemo. But we said all the stuff we needed to say.'

'Was it in Norwich?'

'Yeah. He died at the N&N.'

'How long were you here?'

'Three months.'

I swallow a hot rush of guilt. The email and WhatsApp she'd sent me a few years ago must have been when Billy was dying. And I ignored them. 'I'm really sorry. For not—'

'It's okay, Neve. You weren't ready. That's fine. I don't resent you for it.'

'Still. It's Billy. I am sorry.' *I loved him too*, I want to add, but don't.

'Like I said, we had time together. Which is all that matters, in the end.'

'Is your mum—'

She shakes her head. 'Not in the best of health. She doesn't look after herself too well, and she's barely mobile, so—'

'You're back to help out,' I realise.

I should go and see her. It's less a conscious thought, more a reflex: Corinne was like a mother to me, growing up. I feel momentarily bad for having cut her out of my life, too. But the situation was impossible: I couldn't know Corinne and detest Lara at the same time. I saw Corinne once, in Sainsbury's, examining a bag of apples, and the urge to go and put my arms around her was so fierce, I had to abandon my trolley and walk out of the shop.

'How long are you staying this time?'

'Who knows?' Lara forces a smile, but it looks a bit hollow. I can tell she doesn't really want to talk about it.

I can understand why. It's been nearly a decade since we shared anything personal. I'm sure she has other friends now, people she's closer to. Bonds are forged over time, and we've lost so much of that.

Out of nowhere, a cave opens up in my stomach; dark, cold regret for all the years we've missed out on. The experiences we might have had, the holidays we never got to enjoy. The nights out, the gossip and stories, the jokes and anecdotes we'd have carried with us into old age. I realise I actually don't know very much at all about who she is now. What music she likes, her favourite food. How she celebrated her last birthday. If she cares about keeping fit. Her thoughts on getting older. Whether she can cook, or speak another language, or do a really solid impression of someone famous. If she knows anyone famous. I can't even guess with much confidence which way she'd vote.

'What's Felix's family like?' I ask. A first attempt, perhaps, to get to know who she is today.

'They're amazing. Big. Loving. So loving. I feel very lucky.' Lara's sitting up now, fiddling with the picnic. She rips open a giant packet of crisps, then passes me a pack of chicken empanadas.

I take one, pushing away a dark flutter of envy, as I so often do when I encounter people with functional families.

'How's your mum doing?' she asks, like she can still read my mind after all this time.

'Same as ever. Dating and drinking and doing my head in.' I bite into the empanada. It's good, and I realise how hungry I am.

'Does she still hang around with that guy . . . What was his name?'

'Ralph.'

'Ralph! That's it. I often wondered if they'd get it together. He always seemed like he genuinely cared about her.'

'I think my mother's allergic to people who genuinely care about her.'

She smiles faintly in response, but I can't quite read her expression.

'Lar, what's Felix like?' The over-protectiveness I detected – suspected? – before is bothering me. I need to know more about him.

I shouldn't care, but some instincts you can't control.

'In what way?'

'Well, what's he *like*? I mean, how do you know . . . he's the one?'

Lara nibbles on a single crisp. 'Aside from the fact he's insanely handsome and warm-hearted and has the body of a god?'

'Yeah,' I say, with a smile. 'Aside from all that.'

'Well, mostly,' she says, after a few moments, 'he's a grown-up.'

I think about a boy she once dumped back in uni because he wanted to be a lawyer, which Lara decided was a bit of a red flag, personality-wise. 'Remember Sam?'

She laughs. 'Oh my God. The funniest thing. We're back in touch. He's an entertainment lawyer now. I've come across him at work a couple of times. Such a nice guy. Married, two kids.'

'Small world. You don't regret—'

'God, no. Lovely guy, but you know . . . he's no Felix.'

'Tell me,' I press, because she seems so certain, 'what it is about him.'

She takes two tubs of pasta salad from the hamper, passing one to me. 'Well, he was the first guy I'd met in ages who didn't want to play games. I mean, a lot of guys say they don't want to, because they think that's what you want to hear, but Felix actually means it. I *love* that about him. He's so self-assured. He knows what he wants from life. And he's one of those people who just draws people in, you know? We were on the night bus once and by the time we got off there was this crowd of people just . . . wanting to talk to him.'

Showman? I think, but don't say. Lara used to loathe guys like that.

But now, I can tell her eyes are shining behind her shades. 'That he can draw people to him wherever he is, even on some random bus on a Tuesday night, that's *hot*, Neve. But he cares a lot, too. He's kind and generous and . . . careful.'

'Careful?' I say, through a mouthful of pasta.

'With people's emotions. Their hearts. He's friends with all his exes.'

I'm still unsure, actually, as to whether I think that's a great thing in principle, but decide not to voice this.

'He's perfect, then,' I venture, because that's essentially what she's saying.

'Well, no, obviously. But he's perfect for me.' She pushes the hair from her face, crosses her legs, adjusts her sunglasses. 'Neve?'

'Yeah.' I think I know what's coming next.

'Are you . . . ready to talk about what happened with Jamie yet?'

She says this so cautiously. I don't recognise at all this permission-seeking version of the girl who, as a teenager, once did her best impression of *Riverdance* live on the regional news for a dare, skipping ludicrously into the background of an outside broadcast as the presenter gabbled obliviously on.

'No,' I say, because even though there's a part of me that wants to talk about Jamie – that needs to say his name and even tell her what I think might be going on with Ash – I don't want to let those dark and complicated feelings eclipse this sliver of sunshine we're sharing. I was so lost for so long after Jamie died, and I'm simply not ready to relive all that again.

'I really want to,' she insists. 'It's important. There are things—'

'I . . . can't. Not yet.'

She nods, *Okay*, then sips from her drink.

'Will you marry Felix, do you think? Start a family?' Maybe there's a part of me that senses some transience in her. That I might get close to wanting to be her friend again, only for her to up and leave me for California, a world light years away from this one.

She takes a long while to answer. 'I hope so,' she says, eventually.

We both lie back and angle our faces to the dry blue heat of the sky.

'I meant to say, I'd like to see Corinne.'

'She'd love that. Thank you.'

She asks how it's going with Ash. I tell her good, but that it's still early days.

'Hey,' she says, 'I don't know if it would be too soon . . . but it would be great to have dinner. The four of us, sometime? I'd love you to meet Felix properly. And it would be really nice to get to know Ash, too.'

'Yeah, maybe,' I say. 'I'll have to see how it goes.'

We've hardly made a dent in the picnic. And there is so much still left unsaid. But for now, today, maybe this can be enough.

19.

A full working week has passed since that dynamite kiss with Ash. We both have crazy work schedules: Ash is deep in securing planning and building control consent on a split residential plot in the city, and I'm pitching to win a hefty design contract for a set of holiday lodges in Suffolk. He has some sort of pool league thing going on too, and on his only free night – and mine – I'm seeing the new Greta Gerwig film with an old work friend.

Maybe, on some level, I've resisted making time for him because of what I think I know. That on the night of Ash's accident, Jamie took over his body somehow.

Every time I contemplate it, it sets my mind spinning. It makes me feel out of control.

And I can't imagine continuing to think all this as Ash remains oblivious.

But we agree to meet on Saturday morning. Ash picks me up. I invite him inside, and give him a tour of the house. He takes time to admire the pristine paintwork, the moulding and cornicing, the waxed floorboards, the flow of the rooms.

'I'm getting proper show-home vibes here,' he says, with a smile.

I return his smile and tell him I'm not really here enough to mess it up, which is only partly true, but I don't want to major on the fact that I like to clean as a way to unwind. It's my dirty secret, I guess. It's definitely the least cool thing about me.

In the living room, he peers forward to examine the framed photos on my mantelpiece, and I curse myself for not having thought to take them down.

He turns to look at me, asking the question without words.

'A friend,' I say. 'He died.'

'I'm sorry.'

I smile. 'Thank you. Shall we go?'

I can't help but hope he felt a flicker of recognition when he looked at the photos. Or at the bronze N and J bookends nearby. Or at any of Jamie's old possessions I still keep around my home.

But if he did, he doesn't let on.

As we reach the front door to head out, we both pause, and then he leans forward and kisses me. It hits as fiercely as a flame leaping to life.

It was my suggestion to go to Wells. It's a perfect June morning. The air is warm, heat rising from the sun-baked sand. The beach is busy, but not heaving. Seagulls soar through a blue-domed sky, riding a breeze scented with saltwater and seaweed.

We didn't stop talking the whole way here, about houses, and work, and how badly we are both aching for promotion. Ash wants to be made an associate at his firm within the next couple of years; I'm aiming for head designer, a position Kelley's been threatening and failing to create for years. But this year, with all the hours I've put in and the positive press and winning feedback from clients, I've never felt so close.

'Neve,' Ash says now, as we start to walk. I don't know where we're heading. Just the open mouth of the horizon, I guess. 'I should probably tell you, I . . . Googled Jamie Fraser.'

My stomach pitches sharply. Did he have a sense, somehow, of what I've been thinking this past week? Or did Jamie's name sound inexplicably familiar?

'It was after you asked me about him. I was just curious, I guess.'

I nod. It's fair enough: I idly searched for Tabitha the other day while I was waiting for a client. She's beautiful, of course, works as a personal trainer. Has nearly fifty thousand followers on Instagram. Though a part of me felt slightly sorry for Ash, because even watching a couple of her reels left me feeling like I needed a lie-down.

We keep walking.

'Jamie Fraser is the same guy that's in the photos on your mantelpiece.'

I swallow, feeling suddenly hot, despite the coastal air. In any other situation, I'd get up and walk away, escape the sensation of scrutiny. But I can't walk away from this.

'A friend?' he says gently, because that's what I told him an hour ago, but I suspect he knows it was a lie.

I exhale. Ash has been completely open with me. The least I can do is answer him truthfully. 'No. He was . . . my boyfriend. A long time ago. Sorry I lied before, I just . . .'

'I caught you off guard,' he guesses. 'It's okay, Neve. And I'm really sorry. I can't imagine.' He reaches for my hand and squeezes it.

'Thank you,' I say.

We walk in silence for a minute or so. A pair of Labradors barrels past us, their owner a mere fleck in the distance.

'Do you think . . . Do you think you're completely over him?'

I feel him glance at me as he says this. I fix my eyes on the long crease in the view where sea meets sky.

My mind has been on Jamie constantly over the past couple of weeks, which feels so strange. On the one hand, it's lovely and extraordinary, to think he might – somehow – be back. But I haven't thought about him this intensely in so long. I've built a different life now, and it's a bizarre sensation to unexpectedly be making room for him in my head again.

'I understand if you're not,' Ash says, after a few moments. 'Grief . . . It's the most complicated thing about being human. I'm not going to be all . . . weird and jealous if you still love your ex. It makes total sense.'

I look over at him. I think he might be one of the kindest people I've ever met. Especially given what happened with Tabitha. Being cheated on, made to feel second-best.

I know I owe him my honesty. But I also want to see how he reacts if I start to confide in him about what I suspect may be going on.

'You actually . . . remind me of Jamie, in lots of ways.'

He looks surprised. 'I do?'

'Well,' I say, carefully, 'he was an architect too. Or studying to be one.'

A slow nod, then he waits for more, because he knows – he must know – that there is more.

I try to think how I can elaborate in a way that doesn't sound completely ridiculous and trivial. 'And . . . you have . . . exactly the same handwriting.'

But, of course, this *does* sound ridiculous and trivial. And perhaps it goes to show that I really have been losing the plot.

Maybe I just needed to say it out loud. To expose it to the light, so I can see it for what it really is.

But Ash, being kind, doesn't laugh. 'I have appalling handwriting.'

'So did he.'

He smiles. We pause next to some sand dunes, then sit down together. Our knees touch as we stare out at the streak of beach, the grey-blue stripe of sea.

'And . . . *Nighthawks*.'

'Sorry?'

I turn to face him. His cheeks are flushed pink from the sea breeze. 'It was Jamie's favourite painting, and . . . you have it in your apartment.'

After he died, his father took Jamie's print from the house. It broke my heart to be without it, so I bought my own, which still hangs above my bed.

'I was thinking, you know,' I say, as if I'm changing the subject, though really I'm not at all. 'About your accident, the way you changed personality—'

'Priorities.'

'Sorry?'

'I tend to think of it more like . . . my priorities changed. I just wanted to take myself, and my life, more seriously. I really don't think it goes much deeper than just . . . growing up.' He keeps his eyes on me. 'Neve, can I ask you something?'

'Of course.'

'Will you answer me truthfully?'

And then it happens. The abrupt, mournful wail of an air-raid siren.

I feel cold suddenly, like someone is trickling iced water down the back of my neck.

'Do you . . . know what that is?' I say.

He nods. 'The high-tide warning. They sound it when the tide turns. To let you know to get to dry ground, or you might get swept out to sea.'

I've fully got plans to haunt you, if I go first.

I blink at him. *Come on, Jamie. This isn't funny any more. Stop messing with me.*

'It's nothing to worry about,' Ash says, misinterpreting the shift in my expression. 'We just have to stay on this side of the channel.'

I swallow. 'Yeah. Right. Okay.'

He gets to his feet, reaches out and pulls me up. Without saying anything further, I slip a hand into his.

I feel sure he'd been going to ask if my attraction to him is down to how much he resembles Jamie. But he doesn't bring the question up again once we start walking, maybe because he's not quite ready to hear the answer. And I am thankful, because I'm not sure I can be one hundred per

cent honest with him yet. I don't want him to think I'm
mad. I like him so much.

Anyway. Maybe that is all we need to say for now. It's
not the whole story, but it's a start.

But as we walk, I have to keep glancing over at him, to
check whose hand it is I am really holding.

20.

It's late by the time we make it back to Norwich. Despite the rollercoaster in my head, I've been aching to kiss him for most of the ride home. For most of the afternoon in fact. As we drove up the coast to Brancaster Staithe. As we stopped at the pub for drinks on the terrace overlooking the salt marsh. As we climbed back into the car, and I felt the air between us contract, my mind turning to thoughts that felt irresistible.

I lean over to him as soon as he's switched off the ignition. Our mouths meet, and the wild feeling inside me uncoils. He tastes of hunger and sea breeze. Pretty soon his hands are in my hair, and mine are skating down his back, gliding up beneath his T-shirt.

I feel him smile as we kiss, and I do too, because I know what he means.

I push aside all thoughts of Jamie. Because right now, I know it is Ash I want.

After a few minutes, a group of people passes the car, and we draw apart, catching our breath. His eyes dance across my face. He pushes back my hair with one hand. My heartbeat is ridiculous.

'Neve, can I ask . . . I like you, a lot, and . . . I'd like to see if this could go somewhere. But I need to know ... are you ... looking for something right now?'

I realise, at last, that the answer is yes. I want to do this. I want to make space in my life for this man. 'I think ... I'm looking for you,' I breathe.

'Thank God,' he says, leaning in to kiss me again.

I can't resist any more. I want him too much. I can ignore the complicating factors. Analysis can wait. 'Do you want to come in?'

'Yeah, I really do,' he says, and then we get out of the car and head inside.

I'd been planning to put on some music, make coffee, freshen up. But as soon as we're through the front door, I feel his hands on my waist, spinning me gently round so he can kiss me again, and I think, *Screw the coffee. I only want you.*

We make our way into the living room. I leave the lights off. The house is warm and still. I am molten with anticipation.

I'm not feeling my way now, and neither is Ash. We both want this. He mirrors my movements, letting his fingers skate from the small of my back up to my shoulder blades and then down again, every knot and hollow of my body flexing with his touch.

He lifts my sweater over my head, then takes off his T-shirt. We move towards the sofa, too impatient to make it upstairs. But then I remember Jamie's framed photographs on the mantelpiece, watching us, and I grab his hand. 'Come on,' I whisper.

Upstairs, the bedroom is deliciously dark. He presses

me gently to the wall. I can feel his heart pumping like an animal's. His hand moves to my jeans, unbuttoning then unzipping. I tug myself free, kick them to the floor, and then together we make it onto the bed. I changed the sheets mere hours ago. The scent of fabric softener still lingers. Our bodies are already damp and hot and arching for more, our breathing ragged, our movements primal.

Finally, I move on top of him, feeling desire like I've never experienced before.

Somehow, I seem to know exactly what he wants, and he understands the same in return. I feel as though I am already familiar with every last touchpoint of his skin, the path of his hands, the press of his body.

His hands are on my hips. We quickly get frantic, a blur of bodies and gasped names and sweat-slick skin. We unravel each other entirely, again and again, unable to stop, our gazes locked tight.

Morning. I blink and drink in cold, white light, take a moment to orientate. Then a rush of fresh pleasure as my body remembers. We hardly slept last night. I recall a grey-feathered dawn starting to edge around the blinds, and saying to Ash, through our millionth kiss of the night, 'It's getting light.' And he laughed, and began to say something, then checked himself. So I elbowed him and told him he had to tell me what he'd been going to say, and he laughed some more and said, 'I was going to say, "That's got to be some kind of record," before I realised that would be just about the worst thing that's ever left my mouth.' And I smiled and said true, but that it was a record for me too, so let's just be proud that we're the kind of people who set records in bed, and then we both started laughing until we eventually began to drift off, wrapped sleepily in each other's arms.

I saw his lightning scars for the first time last night, too. Faint pink tendrils, like feathers. They stretched across the ridges of his abdomen, marking the place where nature had struck him.

I drew a finger across the patch of marked skin, marvelling at the madness of it, feeling the scars' tiny seams.

'They usually go away,' he whispered. 'After twenty-four hours, or so. But mine never did. I guess I must scar easily.'

'I guess you must.'

'I like to think they're a reminder to live for the moment. If that's not too corny.'

'It's not corny at all.'

'I've not always loved them, if I'm honest.' He was tracing my skin with one finger too, absent-mindedly, a circle on my shoulder. 'People have made comments, sometimes.'

'You mean, when you've been . . . with them?'

He nodded. 'And trust me, nothing kills a moment of passion like someone exclaiming, *Oh, you're the lightning-strike guy!* I get people coming up to me sometimes, too, asking for selfies.'

'Are you serious?'

'Unfortunately, yeah.'

I returned my gaze to his scars. 'Do they hurt?'

'They did a bit, at first. Not so much now.'

'I think they're beautiful,' I whispered. 'Mad and beautiful all at once.'

He laughed softly. The sound of it touched me deep inside. 'Mad and beautiful. Thank you, Neve. I'll take that.'

And then he dipped his head to my collarbone, the exact same spot Jamie was always drawn to, and kissed me there. The sensation felt so familiar, so much like a love I knew well, I had to swallow away tears.

The space next to me on the mattress is empty now. I check the time – still early, though I can hear the rumble of cars on the road outside.

I ease out of bed and pull on a hoodie. As I do, I catch sight of my old battered copy of *On Decorating* on my nightstand. I retrieved it from the box beneath my bed after I bumped into Lara. It was the first time I'd felt able to look at it since we fell out. Even flicking gingerly through its pages brought her kindness rushing back to me in gusts. How much she believed in me. How she only ever wanted the best for me.

I head downstairs, hoping Ash is there, praying there's no note to say he had to go, or some other evidence of second thoughts.

To my relief, he is barefoot in my small galley kitchen, wearing yesterday's T-shirt and jeans. The air is sweet with the scent of coffee and warming butter. At the edge of the room, I pause and smile, my heart on a high-wire. 'Morning.'

He looks up, concentration subsiding into a smile. 'Morning. Hope you don't mind, but ... thought you might fancy breakfast. Took the liberty of raiding your fridge for eggs.'

I want to assure him that looting my kitchen for ingredients with which to cook me breakfast definitely counts as one of the lesser morning-after crimes.

'That's the opposite of a liberty.' I lean against the door jamb and watch him for a couple of moments.

'You look lovely,' he says.

I run a hand through my unruly mass of bed hair, hoping I don't resemble my mother. I'd been so impatient to get down here, I forgot to so much as glance into a mirror.

'And you,' I say. And it's true – every time I catch sight of him, my stomach skips. Tall and dark, melt-in-the-middle eyes, the suggestion of a smile always moments from his mouth. And the way he was last night – intense and feverish, gripping and teasing me, dismantling me inch by inch.

After so many years of feeling not quite myself – like some component part of me went missing when Jamie died – I feel a strange sense of ease this morning. It's as though I've finally found what I lost, glistening like a gemstone in the mud left by a turning tide.

Ash lines up chives on a chopping board. My attention lurches sharply to what he's holding. 'You're not seriously going to . . .?'

'What?'

'It looks as though you're going to try to chop those with *that*.' I indicate the enormous knife, which is better-suited for skinning elk than it is for chopping herbs. It was part of a mystifying Christmas gift from my mother one year – a knife block I suspected to have fallen off the back of a lorry – and this one, I have never used, because it is terrifying.

Ash smiles. 'Chopping fast is literally my only party trick.'

'If I tried that, I'd have no fingers.'

'It's actually pretty easy. You just need a decent knife. Which, fortunately, you have. Come here, I can teach you.'

I smile, enjoying for a moment the idea of him standing behind me, his hand over mine on the knife, showing me how. 'No, you're all right. I quite like having all my ligaments intact.'

'Come on. It's easy.'

I hesitate, then relent. The urge to be pressed up very tightly to him as he demonstrates is just too strong.

I take a couple of steps towards him. He pulls me close, moving behind me so we're both facing the worktop.

I have no idea what possessed me to buy chives. Then again, I'd be hard-pushed to recall my own name if someone asked for it at this precise moment.

'All right,' Ash whispers into my ear. His body is firm against mine. 'Lesson one.'

I shiver. 'You *really* can't do that if you want me to go anywhere near a sharp blade.'

He laughs softly. 'Okay. Sorry. So, pick it up.'

'How do you know I'm not left-handed?'

'Are you?'

'No,' I admit.

'Just so you know, I'm not going to fall for distraction tactics.' He places one hand over mine, and together, we position the knife. 'All right. I'm going to move it, you just . . . go with it, okay? Don't try and control it.'

'Okay.'

'You sure? Ready?'

'Ready.'

'You trust me?'

'Yes,' I say, realising it perhaps for the first time. 'Yes, I do.'

He guides the knife effortlessly through the chives with a rocking motion that feels very different to the way I usually hack into things with whatever blunt blade I have to hand.

'See?' he whispers, when we're done. The chives are lying in a little pile on the chopping board. 'It's not so hard.'

Against the worktop, I turn to face him. Steam from the stove is starting to wet the air. I start to speak but he smothers my words with a kiss.

Pretty soon after that, the breakfast gets abandoned. I might have felt bad about all the effort he went to, if what we go on to do together didn't feel so insanely good.

21.

Then

That summer, with Lara's encouragement, I decided to start chasing the life I wanted for myself after uni. My first step was securing work experience three days a week, at Kelley Lane Interiors.

It was full on: as well as the requisite coffee runs, diary-organising and photocopying, I helped to create presentations and fly-throughs, liaised with clients and architects, attended pitches and project meetings, and assisted with budgeting. I loved it, and realised I was thriving, even as I was doing it all on top of part-time shifts at the pub. Meanwhile, Jamie was working hard in London, and Lara was on night shifts at a care home while she interned for a local TV production company.

Jamie and I tried to FaceTime a few times a week. He was working long days, too, being paid an astoundingly high wage for someone with no qualifications, and they expected him to graft hard in return. And he was out most nights socialising, at rooftop drinks in the West End, flashy client dinners, secret gigs in Shoreditch. I missed him a lot.

Every time we spoke, my stomach felt like it was hitched right up against my heart.

'Designed the next Gherkin yet?' I would ask him, with a smile.

'Working on it,' he'd always say back.

He'd been in London five weeks before he invited me to visit. Luckily, I was able to swap my pub shifts so I could stay with him for the whole weekend.

I admit I was slightly jealous, when I walked into that flat in Soho for the first time. Yes, it was tiny – probably even smaller than the ground floor of our house in Norwich – but it was stunning. All sleek lines and shiny appliances. Mini chandeliers, remote-controlled lighting. High ceilings and polished floors. A leather sofa I could tell without asking had cost thousands of pounds. I couldn't deny, in that moment, that I wanted what Jamie had – parents who could spoil me and make things happen and open doors for me.

But ultimately, I knew Lara was right. If I didn't have parents who could do all that, I had to be able to do it myself.

Jamie poured us some champagne. Moët, of course. I guessed he had a preferred brand of the stuff, now. The glass was thick-cut and weighty in my hand.

I took a sip, then pulled him close and kissed him.

'God, I've missed you,' he groaned. 'This week has been *long*.'

I thought we might have sex right then and there, perhaps even on the shiny kitchen floor tiles of his dad's flat – which

I couldn't deny would have given me immense satisfaction on multiple levels – but we didn't. Maybe that was another mark of his new-found maturity. Instead, we finished the kiss, then took the champagne and went to stand demurely out on the tiny balcony that led off the living room. There wasn't really a view from it – it faced onto the back end of other buildings – and noise spat up at us from all directions: traffic and doors slamming, the occasional blast of music, conversation and shrieks of laughter.

'It's more frantic here than it is at home,' he said, as we sipped our champagne like we were looking out over Hyde Park or Lake Garda, rather than at soot-stained roofs and grubby brick walls. 'But in a good way, you know?'

'Yeah.' I didn't ask if he was having second thoughts about choosing not to study in London. He'd referred to Norwich as home, and that was good enough for me.

Jamie had bought tickets to see *Mamma Mia!* and had booked a table at a fancy restaurant on Charlotte Street. He wore a shirt with a Ralph Lauren logo. I couldn't work out if it suited him. Still, I was pleased he'd made an effort, as I'd bought a tiny black dress I couldn't really afford on an emergency late-night shopping spree with Lara earlier in the week, after Jamie had told me we'd go out somewhere nice.

We played make-believe all night – imagining we were ten years in the future, out in the West End together, theatre-going, drinking champagne, dining in a high-end sushi restaurant. I kept looking over at him and thinking, *Yes. This is exactly how it's meant to be.*

In the cab home, he leaned over and whispered, 'You look incredible, but I cannot wait to get that dress off you.'

Jamie didn't normally say stuff like that, but I didn't dislike it. 'Actually, I think I might keep it on,' I teased.

'Fine by me,' he replied, his voice practically gravel.

I kissed him in the lift up to the apartment, unable to wait. He kissed me back, then slid a hot hand up my dress.

I laughed, pushing him away despite my pounding heart.

He laughed too, leaning back against the lift wall. 'I quite fancy doing it in a public place, actually.'

'Really?'

'Don't you?'

I thought for a moment. 'We could have done it at the restaurant. Those loos were pretty luxurious.'

The lift doors pinged. 'Next time,' he said, with a smile.

When we got inside, I thought we might go straight to bed, but Jamie shot me an apologetic grimace. 'Just got to call Mum quickly. See how she is. I haven't spoken to her for a couple of days and Dad texted just now, so . . .'

'Your mum?' I was confused.

'Yeah . . . I was meant to be seeing them tonight. But she broke her ankle, so . . .' He trailed off then, realising what he'd said. The words had slipped out, his voice a slope made smooth by alcohol.

I was too surprised to express my sympathies, or ask how his mum had broken her ankle. I sat down heavily on the sofa. Beyond the window, the sheer curtains had turned the glow of the city lights into a hazy solar system. 'What?' I said, eventually.

Still on his feet, Jamie stared at me.

'I thought you got those theatre tickets and booked the restaurant for us.'

'Baby, it *was* all for us.'

Baby? He'd never called me that the entire time I'd known him. The logo of his shirt caught my eye, and I felt something detach in my chest.

'Neve. Sorry.' He shook his head, rubbed his face. 'It's . . . I'm tired.'

He'd seemed wide awake until about thirty seconds ago.

'Your parents did it all,' I realised, out loud. 'Bought the theatre tickets. Booked the restaurant. You only invited me here because *they* cancelled.'

He didn't say anything to that, though he did thrust his hands into his pockets with the faintest hint of defiance.

I stared at him, the truth excruciating. 'You let me think . . .' But I couldn't carry on talking. I was gutted in a way there simply wasn't words for. I thought Jamie had planned the whole night we'd just enjoyed. Put time and effort into thinking about what I might like.

'Neve,' he whispered, sitting down next to me.

I felt two opposing forces at work in my gut – to push him away, and pull him closer. I knew we were short-circuiting, and the sensation scared me.

He put an arm around me, rubbing a slow figure-of-eight between my shoulder blades with one hand in that way he knew I loved. 'Hey,' he whispered. 'What's this really about?'

I wanted to tell him I was scared of losing him. That deep down, I was worried he would end up loving it here so much he wouldn't want to come home. But in that moment, I felt wrong-footed for some reason.

'You have no idea how much I love you, do you?' Jamie said, before leaning forward and kissing me, my face between his palms.

That night, for the first time ever, the sex felt awkward. Jamie's bedroom was so tiny, the king-sized bed practically jammed into it, we kept banging our limbs on the walls. The space was cold as a fridge because of the air-con, so cold it gave me goose pimples. I remember feeling conscious of how I looked in a way I never had with Jamie before, thinking I should have waited before taking off my make-up, worrying that my hair had been worked up into a little beehive by his hands.

But despite all that, I wanted him in a way that felt raw and deep.

And he wanted me too. I kept the dress on.

22.

Now

Ash and I start seeing more of each other. He doesn't revisit the question he'd been going to ask me that day at the beach, and I am relieved.

We have to work to make the time. But when we do, it's always for something that fills my heart, like a long, lazy brunch or a late film, a candlelit bistro supper.

Dating Ash feels romantic. Dating Leo was more like dodging enemy fire.

If Ash has trust issues, after what went on with Tabitha, I never detect them. He is unfailingly open-hearted and thoughtful – messaging if I have a big presentation at work, suggesting a late drink to help me wind down, offering to call his guy when my boiler packs up. There are no obvious clues that he's nervous about getting into something with me, or that he's holding anything back. If he is, he's very good at hiding it.

'Gabi would laugh if she could see me now,' he says to me one Sunday morning, over coffee and pastries at Bread Source.

I smile. 'Would she? Why?'

'All this being up with the lark and eating breakfast like a functional human . . . I used to spend a lot of time just lazing around in bed, waiting till it was time to go out again.' He sips his coffee, meets my eye across the rim of the cup. 'I'm so glad you never knew me back then.'

'But your sister still misses that version of you?'

'So she says.'

'Why, though? If you were basically a jail sentence waiting to happen.'

He laughs. 'That actually sums it up pretty well. I don't know – maybe because she's still kind of . . . back in that place, waiting for me.' He looks wistful for a moment before his eyes return to mine. 'It's nice that I can talk to you about this stuff.'

'I like that you do.'

'Tabitha used to tell people about my accident at dinner parties, like it was an amusing anecdote. My sister actually thought it was funny, too, for a while. Like, *Who gets hit by lightning?*'

I find myself thinking about Jamie's brother Harry.

Could it be possible that in fact, he is Ash's true sibling?

No. The idea is absurd. But still, I can't resist the urge to float it.

'Have you ever wanted a brother?' I say, but lightly, like my mind's just wandering.

'Sometimes. I mean, not really, obviously. But occasionally . . .'

I lean forward. 'Go on.'

He shrugs. 'Everyone fantasises about the sibling they never had from time to time, don't they?'

The moment passes. I take the last bite of my cinnamon swirl. 'Absolutely. I'd love to have someone I could bitch about my mum with.'

Ash tells me Gabi met her current boyfriend at Coachella. 'They're this ... complete toxic whirlwind, from what I can work out.'

'I've been there,' I say, sympathetically, thinking of Leo.

'Right. And so have I. But then ... you get out.'

'Sometimes it's not that easy.'

His forehead furrows. 'Yeah. I guess. I'm being unkind, aren't I?'

I nudge his knee with mine. 'No, you're being a brother.'

I help Ash style his apartment, sourcing rugs, light fittings, console tables, cushions, bar stools, lamps and bookshelves. I ask Parveen to find him some affordable art. And I avoid that scrap of paper bearing Jamie's handwriting like my life depends on it.

We spend long nights together drinking wine, or whisky, and talking till it's almost dawn. He cooks. I rave to him about the *Before* trilogy, so we watch all three back to back. He comes with me to spin class. We revel in the romance of empty beaches. We play poker, at which I have always been terrible, despite the fact I am forever being told I have an excellent poker face. One night, fuelled by rum – and weirdly buoyed by some cigars he has left over from a stag weekend that we decide to smoke for a laugh – it turns into strip poker. And this is the night I realise – with a clarity that I hope isn't down to some hallucinogen in the tobacco – that I have no inhibitions whatsoever with this man.

It's almost as if I have known him for years.

I meet his friends, and they make me feel comfortable straight away, sharing anecdotes and asking me questions and hugging me warmly at the end of the night, even though we came last in the pub quiz, which was largely down to my wrong answers (tzatziki, the Danube, John Travolta). I can see how different they must be to the crowd Ash says he used to run with. Nobody has been rowdy, or got steaming drunk, or picked a fight with a parking meter or ex-professional boxer or whatever it is they used to do.

'I liked your friends,' I say to Ash later.

We're in bed, breathing hard, our skin glazed with sweat. My heartbeat is a long, liquid rush in my chest.

'They liked you too,' he says, stroking the hair from my face. 'No, actually, they *loved* you.' And then he holds my gaze, as though he wants to say something else, before changing his mind.

Later, after he's showered, I go into the bathroom to find a heart traced into the steamed-up screen.

I know he wants to meet my friends, too. And though I've mentioned Lara, I've skirted most of the details. He seems to sense it's a difficult subject, and hasn't pushed it.

But he's a good listener. I can ramble endlessly on about work, or politics, or my neighbours, and not once does he try to hijack what I'm saying, or change the subject. I know I could tell him about Lara, if I wanted to.

Picking up my phone at work to check for messages from him becomes a reflex. I try to hide this from Kelley, and keep finding myself in the ladies', crouched down on the closed lid of the loo, typing away like a maniac, hoping no-one will catch me. I don't have the time to behave like a teenager with a crush, but I compulsively do it anyway.

Parveen notices, of course. 'I've never seen you like this before. Not even with Leo.'

Especially not with Leo, I think. There's not another person on this planet for whom I would even think of risking Kelley's wrath.

We become the kind of couple that people have to side-step. We hear, 'My God, get a *room*,' more times than we can count. We kiss and touch in cars and taxis, on street corners, outside cafes, inside bars. One night, we get so stirred up in a restaurant that I find myself whispering into his ear, 'Meet me upstairs.'

A ripple of laughter, on a caught breath. 'You're not serious.'

I nod and slide away from the table, attempting to keep my composure as I head to the toilets, wondering even as I go what's got into me. This is *so* unlike me. We're just out to dinner. We don't have the excuse of being on a plane, or come to that, amphetamines. Why can't I control myself?

I think back to a particular conversation with Jamie.

We could have done it at the restaurant.

Next time.

Jamie and I never did end up going through with it. Possibly because we only ever usually went to fancy restaurants when we were in the company of Jamie's dad.

A couple of minutes later, Ash approaches me at the top of the staircase where I'm pretending to look into a mirror. He is smiling disbelievingly, yet he knows this is happening, and is no more likely than I am to suggest we pull ourselves together and get the bill.

Thankfully, the ladies' are empty, and – crucially – clean, because this is a nice restaurant (recommended to us, ironically enough, by Ash's boss). We make for the end cubicle. To my relief, it smells only pleasantly floral, a bit like the perfume section in a department store.

Inside the cubicle, I put my back to the door and lock it, and in the next second we are kissing, fumbling, lips and hands everywhere. I am wearing a knee-length satin dress, which contains a useful amount of stretch. Ash hikes it up around my waist, and then there is the tug of a zip and my legs are around him. As we start to move, something begins squeaking inelegantly – I have no idea what – and if anybody were to walk in, they would be in no doubt at all as to what we are doing.

The trust between us is implicit. I'm confident he won't message his mates to report on our bathroom encounter; that it won't become an anecdote (except maybe between us). I never feel self-conscious with him, or awkward. He doesn't crack jokes that make me want to crawl inside my handbag. And after dark, when the drug of him hits hardest, the connection we share feels once-in-a-lifetime.

Except that I know it isn't. Once-in-a-lifetime, I mean.

Whenever I'm with Ash, I try very hard to push all thoughts of Jamie out of my head. But sometimes – usually as we're drifting off to sleep, my head on his chest, our bodies knotted together – I catch myself thinking of Jamie's joke that he'd come back to haunt me. And how I assured him nothing would ever come close to the physical connection we shared.

Pretty soon, I know I have to let Ash in on the most painful story from my past.

I mean, I don't *have* to. I want to. It's something I think he should know.

I do it as he's shuffling a deck of cards one night. We are drinking Old Fashioneds, which helps.

'Do you reckon you might . . . want children one day?' It all comes out clumsily, but it's the only way I can think of to start the conversation.

He glances up from the cards. 'I mean, eventually I would. I think I want . . . a family life, at some point. I'm probably quite conventional like that.'

'Have you ever . . . got anyone pregnant?'

He clears his throat, like he thinks (hopes) he might have misheard. 'Have I ever what?'

'Got anyone pregnant,' I say more slowly, begging him silently, *Think. Think. Think.*

He does a little double-take with his eyes. 'Is this . . . a trick question?'

'In what way?'

'Not sure.' He laughs uncomfortably. 'Do you know something I don't?'

Maybe, I want to reply. But I manage to hold back. 'Just curious.'

'Nope, never got anyone pregnant.' He punches out a breath. 'Sorry, teenage flashback.'

I smile.

He throws me a look. 'My parents convinced themselves I was going to get someone pregnant. Or should I say, they were apoplectically terrified. Mum used to sit me down at least once a week and remind me about safe sex. My dad used to buy me boxes of condoms.'

'Oh. So you were—'

'No! Actually, they had it all wrong. My crazy nights back then were more about drinking and prat-ting around. No legions of illegitimate children out there, I promise.' He glances at me. 'Might stop talk-ing now.'

Weakly, I smile. 'Actually . . . there's something I wanted to tell you.'

And now the words are tumbling from my mouth, and his face is contracting in sympathy, and I would love to know if this is ringing any bells for him, if he has even the faintest sense of recollection as I'm talking. I tell him about what Jamie's mum did, and the flesh wound of that conversation, the scar that still remains, all these years later.

When I'm finished, Ash sets down the cards. He reaches for my hand and says, 'Neve, I'm so sorry.'

I feel a confusing flicker of disappointment when I see there is nothing at all in his eyes except surprise and sadness on my behalf.

I don't tell him, of course, about the box I keep under my bed. The box that's still filled with memories of Jamie. The tickets from *Mamma Mia*. Birthday and anniversary cards. The corks from the champagne his mother bought us, that first night in Edinburgh Road. Beer mats, even parking tickets. Answer sheets from pub quizzes. Cinema stubs. Things that would mean nothing to anyone but me. And finally, our pregnancy test, the one which once bore two tiny yet unmistakeable stripes.

23.

We're in our daily stand-up meeting when Kelley says she can't make the awards do she's been scheduled to attend on Friday night due to childcare issues, and would anyone like to take her place? The room shifts uncomfortably. Eyes avert, arms cross and uncross. Each year, KLI sponsors the Business Person of the Year category at a local business awards, an event which most of us have attended at least once. But it's the kind of do you endure rather than enjoy, because of the inevitable small talk and clapping for an infernal number of awards for so long your palms start to burn, and then shouting to be heard above the over-enthusiastic DJ. It isn't anyone's idea of a decent Friday night, except maybe someone newly discharged from a long stay in hospital. I usually enjoy a chance to network, but I've found in general it's much better done over breakfast, because of the pastries and strong coffee and a definite end point at which everyone can legitimately leg it.

But with the prospect of promotion ever-present in my mind, I stick up my hand and say, 'Love to,' to which Kelley smiles frostily, because she knows no other way.

'You'll be presenting the award,' she reminds me. 'Touch base with them today, introduce yourself.'

'Absolutely,' I say brightly, making a note to do so. On the other side of the room, Parveen forms an L with her thumb and index finger, then raises it slowly to her forehead.

I do actually have another more enticing reason for volunteering to take Kelley's place. Ash's company is sponsoring the Green Business of the Year award, and sure enough, when I mention it to him, he reckons he can wangle a ticket. I remind him it's black tie, then spend the rest of the morning fantasising about seeing him in it.

For all her jibing, Parveen's going too, and our HR guy, and Kelley's assistant. We share a table with the business development team from a local hotel, who seem up for a laugh. For an awards do on a budget, the room actually looks pretty nice – lots of crisp white table linen and creamy floral centrepieces and grey-shirted waiting staff gliding smoothly around with platters and bottles.

Parveen raises her eyebrows as I reach our table. 'Wow.'

'Is that a compliment?'

'Yes, obviously. You look amazing.'

'So do you.' Parveen's wearing a long-sleeved dress in sequin-studded blue chiffon, which is arguably much more elegant than the dress I've picked out.

It's the same one I wore years ago, on my trip to London to see Jamie that first summer. Tiny, black, bold. I stood in front of the mirror for an inordinate amount of time before leaving the house earlier, feeling the dress's ruched fabric between my thumb and index finger, remembering the day Lara took me shopping and insisted I splash out all that money on it. Even now, I don't think I'd spend so much on a dress. But back then, I hadn't cared.

'Is it too much?' I ask Parveen, sitting down quickly.

Parveen smiles, grabbing a bottle of white wine from a cooler. She fills my glass. 'Not to be a bad feminist, but we both know you're wearing that dress for Mr Heartwell's benefit. And, trust me – he is going to *love* it.'

I whack her playfully with my clutch bag. 'You're wrong, actually. And can you stop calling him that? You make him sound like a geography teacher.'

She sets the bottle back in the cooler. 'Quite jealous right now. Everyone's got a crush on Ash. I bet he looks hot in black tie, too. When Maz wears it he just looks like a slightly awkward member of a chamber orchestra.'

I smile, on the verge of reminding her it's still early days with me and Ash. That, objectively speaking, we have barely got started. But somehow, I already know that would be a lie.

I catch his eye about ten minutes later as he arrives at his table, greeting colleagues. We exchange a smile, and thirty seconds or so later, meet in the middle of the room. The awards aren't yet underway, and everyone's still milling around. I know that's what I'm meant to be doing, too – networking and making contacts and paying compliments. But all hope on that front is lost, because the man standing in front of me is far too much of a distraction.

'Black tie suits you,' I murmur into his ear, as we air-kiss.

'And you. You look incredible. I've missed you.'

I smile. 'Since yesterday?'

He looks at me in a way he usually saves for dark corners in bars, the suspended seconds before we kiss. 'Yeah, actually. It's getting more and more difficult to be apart from you.'

Trying not to think too hard about getting to undress him at some point tonight, I tell him I'm presenting an award on behalf of Kelley, necessitating impeccable behaviour all evening.

'What – no kissing on the dance floor?'

'None.'

'Or sneaking off to the loos?'

'Only if you want to get me sacked.'

He moves a step closer, murmurs, 'Really? That's a shame.'

I feel the tick of desire deep in my belly.

'All this actually reminds me of the first night I met you.'

I smile, feel the heat of his palm at my back. 'Yeah?'

'Yeah. I couldn't take my eyes off you that night. And neither could anyone else. They all wanted to be close to you. They always do.'

I present the award on behalf of Kelley, which all goes smoothly until its recipient – the owner of an all-female recruitment consultancy – whips out cue cards to deliver an acceptance speech better suited to the Oscars than a regional business awards. I miss the opportunity to leave the stage, so end up standing awkwardly next to her while she rambles on, not knowing whether to nod enthusiastically at every minor juncture of her story, or stare detachedly towards the back of the room like I'm her personal security detail.

Afterwards, the DJ gets going, and everyone starts moving towards the dance floor. I can see Ash getting to his feet, drink in hand, hopefully to come and find me. I'm no Shakira obviously, because no-one is, but I've necked the requisite amount of wine now to believe that maybe a quick dance with my – date? Boyfriend? – might not be the worst idea in the world. I'm sure we can keep it clean. No grinding or twerking. We're not animals.

But as Ash approaches, my phone starts to ring. I groan internally when I see my mother's number. She only ever calls this late at night when she's having a crisis, or needs a favour.

'Mum?' I struggle to hear her over the music.

But it is a male voice on the other end of the line. 'Mother . . . taxi . . . address.'

'Sorry? What? Hang on.'

I find the nearest door, push it open. The music fades to a thump as I step into the hush of the corridor. 'Hello?' I repeat, terrified it's the police, praying the whole drama with Bev hasn't somehow resurfaced.

'I have your mother in my taxi. She's very . . . She's had a lot to drink, and she can't remember her address. She said your name, told me you'd know. I'm borrowing her phone.'

I lean against the wall next to me and sigh heavily. This isn't the first time this has happened. I give him Mum's address. 'I'm so sorry. Will you tell her I'll be there as soon as I can?'

'Will do.' He rings off, sounding slightly irritated that picking up a middle-aged woman has turned out to be more of a ball-ache than a group of steaming teenagers clutching post-club kebabs.

I feel a hand on my shoulder and jump.

'Sorry.' Ash looks worried. 'I saw you come out. Everything okay?'

'It's my mother. Mum. She's . . . Well, she's had a bit too much to drink, I think.'

'Is she all right?'

'Er, yes. I think so. But I should probably go and check on her.'

'I'll come with you.'

'You don't have to do that.'

'I want to. I'll come.'

I just look at him for a couple of moments, determined to refuse. There is no way I'm inflicting my mother in this state on someone I really, really like.

Then again. If Ash is anything at all to do with Jamie, then maybe it would be a good idea to bring the two of them face to face. Won't there be some glimmer of recognition, from one of them at least? Some clue that in fact I'm not going crazy?

'Well,' I say. 'If you're really sure. My mother is . . . Well, she's quite unique.'

'That's okay. Most parents have their quirks.'

I smile. He's being sweet, but 'quirky' doesn't really capture the years of lacklustre parenting, the succession of appalling men, the police, the restraining order. My mother is what happens when quirky self-destructs.

Outside, as we're waiting in the darkness of the car park for our cab, Ash rests a hand on my back. At one point, he rubs the spot between my shoulder blades in a slow figure-of-eight motion, and despite the warmth of the gesture, I feel myself freeze.

'You okay?' he asks. 'Cold?'

'Fine,' I manage to mumble. But inside, I'm thinking, *Jamie used to do that. Just there, just like that.*

24.

'Don't judge me,' I whisper, as I put the key in my mother's lock.

'For what?'

'The way my mum is.'

'You're not your mum, Neve.'

True, but still. I know how easy it can be to judge someone by association.

We head inside, then make our way to the living room. Mum's curled up on the sofa in the gloom, thankfully fully clothed in a long sequinned dress and high heels, half covered with a cashmere wrap. The overhead lights don't work in here, so I snap on the House of Hackney standard lamp I bought her two Christmases ago, which still has a functioning bulb.

'Mum.' I crouch down beside her, making the floor-boards creak. Ash remains standing at a respectful distance behind me, in the doorway. I catch the scent of strong perfume and alcohol, but nothing resembling the contents of her stomach, thank goodness. 'Are you okay?'

Her eyes flutter open. Her hair is twisted into a giant topknot that's been lacquered into submission by what must have been an entire can of hairspray. She still smells slightly flammable. 'Neve?'

'What happened?'

'Oh,' she says, eyes drifting closed again. 'Load of fuss about nothing.'

'The taxi driver said you couldn't remember your address.'

'I told him . . . Senior moment . . . No need for all the . . .'

Most of her make-up has migrated to the folds of her face. Her teeth are patched dark red in places, and for a moment I think it's congealed blood, before I realise it's lipstick.

I glance at Ash and shrug, lightly. He responds with a supportive smile.

'Mum, how much have you had to drink?'

'No idea.'

'We need to get you to bed.'

She opens her eyes again, then looks over in Ash's direction and smiles. 'Hello, Jamie.'

My stomach drops off a cliff. 'Mum, that's not—'

'What's Jamie doing here?'

'No, Mum, it's . . . This is Ash. He's . . .' I glance back at him, and he gives me another reassuring smile. A *just say what you've got to say* smile. 'He's a friend.'

'Nice to meet you, Daniela,' he says softly, patiently.

'Are you my taxi driver?'

'No, Ash is my friend. He's an architect, Mum.'

'Jamie's an architect.'

I feel a flare of panic. Maybe bringing Ash here was a stupid idea. I remember how weird Mum used to be towards Jamie. How awkward the room felt whenever they were in it together.

'Would you like a drink of water?' Ash says. Without waiting for a response, he disappears into the hallway, and I hear him making his way to the back of the house. My panic recedes a little.

'First time Jamie's ever been helpful,' Mum slurs, shooting me an enormous, exaggerated wink, the supposed inference of which I don't even begin to get.

I draw in a couple of steeling breaths. She's way too drunk to make it upstairs, so instead I fetch a blanket, remove her heels and encourage her into the recovery position. Is that what they still recommend? I fetch an ornamental bowl from a shelf – something she bartered for on holiday in Turkey years ago – and decide that if she wakes up tomorrow and discovers it's full of puke, then that can be her punishment.

'Duke's back with his "wife".' She makes air quotes with her fingers – though I'm not really sure why, since it's reasonable to assume the man hasn't invented being married.

My impatience gives way to pity. Because, despite everything, I know Mum's heart is too fragile to be dating some arsehole who thinks wedding rings are optional. Especially an arsehole who has a nickname more suited to a 1980s porn star.

'Then he doesn't deserve you,' I whisper, squatting down next to her and gently squeezing her arm.

Ash reappears with a pint of water and some paracetamol, setting them down between the newspapers and unwashed mugs on the coffee table.

'Thanks, Jamie,' Mum says, with the heavy sincerity of the very drunk, looking up at him, eyes rolling as she attempts to focus. 'All right if I call you Jamie?'

'No,' I say, sharply, 'it isn't.'

He reaches out to touch my shoulder, mouthing, 'It's really okay.'

I get to my feet. 'I'd better stay with her.'

A beat. 'I can stay too. If you like.'

'Here?'

'Yes, if . . . If that's okay.'

I glance down at Mum. Her eyes have fluttered shut now, her breathing becoming weighted.

I realise I feel relieved. I don't want him to go. 'Only if you don't mind.'

He puts an arm around me, and my heart unclenches.

My bedroom door probably hasn't been opened since I was last here, and the space has that locked-room smell. I go straight to the window and yank it open, letting in a warm gust of night air and the faint sound of traffic moving along Earlham Road.

'It's a gorgeous house,' Ash says, sitting down on the edge of the stripped single mattress.

'Well, it could be. Or should be. She won't let me touch it. It's her special way of tormenting me. What would you do with it?' I say, with a smile.

'Architecturally? If it were down to me . . . not much, actually. A few tweaks, maybe. I might frame the view of the garden from the kitchen a bit differently. Redesign the lower part of the rear elevation, create a better entertaining space.'

I laugh softly. 'I don't think my mother needs any more encouragement to entertain.'

'Was this your bedroom?'

I nod. 'It hasn't changed much since I was a kid.'

'A Timberlake fan,' he observes approvingly, nodding at my posters.

Occasionally, Jamie would have a go at the dance moves to make me laugh, so badly I'd always threaten to break up with him. 'I mean, who isn't?'

'Well, quite.' He leans back on his arms and smiles, looking every inch the double-O in his black tie. 'And is that Lara?'

I follow his gaze to the photos still clinging doggedly to the wall. In every shot, we're squeezing each other tight, our skinny arms wrapped around each other. There's one of us in this house, downstairs in the kitchen. One on a pair of canvas chairs, at a caravan park in Devon. One at school, on our last-ever day, white shirts graffitied with messages from our friends. We're sticking our tongues out, and for some reason they're stained green, but I can't remember what from. 'Yep. That's her.'

'You look close.'

'We were. We were . . . inseparable.' And then, before he can ask more, I say in a rush, knowing I have to confront what happened downstairs, 'I'm sorry, by the way. About my mum calling you Jamie. She's just drunk.'

He nods. 'I know.' But I wonder if his eyes are saying, *Are you only with me because I remind you of him?*

I feel sure this is what he'd been going to ask me at the beach that day.

But I can't tell him he does far more than just remind me of Jamie. That all the stories I read online about souls swapping over, and the countless similarities between Ash and Jamie – way too many for it to be coincidence – have continued to beetle at the back of my mind.

And now my mum – based on two seconds of conversation – has made the link too. And yes, she is bonkers and drunk and generally about as reliable as a helicopter in fog. But how can I ignore it being the first thing she said, unprompted; the first thing she thought when she saw him?

'Do you recognise this dress?' I ask him.

'In what way?'

'Can you remember . . . ever seeing it before tonight?'

It's the same question I wanted to ask when I told him about the baby, and when we walked into this room just now. *Does this memory seem in any way familiar to you?*

He stares at me for a couple more moments before his expression becomes a smile. 'I mean, I love it, if that's what you're asking.' From where he's sitting on the edge of the mattress, he reaches out, places his hands on my hips. 'Why do you ask? Has someone famous worn it, or something?'

'So you do think you might have seen it before?'

'You carry it off *way* better than any celebrity I can think of.' Misunderstanding complete, he moves one hand to the dress's hem, then starts to push it upwards, bunching its fabric over my thighs. Slowly, he starts to roll down my tights, his gaze gripping mine the whole time.

But just as I'm about to shut my eyes and abandon earth, I feel him hesitate, let out a punch of breath. 'Sorry, Neve. Is this a bit . . . weird, with your mum downstairs?'

'No. No, not at all. She wouldn't care. She'd do the same.' Of this, I could not feel more confident.

'You looked really good, you know, up on that stage tonight,' he murmurs, returning his attention to my legs, my dress. 'CEO would suit you.'

I smile, though I'm struggling to fully focus. 'Kelley's going nowhere.'

'You could start a rival business.'

'Never. She'd bury me.'

He pauses. 'Just so you know, this isn't my idea of dirty talk.'

I look down at him, lifting an eyebrow. 'But ambition turns you on.'

He laughs. 'Never really thought of it like that before but . . . yeah. I guess it does.' He bends forward to kiss my stomach, begins to hitch up my dress again. He takes my tights down just enough. Struggling to stay rooted, I grip on to his shoulders. The room, suddenly, is soundless as a cave. I can hear only my ragged breathing, the failing brakes on my heartbeat.

'Ash,' I manage, as his fingers inch closer to my underwear, 'can I ask you something?'

'Yeah,' he breathes, 'yeah, anything.'

'Do you feel like you've met her before?'

His hands still. He pulls back and looks up at me. 'Who?'

'My mum.'

'What?'

'Does she seem . . . familiar to you?'

He shakes his head. 'Um, Neve, I know I brought it up – but any chance we could stop talking about your mum?'

At this, I finally shut up, to let him finish what he started.

The whole time, as I suspected he might, he insists I keep the dress on.

25.

Then

Lara was dating someone. Sam. She'd met him over the summer, while she was interning. He was a few years older, worked in prosthetics for film and TV. Maybe she'd been hoping to make a good contact, or maybe she liked him because they had stuff in common. Perhaps a little of both. They'd been out a few times. Nothing serious yet, as far as I knew – although it was the most dates she'd ever had with one guy. So maybe there was something there.

Every time she came back from his place – a house share up on Pottergate – she and I would climb into her bed together with mugs of tea, and she would tell me everything.

That morning, we were listening to Coldplay. Jamie was already on the phone to his mum, reassuring her about God knows what.

'He doesn't laugh much,' Lara said about Sam, wrinkling her nose. 'Takes himself quite seriously. And he wears T-shirts in bed.'

'So?'

'My *dad* wears T-shirts in bed.'

'But he's hot. Sam, I mean,' I clarified, quickly.

'I know. It's quite annoying.'

Next to me, her tumble of blonde hair was splayed like a mermaid's on the pillow. *She is so beautiful*, I thought. I hoped Sam thought the same, when he looked at her.

'Neve, do you ever worry . . . that you've settled down too soon?'

I stared at her, surprised. Lara was almost as close to Jamie as I was. 'No. What? Why would I?'

She shrugged. 'I don't know. Because everyone has flaws? Even Saint Jamie.'

I rolled my eyes. 'I never said he's perfect.'

'But that's what you think.'

'No, I don't.'

'Okay. Name one . . . imperfect thing about him.'

I had to think really hard before deciding that maybe, sometimes, Jamie could be a tiny bit stubborn. Like when he knew he wouldn't enjoy a certain TV show before he'd even seen it. Or refused to ever get Indian takeaway because of one bad experience with a too-hot jalfrezi.

'I'm waiting,' Lara said.

'Okay. Maybe sometimes he . . . can be a bit stubborn.'

She rolled her eyes. 'That's not an imperfection. That's a superpower. Take it from me.'

'Being stubborn is your fatal flaw, and you know it.'

'Anyway. That's it? That's seriously the worst thing you can think of?'

'You asked me to name an imperfection, not the worst thing about him.'

Morning was seeping through a crack in the curtains, a slow buttermilk trickle of daylight.

She sipped her tea. 'Okay then. What's the worst thing about him?'

'Probably his dad.' I felt bad, even as I said it. 'I really can't stand his dad.'

'Wow, you two really are off-the-charts scandalous, aren't you?'

I stick out my tongue. 'I can't help it if he's the best person ever.'

'Okay, get out of the way. I think I'm going to puke.'

I wondered about that, later. Why I'd let Lara talk me into bad-mouthing Jamie, even though it was really only his dad I'd criticised. Still, when I curled up in bed with him that night, I felt guilt for not being as loyal as I could have been. I could have just said, *I can't think of anything. He's perfect.*

The following afternoon, Jamie popped out for some bread and milk. He left his phone on the coffee table in the living room. I only glanced at it when it flashed with a call. Probably his mum.

But it wasn't his mum. *Heather* was the name on the screen.

To this day, I have no idea why I picked it up. Why I thought it was even remotely my place to answer.

'Hello?'

A held note of hesitation. If slipping up had a sound, I felt sure this was it.

Then she asked for Jamie, in a voice as cool and smooth as cream.

'Sorry. He's out right now. Can I take a message?'

'No, that's okay. Thanks.' And then she rang off.

I don't know why the call made me feel so uneasy. I stayed where I was on the sofa, the phone a mudweight in my hand.

Jamie had never mentioned anyone called Heather.

'Heather rang,' I said, when he got back. I don't know why I said it like she was someone we both knew. The words were out of my mouth before he'd even shut the back door.

I listened to him sling his keys onto the kitchen worktop, put away the bread and milk. Then he called out, 'Oh, really? Okay. Cheers.'

'I picked it up . . . because I thought it might be important.'

He wandered through to the living room, set his wallet on the coffee table. He nodded, but didn't seem bothered about retrieving the phone from my hand. He didn't pass further comment, appeared completely unconcerned.

'She didn't want to leave a message.'

He nodded again. I noticed his cheeks were ruddy from the walk. Or was he slightly flustered? 'Fancy the pub?'

'Okay.' I took a breath, passed him the phone. 'Who . . .? Who is she? Heather.'

He started scrolling, I couldn't tell on what. 'Oh, just someone from A&L.'

Archibald & Leicester, the firm in London where he'd spent the summer.

I waited.

He looked up. 'You okay?'

'Yeah, I was just . . . wondering who Heather is, that's all.'

He frowned. 'I told you. Someone I worked with at A&L.'

'You never mentioned her.'

A beat. Tension clung like sweat to the space between us. 'Why would I?'

'I don't know . . . because you have her number in your phone?'

'Well, she was my mentor, so she gave it to me.'

I could feel my skin prickling. I wasn't the jealous type, never had been. I wouldn't have dreamed of policing Jamie's calls, or his friendships, or anything. In the last days with my dad, we'd all lived on a boiling tide of my mother's accusations, each one wilder and more devastating than the last. It was hard to witness, and I'd sworn to myself I would never be like that.

Still, some new reflex was compelling me to dig deeper. 'But how come . . . you never mentioned her? If she was your mentor, I mean.'

Jamie shrugged. 'I hardly had anything to do with her. She didn't take the role of mentor that seriously, if I'm honest.'

'So why is she calling you?'

'I have no idea, Neve.'

'Aren't you curious?'

'Not really.'

My insides bunched with frustration. What aspiring architect receives an unexpected call from the company they spent the summer with – a prestigious architectural firm – yet claims to be not in the least bit curious why? 'What if they're ringing to offer you a job?'

'Heather's not senior enough to offer me a job. And I wouldn't be interested anyway. I don't want to move to London. I told you that.'

He was so casual, so bemused by my apparent concern. But I simply couldn't understand it – why she was in his phone, why she was calling, why he apparently didn't care what she wanted. 'Aren't you going to ring her back?'

He groaned. 'Neve. Maybe later. Come on, are we going to the pub or not?'

The thing was, I did trust him. He'd never given me reason not to. I knew how affairs looked – the way they sounded and smelt and felt. I would *know* if he had something to hide. So I resolved to put it to the back of my mind. Heather was his mentor, that was all there was to it. Heather was his mentor – but I was his girlfriend, and we were in love.

26.

Now

Lara suggests dinner at a Thai place on Tombland. 'I want to meet Ash. And you can get to know Felix better.'

Once again, my instinct is both to accept her invitation and reject it. I have no idea how to balance the simultaneous desires I have to love her, and deplore her.

But I agree, partly because I've always adored the restaurant's building, next to the thirteenth-century gate on the south side of the cathedral. It's Grade II listed and beloved by building nuts for its mansard roof and decorative tiling, dormer gables, mullion windows. There are lampposts on the cobblestones at the front of the building too, which always makes coming here feel a bit like stepping back in time. I suppose tonight, in lots of ways, it is.

Inside, it's busy, but Lara raises a hand, so we spot her straight away. She stands up when we reach the table. Her angel-blonde curls are loose around her face, skimming her shoulders. She's wearing the skinniest jeans I think I've ever seen.

A couple of nights ago, I told Ash why Lara and I fell out. He listened quietly, then said, 'Well, I think it's great you've been able to get past it.'

I didn't know quite what to say to that.

'Wine?' Ash asks, once we've all said hello and sat down, and Lara's complimented Ash's shirt, and Felix has told us about their taxi driver, who jumped every red light on the way here before nearly rear-ending a bus. 'Felix, Lara – red, white, rosé? Or beer?'

'Actually,' Felix says, 'just sparkling water for us, I think. We're detoxing.'

'From what?' I say, looking between him and Lara.

'A touch too much fast living,' he says smoothly, which though it answers my question, still feels like an evasion, a response prepared beforehand.

Back at uni, Lara used to sneer at people like Jamie's mum, with her juicer and personal trainer and quarterly commitment to water fasting. *Every time she does it I swear she shits out a little bit more personality*, she'd say.

Still. I know it's far from my right to judge a single thing about her lifestyle now. 'We can stick to soft if you—'

'Oh, no, please,' Lara says, quickly. 'No point all four of us suffering.'

So Ash and I order white wine, and Lara and Felix get sparkling water.

Ash asks Felix more about the company he founded. He tells us about the tech, which is something to do with AI-powered robots. Its primary application, he says, is infrastructure inspection within the mining and oil and gas industries. They were taken over by a multinational two years ago, but Felix stayed on as CEO, pocketing a hefty windfall in the process – though he's far too classy to say how much, of course.

He really is California-handsome, I think, as he talks, with his designer smile and twenty-four-carat charm. Lara was never in a hurry to meet her soulmate, but I always felt sure that when she did, he would be a Felix.

'But you played tennis professionally before that?' Ash says.

'I did. The two careers overlapped for a little while, actually.'

'Do you ever miss it?'

'No,' Felix says, thoughtfully. 'I still play. And believe it or not, I'm even more passionate about what I'm doing now. It feels useful in a way that tennis didn't. And the field I'm in is just so exciting. But I'm still involved in sport. I'm actually hoping to set up some kind of a tennis academy one day. But that's more of a long-term goal.'

'What brought you to London? When you met, I mean,' I ask, keen to hear the story from his side.

'I was here on business,' Felix says, sipping his water. 'I had some meetings lined up, and a friend of my agent invited me to a party.' He looks over at Lara. 'And we got talking, and . . . well. Let's just say, I didn't go home for the next six weeks.'

Ash laughs appreciatively.

'We had five nights in the Savoy,' Lara says, 'then he came to stay with me in Twickenham. You'd love my flat, Neve. It's on the top floor of one of those lovely old mansion blocks. And it has views of the Thames.'

'Mmm,' Felix says. 'If you squat at an exact height, tilt your head and squint.'

Ash laughs, and I want to too, but something about the way Felix says this makes me bristle. Even though I'm sure he's not intentionally being unkind. It takes me back to what she said about him being the first guy she thought I might approve of. But am I seeing what she sees?

Lara tells us more about being a production designer, the various shows she's worked on, the ups and downs of freelancing in the entertainment industry. She says she's between projects at the moment, which is why the timing's been perfect for her to come back to Norwich for a while.

At this, I notice her exchange a glance with Felix. She squeezes his hand, and I wonder what it means. Whether the truth is that in fact, he doesn't really want to be here at all, marooned in this small English city, sleeping in the spare bedroom at her parents' house. I wonder if perhaps she had to beg him to come; what she had to promise him in return.

Is that a man who knows her worth?

'How long are you taking a break for?' Ash asks.

'Oh, you know. Pieces of string, and all that.' By her side, Felix doesn't take his eyes off her. She shifts in her chair, sips her water. Then she asks Ash what he does for a living.

He turns to me in slight surprise, then back to her. 'Oh. Well, I'm an architect.'

Is it me, or do her eyes double-take slightly? 'Really? In Norwich?'

'Yep. At a company called Crave & Co.'

'Great name,' says Felix, finally shifting his gaze away from Lara.

'Do you enjoy it?' Lara asks.

'I do. I love it. I was born to it, I think.'

'What kind of stuff do you like to work on?'

'Well, mostly I just love a challenge.'

'What sort of thing?' asks Felix.

Ash sips his wine. 'Well, an example might be ... persuading a client to go for a rebuild, instead of refurbishing. Or adding modern design to period properties in a way that feels really innovative, but still does justice to both elements, you know? And clients with particularly niche requirements – they're always fun.'

'Like what?' Lara says.

I smile into my drink. Knowing Lara, she's probably thinking *sex dungeon*.

'Well, right now, I'm designing a property around the precise movements of the sun. And the clients want a moat to swim in, too.'

'A *moat*? What the hell are you designing, a castle?'

'I suppose you could say it's the modern-day equivalent.'

'Has Neve shown you pictures of Felix's place?' Lara says, excitedly.

Ash turns slightly in my direction again, then smiles at her and shakes his head. 'Not yet, no.'

'Oh,' she says. I can just detect the brightness fall from her voice. 'Well, I'll show you some other time. But the design is just ... breathtaking. Open-plan, four-storey, views of Monterey Bay. And a tennis court, of course.' She puts her elbows on the table, making a cradle for her chin with her hands. 'So, what's your absolute dream project?'

Don't say it. Don't say it.

'Well, the ultimate would obviously be to design an iconic structure. To have my name on something world-class, like . . . a concert hall, or a museum, or—'

'—the next Gherkin,' Lara chips in, speaking slowly. And then she looks directly at me, and her eyes say, *What the hell?*

Luckily, at this point, our main courses arrive and the moment moves on.

Before we eat, Lara throws back a handful of brightly coloured tablets from a rose-gold box retrieved from her handbag.

Next to her, Felix is doing the same. 'Orders of the detox,' he says. 'You wouldn't believe how many rules we're breaking tonight just to have a stir-fry.'

I notice Lara squeezing his hand again, looking right into his eyes. Reassurance, perhaps, that she's fully on board with his health obsessions?

The noodle dish she's chosen has pretty much zero kick. In the old days, she would have been the one ordering a curry with three chili symbols and a warning triangle on the menu, furiously refusing any fluids that might counteract the heat.

As we start eating, Lara suddenly looks up and lifts her fork, tapping it against the air. '*Oh*,' she says, to Ash. 'I knew I was missing something. I remember you.'

My heart leaps to my throat.

'Weren't you the guy who got struck by lightning?'

'What?' Felix says, incredulously.

'Yes!' she says. 'I read about it at the time. My mum cut something out of the paper for me. She was trying to distract me, probably. I think the headline was something like, *ASHLEY'S MIRACLE ESCAPE.'*

'Your real name is Ashley?' I ask him, wondering how I managed to miss that.

'I mean, only officially. Nobody ever calls me that. Not even my parents.'

'Hold on,' Felix chips in. 'You . . . got struck by lightning?'

'Yep,' Ash says, politely. 'It was a long time ago, though.'

Felix gapes for a couple of moments. 'What . . . in the hell does that feel like?'

'I don't actually remember, fortunately.'

Felix nods, holds up a hand. 'Apologies. Didn't mean to pry. Just . . . wanted to make sure getting struck by lightning wasn't one of those British turns of phrase I don't quite get.'

By now, opposite me, Lara is sitting up very straight. 'It was just around the corner,' she says slowly, like the pieces are slotting together in her mind. 'It was the same night, Neve. It was the same night as—'

I shake my head at her silently, pleading with my eyes.

'The same night as what?' Ash says, looking between us both.

Despite having searched for Jamie online, I guess he never checked the dates. And I know he hasn't made the connection between his accident and Jamie's death. Why would he?

'Nothing,' Lara says quickly, rearranging her shocked expression. 'Sorry. Nothing. Crossed wires.'

★ ★ ★

Back at my place, Lara calls as I'm in the kitchen getting water. Though her avatar is blank, it still feels strange to see her name on my phone screen after all this time.

Ash is upstairs, stuck messaging in a group chat, but I shut the kitchen door, just to be sure.

The world has quieted, the only light the diffuse orange glow of the streetlamp from the alleyway behind my garden.

'Are you by yourself?'

'Yes, I'm in the kitchen.'

'Okay. I'm going to say something now, and I want you to promise you won't flip out.'

The floor tiles feel cold as concrete against my bare feet. 'He reminds you of Jamie.'

She exhales. 'Is that why you like him?'

Absent-mindedly, I slot my phone between my ear and my shoulder. Then I shake out a cloth, spray disinfectant onto it, run it across the surface of the worktop. 'No . . . I mean, maybe that was what drew me to him at first, but . . .' I trail off. I want to tell her the truth. About what I really suspect happened that night. But she'll think I'm crazy. Won't she? Or has a part of her mind started to make the same impossible connections, too?

'They are . . . incredibly alike. It's kind of weird,' she says, but then nothing further. And I can tell there is so much more she is holding back from saying, because we still haven't talked about what happened when Jamie died.

But she knows how raw it still is for me. How hot and toxic it remains, all these years later.

'There's something I have to tell you,' I say, rubbing at the worktop in an attempt to bring up a shine.

She waits.

'It's about Ash.'

'Go on.'

Above my head, the floorboards creak. 'Actually, you know . . . I can't do this over the phone. Let's meet next week.'

'Okay.' A moment passes. 'Neve?'

'Yes?'

'What do you think of Felix?'

I release a breath. 'I like him.' This much, on a base level at least, is true.

'But?'

'Who said there's a *but*?'

'If there wasn't a *but* you'd have said, *I love him, Lar, he's perfect for you.*'

I smile into the phone. I appreciate her attempt to pretend we're ten years in the past, enjoying the kind of late-night gossip we used to live for.

I think about how intensely Felix kept looking at her, earlier. The way she kept squeezing his hand, and what it might have meant. Is he controlling? In need of constant placation? And if so, how the hell is he the right guy for the Lara I used to know – or, come to that, anyone?

'He's . . . I don't know.' I sigh. 'Maybe you're just very different to how you were when I last knew you.'

'Stop being cryptic. I actually want to know what you think.'

But how is what I think relevant, really? I have a vague, nagging sense that perhaps he's overprotective. That he might have crazy ideas about health and diets (not least that a stir-fry is the devil's work). But these are merely impressions. Hunches. He's pleasant enough. Cordial and perfectly charming. And the reality is, until a couple of months ago, Lara and I were estranged. I'd need to spend hours, days, weeks with both of them before I could arrive at any kind of fair conclusion about how well-suited they are for each other.

'Why?' I ask softly, in response to her question, blinking into reflected lamplight. I rinse the cloth, fold it over the tap, straighten its rumpled edges.

'Because it's important to me. Because you're my oldest friend.'

Was.

'And I know we still need to talk about what went on with Jamie, and everything … but what you think will always matter to me, Neve.'

I exhale. 'Let's talk next week.'

'Okay. Neve?'

'Lar.'

'I really do love him, you know.'

'I know,' I say, because that's not what I feel hesitant about.

'And for what it's worth? I think Ash is in love with you. It's written all over his face, the way he feels.'

I feel a blush of pleasure creep through me, thinking about the heart he sketched onto my steamed-up shower screen before we left the house tonight. 'It's only been a couple of months.'

'So? Do you love him?'

It surprises me, the swiftness with which my whole body says yes. The certainty is like a tiny wingbeat inside me, right in time with my heart.

'Yes. But it's so fast to feel this way,' I confess. I think of my mother, how quickly she gets in deep with people. How fiercely I've resisted doing that, since all the devastation with my dad.

'Want to know how long it took me to fall in love with Felix?'

'Go on.'

'A *day*. Well, a night, actually. Well, about five hours.'

'That's not like you.'

'No,' she agrees. 'But that's how you know it's love.'

Upstairs, after Ash has dropped off to sleep, I stay awake for hours, blinking into the blackness, listening to the gentle percussion of his breath. Wondering for the millionth time if I'm losing my mind.

I have a craving to get up and clean something – anything – to try to stem the overwhelm of my thoughts. But I resist. I don't want Ash to wake up and find me scrubbing down the toilet at three a.m. in a pair of rubber gloves.

By nature, I'm a sceptic. I've never been into ghosts, or past lives, or those psychics who tell you your dead nan's got a message for you. I've always believed that when you're gone, you're gone. Which was maybe why losing Jamie was so hard. I could never really draw comfort from the idea that he was looking down on me, or that if I talked to him, he was listening. When he died, it was as if he'd simply vanished – evaporated like morning mist as the sun rose without him. He was dead, gone for ever.

So how can I possibly turn my back now on an unexpected chance to reclaim him? To live out the future that was stolen from us? Ash is, in a million tiny ways, the person Jamie was destined to become.

I'm pretty sure Ash won't take it well, if I tell him any of this. But I'd never forgive myself if I didn't try. I need him to know that on the night of his accident, I believe that – mad as it sounds – Jamie's spirit occupied his body somehow. That what Jamie and I had was too good, too magical, for our premature goodbye. That our love simply shed its leaves for a season – a winter that arrived without warning – and now our summer has come again.

27.

On a hot Friday night after work, Lara picks me up in a silver convertible.

I afford the vehicle the staggered gawp it deserves. 'What is *this*?'

She pulls a face, despite the fact that with her shades and floral headband, the whole look really quite suits her. 'It's Mum's, she loves it, she bought it right after Dad died, so no-one can say anything. It's horrible, it's embarrassing, get in.'

I smile, and do as I'm told.

'Felix thinks she'd be offended if we got a hire car while we're here. So . . . we're just going to act like delusional OAPs for the evening, okay?'

'Why act?' I say, pulling on my seatbelt. 'I'm knackered. I quite fancy early retirement.'

Lara laughs, and starts the engine.

It doesn't escape me how carefully she pulls away from the kerb.

There is a nature reserve a ten-minute drive from Norwich, on the south bank of the river Yare. Lara tells me she can't be arsed to walk, that she knows a good bench. At this, I'm relieved – being July, it's way too hot for hiking, and anyway, I'm wearing sandals.

She leads the way along a winding grassy path to a bench overlooking a glistening web of silver streams spun into the heart of the reed bed. It's a private and tranquil corner of the reserve, a summer-lit segment of solitude, our only company the frogs and grebes and reed warblers and coots.

'This is actually my dad's bench,' Lara says, as we gaze out over the cluster of lush green wetland. Above our heads, tiny vaporous clouds roll past, soft like kettle steam. 'He loved this place.'

I turn to look at the brass plaque behind my right shoulder.

For Billy, who liked to watch the world go by.

My throat clots with emotion. I swallow it down. 'That's beautiful. He'd have loved it.'

She smiles. 'He'd have told us off for being sentimental tosspots, actually, don't you think? But yeah. Deep down, you're right – he would.'

I don't have the monopoly on grief here, I think, suddenly. *How long should I go on punishing her for what happened to Jamie?*

The thought comes out of nowhere, and it feels foreign and alarming. Did I get everything wrong? Was my anger misdirected? Over the years, it has kept me safe, in lots of ways. Has given me focus when the pain of losing Jamie became too much.

'It's so weird,' she says. 'That Dad dying was the thing that eventually brought me and Mum together again, after a decade of me acting like a total brat. We're closer than we've ever been now.'

'Billy would be happy about that.'

'Yeah. But he'd probably also want to know what took me so long.' She shakes her head. 'Anyway. Talk to me, Neve. What was it that you couldn't say on the phone on Saturday night?'

Talk to me. Just three words, but they flicker to life at the back of my brain, like an old bulb I'd forgotten was there. She used to say it all the time, instead of, *All right?* or *What's up?*

I feel the urge to backtrack, tell her it was nothing. But Lara is the only person on the planet who might be able to help me understand what's going on with Ash. Because she knew Jamie too, and she loved him. There's no-one else who can reliably discern whether or not I'm going mad.

'This is going to sound . . . a bit out there, okay? You might think I'm nuts.'

She's probably expecting me to say I still miss Jamie. That Ash reminds me of him a little too much. But she doesn't yet know how deep it goes. How messy it's all become.

She slips me a smile. 'Come on. That ship sailed when you confessed to fancying Attenborough.'

I smile back at her. I once admitted to finding David's voice soothing, and she's never let me forget it.

'I feel as though Ash . . . might be Jamie.'

She blinks a couple of times, takes a breath, lets it out. 'No. Sorry. Don't understand.'

I shake my head. 'I know that sounds insane. Believe me, I *know* it. But I think . . . Jamie might have come back to me. He always said he would.'

Lara touches my hand with her fingertips. She's wearing a stack of gold bangles that reaches halfway up her forearm. 'Talk me through it,' is all she says, very calmly.

So I tell her everything. About Ash's job and flat, and taste in art and music, about his handwriting and favourite aftershave, and the myriad other weird little similarities between them. I describe all the ways in which he already seems to know me so well. I tell her about the lightning strike, about Ash becoming a completely different person afterwards. I insist it can't be coincidence, in the hope that she doesn't try to tell me that's what it must be.

It's comforting as it always was to talk to her. Like no time has passed at all. It's as though we're back in the bedroom at Edinburgh Road, lying on her bed with our feet propped up against the wall, taking it in turns to offload and trying together to make sense of how the world works.

When I'm finished, she draws a deep breath. 'And what does Ash think about this?'

'I haven't told him yet.' I shake my head. 'Honestly, Lar, I feel like I've gone back in time. Thinking about Jamie constantly, unable to forget him. I moved on from all that. But now I'm right back there.'

'That must be tough.'

'I mean, it is . . . but at the same time, Jamie was the love of my life. So, in a way . . .'

She nods, waits patiently, like there's nothing at all unusual about the things I'm saying.

'What do you think? I mean, you've met Ash, and you . . . knew Jamie, too.'

I notice her eyes pool briefly with tears before she swallows them away. 'You know as well as I do there's only one way to get to the bottom of this. You need to talk to Ash. Tell him everything. You never know, it might make complete sense to him.'

I consider this for a moment, then shake my head. 'What would you say, if someone said that to you?'

'Well, that would depend.'

'On what?'

'On whether I felt on some level like I wasn't myself, I guess.'

'His personality changed completely. He admits that. But he just puts it down to the accident. I swear, this walk-in thing makes *total* sense. Everything – *everything* – about it adds up. If I could just show him some of the things I've read . . . he wouldn't be able to dismiss it. I know he wouldn't.'

'Maybe not.'

'So you think it's possible?'

'I mean, who knows if it's possible?'

I swallow. 'Do you ever . . . think Billy's still about?'

At this, she laughs, loudly. 'Oh God. All the *time*. Remember that thing he used to do with peaches? He'd leave one on my pillow, or on my chest of drawers, because he knew how much I loved them. Well, after he died, I found a peach in my fruit bowl at home, and I swear – *I swear* – I didn't buy it, Neve. To this day, I have *no idea* where it came from. And once, a lightbulb blew when I was helping myself to his whisky, back at Mum's. Literally as I took the stopper out. *Bam*.' She shakes her head. 'I'd bet my life savings that was Dad saying, *Hands off*.'

I smile. If Billy were ever to reach out from beyond the grave, of course it would be to protect his precious drinks cabinet. 'So, you do believe in that stuff? People's souls still being around.'

I don't think we discussed this kind of thing much when we were younger. I suppose we never really needed to.

Lara shrugs, gently. 'The point is that nobody knows. We can guess, but we don't know.'

'What Ash and I have is really good. I don't want that to change,' I admit with a frown, watching dragonflies skim the surface of the stream by our feet.

'But what you have isn't real if you're not being honest.'

A beat. 'Just so you know, this is more than me just missing Jamie. I . . . believe this.'

'I can tell.'

'I actually wish it was that simple. That I just missed him.'

'Since when was grief ever simple?'

After that, we just sit there together for a while, watching the iridescent beauty of the dragonflies making rainbows among the golden beams of evening.

28.

Lara's right. I need to talk to Ash. But I don't know where to start. How does anyone go about confessing something so outlandish?

We have a date on Wednesday, but I end up cancelling because I'm working late. Thursday night, Ash forgets he's made plans for a poker night. So by the time I think I might be able to talk to him, it's a full week after my conversation with Lara.

Friday is boiling, a thick soup of heat. We drive out to Suffolk after work, to cool off in the lido.

We swim lazily for an hour, then pull up a couple of loungers to soak up the last of the sunshine. Swifts swoop above our heads, snatching insects from a sticky web of sky. The air sparkles with water thrown up by other swimmers. Next to me, a handsome man is prone topless on a sun lounger, and he is mine. Despite everything that's been going on in my head, if I had to define contentment, this moment would come pretty close.

'Neve,' Ash says, after a few minutes. Though my eyes are shut, I sense his voice turn towards me. 'I'm going to say something now, and take full advantage of us being in public, and you not being able to run away. Are you ready?'

I open my eyes and smile. 'Should I be scared?'

He extends a hand, running one finger along my bare shoulder. 'That depends.'

'On?'

'Your appetite for soppiness.'

I feel the traffic light of my heart turn green. 'I'm the one who suggests soppy movies for first dates, remember?'

'All right then. Do you know what tonight is?'

'Tonight right now . . . or tonight when we get home?'

Our gazes collide. He smiles. 'Tonight right now. Two months ago today, what we were doing?'

I frown, feigning bemusement. 'Were we . . . discussing where you got your wine glasses?' I'm just teasing, of course. I know exactly what we were doing. Listening to London Grammar, kissing for the very first time.

'Nope.' He leans over, putting his lips to mine. And tonight, his kiss feels different. Long and lingering, tender like a message. A love song. 'Neve, I need to tell you something,' he whispers, but then the air grows suddenly cool and dark, as if a cloud has just swallowed the sun.

We peel apart and look up. A short, stout woman in a striped halter-neck swimming costume is standing over us.

'Excuse me. I hope you don't mind me asking, but are you the man who got struck by lightning?'

Perhaps reflexively, we all glance at Ash's torso. He can hardly deny it – the scars are on show for anyone to look at, if they're nosy enough.

Ash looks back up at her. 'Er, yep. That's me.'

She grins like she's won a bet. 'Would you mind if I took a selfie?' She waggles her phone at us.

Why? I want to say. *He had a horrific accident and nearly died. He's not a celebrity.* I mean, I think his scars are kind of beautiful, but that doesn't mean I'm excited by what happened to him. This woman is probably the same class of ghoul who'd stop to video a road traffic accident rather than dial 999.

She passes me her phone. 'Would you mind?'

Ash slips me an apologetic expression and shrugs.

'You're not allowed to take photos here,' I tell her, gesturing to the bright red notice fixed to the railings behind us.

'Oh, quickly,' she pleads. 'While the lifeguard's looking the other way.'

I glance again at Ash, who mouths, 'It's fine,' which I suspect is code for *Just do it to get rid of her.* So, reluctantly, I check the lifeguard's head is turned before snapping a picture of the woman with her arm around Ash. She's grinning widely, all teeth and no inhibitions.

We watch as she walks back to her friends, shows them the photo on the screen, gestures back over towards Ash. We are both sitting upright now, relaxation suddenly a distant memory. I notice Ash has arranged his towel over the patch of skin where his scars are.

'How can people be so insensitive? That was awful.'

'Ah, it's okay. I blame the papers, really. They made such a big deal about it at the time.'

'But to be so crass like that—'

'Well, people are, aren't they? Everything's currency these days. Even other people's trauma.'

I admire him for being so polite. Feeling oddly close to tears, I decide to try to change the subject, take our minds off it. 'So,' I say gently, 'you said you had something to tell me?'

He hesitates, glancing back over to the woman. The group of people surrounding her seems to have grown. People are glancing towards us. A man's even shading his eyes against the sun to get a better look.

'Yeah,' he says, 'but I'd prefer to do it without an audience. Shall we get out of here?'

Back at Ash's apartment, the last of the furniture and fittings I helped him order have arrived. So I delay my shower in favour of spending a satisfying hour or so making everything look beautiful, while Ash stays in the kitchen, cooking a pad thai.

'You were so nice to that woman, earlier,' I say, once we're sitting cross-legged on the floor, bowls of noodles in our laps, surrounded by bubble wrap and cardboard and paper guarantees. I'm just about done unboxing and arranging a standard lamp. 'Not sure I'd have been that calm.'

'Wasn't really worth picking a fight over.'

'People are so entitled these days. Do you think this is how celebrities feel?'

'Yeah, except I don't get any of the perks of being a celebrity, do I? I'm just half known for something a bit shit.'

'I'm sorry,' I say.

'It's fine, really. Anyway, you being there made the whole thing infinitely more bearable.'

Setting down my empty bowl, I plug in the lamp. It springs to life. 'Ta-da.'

The rugs, console tables and lamp are the finishing touches: the area has at last been transformed from echoey vault into stylish space. 'You see,' he says, swivelling round to survey the end result. 'I could never have done that.'

I smile. 'You could. You must pick up ideas when you're working on projects?'

'Yeah, but . . . I can never translate them into what would look good *here*. I just don't have the right kind of brain.'

I get what he means. A fair amount of my job involves working with – and sometimes adjusting – architects' plans, but that doesn't mean I could do what they do.

'Well, I love your brain,' I say.

A couple of moments pass. His expression becomes serious. He sets down his bowl, reaches out and takes my hand. 'On that note.'

My heart waits, hard.

He clears his throat. 'What I was trying to tell you earlier was that . . . I've never felt about anyone the way I feel about you, Neve. I've never . . . tracked the days and weeks. I've never wanted to spend every spare minute I have with another person. And I know it's all been a bit of a whirlwind, but . . . I really think this could go somewhere.'

Or maybe it just feels like a whirlwind, because, actually, we were already there. We already knew and loved each other. We just got to skip to the good bit.

He lets out a breath, then looks me right in the eyes. 'What I'm trying to say is that I . . . I'm falling in love with you. I love you, Neve.'

Before he's even finished speaking, I know I feel the same. Albeit in a more complicated way, but that doesn't make it any less true. 'I love you too,' I say, the words coming easily.

He leans forward to kiss me, like he can't hold back for one second longer. His skin still carries the scent of chlorine. I can taste lime on his tongue. He moves a hand to the back of my head, gently grasping my hair, which is still softly tangled from the water earlier. The kiss becomes long and full, and after a minute or so, he runs a hand beneath the blue cotton of my dress. I respond, sliding my fingers inside his T-shirt, over the spot of skin where I know his lightning scars to be. The heat of his touch skims my thighs. As I shut my eyes, he dips his head to kiss my collarbone. 'Jamie,' I murmur.

Everything freezes. Instantly, the room is gripped by a chill.

Ash pulls sharply away. He stares at me as though I've slapped him.

'I'm sorry,' I say, knowing even before I speak that no words can make up for what I just did.

He runs a hand through his hair, fighting to regain his stolen breath. 'Wow,' he says, eventually, not looking at me.

A few moments pass, stiff and tense and devastating. I have no idea what to say or do next. I can't understand what just happened. I wasn't thinking about Jamie, not in that moment. I wasn't imagining it was Jamie touching me, or Jamie I was kissing.

'Ash, I honestly don't know why I said that,' I whisper, my voice shaking.

His dark eyes regard me. 'Well, my guess is that you were thinking about your ex-boyfriend Jamie.'

'I wasn't. I really wasn't.' I put a hand on his arm, but he flinches away. 'I think I just … He's been on my mind lately because you do remind me of him—'

He lifts a hand to his face and rubs vigorously. 'Argh. Why did I just—' And then he breaks off, and I feel my heart curl up into a ball, because the time between Ash telling me he loved me and me calling him Jamie must have been less than thirty seconds.

What the hell is wrong with me?

He jettisons a breath. 'Look … I get … that you loved him, Neve. I do. But if you're saying his name while we're together, I can't … I can't really deal with that. Especially after Tabitha, I—'

'I know,' I say, feeling the shame like a punch. 'I honestly don't know why I said it.'

He looks at me, long and hard. 'Far be it from me to psychoanalyse you, but if you genuinely don't know why you said it, maybe you need to ask someone who does.'

This is what I was scared of. Being seen as crazy. In need of professional help.

'I wasn't lying, Ash,' I whisper. 'I do love you.'

He nods, but slowly, sceptically. 'Or maybe I just remind you of someone you used to love.'

The words crash-land in my chest.

'*No*,' I say. Because even though I can't deny that, I am also sure that if I'd never met Jamie, I would still want all this. I would still have fallen in love with the man in front of me right now. Wouldn't I?

His head is in his hands now. 'This felt real to me, Neve.'

'It was. It is. I—'

'But it turns out I'm just second-best to your ex.'

'*No*,' I insist again.

'Okay. So if Jamie walked back in here right now, what would you do?'

I swallow, hard. My voice can hardly make it up for air. 'That's not fair,' I whisper.

'Maybe not. But the fact the answer doesn't come easily tells me everything I need to know.'

'Ash—'

'We should call it a night,' he says coolly, clearing his throat. 'I need some breathing space.' He gets to his feet, picks the bowls off the floor, then heads over to the sink, likc he doesn't even want to be near me any more.

My whole body becomes a silent scream. *Just tell him – tell him what you believe! It could change everything!* But somehow my brain won't co-operate and free the words from my mouth.

'Okay,' I say eventually. 'I'll call a cab.'

He nods then disappears towards the bedroom. I book a cab, then gather my things and wait mutely on the sofa.

After a while, it becomes clear he won't be coming out to see me off.

Frustration loops through me, a murky cycle of recrimination. We've had the perfect couple of months, but now everything is a mess. And I have no idea how to fix it. If I even can.

29.

Then

'Where would you like to go most in the world?' Jamie asked me one night, after getting off the phone to his dad. It was the January of our second year at uni. Chris had just booked a cruise, fourteen days in the Caribbean with Debra and her mother. He'd invited Jamie too, but Jamie had had to remind him it would be his final year of undergraduate study that winter, that he couldn't possibly take two weeks off to lie on a pool deck and drink piña coladas in thirty-degree heat. It amused me, overhearing him making the trip of a lifetime sound frivolous, like something he couldn't possibly spare the time to indulge. I knew his dad would have hated that.

I lay back against Jamie's chest, enjoying feeling secure in his arms. We were in bed, listening to Ellie Goulding. His hair was damp from the shower, the linger of mint bodywash still on his skin.

I felt so loved, in that moment. Cared for. Safe.

'I don't know,' I said, in answer to his question.

'Well, where's your favourite place you've been?'

'I quite liked Devon.'

He nudged me playfully. 'I meant abroad.'

'I've never been abroad.'

Next to me, I felt him draw away. 'Shut up.'

'You know this. When have I ever been abroad?'

A couple of moments passed. 'Oh,' he said slowly. 'Right. Okay.'

I shrugged. 'Anyway, I don't have a passport.'

'You don't have a passport,' he repeated, like I'd just confessed I couldn't read, or didn't have a legal name.

'Nope,' I said, bristling defensively, trying not to think about what his father would say, if he knew. *You need to be with a girl who's well-travelled, Jamie. How can someone have a broad perspective on life if they've never even left England?*

The more I'd come to know about Jamie's dad, the more I wanted to avoid him. I'd started to have doubts about exactly the type of man he was. Was he, for example, one of those dads who delighted in doing slightly perverse, alarm-bell things like taking his son to strip clubs, or setting him up with the daughters of family friends? I imagined him grilling Jamie about me, probably in one of those pubs with stags' heads all over the walls, demanding to know – again – why he'd insisted on committing so young.

I had no evidence for any of this, of course. But I distrusted him deeply, and found that hard to hide. So whenever Jamie mentioned him, I would change the subject. And every time he went to visit him – which he'd done a few times recently, spending several weekends in Putney in the four months or so since his internship had ended – I'd started to feel not disappointment, but relief, that we'd both begun to assume he would make each trip alone.

'Don't you want to?' Jamie said now.

'Don't I want to what?'

'Go abroad.'

'I can't afford it.'

'Forget the money.'

'Only people with money say, *Forget the money*.'

'I mean, theoretically. If you had the money, would you go?'

On holiday with you? In a heartbeat. 'Obviously.'

He broke into a smile. 'Okay. Get a passport, and we'll catch a plane somewhere for a long weekend.'

'Just like that?'

'Yeah. Just like that.'

I loved how easy he always made life sound. Nothing was ever a barrier, no suggestion too much trouble. Which largely came down to being rich, of course. After all, as Lara would say, optimism was easy when you could pay your way out of pretty much any problem.

From downstairs, the timer started to sound on the oven. The lasagne he'd made us was ready.

He got up, then leaned down to kiss me. 'I'm serious. I love you. Let's go somewhere.'

'You just told your dad you couldn't go on that cruise. He won't be too impressed if you turn around and—'

He paused by the door. 'For the last time. I don't care what my dad thinks.'

But you do. You care a lot.

'You're serious, aren't you?'

'Yeah. I'd love it. Wouldn't you?'

I'd mini-break to a war zone, I thought, *if you were by my side.*

A month or so later, I was working on a uni project, creating sketches for upholstery using Islamic pattern structure. I was fully absorbed, switching smoothly between compass and ruler, virtually meditating. It was probably the project I'd loved the most since starting my course.

Jamie walked into the living room. 'Shut your eyes and hold out your hands.'

This wasn't a good way to distract me from my sketchbook. My dad used to play this game, insisting the surprise would be good, and when I opened my eyes there would be a cold clump of soil in my palms, alive with wriggling worms, or a meaty tangle of last night's spaghetti. I always fell for it, let him persuade me that this time, I could trust him.

That was one thing I didn't miss about my father – the way he sometimes liked to toy with me. Press buttons I didn't know I had.

'This is a very intricate project, actually. I can't shut my eyes.'

'All right. Then just . . . look at me for a minute.' So I did, and Jamie held up a piece of paper. 'I booked it. A long weekend, this September.'

I discarded my sketchbook and got to my feet. 'Are you serious? Where?'

'Amsterdam.' He was beaming. 'We can fly from Norwich. Harry's been, he says it's ace. I know it's a while off, but you get a better hotel if you book ahead.'

I put my arms around him, burying my face in his neck. Visions of canals and gabled buildings, of cobbled streets filled with bikes and flower stalls and pavement cafes were already reeling happily through my mind.

'And . . . I got you this, too.' He removed a book from the deep pocket of his woollen coat and handed it to me. The Lonely Planet guide to Amsterdam. 'Better gen up,' he said, catching my eye in a way that only he could, and I knew he got a kick out of making me feel special.

'I love you.' Every time I said it, it felt more true.

'He's going to propose.'

'What?' I laughed. Lara and I were in Frank's Bar while Jamie played pool with friends. I liked Frank's and its emporium feel, the cosy jumble of tables, the timber-beamed ceilings and offbeat lampshades, the intimate bohemian vibe. It was somewhere I always felt at home.

'I'm telling you,' Lara said, sipping her beer, leaving a thick print of bright pink lipstick on the neck of the bottle. 'Why else would he suggest a holiday?'

'To be romantic?'

'Yeah, and what's more romantic than a proposal? You've been together – what, nearly five years?'

'Nearly,' I said – but did all those years count? I did wonder, sometimes. We'd been kids for three of them. It wasn't like we'd met when we were thirty.

Jamie and I constantly referenced our future, though, saying things like *When we're married*, and *When we have kids*, and *Once we've got our own place*. I guess I kind of took it for granted that we were planning to spend our lives together. But a ring? A proposal? An actual wedding? I hadn't expected any of those things to be imminent, at least not while we were still studying.

Then again, we'd always been the exception to the norm, hadn't we? Most people our age hadn't been in a relationship since they were fifteen. Most of them wouldn't have *wanted* to be. That we might be arriving at convention ten years ahead of time felt ... unconventional, somehow. So in that sense, really, it suited us.

'You should think about what you'd say. If he got down on one knee.'

There wasn't an ounce of hesitation inside me. 'I'd say yes, obviously.'

'Definitely?'

'Definitely.'

'I'd be happy for you.'

A beat passed. 'But ...?' I prompted.

'But ... don't forget what I said, okay?'

'About what?'

'Not making your ... whole life about Jamie.'

I swallowed. 'I haven't forgotten.'

Her blue eyes found mine. 'Marriage isn't everything. It's not ... automatic security.'

'Lara, stop. I know that. Don't you think I know that better than anyone?'

'You still need a career, your own money—'

'I know. This isn't the 1950s. Look at my mum. I *know that.*'

'Good. Just as long as you do.'

I shook my head, changed the subject. 'What about you and Sam?' I sipped my pisco sour, enjoying its slightly savage tang. 'Is it going anywhere, do you think?' They'd been seeing each other on and off since the summer.

'Nah. I'm going to let him down gently.'

'What? Why?'

'He told me last week he's considering retraining to be a lawyer.'

'Oh.'

'He said a career in film and TV is too "unpredictable".' She shook her head. 'Imagine jacking in your job because it's not quite boring enough.'

At that, we both started laughing, and ordered in another round of drinks.

Lara and I went on holiday together once, when we were fourteen. Her aunt had gifted Corinne and Billy a week in a caravan in Devon, only the third chance they'd had to get away since Lara was born.

Jamie had already been on more holidays than I could count, to places like Florida, Switzerland, California. Chris had even bought a villa in Tuscany. There had recently been talk about sending Jamie to private school, too, but straight away Jamie had said he would refuse to go.

I was probably already in love with him by then, though we hadn't yet kissed.

The sun blazed beautifully, untroubled by clouds, for the whole seven days we were in Devon. Being teenagers,

Lara and I were in the mood for spending time together, alone, sunbathing and gossiping and not having our style cramped. Her rebellious phase was just kicking in, so we'd sneak cigarettes from Corinne's handbag and little nips of wine from the bottle in the fridge.

One evening, Corinne sat down next to me outside the caravan while Lara was having a shower. It had been blisteringly hot for the past few days, and my pale skin was poached pink with sunburn. Corinne and Lara, on the other hand, had developed deep, beautiful tans.

Our caravan was next to a dense run of gorse bushes, and I'd been enjoying the coconutty scent of the yolk-yellow blossom, the freeing feeling of being out from under my mother's feet. I was slightly dazzled by the peace and quiet, too. Life rarely felt calm back home, what with all Mum's singing and crying and chucking stuff at hard surfaces. Here, there was only birdsong and the occasional crunch of car tyres against gravel, people chatting and laughing behind windbreaks.

Corinne sparked up a cigarette, passed it to me, and said, 'You're a good friend to Lar.'

'She's a good friend to me,' I said, meekly taking the cigarette from Corinne like I hadn't been nicking them from her bag all week.

She lit one for herself. I noticed her hair was greying around the sides and on the crown. Lara had told me she was in her late fifties – as old as my actual grandmother. Maybe that was why she was so kind. Because grandmothers were, weren't they?

'How are things with your mum?' Corinne asked me.

'Fine, thanks,' I lied. It had been two years since Dad had left Mum for Bev. Mum was still prone to bursting into tears out of nowhere and prank-calling Bev after she'd had a few drinks. Last month, she'd turned up at parents' evening with a hip flask.

Our mothers had only crossed paths a handful of times, since Mum was mortally averse to anything school-related like picnics or playdates or birthday parties. Maybe there was a mutual acknowledgement that they would have nothing in common. Or perhaps it was partly down to their age gap. Mum once said to me, 'First baby after *forty*. You tell me what went wrong there.'

I remember thinking that *wrong* was an odd choice of word.

'You know you can come to me about anything?' Corinne said then. Her blue eyes were resting on me, crinkled at the corners. I wanted to squirm away and throw my arms around her all at once.

Maybe word had got round about the hip flask. 'Okay,' I said, stiffly.

'You know, no parent is perfect, Neve.'

But I had never wanted a perfect parent. Just one who at least gave the impression she could be arsed, like Corinne.

I didn't know Jamie's mum very well at that point, but she too seemed loving and attentive and kind. There were always chocolate biscuits in her cupboard and cans of proper Coke in the fridge, and to my knowledge she'd never screamed at Jamie to do his own laundry, or been arrested, or propositioned his maths teacher.

'Thank you,' I told Corinne.

'For what, sweetheart?'

'Being there,' was all I could think of to say, because it was true.

'You're lucky,' I said to Lara later. 'To have Corinne.'

We called her that sometimes, because Corinne had once told Lara she could if she wanted, even though Lara had scoffed at first. *Like she's a social worker.*

'Even though she's ancient?'

I smiled. 'Yeah.'

'You know she makes sounds when she gets up now? Like, *Oof*. And her knees creak.'

I laughed softly. 'Don't be mean.'

'And she's all wrinkly, and so is Dad.'

'Stop it.'

Lara lay back and sighed. 'I am never getting old.'

'I don't actually think that's your decision.'

'Yeah, it is. First sign of a wrinkle, Botox me up. And we should probably stop smoking.'

I quite liked the idea of eternal youth. Life just seemed to get more complicated the older you got.

I held out my pinky. 'We should make a pact, then. We're never getting old. Swear?'

She took it and grinned. 'Swear.'

It kind of became our refrain, after that. For years afterwards, right up until the day we stopped speaking altogether, we would periodically agree: we were *never* getting old.

30.

Now

Over the next week or so, Ash fails to respond to my messages, or answer my calls. He hasn't gone as far as to block me, but every time I ring him, I imagine he's probably getting close. My brain bumper-cars between emotions – guilt, frustration, desperation. I drift off frequently at work, raking over what happened, wondering if we can come back from it, whether he'll end it for good. If he hasn't already. I fail to sleep, busying myself with chores into the early hours, because I know if I get into bed, all I'll think about is the fact that he's not in it with me.

I consider calling Lara for advice. But something stops me. The thought, perhaps, that I rejected her for nearly a decade, and wasn't even there when her dad died. My feelings for her still lie somewhere in the baffling no-man's land between guilt and resentment.

Eventually, Ash responds, telling me work's been crazy and he just needs some time. Not long after that – a full fortnight on from when I last saw him – he arrives at the office for a meeting with Parveen. I know they've been due to review and check the lighting and electrical layouts for Millbrook, and I've been restless and fidgety for most of the day, waiting for the clock to hit three p.m.

Parveen knows something's happened, but I've told her it's complicated, that I'm not ready to talk about it – though I have made it clear the fault lies with me. So, other than bringing me endless cups of tea and telling me she's here if I want to chat, she hasn't pressed me on it. I'd love to confide in her – but I really respect Parveen, and have no immediate desire to confess something that might make her feel the opposite way about me.

When I finally see him, it feels as though someone's hot-wired all my limbs. Forty agonising minutes later, I try to catch his eye as he walks out, but he keeps his gaze trained firmly towards the door, and because I'm on the phone to a client, I can't run after him. As I watch him go, I hear my voice waver. Fortunately, my client only takes this to mean I'm getting highly emotional about her Venetian plaster walls.

Seeing him has confirmed what I already knew, deep down – that I'm not ready for this to end. I want to save this. I want to save *us*. Even though the situation seems so complicated. In the compass of my heart, I know he is true north.

I message him again.

I don't want this to end

I love you

Please let me make this right

The Spark

I am fully prepared for the double-tick of doom, made all the more torturous by a lack of response. But to my surprise, this time, the typing dots spring to life.

> Don't want it to either

My heart soars.

> Just needed some time
> Sorry. Wasn't trying to make you feel worse.
> Can I see you?

We meet after work in an underground bar. Outside, it's a sultry evening, the air bloated with heat. Inside, it is packed. We order cocktails, find space to squeeze onto two stools in a shadowy corner. I wish more than anything I could turn back time to when we were last in here and Ash had his hand on my leg, his lips to my ear.

'Talk to me,' I whisper, as we sit, borrowing Lara's favourite phrase. Even though I am nervous, the relief I feel to be finally given a chance to explain myself is immense.

But his usually warm eyes look cool and grave. His face is wearied in a way that suggests a run of sleepless nights, though whether that's down to me or work pressures, I have no idea.

'I feel like an idiot, Neve.'

'It's me who should be feeling that way, not you.'

'Can I ask you something?'

'Of course,' I say.

'Were you . . . thinking about him, when you were with me?'

I know he means in bed. Thankfully, this is easy to answer. 'God, *no.*'

I can't deny there were fleeting points when Jamie drifted into my mind in those moments. But they were only ever transient. Scraps of unbidden memory, half-seconds at most, by no means some kind of enduring fantasy.

Ash frowns, looking past me towards the cluster of people at the bar. But I can see only him: the brush of his collar against his neck, the splay of his legs on the bar stool, the turn of his wrist as he lifts his glass.

'It's been hard for me,' he says. 'To trust again. Since Tabitha.'

I wonder if perhaps Tabitha called Ash by the wrong name once, too. If that was his first clue to her affair. He says he stumbled across a thread of messages buried deep in her WhatsApp, but maybe she made the same mistake I did, and he felt too crushed to tell me.

The thought that I'm effectively putting him through that again makes me feel sick.

'I promise,' I say, 'nothing like that will ever happen again.'

'I mean, it can't,' he says, meeting my eye. 'I'm sure you can understand that.'

'Of course I do,' I assure him, softly.

Ash sips his cocktail. It is something dark, rich with walnuts and rum. 'I mean, ultimately, I want to be with you, Neve.'

Without warning, a few tears spill down my cheeks.

'Hey,' he says, softening, leaning forward to wipe my face with his thumb, the tenderness with which he does so making my stomach swim. 'Don't get upset. I'm sorry. I wasn't trying to be an arsehole. I don't want to make you feel bad.'

I shake my head, because what I'm actually feeling is a mess of remorse and relief.

'The stupid thing is, I get it, Neve. Weirdly enough, I do understand. And I want to move past this.' He leans into me then, puts a hand to my face and kisses me, tentatively. 'If that's what you want. Which is why I need to ask you—' He breaks off, punches out a breath, looks down at where our legs are now nudged tightly together.

I stare at him, unable to imagine what he might be about to say.

'Before all this happened, I booked . . . a trip for us. It was going to be a surprise.'

'A trip?' I say softly.

'Yeah. I asked Parveen to help arrange it all with Kelley. A long weekend in September. I thought . . . we could go to Amsterdam. I mean, you have the guidebook at home but you've never been, and you haven't had a holiday in way too long either, so I thought . . . Well, I wanted to surprise you.'

A surge of conflicting emotions. *Amsterdam. Amsterdam.* 'That's . . . that's . . .'

He stares down at his half-finished cocktail, lets out an uneasy laugh. 'Anyway. Parveen asked me today if we were still planning on going, and . . . I knew straight away that I wanted to. That I do want to. That . . . actually I'd love to just get past what's happened and put it behind us.'

Despite everything that Amsterdam means to me, my heart goes into orbit. 'I'd love to,' I say, kissing him back. 'I'd love to go away with you.'

Our houses are pretty much equidistant from the bar, but without discussion, we find ourselves walking back to mine. Above our heads, the sky rumbles, and I realise a storm is coming.

I try not to think about rain. The way it always feels like it's hammering on my heart.

Back at the house, we head wordlessly upstairs, turning to each other in the dark heat of the bedroom. Next to the fireplace, he drops to his knees, pushing my dress up and my underwear down, gripping me from behind. Beyond the window, the storm finally breaks, the rain hitting the glass as hard as hail. I try to let what we're doing drown out the sound of it. I reach out for something to hold on to, swiping through empty air until my fingers find the top of the fire surround. I cling to cold metal as he draws me to a precipice, again and again. My eyes roll back. My limbs go weak. My blood becomes a rush of repeating pleasure. But the whole time, I am biting my lip, so I don't say something I can't take back.

31.

Over the next few weeks, I resolve to put Jamie firmly out of my mind. But whenever I catch sight of the Amsterdam guidebook on my shelf at home, it seems to wink at me, like an old message on an answerphone, drawing me back to the moment he gave it to me. It's starting to unsettle me, that memory. As is the prospect of Amsterdam at all. Just the fact Ash picked it too.

Eventually, I banish the book into the bottom drawer of my sideboard, where I've also stashed the framed photographs of Jamie.

One rainy morning at the start of September, I dive into the loos at work to call Lara.

'Hi?' she says, sounding slightly surprised.

'Hi. Can you talk?'

'Yeah, just on our way to . . . Never mind. What's up?'

'I don't think Amsterdam is a good idea.'

I told her, eventually, about calling Ash by the wrong name. She seemed sympathetic, and also relieved we'd made it up, because at her core, Lara is a die-hard romantic. Not everyone knows that about her, but I do. I've always known.

'Oh, why?' she says now.

'It just feels wrong.'

'Okay,' Lara says. 'Then here's what I think you should do. Go to Amsterdam, and just . . . forget about the Jamie stuff for a bit, so you can go and enjoy this trip. But when you get back, you do need to talk to him.'

'That doesn't feel like the right thing to do, though. It doesn't feel honest.'

'Isn't this more about confusion now than it is dishonesty?'

I pinch the bridge of my nose between my fingers, draw a couple of breaths. *Get it together, Neve, for God's sake.*

I hear the main toilet door swing open, then Parveen's voice, tentative. 'Neve?'

'Yes?' I say, quickly. 'Yes, I'm here.'

She hesitates briefly. 'Hate to do this, but Mrs Ogilvy's on the phone, and she's refusing to hang up until she's spoken to you. Apparently, I won't do. She says it's an emergency.'

'Oof. She sounds needy,' Lara says, in my ear.

'You have no idea,' I say darkly. Mrs Ogilvy's last 'emergency' was an eleventh-hour panic that the kitchen floor tiles we'd agonised over might clash with the colour of her chihuahua (no joke).

'Tell her I'm coming,' I say to Parveen, and then, to Lara, 'Thank you. Sorry. Better go.'

'Yeah, go. And by that, I mean to Amsterdam. All the other stuff can wait.'

★   ★   ★

A week later, Ash and I check in to our hotel on the south side of the Vondelpark. I haven't a clue if it's the same place Jamie chose. I've long forgotten the name of it, and have no way of finding out.

But I know I shouldn't care. That I have to try to just enjoy being here, in the moment. I mean, I know I owe Ash more than that – a lot more – but it's a start, at least. He went to the trouble of organising a secret long weekend via Kelley of all people, who was taking conference calls on her honeymoon and thinks bank holidays should be banned.

So I ignore the occasional spikes of voltage that I know to be my conscience, burying them beneath all the better, more pleasurable feelings.

I don't doubt that what I feel for Ash is love – I recognise all too well the crushing, stomach-skewering power of it. But whether I am in love with Jamie, or Ash, or a strange entanglement of the two, is becoming harder for me to say.

On our first afternoon, we spend several dreamy hours walking through cobbled streets and beside canals burnished with sunlight, among the jangling rush of bicycles, beneath the dolls' house façades of the buildings, between passing trams and centuries-old bridges. There is a fairy-tale quality to it all, and I get so caught up that I lose count of how many times Ash has to pull me out of the path of a bike. We talk and talk, about work and our friends and family, about books we're reading, and politics, and Ash's nightmare landlord at uni, and the most embarrassing stuff we've ever done, and the curse of group chats, and our best ever finds on the Lidl middle aisle. He makes me laugh to the point where I have to plead for breath: I particularly enjoy his killer impression of the woman from the next apartment but one, who's had so much facial filler she can no longer enunciate.

We neglect to eat, forget time and directions. The city tingles with late-summer heat and high spirits. The pavement cafes are jammed full, the streets flocking with people. As dusk descends, above the jumble of rooftops, a pale rhubarb moon climbs through the sky. Eventually, in the darkened corner of a waterside bar, the heat between us ramps up, and then it is a race to find a taxi, our hotel, our room, our bed.

He tells me he loves me as he moves against me, my legs wrapped tight around him. And as I say it back, through a dark square of window, I see the night sky blaze with a million stars.

After bagels and coffee the next morning, we set off together along the canal. Which is when something peculiar happens. I find myself telling Ash all about the leaning houses, the hoisting hooks and hidden gardens, the family crests on houses flaunting the wealth of seventeenth-century merchants. I describe the design style of the Middles Ages, the Dutch Renaissance, the introduction of French interior design in the eighteenth century. We walk the patchwork of lanes, beneath lines of fleshy trees, to the Amsterdam School and the Rijksmuseum, the Centraal

Station, and I talk him through the engineering of the city's bridges. I do the same at the Nieuwe Kerk, the Gothic Oude Kerk. I'm unable to stop, the words spilling from my mouth like confessions.

I'm no architecture expert. But over the course of seven months, ten years ago, I think I read more about Amsterdam than a single one of my degree course topics. I was so engrossed and excited by the idea of my first holiday with Jamie, that somehow, the information all stuck, the way obsessions often do.

Eventually, opposite the Stedelijk Museum, we stop for coffee. Our window seats have an elevated view of the street crosshatched with tramlines, the turrets of the Rijksmuseum.

'So, if you don't mind me asking,' Ash says, running a hand over his jaw as he looks at me, 'what the hell was that?'

His dark T-shirt matches exactly the deep pigment of his eyes. 'What?'

'I'd have *paid* to do the tour you just took me on. How do you know so much about architecture in Amsterdam?'

'I'm just . . . a bit of a sponge when it comes to stuff like that.'

A pause. 'You can tell me, you know. If you've been to Amsterdam before. Did you come here with Jamie?'

I gaze down at the street, at the commotion of taxis and trams and people. 'No, never.' This much, at least, is true.

His expression relaxes slightly. 'Well, anyway. It's nice that I don't have to hide this part of my personality with you.'

'Which part?'

'The part that gets turned on by a really good building.'

I laugh.

'I nearly cancelled this trip, you know. After . . . what happened. I'm so glad I didn't.'

I swallow down the mess of feelings in my throat. It takes a little effort. 'Me too.'

32.

On our last night, we go for dinner at a restaurant recommended to Ash by Gabi. It's pretty tiny – there are just two lines of tables inside – but it is romantic, and rustic, and feels comfortingly and distinctly European. The walls are papered with vintage French posters. There are bottles of wine everywhere, and warm flickering candles, and plenty of dark corners for getting cosy in.

I'm surprised to learn it was Gabi's idea to come here, given how infrequently Ash says they speak now.

'She called me not so long ago,' he says, dipping a chunk of celery into the vat of fondue between us. 'She still does occasionally, if she's having a crisis.'

'What was the crisis?'

'Toby.'

'The Coachella guy?'

He nods. 'She thinks they should live together. Terrible idea, obviously. I probably wasn't as tactful as I could have been.'

'Why is it a terrible idea?'

I can tell Ash still cares by how quickly his forehead furrows. 'It just seems like every conversation they have is a row. And they don't have much in common. He hasn't got a job. Not sure if he ever has, actually.' He pauses, then picks up his wine. 'I mean, if you move in with someone, the starting point should at least be that you get on, don't you think?'

'Of course.'

'Like, you should have fun all the time and a mad attraction and have similar life goals . . . right?'

'Definitely. I mean, maybe you should say that to her.'

'Yeah, maybe,' he says, thoughtfully. 'I thought I'd try . . . saying it to you first, though.'

I look up from my plate and frown, confused.

He takes in my expression and laughs. 'Okay. I'm trying to ask if . . . you'd like to live with me, but clearly I'm completely cocking it up.'

'Oh,' I say, feeling a rush of pleasure and surprise.

Across the table, he grabs my hand. 'I know it's only been a few months, but . . . this doesn't scare me, Neve. It feels right.'

A beat. Despite everything, I can't disagree. Maybe moving in with Ash – properly committing – will be a way to finally banish Jamie from my mind, to break free from the past, to get back to who I was before all this happened.

'Yes. Okay. Yes.'

His eyes gleam. 'Seriously? You want to do it?'

I smile. 'Well, I do need to check one thing with you first.'

'Go on.'

'What would you consider to be your most horrifying domestic habits?'

He takes a second to mull it over. 'Okay, I only have one.'

I sip my wine. 'Let me be the judge of that.'

'Well, I'm a rubbish-squasher. I leave the bin till the lid's popping off before I can be arsed to go down and take it out.'

'Hmm. You do live in a top-floor apartment. So that's not too bad, considering.'

'You're excusing my bin crimes?'

'There are mitigating factors.'

'All right. You? I bet you don't even have one bad habit.'

'Oh, I do. I stress-clean.'

'Nothing wrong with that.'

'Ordinarily, no. But some of it's a bit . . . next-level.'

He smiles at me over his wine glass. 'Examples, please.'

'Well, the worst one is probably that I . . . steam my bedsheets. Once they're on the bed. Like, every single crease.'

'That sounds . . . labour-intensive.'

'It's a sickness,' I admit.

'Still. Hardly what I'd call horrific.'

'But what if you're waiting to go to bed and I'm steaming?'

'Then . . . I'll just have to present you with a more appealing alternative.'

I smile. Beneath the table, he grazes my calf with his foot. Above it, he squeezes my hand. He can't stop touching me, and I feel the same way.

'So,' he says. 'Bin-squashing and sheet-steaming aside, reckon we'd be good housemates?'

'Yes. I do, actually.'

He leans across the table and kisses me, almost dislodging the pot of fondue in the process. Someone claps. My heart does cartwheels.

33.

Then

It was May. Jamie was spending long hours at uni, refining his proposal for his final-year research project.

Norwich was blooming, the trees fat with leaves and frizzing with blossom. We had house sparrows nesting in the eaves that year. Starlings were frequent visitors to our tiny knotted jumble of back garden. The evenings had got lighter, the jasmine-scented hours long and golden, the nights swimming-pool warm.

One lunchtime, Lara came home and found me curled up on the sofa. I should have been at uni, putting the finishing touches to my second-year written project on textile waste. But instead, I was watching *Gavin & Stacey* in my pyjamas beneath a blanket, despite the warmth of the day outside.

'Oof,' Lara said, when she saw me there, not moving. 'I told you never to mix ouzo with . . . well, you.'

She sat down next to me. There was a faint sheen of sweat on her skin from her walk home. Her summer freckles were kicking in.

On screen, Nessa was berating Smithy. Lara exhaled happily. 'My queen.'

I smiled weakly. 'Yeah. Pam's still the best, though.'

I'd always wished I had a mum like Pam.

We watched together for ten minutes or so before I said, 'It's not ouzo, by the way.'

My voice sounded offbeat, even to me. Lara picked up the remote and muted the TV.

A few seconds passed. She took me in. 'Talk to me,' she said, eventually.

'I'm late.'

'How late?'

'Three weeks.'

'What?'

I knew I didn't need to repeat myself.

'How the hell did you not notice?'

'I don't know. I've just . . . been thinking about other stuff, I guess.'

'Wow. Okay. What stuff? Well, let's get a test.'

'Three weeks is a really long time, isn't it?'

She met my eye. 'Have you told Jamie?'

It will be all right, I thought. *Lara is here.*

'Not yet.'

'Good. Come on. Let's go.'

'I don't think I'm ready.'

'Screw ready,' she said. 'It's been three weeks. We're going.'

We got the test from the supermarket on Earlham Road. That day was the only time I'd ever left the house in my pyjamas, except for maybe when I took the bins out, which didn't count. I thought about what Jamie's mum would say if she could see me, and felt a flash of petty, teenage-like triumph.

I suggested getting more than one test, just to be sure, but Lara said taking lots of tests was just something they put in films and TV shows to keep us all captive to capitalism. 'As if they're not enough of a rip-off already,' she muttered loudly, right in front of the checkout guy.

At this, a woman behind us in the queue laughed. 'A high like that usually costs way more than six quid. Believe me. Best money I ever spent.'

'Do you think she was positive or negative?' I asked Lara, as we left the shop.

'Not sure,' Lara mused, frowning. 'But someone should probably tell her she's taking the wrong drugs.'

Back at the house, I peed on the test, then we sat on the sofa together and waited.

'What do you think Jamie will say, if you are?' Lara asked. She was holding my hand for support in a way my mother had never quite got the hang of.

I'd been thinking about my mum all morning. About whether she'd wanted me. About whether a pregnancy test had been her *Sliding Doors* moment. I'd never asked her outright, because I wasn't sure I actually wanted to see the tell in her face that gave it away: the confirmation I hadn't been wanted. Not wholeheartedly, anyway. That I'd started life as a weighing-up, a list of pros and cons that, knowing my mother, was probably still crumpled up in a drawer somewhere. I was surprised she hadn't whipped it out for fun on my eighteenth birthday.

I released a breath. For some reason, I was having trouble picturing Jamie's reaction to my being pregnant. 'I have no idea,' I said, in reply to Lara's question.

She nodded at the test, face down on the coffee table. 'That's it. Three minutes.'

But I didn't even need to look. I knew what it would say. The bell in my body had already chimed.

I turned the stick over, swore, then surprised myself by laughing.

Lara swore too, her fingers squeezing mine.

I realised later that my laughter must have been instinctive. My body's subconscious expression of a joy I hadn't been fully certain I would feel.

Jamie and I had made a whole other life. There was a baby inside me that was half him, half me. We were going to be *parents*.

If I hadn't dared to admit how I felt until that point, I knew it then. I was exultant. I thought back to what the woman in the shop had said, and realised she must have wanted what I had now.

'Are you happy?' Lara ventured.

'Yes.' I started to cry.

She wrapped her arms around me. 'I'll be here for you. Whatever happens. You and me – we can get through anything.'

You mean, if he doesn't want this.

'You don't have to tell him straight away,' she said. 'If you need a bit more time to think about it.'

I pictured Jamie, head bent over his work at uni, oblivious, and felt a tug of love as I thought about the things he always said, like, *When we're parents*, or *When we have kids of our own.* And yes, maybe this was all happening a bit earlier than we'd anticipated. But I was starting to feel more sure that he would want this. Or, to be more accurate – that he loved me enough to want it.

'I know it seems mad, Lar, because we're students, and we don't have proper jobs yet, or anywhere permanent to live. But we're in love. We can do this.'

Jamie was going to see his parents that weekend. Even Harry was apparently going to put in an appearance, home on a rare sojourn from Zurich. I couldn't quite imagine Jamie telling Chris and Debra they were going to be grandparents. I was pretty sure they would hit the roof. Should I go too, so we could make the announcement together?

Lara disappeared into the kitchen to concoct a sugar-hit we usually reserved for hangovers, bad grades, time of the month. Microwaved chocolate puddings, half a Mars bar melted over the top of each one.

After a couple of minutes, she returned and passed me a bowl. I was still experiencing a slightly unsettling, uncontrollable urge to laugh.

'What will you do, though?' she said, sticking a spoon into her pudding. 'About a career, and stuff? It'll be harder, if you have a baby.'

I thought straight away of the brilliant time I'd had at Kelley Lane Interiors last summer. Lara had been right, before – I'd felt more fulfilled during my internship there than I had in a long time. Possibly ever.

But a baby didn't mean I couldn't have a career. It just meant it might be slightly more complicated.

'We can make it work. We'll find a way.'

'Do you think,' she said gently, 'that you want this because of everything that happened with your parents?'

This wasn't the first time she'd said this to me. I knew she thought I was looking to Jamie for the stability and loving family unit I'd never experienced at home.

But even if I was, so what? I felt almost blissful in that moment, high on some sort of hormone, one that made me believe my baby and I – or the clump of cells inside me, at least – were already protected by a kind of shield, a bubble, something that would keep all negativity at bay. 'Does it matter?'

She shrugged. But then she seemed to be readying herself to say something else.

'Go on,' I said.

'I saw Jamie . . . punching a wall earlier.'

I blinked. 'What do you mean?'

'Just that. I saw him . . . punching a wall. Or, not punching. Sort of pounding, with his hand. I don't think he broke anything. But he looked . . . pretty angry.'

A beat. 'My Jamie?'

'Yeah. In the corridor, in the main building. He was on the phone to someone called Heather. He kept saying her name, over and over. Well, sort of shouting.'

I felt my joy turn cold. The bubble burst.

Heather. The girl who had called him at the start of term. Who he said was his mentor.

'Who is she?' Lara said.

'I don't know. I mean, I do. Sort of. I've not met her. He worked with her.'

'In London? Last summer?'

I nodded.

There was a long silence, during which I could feel Lara's eyes tracking my face. 'Neve. Do you think—'

'Never. He wouldn't.'

'Okay.'

'What does that mean?'

'It means, okay.' She held up her hands. 'For what it's worth, I actually don't think he would either.'

Though I was clearly in the dark about something, I felt a flicker of reassurance to know that Lara didn't think I was being naive.

'I wouldn't have said anything if I thought . . . I assumed you'd know what the argument was about.'

I just shrugged then, because it was clear to us both that I didn't.

'You've got to talk to him about the baby.'

'I know.'

'Don't be scared.'

'I'm not.'

But of course, I was. It was impossible to know which pin to pull first: an argument with another girl, so impassioned it had had Jamie thumping the nearest wall? Or the fact I was carrying our baby?

In the end, Jamie made the decision for me. We walked into the city that night, to catch a film he'd been wanting to see, and he flinched slightly when I grabbed his hand. I wondered if it was the result of his fist having met brickwork earlier that day.

The evening sky was making its lazy, lilac shift into night-time. A rich weight of blossom, mown grass and gathering dew clung to the air. I thought of the budding new life in my womb, how apt that it was springtime. The timing already felt poetic.

'Lara heard you arguing earlier, on your phone,' I said, as we walked. I kept my voice light, free of accusation. 'With Heather.'

I'd thought maybe he'd freeze or clam up, start stammering. But instead, he said, 'Oh God. Did she hear that?' He seemed embarrassed, but not afraid. Not like someone hiding a secret.

'I think half the building heard it.'

He shook his head, as if in frustration. 'Heather . . . called, out of the blue. She said she'd sent my CV up to HR at A&L. They've offered me another internship, starting next month.'

I fought the urge to set my hand on my stomach. I'd suspected for a while that he would go back to London for the summer. I knew his dad would have tried to persuade him. But Jamie had been stalling, saying he hadn't decided yet. Which was very unlike him. Dithering wasn't in his DNA.

'Yeah,' Jamie continued. 'Apparently, Heather's boss had lunch with my dad and they sort of agreed I was coming back before they'd even spoken to me. I guess I just felt a bit . . . annoyed, you know. Like everyone was planning my summer for me.'

At that, I felt slightly conflicted. I didn't want Jamie to go, obviously. But I still thought he should be thankful that another well-paid internship had apparently been conjured out of some upper-crust top hat by his dad.

'Anyway, Heather started making out like I was being ungrateful, and I just . . . Well, it wasn't exactly an argument. I just raised my voice a bit when I shouldn't have, probably, because she kept talking over me.'

Already, I could see that Jamie's version of the conversation differed massively from Lara's. But I was inclined to believe him. Lara must have exaggerated. She was prone to doing that from time to time. I'd never seen Jamie thump a wall, or a table, or anything. He just wasn't that type of guy.

I knew then that unless I told him my secret – *our* secret – I'd soon be kissing goodbye to him for another whole summer, while our baby grew inside me.

At the cinema, I drank a large lemonade, and we shared popcorn in lieu of a proper meal. My eating habits – not to mention just about everything else in my life – were going to have to change.

But, for some reason, even later that night, and for several nights afterwards, I simply couldn't find the words to tell him.

34.

Now

After Amsterdam, Ash and I go back and forth a bit over where we should live. Eventually, we decide that him moving into mine makes the most practical sense. We're not ready to buy somewhere together, and there's a part of me that would find it almost impossible to leave my house. It's my sanctuary if I'm struggling, the place I escape to when I need to make sense of the world. My heart lies within its walls. Every day, I lavish love upon it. Only yesterday, I spent hours painstakingly oiling the kitchen worktops, and scrubbing the first copper tinges of autumn out of the back patio.

By contrast, Ash – though he loves his place – is able to contemplate moving on one day. Finding his forever home. 'A wreck that needs doing up,' he tells me one night, over spaghetti. 'That would be the dream.'

'I reckon you might be quite good at that,' I say, privately thinking that I would, too.

He smiles, twirling pasta around his fork. 'It's getting hold of one that's the tricky bit.'

'You must have loads of contacts.'

'Yeah. But you can't get mates' rates on old houses any more.'

I think about my mother's house, the crimes against period charm she commits every day.

'You're crazy,' Parveen says, when I tell her Ash is moving in.

'You think it's too soon?'

There is a part of me that does feel this is quick. That it's exactly the sort of thing my mother would do – move in with someone because it feels romantic, not because it's the sensible choice.

Parveen laughs, and says, 'No, I mean you should buy a place together.'

'It's way too soon for that. And I'm too attached to mine, anyway.'

'Do you know how long me and Maz were dating, before we decided to buy our place? Six weeks.'

'You were not.'

'We were. We just knew.' She pauses, sips her coffee. 'Plus, you know – I was pregnant.'

I manage a smile, even though after all these years, the word still has a habit of hitting me square in the stomach. 'Well, exactly. We don't have quite the same imperative as you did.'

She turns back to the 3D rendering she's looking at. 'I just think, when you know, you know. People get sneery about whirlwind romances, but only because they're jealous.'

I think of my mother. To her, love isn't love unless it feels storm-gauge. 'Or sensible.'

'God, wouldn't life be so boring if we were all sensible, though?' She shudders. 'I'd choose the whirlwind any day.'

She reminds me so much of Lara, when she says things like that.

Lara and I go for lunch at the waffle place on St Giles Street. I'm wolfing mine down because I'm on a tight deadline at work and don't really have the time for long lunches. But I wanted to see her.

'Aren't you hungry?' I ask her eventually, gently, because for the past ten minutes she's mostly been pushing the food around her plate.

'How are things with Ash?'

I can't hold back any longer. 'Is it this diet you're on? Was it your idea?'

'What? I'm not on a diet. What?'

I set down my fork and attempt to make eye contact. She avoids it. 'Lara. That detox—'

'I miss work,' she says, the words falling from her mouth in a rush. 'I miss London, and work, and my flat, and my dad, and my old life, and knowing—' She breaks off, then shakes her head.

I lean forward, feeling stupid for thinking her lack of appetite was just about food. 'Knowing what?'

She just shakes her head again.

'Lar. Is it Felix?'

Seeming to recover slightly, she takes a sip of water. 'Is what Felix?'

'Is Felix why you're feeling so—'

'Felix is the love of my life.' She looks me right in the eyes as she says this.

'I know. But sometimes . . . that makes things harder, not easier.'

She considers this for a moment or two, then shakes her head for a third time. 'Come on. Talk to me. How are things with Ash?'

I haven't told her that Ash is talking to an estate agent today, enquiring about letting out the Old Yarn Mill, and calling the mortgage company to see if he can switch his loan. He's doing all this . . . yet I still haven't confessed my theory about what really happened on the night of his accident. I've been kicking it down the road for weeks, not wanting to derail us getting back together, or Amsterdam, or moving in. Every day it seems, there's another reason to hold off.

But there's no good reason not to fill Lara in.

I open my mouth to tell her everything; but I can sense from her demeanour that she has too much on her mind to hear it all right now. Though whether that's because of Felix, or her mum, I'm not too sure.

So instead, I just tell her about our most recent nights out and what we're watching on Netflix and his friends teaching me darts, for which – it turns out – I have an unexpected gift.

'I know,' I say, as Lara laughs. 'Why couldn't I be secretly talented at something really cool, like snowboarding, or poker, or being fluent in seven languages, or something? The land-lady kept trying to get me to join their ladies' league. She's got my number. She WhatsApped me all the details.'

Lara shakes her head, trying to regain her composure. 'Well, what's wrong with that?'

'My *mum's* a member. And . . . last Christmas, they did a darts league calendar.'

Her mouth drops open a little. 'Oh my God.'

'Lots of strategically-placed dartboards,' I say, my insides shrivelling at the memory.

'I *have* to see this. Does she still have it?'

'Obviously. Pride of place in the downstairs loo.'

'Which month was she?'

'February, May *and* August. Of course. Couldn't get enough.'

We carry on laughing, which means I can leave all the more complicated stuff – the emotional heft of loving a man who only knows half the story – for another time.

Ash and I are in bed, delaying getting up because for the first time in months, the air is shot through with an autumnal chill. We've been laughing because we got in late last night, drunk on espresso martinis, and Ash made us cheese toasties, which we ate in bed. Only now that we're sober have we realised the mattress is sprinkled with crumbs. Ash shook his head and said we were animals, but I didn't care. It was the best cheese toastie I'd ever eaten, because he made it for me in a sweet late-night effort to mitigate my hangover.

Once we've stopped laughing, he turns towards me on the pillow and says, 'Hey, I want to ask you something.'

'Okay,' I say, my heart thumping a little harder, as it always does when he looks at me this way.

'Will you come to my parents' house with me, for dinner? Saturday after next?'

I smile cautiously. 'What's the occasion?'

'The occasion of me wanting you to meet them.' He shuffles a little closer, then rolls onto his front, propping himself up on his elbows. I feel his breath skim my skin. 'Well, that, and it being my mum's birthday. Gabi's going to be there too.'

I have often tried to imagine how life has felt for Ash's family since his accident; the peculiar agony of losing someone still living and never quite getting them back. What would they say, if I told them what I believe? Maybe they'd be relieved. Perhaps they'd finally feel as though – for the first time in nearly a decade – everything at last made some kind of sense.

But disclosure isn't an option. I haven't even talked to Ash yet.

He'd been going to introduce me to his family at a barbecue back in August. But before it could happen, I called him Jamie by mistake. This morning is the first time he's mentioned me meeting them again since.

'What have you told them about me?' I ask him.

He sneaks me a look. 'I don't want to say.'

'Well, you have to.'

'Why?'

'So I can prepare. Or, you know. Cancel.'

'Well,' he says, 'I've told them I love you, and that I want to make a life with you.'

'To which they said?' I whisper.

He bends down to kiss me. 'Actually . . . they said they'd never seen me look so happy.'

Even as I melt into the kiss, I know a confession is long overdue. Because if I believe he is not entirely who he appears to be, then I cannot be who he thinks I am, either. We are both living a lie – but only one of us knows it.

He pulls gently back, his pitch-blue eyes seeming to search mine. Does he sense, somehow, that I am fermenting with secrets, with half-finished sentences and hidden sentiments?

I open my mouth to speak, but at the last moment, change my mind.

The timing's all wrong. I'll talk to him once I've met his family. It's just a couple more weeks. Maybe meeting them will help me to zoom out of the situation, to view its whole context, make sure I've missed nothing. And then I'll tell him what I believe, the thing that is feeling increasingly like tentacles wrapped around my chest.

35.

'Hair of the dog,' Ash's sister Gabi says, passing me a glass brimming with prosecco.

Ash shakes his head. 'I'm not even going to ask.'

'Let's just say it was something that would have been right up your street, back in the day.'

'Then I definitely don't want to know.'

'Probably for the best.'

When we met at the front door, I liked Gabi instantly. She hugged me warmly, made full eye contact. I could see straight away that beneath her brisk demeanour, she was kind, affable. The similarity between her and Ash caught me off guard, which is ridiculous, given they're twins: same dark blue eyes, playful smiles, rolling laughs. She's dressed all in black, her hair cropped into a sleek dark bob that reminds me, unexpectedly, of Bev. I could just picture Gabi in a BMW, idling coolly by the kerb, waiting for her lover to get the hell out of his wife's house. I know this should probably alarm me, but I never hated Bev. Bizarrely, the way I felt about her always came closer to private admiration.

We're in the Heartwells' family living room, in a large detached house just south of the city. Everything in here seems to want to swallow me up: I'm trying not to disappear into their enormous gold damask sofa, and the pile of the cream carpet beneath my feet is so deep, it's practically quicksand. I am paranoid about spilling something, even though Ed and Juliet, Ash's parents, are all beams and cordiality and welcoming smiles. I've been urged to help myself to nibbles several times since we got here. There are bowls of them everywhere – smoked almonds and garlic-stuffed olives, little cubes of Manchego cheese. Classical music is coasting smoothly from a stereo in the corner of the room. I can tell this is a big deal for them – a real occasion. And not just because it's Juliet's birthday.

As yet, I've seen no evidence of the disconnect between them all that Ash described before. But I know better than anyone that family tensions can run deep.

It's obvious that the Heartwells have money – that they are what middle-class people would describe as being *comfortable* – but they're not showy about it like Jamie's parents were. I'd be willing to bet they'd be happier in a decent pub than at a Michelin-starred restaurant. I don't think they own more than one house, nor do I imagine they have a wine fridge reserved especially for champagne.

'Ash tells us you're moving in together, Neve,' Juliet says warmly, once we've all chinked glasses. She's demurely dressed, in a lace-edged top and slim, pale trousers. Her manicure looks expensive. I bet she never loses her nails down the back of the sofa like my mum does.

'Very happy for you both,' Ed chimes in. I can tell he is kind, like Ash. A good man. The type of person who'd rush into a burning building without a second thought. He and

Juliet are sitting across from us with beatific smiles on their faces, as if they can't quite believe Ash is in the same room as them, let alone introducing them to his girlfriend.

'Five months,' says Gabi, shaking her head. 'I've been with Toby longer than that and he still refuses to leave more than a toothbrush at my place.'

'It's nearly six, actually,' Ash says, quietly. And though I don't have a sibling, I still recognise that compulsion to become a teenager again – to score petty, paltry points – that kicks in whenever a family member happens to hit the right button.

'That's probably because your place is in need of – how can I put this? – a little TLC, darling,' Ed says to Gabi, which makes everyone laugh, even her. It's clearly a family in-joke. I always wondered what it would be like to have those. I bet my dad and Bev have them. Their own private language, shorthand for, *I get you.*

'And because Toby's – how can I put this? – a bit of a flake,' Ash says.

Gabi ignores him, throwing a handful of almonds into her mouth, then turning her attention to me. 'Well, here's an idea, Neve. You should come round and feng shui my place. Maybe Toby would actually deign to move in, if you worked your magic on it.'

'Neve's job is nothing to do with feng shui,' Ash says. Though he speaks calmly, the tone of his voice has darkened a little. He is slightly gruff with his family, I've noticed. Less upbeat than he is in private.

I appreciate the gesture, but he really doesn't need to wade in on my behalf. I'm well-versed in correcting people who assume I spend my days looking at fabric swatches and overcharging clients for advice on curtains and carpets. It goes with the territory, but I generally find that when people try to put down what I do, it says more about them than it does about me. I smile sweetly at Gabi. I want her to like me, of course – she's the twin of the man I love – but that doesn't mean I can't establish a gentle boundary. 'If you want to feng shui, there are loads of great books about it,' I say, as affably as I can. 'It's not really my specialism, to be honest.'

This isn't quite true. If a client was interested in feng shui, I would make it my specialism, fast. But I think Gabi and I both know she has no intention of becoming my client any time soon.

She returns my smile. 'So. Remind me how you two met.'

'Well, we kind of knew of each other through work. But we actually met for the first time at an art gallery.'

'Really? I thought my little brother was allergic to culture.'

'They're actually twins,' Juliet says to me with a smile, reaching over with the prosecco to top us all up, 'but Gabi's eighteen minutes older.'

I can tell Juliet is a born peacekeeper, that she's probably spent the past few days worrying about tonight going well. My heart flexes for what I know instinctively to be her innate kindness, her unconditional love.

'Ash says you met Toby at Coachella?' I say to Gabi.

'Yes, but I'm starting to think that wasn't such a bright idea. He is a flake, actually. Which I was too off my face to realise when we met, of course.'

Ed gets up to refill the nibbles. Juliet asks what I'm doing at work at the moment. I tell her about the city-centre bistro I'm refitting, and the Suffolk holiday lodges, and my latest project, interior specs for an exclusive development of new-build homes in South Norfolk.

'And Ash is such a talented architect,' I finish by saying. 'You must be very proud.'

'Oh yes,' Juliet says. Then, with a laugh, 'As far as we can make head or tail of what he does.'

'We're all medics in this family,' Ed clarifies.

'Oh, please no med chat today, Dad,' Gabi says with a groan. 'It's my day off.'

I still can't quite get my head around the idea of Gabi being a fully qualified doctor, mostly because she has the energy of a rebellious adolescent. She's exactly how Ash described himself to be, before his accident. I can't imagine her focusing for long enough to take a single exam, let alone monitor a patient's vitals during an hours-long operation.

'Probably a good thing, though, isn't it?' Juliet says to Ash. 'That you never became one too. Four medics around one table might have been a little too much for anyone to handle.'

'He'd never have lasted,' Gabi chips in. 'All doctors need a spark of madness, isn't that right, Dad?'

'Well, it definitely helps,' Ed replies, with a smile.

'You're thinking of comedians, there, Gabi,' Ash says, straight-faced. I can't work out if he's annoyed or being dry.

'Whatever. It applies to doctors too.' She beams at him, then turns to me. 'My brother is the exact opposite of mad, you'll be pleased to know, Neve. He no longer has a single spark of any such thing.'

For dinner, Ed and Juliet have served up a huge spread of Middle Eastern-themed food (I detect Ottolenghi). The dining table – which is huge, and Regency mahogany – is piled with bowls and plates bearing heaps of glistening vegetables, creamy hummus, couscous, roasted meat and glazed fish. There's easily enough food here for twenty people. It all feels beautifully lavish and delightful and *warm*. So warm. An occasion like this at my mother's house would never get beyond aperitifs, with some salted peanuts if her guests were lucky. I can't remember the last time she put effort into anything.

'So, Neve,' Gabi says, as Ed spoons tabbouleh onto my plate, bookending the little mound he's made with a chicken thigh and prawn skewer. 'If you had to describe yourself using three words, what would they be?'

Ed chuckles. 'She loves these questions.'

'You do *not* have to answer that,' Ash says, turning to me.

'Come on,' Gabi says. 'It's just a bit of fun.'

'Stop interrogating her,' he says.

I put my hand over his, to let him know he doesn't have to jump in to rescue me.

Gabi nods down at my hand, then looks back at Ash. 'See? She doesn't care.' But before I can answer the question, she picks up her glass and says, 'This guy used to be *wild*, you know.'

She is slightly tipsy now: I can tell from the slight glaze to her eyes, the insistency of her posture.

'They were thick as thieves,' Juliet says dreamily, clearly lost in nostalgia, completely missing the about-turn in her daughter's tone.

'I know,' I say, gently.

'Can we not,' says Ash.

'Mad, the stuff we got up to. God, remember Manchester? Creamfields? Glasto?'

'Not really,' he mutters. 'I was off my face for most of it.'

Gabi looks at me again. 'I'm genuinely surprised he never ended up in jail. He was arrested a few times. My mates used to call him Mr Breach Of The Peace. Except, they were your mates too, weren't they, Ash? From back when you still gave a shit.'

He doesn't reply.

'Gabi,' Juliet says gently. 'Would you like a glass of water?'

Gabi ignores her mother. 'We used to be best mates. I could tell him anything.'

'Gabs.' Ash's voice is soft and sad. 'I just . . . grew up. That's all it is.'

She looks at me again. 'This is actually the first time we've got together in one room – the four of us – in an entire year.'

They live in the same city, yet it's been a year since they've all had dinner together? I'm surprised by this. I'd no idea it had been so long.

'Because of your shift patterns,' Ash says. 'And when you're not working, you're always out, or away, or not answering your phone.'

The room falls quiet. I'm pretty sure Ed and Juliet have never wished so hard for the doorbell to go, or the smoke alarm to sound.

Gabi stands up, grabs her wine glass and leaves the room without saying anything.

Next to me, Ash lets out a long breath. 'Just going to go and see if she's all right. You okay?'

'Of course,' I say, with a smile to let him know it's fine.

'Gosh, I'm sorry about that,' Juliet says to me. We have retreated to the kitchen to clear up from dinner. Ed has disappeared into the garden to – as he says – 'attend to the hanging baskets', though I do wonder if that might in fact be code for 'spark up a cigarette'.

The Heartwells' kitchen is huge – almost the size of the entire ground floor of my house. The amount of cupboard space – and granite worktop – in here would be sufficient to service a mansion. I can tell it's the kind of place where there's always a stack of clean tea towels ready to go, as many as you need, rather than the same two on rotation.

The room is quiet except for the occasional splash of hot water, and the chink of glassware and crockery as Juliet sets things on the draining board. I wish I could hear what Ash is saying to Gabi. I bet he's being his usual sweet and calming self.

Juliet passes me a crystal coupe. 'It's always been very difficult with them. Well, I say *always*. I mean, since Ash's accident.'

I nod, taking extra care as I dry the glass, hot in my hand from the water. 'I know. He said he knew he'd changed.'

Juliet exclaims softly, the kind of noise you make when you tweak a muscle. 'That's an understatement.'

'Didn't it make you happy, though?' I ask, leaning forward as she passes me a ceramic bowl. 'I mean, if he was such a wild child before.'

She shakes her head. 'It wasn't so much that he calmed down. It was more this sense of . . . detachment. I mean, he'd always been a very tactile child. Used to throw his arms around me and pepper me with kisses. And his dad. So loving, always. Even as a teenager. Even the night before his accident. But now . . . he's very self-contained. Which just isn't our Ash. You didn't know him before, Neve. He was always so exuberant, so full of life. If Ash walked into a room, *everybody* knew about it. Just like his sister. They were this . . . extraordinary double-act, I suppose you could say. But since the accident . . . There's that phrase: "being a shadow of your former self" . . .' She looks across at me. 'Does he ever talk to you about it – feeling different to how he was?'

I swallow, try to find the right words.

She pushes her dark hair back behind her ears, leans forward. 'He does, doesn't he?'

'Juliet, I—'

'You can talk to me, Neve. I promise I'm not trying to interfere in his life, I just want . . . to understand, I suppose. We were always so close, as a family. Growing up, Gabi and Ash were inseparable. And now there's this distance between them . . . and it's been very hard for us all to accept.'

I take a breath, on the verge of confiding, then change my mind. No. She'll think I'm nuts. And it wouldn't be fair on Ash.

She reaches out, puts a hand on mine. I realise she is shaking slightly. 'Is it something we did? Please tell me, Neve.'

I glance behind us, towards the doorway. 'I really shouldn't be talking about this. Ash would be . . . Well, he wouldn't be happy. Maybe we could all sit down and discuss it together.'

She shakes her head despairingly. 'He always clams up in front of us.'

'Juliet, I don't—'

'Please, Neve.' There are tears of desperation in her eyes now.

I let out a long breath. 'Okay.'

She waits.

'There . . . There is something.'

'Tell me. Is he ill?' Her voice is pinched with fear.

It is when she says this that I know I have to at least try to help. To offer up something that might make sense to her. Some way of explaining why her son seemingly left their lives, never to return.

'No,' I say, quickly. 'No. It's nothing like that. He's not ill.'

Her eyes glimmer briefly with relief. 'But there is . . . something?'

I realise now that she's not about to let this go. And why should she? She's his mother. If I were her, I'd probably be doing exactly the same thing.

'Okay.' I exhale again. *Here we go.* 'I read this thing about . . . when someone dies, another soul can . . . walk into their body.'

Juliet frowns. 'I don't understand.'

'I know it sounds crazy . . . but I think that might have happened with Ash.'

A pause. 'I don't think you're crazy, Neve. I just want to understand.'

And I believe her. So I tell her everything. About Jamie's accident, just a street away from where Ash's heart momentarily stopped beating. About the million ways in which her son resembles Jamie. About how it all adds up, given everything the Heartwells say about Ash's personality change, and his disconnection from family, friends, old memories. I suggest it might be because none of those things actually belong to him. Because he might, in fact, *be* Jamie.

I don't know if Juliet would have been able to tease it out of me at all, were I not at least half a bottle of prosecco down. Maybe the alcohol spurred me to confide in her, but it is my sane and temperate mind doing the talking now. The words are out there – there is no going back – so all I can do is try my best to get her to understand.

But just as I near the end of explaining my theory, I look up to see Ash standing behind us, in the doorway to the kitchen.

I didn't hear him come downstairs. I have no idea how long he's been standing there.

He is staring at me, his gaze hardened to flint. 'Oh, Jesus. You actually think I'm him. You really believe everything you just said. Don't you?'

But he doesn't wait for me to reply, just turns and walks away. In horror, heart pounding, I drop the tea towel and leave Juliet in the kitchen, following Ash into the hallway. 'Ash, wait . . .'

He turns to face me. The space suddenly feels too small. It is scented with furniture polish and the faint smell of cut flowers from a vase on a tiny sideboard. One wall is covered in framed photographs of Ash and his sister. I glance sorrowfully at the sweetness of him in his school uniform, aged maybe ten or eleven, side by side with Gabi, whose hair is in bunches. Both their faces are already sparky and defiant, plucky with determination.

I move my gaze back to him. His eyes are hot with hurt. For a moment, we just stare at each other, my betrayal smouldering between us. And I know that what I say or do next will determine whether or not we burn.

'Be honest with me.' His voice sounds off-key with anguish and shock. 'Do you actually believe I'm . . . Jamie?'

'Ash,' I plead, 'if you just—'

'I think you'd better leave.' His jaw is locked firm. He is clearly devastated.

I stand numbly in front of him, wishing I could take back every word of the last twenty minutes. Because though I'd been planning to talk to him, this is not how I wanted to have that conversation.

'I'm calling you a cab. You can wait here. I'll get your stuff.'

'Ash, you're being—'

'What?' His cheeks are wet now with tears, his voice contorted. 'What am I being?'

I don't even know what I'd been going to say. *Ridiculous? Unfair? Irrational?* Because he is, of course, being none of those things. He is never any of those things.

He seems to gather himself. Then, so there can be no confusion: 'It's over, Neve.' His voice is cool and newly calm, unruffled as the air the morning after a storm.

36.

I don't sleep. Of course I don't. I spend the night emptying and scrubbing down my kitchen cupboards, a futile attempt to circuit-break the turmoil on loop in my mind. Eventually, as dawn unfolds, full mortification kicks in, more brutal than any hangover I have ever experienced.

I can't stop picturing Ash's face, last night. The way he looked at me. The man I love, thunderstruck with hurt and bewilderment. And I *do* love him. Don't I?

Or is it Jamie I love – Jamie I am still, after all these years, trying to build a life with?

Though my mind is foggy with muddled logic, I try calling him, as I did four times when I got home last night. But his phone is off. So I message him again, though I can't find a way to word my feelings without sounding as if I am guilty of a crime.

| It isn't how it sounded |
| I love you |
| Please call me |
| Can we talk? |

I sent him similar messages in the early hours of this morning. A total of twenty-two now sit delivered but unread at the end of our message thread. I look at them all, then replay my conversation with Juliet, over and over. And of course I see how Ash could think that in fact, I have lost my mind. How he might think he has fallen in love with someone who's entirely detached from reality.

By eight o'clock, I have been churning with disquiet for so long, I feel as though my brain is filled with mud. So I take a shower then leave the house to walk the thirty minutes or so to Ash's apartment. Sunday mornings in the city always feel slightly mournful – deserted streets, bags of rubbish in shop doorways, empty bottles abandoned the night before. The clouds today are the colour of wet cement.

I stop at Costa for two coffees, then walk the last five minutes to the Old Yarn Mill, heart pounding with anticipation.

'Yep,' he says gruffly, when I buzz.

'It's me.'

He doesn't say anything, and for a moment I think he's just going to ignore me. But then he buzzes me up, so I head inside and take the lift to the top floor.

He is a long time answering the door, and when he does, he blocks the space with his whole body, as if I'm a religious fanatic, or a charity worker who won't be told no.

'Can I come in? I brought coffee.'

A semi-surprised laugh. He doesn't move. He's wearing a crumpled T-shirt and tracksuit bottoms, and all his features look strangely flat and colourless.

'I don't think there's anything to say,' he replies.

Standing in the clinical dead space of the building's hallway, as though I'm trying to sell him something – which I guess I am – I feel my heart slide into my shoes. 'Please let me explain.'

He starts to speak, then hesitates, and for a moment I think he might invite me in. But then he says, 'Do you know how long I was standing behind you last night, listening to what you were saying to my mum?'

I shake my head, the shame of it all gripping me again.

'Ten minutes. Ten actual minutes while you were talking to her, telling her you think I'm the reincarnation of your ex. Trying to *convince* her, too. Do you know how humiliating that was? Not just for me, but for Mum. It was her birthday, for God's sake. And they were so excited to meet you, Neve. They put a lot of effort into last night. And you ended up telling her you're essentially in love with someone else. She saw what I went through with Tabitha—'

'This isn't that,' I counter.

'Look, I don't want coffee, or to talk. I want you to leave.'

'I wasn't trying to convince your mum,' I say, in an attempt to penetrate the stone wall of his expression. 'I didn't plan to say anything to her. I swear. But she seemed so worried about you, and we were talking in the kitchen, and it just . . . came out.'

'Well, at least I know now how you really feel, Neve. This whole time, we've been together because you believe – and don't even get me started on the logic of this – that I'm your ex. You don't love me for me. You don't even love *me*. You love your ex. The guy you were going to—' But then he breaks off and shakes his head, drawing a hand down his face.

'I take it she didn't—'

'Believe your theory?' He lets out a half-laugh, but he's not smiling. 'No, Neve. She didn't.'

I nod. 'Right. Okay. Fair enough.'

'Yeah, it is. This feels no different than if you'd told me . . . you'd been shagging someone else.'

'Ash, I know it's complicated,' I insist, trying not to think about Tabitha. 'But I do love you.'

'No. Complicated is when . . . one person lives in Norwich and the other lives in Aberdeen. Or when one of you votes left, and the other right. Compared to this, complicated is actually pretty simple.'

His words are fierce, but at least he's talking. There might be hope. 'Can I just come in, for five minutes?'

'Sure – if you tell me you don't believe I'm Jamie.' He steps aside, opens the door wide enough for me to pass.

It's the simplest of tests. And of course, I fail straight away. 'The point is, you might not actually *know* you're him . . .'

I read about something similar to this in an article online – people living with personality changes brought on by traumatic brain injuries. They know they have changed – because everyone keeps telling them – but they can't *feel* it themselves. Can't inhabit the person they were before.

Ash shakes his head. 'Look, I'm going to save us both a lot of time, pain and confusion. I don't believe what you told my mum last night. All right? I'm categorically not

Jamie. Obviously. I don't buy into reincarnation and ghosts and the afterlife and all that malarkey. Never have. It's claptrap, nothing more.' He swallows, and I watch him force out what he says next. 'I don't see how we can come back from this. I'm going to stay here. There's no way I'm letting the flat out now.'

I should have been expecting this. But somehow, the shock of hearing him say it still feels brutal as whiplash. For a couple of moments, I can't speak.

'Can you drop off my stuff when you get a chance? If there's anything here of yours, I'll do the same.' All the warmth has left his voice. It's now just logistics, like we're estranged relatives planning a funeral, or neighbours discussing a party wall.

It was a bad idea to bring coffee. With both hands full, I am unable to do anything but stand helplessly in front of him, when all I want to do is pull him into a hug. 'I don't want this to end,' I say.

'I don't know why it would be a surprise to you,' Ash says softly, 'that I want to be with someone who loves me for me. Because you know what? I still want that, Neve. I still want to find that person. I thought you were her, but—'

'I *am* her. It's not that simple, it's—'

'What if it was the other way around? How would you feel if you found out that all this time, I'd been thinking of . . . Tabitha, while I'd been with you?'

'Please hear me out,' I say, a final time. 'What I believe . . . It would explain so much. Stranger things have happened, Ash.'

'Um, they absolutely haven't. Not in my world, anyway.'

'You're being extraordinarily small-minded.'

'And you're clearly still grieving that guy. You never resolved it. You should go and see someone about that, Neve, before it ruins the rest of your life.'

I feel a swift spark of anger, the first since we met. 'Don't try to make out I'm crazy.'

'I'm not. You're doing that all by yourself.'

Behind us, the lift rumbles, indicating the arrival of a neighbour, or delivery person. I have mere moments left.

'I'm *not mad*,' I insist, looking him right in the eye, a final attempt to weaken the barrier he has put up. Or, to be more accurate, the one I have created between us.

But he doesn't say anything else. He just gently but very firmly closes the door in my face.

37.

Then

Just seven days after I discovered I was pregnant, Jamie's parents came to Norwich for the weekend.

I still hadn't told Jamie about the baby.

They'd made reservations at an uber-expensive restaurant on Upper St Giles – one that offered tasting menus and paired wine. I wondered if they'd done that partly to try to intimidate me – to prove I didn't belong in their world, and, by extension, Jamie's.

I wasn't intimidated, but I was apprehensive. I didn't often see Chris and Debra, and I was worried they might be able to guess I was pregnant. What would they say? What would they do? Would they expose my secret in the middle of the restaurant, a hushed and intimate space, where people booked tables months in advance for special occasions? I couldn't bear to be struck by the ugly brunt of Chris's rage in such an elegant, civilised setting.

I knew I should have told Jamie by then. But the mention of Heather the previous week had thrown me. As had the idea that, unless I did something about it, Jamie might be heading to London again for the summer.

My hesitance had turned into anxiety, withdrawal. I couldn't sleep. I couldn't eat. I would push Jamie away at night, and he'd ask if I was okay. But I couldn't tell him. Somewhere inside me, a kernel of doubt had taken root and was growing.

None of my misgivings were to do with becoming a mum, though. I pictured it obsessively: giving birth rosy-cheeked on a damp-misted day in January. Surviving night feeds and dirty nappies and lack of sleep with cheerful, full-hearted optimism, muddling through till we graduated in June. Finding somewhere to live, the three of us. Securing another part-time internship, maybe, then working as an interior designer while Jamie completed his architecture training and we both rode the juggernaut of early parent-hood. It would be a messy and chaotic but exhilarating blur.

But what if, I thought, Jamie's parents got to him before all that? What if they persuaded him the whole thing was just too huge, too soon? That becoming a dad would be unbearably tough?

I tried to imagine my life if we couldn't make it work. Without him waking me each morning with a kiss and cup of tea. Without his messages filling my phone – jokes and funny anecdotes and ridiculous gifs. Without the hearts he would draw for me on the steamed-up shower screen. Without him catching me whenever he came home, pressing me gently to the wall with a kiss. Without meeting his gaze and enjoying the pleasant voltage of our shared smile, knowing he was mine.

But most of all, I couldn't imagine losing the certainty of loving him. A future with Jamie had always felt sure as the sunrise to me, a flare of orange-skied warmth in my mind. Nor could I picture parenting alone. I didn't want to do it without him. Our baby was half him, his cells mingled with mine. I imagined the baby as a silkworm inside me, spinning a new life for the three of us, intricate and breathtaking. And all we had to do for that miracle to unfold was wait.

Alone was a prospect I simply couldn't contemplate.

At the restaurant, Jamie's dad was being especially obnoxious. We'd barely passed the menus back to the waiter before he started harping on about Jamie's future.

'You should really consider doing your masters in London,' he said, his voice abrupt, his expression expectant. 'I'm serious about this, Jamie.'

He and Jamie were wearing matching designer shirts that night. His was white, Jamie's dark grey. I'd been trying to decide if I thought that was sweet or a bit absurd. Still, Jamie was on good form, which helped to distract me from the hornets' nest in my head. He looked so handsome, and had layered on the Tom Ford Noir. I was wearing the tiny black dress he liked, though I could feel his parents' disapproval of it the moment I removed my coat.

'Yeah, I know,' Jamie said, in reply to Chris, sipping his water without looking my way.

I wished Jamie would assert himself. But I understood why he felt he couldn't. His father was implacable when he was in this kind of mood.

'And you, Neve?' Chris's pick-axe gaze swivelled onto me. 'What is *your* plan, for life after graduation?'

I wished I'd thought to have an answer ready for this question. Because I could hardly say, *Well, that really depends on how things go with your first grandchild, Chris.*

The wine arrived. I put my hand over my glass as the waiter made to fill it. 'Hayfever,' I said. (This bit I had practised.) 'I'm on antihistamines.'

Jamie touched my arm in sympathy, not seeming to realise I wasn't presenting with a single symptom of hayfever, nor had I mentioned it before now. As he did so, his designer watch caught my eye, the one Chris had given to him the previous Christmas. It was so expensive, he'd pretended when I asked that he didn't know how much Chris had paid for it. But I Googled it the same night and felt faintly appalled. It had cost as much as a small car.

'Ah, well,' Chris said briskly to me, as if hayfever was a personality defect. He was probably the type of guy who didn't believe in depression, or menstrual cramps. 'All the more for us.'

I could feel Jamie's mum staring at me then, for just a second longer than felt comfortable. But shortly after that, the conversation moved on, and she looked away.

She caught me outside the toilets a couple of hours later, just after Jamie's dad had ordered coffees for everyone without asking if we wanted them first.

'Neve.' Debra's voice was hushed, but her eyes were urgent. She was wearing a slash of lipstick in a violent shade of red I suspected to have been an ill-judged gift from Chris. 'I know we don't know each other very well, but I can see how much my son . . . admires you.' (It didn't surprise me to discover that Debra was apparently allergic to the L-word.) 'I'd like to ask you a question, and for you to answer truthfully.'

'Okay,' I said, even though I already resented everything about this conversation – my assumed dishonesty, her interrogative manner, what I knew was coming next.

'Are you pregnant?'

I could feel colour blooming across my skin. So many things were going through my head in that moment. But among them was how Debra could talk to me as if I'd been her son's girlfriend for a matter of weeks, when in fact she'd known me since I was a child.

Seemingly unwilling to wait for my response, she said, 'I see.'

No congratulations, or impassioned hug. Just stone-cold panic, a silent scream.

'It's still early.' My mouth was dry. She was standing so close, I could taste every cloying layer of her perfume. 'Jamie doesn't know yet.'

Debra activated crisis mode. 'Then I need to ask you . . . please . . . to consider not having this child.'

I stared at her, horrified. 'It's not your right to ask me that.'

She glanced over her shoulder. It seemed mad to me that she could have said something so ludicrous just inches from where people were enjoying romantic nights out, celebratory dinners. 'Jamie has another internship in

London this summer. Archibald & Leicester is an incredibly prestigious firm, Neve. He has big plans for his future.'

'So do I.'

At this, she tilted her head, as if to say, *You wish.* 'Neve. Parenting is a tough, tough job. And Jamie . . . He's not mature enough to cope. You don't have jobs. You don't even have anywhere to live. Please, *please* don't do this to him.'

'I haven't done anything *to* him,' I said, appalled by her outdated assumptions. 'It takes two people to—'

'Chris will . . . *never* recover from this. He wants the world for Jamie. He adores him.'

I just looked at her then, unsure how she expected me to consider the feelings of a man who had never been anything other than dismissive of my very existence.

'I understand that Chris can come across as a little . . . domineering. But we tried for a long time to have a sibling for Harry. And it was very hard and very . . . heartbreaking. Then, just when we'd given up hope, Jamie came along. I suppose you could say he was our "miracle baby". Anyway. For that reason, Chris has always wanted the very best for him. I hope you can understand.'

'I do,' I said, determined to maintain my composure in the face of such outrageous intrusiveness. 'But *I* want the best for Jamie too. And this is really between me and him.'

'So why haven't you told him?'

'I haven't found the right moment. But Jamie will be an amazing father.' The fervent need to stand up for Jamie's rights – not to mention my own, and my baby's – began to really kick in then. 'I *know* he'll want this.'

'Yes, in fifteen years' time, maybe. Once you've both had a chance to live a little and discover . . . what it is you want from your futures.'

I suspected she was hoping Jamie would meet someone else in the interim. Someone from a wealthy family, with parents who played golf and understood things like cigars and wine, who holidayed in Mustique and held membership at Annabel's. Who had connections. Who dined every week at places like this.

A thought occurred to me. 'Do you know someone called Heather?'

'Heather? No,' she said sharply and too fast, which indicated to me that she very much did know someone called Heather. That Heather was perhaps even who she had in mind for her son.

A woman passed us then, to go into the toilets. She smiled neutrally at us, and I wondered what she would say, were she privy to our conversation. How absurd she would have found it. How absurd any normal-thinking human would surely have found it.

'You know, Jamie's father wanted to send him to private school. And the reason Jamie refused was because of you.'

'I never asked him to do that.'

'He's already made big sacrifices for you, Neve.'

But isn't that what love is? I wanted to say.

'I'll pay you,' Debra said then, her voice so low I wondered for a moment if I'd misheard. She reached out to touch my arm. Her skin was marble-cold against mine. But it wasn't a gesture of tenderness. I knew it was the precursor to something harder, uglier, far more forceful.

I met her gaze, asking her to repeat herself with my expression alone.

She did have the decency to look ashamed, even as she whispered her insistence. 'I will *pay* you to take care of this, Neve. However much it takes. However much you want.' Her voice cracked then. But she remained every inch the villain to me, with her scarlet lipstick and formaldehyde-strength perfume, behaviour spinning rapidly out of control.

I felt myself burn with sadness for Jamie – my good, sweet boyfriend, who loved and respected his parents, who would have been devastated to hear the words coming out of Debra's mouth.

It was a gamble on her part, I could see that. If I told Jamie what she'd said, there was a chance he might never speak to her again. But Debra was obviously no stranger to manipulation. She was banking on me loving her son too much to break his heart so completely. She was sure I would take this secret to my grave.

'This is *your grandchild*,' I said softly, placing a hand on my stomach, hoping to shame her back down to planet earth.

It didn't work. She shook her head, disturbingly focused. 'Just name your price,' she said, one last stab at exerting her control.

I could have walked away, then. But instead, I imagined what Lara would say – *You're better than being treated this way, Neve* – and in that moment, I knew I could channel some of her assertiveness.

I took a single step forward. 'I wouldn't expect you to understand, Debra, that some things in life are more important than money.'

I walked back to the table then. She followed a few moments later. By now Jamie and Chris were laughing about some friend of the family, merry enough not to notice that Debra and I had become pale and voiceless, utterly absent for the rest of the night.

38.

Now

I grieve for every part of who we were. For the hearts drawn in shower steam, and the evenings in dark bars with espresso martinis. For walks through the city late at night, his hand in mine. For the cheese toasties in bed, and weekend coffee. For the trips we'd started to plan (a week in Iceland? Or maybe New York). For coming home from work at ten o'clock to find he'd cooked me dinner. For the steady tempo of his breath as he slept. I even miss how he'd watch me steaming the creases from my bedsheets, not laughing, but looking at me fondly, as though it was the most adorable thing he'd ever seen. For the painful poker losses, and the hours spent in bed on Sunday mornings, experiencing a different kind of agony, one that was addictive and beautiful. For our future plans. For all my private dreams about house-warmings and promotions and – who knew? – maybe one day, even a family of our own. For every adventure to come.

One minute, the future felt like solid ground. The next, it was litter on a wave.

Before that night at his parents', I'd started sorting through my things, seeing what I might be able to donate to charity, or stow in the loft, to make room for him. And so my house is filled with boxes and piles of stuff that I need to unpack again, a task I'd normally enjoy. But now I can't even look at them.

I am reminded, sharply, of the early days after Jamie died. Of the double-takes my brain kept doing as it tried to retain the fact that he wasn't coming back.

I tell Parveen it's over. When she asks why, all I can say is that it's complicated, but I've messed up monumentally. 'But you were so good together,' she says, her eyes going glossy, which makes me tearful too.

For maybe the first time ever, I start to experience something resembling resentment towards Jamie. It's almost as if he has sabotaged Ash and me, deliberately stood in our way. On more than one occasion, I find myself staring intently at the print of *Nighthawks* above my bed, thinking, *You weren't wrong about coming back to haunt me, were you?*

And yet. Late at night, the thought still – even now – nags at me that Jamie's spirit, somehow, set up home in Ash one night a decade ago. That it came to shore in his blood, his bones. That it altered his chemistry, infiltrated the essence of him. That Ash is a hybrid of my past and my future, and I have no way of telling which is which.

★   ★   ★

My mother calls to say she has two almost-expired passes to a day spa, but she's come down with flu, so do I want them?

I don't, because I never did quite get the hang of spas. I'm just not very good at lounging about. My mother, on the other hand, could probably live in a spa, wafting around in a towelling robe and having people bring her things on trays.

But it's a posh place, and it's free, and it's Lara's birthday soon. So I could take her for an early treat, I guess. My first gift to her in nearly a decade.

Plus, the more distraction from missing Ash, the better.

I call Lara to ask. She sounds so touched I half expect her to burst into tears.

'Sorry, sorry,' she gasps, rushing into the lobby where we've agreed to meet. (She's only ten minutes late, but I guess she still remembers that I am almost pathologically punctual.) She's out of breath, clutching her phone, manic-eyed. 'I let my flat out to friends of a friend while I'm here, and . . . long story short, they've dropped a bottle of red wine on the floor.'

I wince. 'Carpet?'

Her face darkens. 'Solid oak parquet.'

'Oh God, when?'

'Last *month*. They've only just got around to telling me. And I don't usually get excited about things like floors, but my heart is hurting a little bit because mine was *beautiful*, Neve.'

'Have they tried to get the stain out?'

'Oh yes. You'll love this – I'm not joking: they tried *the white wine technique.*'

I cover my mouth.

'Upturned half a bottle. I mean, seriously.'

I smile. I can't help it. 'I'm sorry. It's not funny.'

She smiles back at me. 'No, it kind of is.'

Our eyes meet, and the moment of shared amusement-slash-horror feels oddly emotive.

I shake it off. 'You'll need a specialist. I know a good floor guy. I'll ping you his number.'

She looks relieved. 'Oh God, yes please.'

'I assume you've unleashed the requisite wrath?'

'On the lodgers?' She smiles at me faintly. 'Actually, believe it or not, I'm a lot more zen than I used to be.'

Lara has this spa thing down. We get a free treatment each, so she suggests we do those first, for a quick dopamine hit, before spending the rest of the day between the pool and the 'relaxation zone'. (Though this phrase alone makes me prickle: to me, zones infer activity. I already feel as though I should be checking my emails, or doing a spin class.)

In the lobby, a group of shiny-faced people walk by in robes, carrying glasses of prosecco. To be fair, they do look like they're having quite a good time, being lazy just for the hell of it. In fact, they all have that glow that spas keep waffling on about being good for. Maybe I have been getting relaxation wrong over the years after all.

Lara doesn't want a treatment that lasts too long, or she

says she'll get twitchy, so we book a basic back massage each, and agree to meet afterwards in the conservatory.

I wait for her for what feels like ages. But just as I'm starting to worry we got our wires crossed about where to meet, she appears.

She's dabbing at her eyes with a tissue.

'Lar?'

She sits down on the sofa next to me, arranges her robe across her knees. It's clear she's been crying.

'What happened?' Out of nowhere, I start to have visions of her having been body-shamed by the therapist.

'Oh God, nothing.' She blows her nose, forces a smile. 'The masseuse said it happens all the time, people bursting into tears for no reason.'

'Did she? Does it?'

Lara shrugs. 'Apparently. Did you?'

'No, I nearly fell asleep. It was nicer than I expected.' (I surprised myself, actually. I can't remember the last time I shut my eyes in the middle of the day and stayed put for longer than five minutes.)

Lara catches the eye of a passing server. 'Drink?'

'Shall we have prosecco?'

She makes a face. 'Ah . . . I shouldn't. You go for it, though. One prosecco and one sparkling water,' she says to the server.

Felix floats into my mind again, and I wish he wouldn't, because I have no real evidence for any of my doubts about him, or the way he is with her in private.

'Are you okay?' I ask her, gently. 'I wish you'd talk to me.'

She turns to look at me. Her eyes are still pink from crying. 'Do you?'

'Of course. I want to help.'

She hesitates for a long time, then says, 'Thank you. But if I'm honest, I . . . don't know where I stand with you, Neve.'

I look down at my lap. 'I know.'

'I mean, we didn't speak for nearly a decade. And don't get me wrong, I am so, *so* happy to be back in your life, but . . . that anger didn't just disappear, did it? I know it's still there. I see it in your eyes, sometimes.'

She's right, of course. The anger's been with me ever since that night. In some ways, it's always felt like the easiest emotion to reach for, whenever I think of Jamie's death.

'Was that why you were crying? Was it to do with . . . you and me?'

She takes a breath, as if we're about to really get into it, then seems to change her mind. 'No, it . . . Like I said. People get emotional when they're being massaged. It's something to do with all the toxins, apparently.'

She's clearly not ready to open up, which I can't really blame her for. Besides, this hardly feels like the right moment, on what is supposed to be a pre-birthday treat – not to mention the space we're in being quieter than a library.

'I think we should talk. About Jamie, you and me, everything,' I say. 'But this . . . doesn't feel like quite the place to do it.'

She smiles. 'Agreed. I heard someone fart earlier and it was louder than a jumbo jet.'

Our drinks arrive.

'What are you doing for your actual birthday?' I ask, taking a sip of prosecco. I don't usually drink during the day, and I feel the alcohol spin straight to my head.

'Felix is taking me to Rome,' she says, slightly bashfully.

'Wow, Lar. That's exciting.'

'I know. I've always wanted to go, properly. I worked there on a TV show when I was starting out and never really got to enjoy it, so it's always been kind of a bucket-list place for me. Spanish Steps, Colosseum, all that history and romance and culture. We've got tickets to the opera. And our hotel room has a private terrace and *the* most insane views . . .'

'Sounds incredible.'

'I know what you're thinking.'

'What am I thinking?'

'That he's flash, all about the money.'

'I wasn't thinking that,' I say, even as I'm wondering, *Was I?*

'You're wrong, anyway.'

I shake my head. 'Lar, he's your boyfriend, he's spoiling you. Why shouldn't he? It's romantic.'

She smiles faintly. 'Yeah. Anyway. It wasn't so long ago that Ash was sweeping you off to Europe on a romantic break.'

Even his name feels like a corkscrew to my stomach. 'Actually . . . Ash and me . . . We're not together any more.'

'What? Why?'

'Ah, it all came out. About Jamie.'

She releases a long, disappointed breath. 'He didn't take it well?'

'Let's just say my delivery could have been better. I didn't actually tell him directly. He overheard me talking to his mum about it.'

Lara looks mildly horrified. 'His *mum*?'

'There was prosecco.' Sheepishly, I lift the glass I'm drinking from. 'And it was a family dinner. Although to be honest, it felt more like a funeral by the time he threw me out.'

I can't bring myself to mention that Juliet practically dragged it out of me. Because it wasn't her fault. I didn't have to say a word.

Lara makes a face like she's watching a road traffic accident in slow motion. 'So, he overheard you telling his mum . . . then what?'

'Well, he kind of lost it, then ended it.'

She swears softly. 'When was this?'

'Last weekend.'

I see her take this in: seven whole days. In another life, I'd have been messaging her from Juliet's front porch while I was waiting for the cab.

Beyond the conservatory window, a cluster of clouds moves across the sun, and for a few moments the air turns cool.

'Has he been in touch?'

I shake my head. 'No, and I actually think . . . he doesn't *want* to work things out. And I can't exactly blame him. He says he doesn't believe in reincarnation or the afterlife or ghosts, so he's definitely not buying my theory. He called it *malarkey* and *claptrap*.'

Lara's eyes narrow. 'Does he also say things like *codswallop* and *brouhaha*?'

I smile, despite myself. 'No.'

'All is not lost, then.'

It is, actually. 'He was so angry, Lar. He said it was like I'd been cheating on him. Which given what happened with Tabitha, is probably the worst thing he could think about me. But the thing is, I really did love him.' I shake my head in frustration as a wave of sadness crests in my chest. '*Do* love him.'

She leans forward, puts a hand on my knee. 'Okay, I'm going to ask you something now. Promise not to get offended?'

I smile faintly. This is the kind of question my mother usually opens with when she's about to lay into my life choices.

'Do you really love Ash? Or do you love him because you think he's Jamie?'

'That's what he said.'

She holds my gaze. 'Well?'

'Both. Is that possible?'

'Not really.'

I sigh. 'Ash said I should see a therapist. He thinks this is . . . unresolved grief.'

Lara just nods, then waits.

'And ordinarily, I'd agree, but . . . I still can't get past the facts. There are too many similarities. Too many coincidences. There are just . . . too many. And every time I read about the walk-in theory . . . it's truly the only thing that makes sense.' I shake my head. 'Even down to little things, like . . . Ash would always kiss that same bit of my collarbone that Jamie liked to kiss. The *exact same spot.*'

Lara raises an eyebrow. 'Not to be captious, but Felix likes to kiss that exact same part of me, too.'

As she says this, an elderly couple shuffle past in their robes, slippers slapping against the tiled floor. The woman glares at us, then looks at her husband and shakes her head.

Lara laughs as they walk off. 'Wow. It's been a long time since I've been the most salacious person in the room.'

'So, what are you saying?' I ask her.

'I'm saying, maybe speaking to a counsellor isn't such a bad idea.'

'You think it's all in my head?' I'm not accusing her. I genuinely want to know.

'No,' she says, equably. 'I think what I've always thought – that we have no idea what happens when someone dies. But I do know that you and Ash had – have – something worth fighting for, and a counsellor could help you figure out how to do that.'

I picture the way Ash looked at me last Sunday. The love had drained from his face and eyes, replaced by cold indifference.

'And look – maybe you just need to force him to sit down and talk to you. Maybe you just need to thrash this whole thing out. Maybe . . . you just don't give him the option, Neve.'

It's only when she looks up and I meet her eye that I realise it's possible we're not talking about Ash any more.

★   ★   ★

When I get back home, still smelling faintly aromatic from the massage oil, I consider how a day can be pleasant and weird all at once. Even now, I'm so base-level angry with Lara, yet it's been surprisingly easy to resurrect something bearing all the hallmarks of friendship. Because the short-hand, the history, the groundwork, is already there. I never have to explain myself to her. She knows me inside out, as I do her, despite that missing decade. Which makes the illusion deceptively easy to believe.

But just because something's easy, doesn't mean you should do it. Maybe, in fact, the opposite is true. It's a bit like getting back into bed with an ex. Easy because it's comfortable, safe, effortless. But usually a bad idea.

She pulled me into a hug as we parted ways in the car park earlier. 'When I'm back from Rome, you and I need to talk. Properly. Okay?'

'Okay,' I said. But something about the intense way she looked at me struck a strange chord inside me. A jumble of notes clashing deep in my belly. The chime in a film score that tells you to panic; the moment when everything changes.

39.

I mess up at work. A developer calls one morning to ask where I am: the meeting we'd arranged slipped right out of my head. The drive to site is forty minutes, and the developer can't wait, so after grovelling my apologies, we reschedule for next week.

Kelley summons me to her office, demands to know what's going on. She's tapping her pen against the giant jotter she keeps on her desk, fixing me with minty-green eyes as she waits for my reply. Her blonde bob is a blade against her set jaw. I feel like a contractor who's got all their measurements wrong.

To my dismay, as I apologise, I realise I am fighting tears. I've never cried at work before, and I wasn't intending on starting today, and certainly not in front of Kelley. 'I took my eye off the ball.'

'I shouldn't need to tell you that forgetting a meeting is incredibly unprofessional, Neve.' Kelley never raises her voice, because she doesn't need to. Her power comes from her cast-iron composure. She's like a monk out-staring a fly.

'I know—'

'If you need some time off, please take it.' Her voice has softened, but only minutely. You'd have to know her to pick up on it. 'But I'd ask you not to let your personal problems affect your work, and by turns, our reputation. It's unfair on me and everyone else who works here.'

'I know. I won't. It won't happen again.'

Back at my desk, I stare blankly at my copy of *On Decorating*. I brought it in, once Lara and I started talking again, propping it up on my desk as a reminder of how far I'd come. But now, it seems, everything's going wrong. And I can't find a way forward, of making things right.

Since she has to get her kicks where she can, I guess, my mother calls out my low mood. 'You look very down in the dumps, Neve.'

I've dropped in after my spin class with some chicken soup, because that's what you're supposed to do when someone has flu, isn't it? But Mum's evidently made a quick recovery. I find her in her bedroom – not ill in bed, but trying on dresses for a gig at the weekend. She looks hot and sheened with sweat, like she's been taking garments on and off for hours. Her hair is wild, a slow-motion explosion. I resist the urge to pass her a headband.

'Just tired,' I tell her.

She peers at me. 'Boy trouble?'

'Man, not boy.' Sometimes, I really do think her need to get on my tits is bordering on pathological.

'Forget him, darling.'

'Wow. Thanks. Wish I'd thought of that.' I sit down on the edge of her bed.

'I'm being serious.'

'You met him for about five minutes when you were hammered. You don't even know him.'

I hadn't got round to telling her we were moving in together. I foresaw her condescension, the crap impression she'd do of a relationship expert, telling me it was far too soon and blah, blah, blah.

She shrugs, sways gently back and forth in front of the mirror. The dress she has on is smothered in silver sequins. It's nice – though more Academy Awards than 3-star hotel bar. 'I wasn't talking about Ash.'

'What?'

She makes eye contact with me via the mirror, because she prefers it that way. 'I was talking about Jamie.'

'You've lost me.'

'From what I can work out, Ash is a nice boy. So he deserves you to appreciate him for who he is.'

'Please stop calling him a boy. Also, you don't know anything about it.'

'Tell me I'm wrong, then.'

I feel a prickle of irritation at the back of my neck. 'You said yourself Ash reminded you of Jamie, when you met him. You actually *called* him Jamie, several times. See, Mum, this is why when you drink, you never—'

'Do you want to spend the rest of your life looking backwards?'

'Like you did with Dad, you mean?' A cheap shot, yes, but she does set them up for me.

'Well, quite. I don't think you should aspire to be me, darling.'

288

I resist agreeing too hard. 'You can't exactly talk about appreciating people for who they are. Ralph's been around for longer than you were even with Dad, and you don't appreciate him, not one bit.'

A smile teases the corner of her lips. 'You're suggesting I get together with Ralph?'

Her amused expression strikes a match inside me. 'What – you're too good for a man who's been nothing but loyal to you?'

'A cynic might suggest you're deflecting the issue here, Neve.'

I sigh and get to my feet. 'I'm going.'

'No, hang on. Which one – sequins, or satin?'

I'd love to say neither. But the fact is, if Mum only knows one thing – which might conceivably be the case – it's how to make the most of her figure. 'They both look good.'

'Neve. Do you want to know the trick to life and love?' she says, as I'm turning to leave.

The urge to laugh is solid. My mother is the most emotionally chaotic person I've ever met. 'Enlighten me.'

She pauses dramatically. 'The trick is to work out who actually *deserves* your devotion. You can give your heart and soul to whoever you want, but very few people will actually be worthy of it.'

I roll my eyes. I can't help it.

'It's time to let Jamie go, darling.'

I swallow. 'I told you. You don't know anything about it.'

40.

Forty-eight hours later, in the middle of the night, my phone rings.

It's a number I don't recognise. I stare at the screen for a couple of seconds, then answer it. I am praying it's Ash – that he's out somewhere and has run out of charge and got all nostalgic and borrowed a phone to call me and say he cannot, in fact, possibly conceive of a life without me. 'Hello?'

The buzz of static. Then a female voice says, 'Neve?'

'Yes?' My heart is in my throat.

'It's Gabi. Ash's sister. Listen, I didn't know whether to call you, but . . .'

I hold my breath.

'. . . there's been an accident. Ash has been run over. We're at the N&N.'

I can hardly speak. 'Is he—'

'In theatre. Will you come?'

Tears spring to my eyes. 'Oh my God, Gabi. What happened? Is he going to be okay?'

'I'll tell you everything when you get here. Just . . . I think he'd want you here, Neve.'

Earlier this evening, I was at a wine bar with friends, being morose into a bottle of merlot. I definitely can't drive, but if a cab doesn't come quick enough, I'll run to the hospital.

'I'm on my way,' I yell into my phone, as I jump out of bed and into a pair of tracksuit bottoms. 'I'm on my way.'

Fragments of what follow remind me of the night Jamie died. Getting the call. Starting to shake, losing my ability to think as my mind became a wind tunnel of fear. I had to get a cab that night too, and I remember almost heaving as I breathed in the pungency of the driver's air freshener. He tried to make conversation, but I only felt capable of throwing out the odd syllable here and there. Eventually he gave up. At the hospital, I stuffed a handful of notes into his palm – I had no idea how many – then ran into the foyer, looking wildly around for someone who might be able to tell me Jamie was okay. But then I spotted his parents. Their faces were stark and haunted. And that was the agonising moment I knew. I'd never experienced pain so vicious, so cataclysmic before, and I instinctively wanted to run from it, because I knew I would not be able to endure it. I can still remember the way it felt, to realise I couldn't escape the fact that Jamie would never return. That grief like I'd never known was coming for me, and there was nothing I could do to stop it.

As the cab pulls up at A&E, I spot Gabi outside, vaping. She regards me as I jog-walk towards her.

Even during an emergency in the early hours of the

morning, Gabi's bob is sleek and groomed, her clothes pressed, her face made up. She's even wearing earrings. I, by contrast, must look positively feral – hair scraped back, crumpled top, tracksuit bottoms and hoodie, whatever I could lay my hands on when she called.

'Have you seen him? Is he okay?'

'He's okay. He's still in theatre, but he's going to be all right.'

Inside my heart, a parachute opens. 'Thank God. What happened?'

'Got absolutely shitfaced after work, apparently. Wandered into the road and a car clipped him. He's lucky he wasn't killed. He broke his leg and ankle, fractured a couple of ribs, punctured a lung.'

She talks like a doctor, I realise. Headline facts, emotion at arm's length. 'Thank you for calling me,' I say, when she's done. 'Really. I'm so glad you did.'

We stand quietly together for a couple of moments. It's a clear night, the sky cluttered with stars and a bright coin of moon.

'Have you quit the real thing?' I ask, nodding at the vape and leaning back against the wall we're standing next to. It's cold, but I need a bit of help staying vertical right now.

'Depressingly, yes,' she says, then glances at me. 'Ash used to chain-smoke. I'm guessing that would have put you off, if you'd met him back then?'

'No,' I say, honestly, because I like Ash far more than I dislike smoke.

'What about all the drinking and the drugs and the

fighting?' She smiles faintly, nods at the hospital building. 'This used to be a fairly standard Friday night for us, you know, back in the day.'

Her question must be rhetorical. Because who, really, would opt for any of that?

I survey the slow procession of cars in and out of the A&E car park, the people making phone calls or sitting on the kerb staring blankly into space like life's just mugged them of everything they love.

'I'm so sorry,' I say, turning to face her. 'About what I told your mum when I came over. It was completely inappropriate and insensitive. I should never have said anything.'

'Yeah, yeah,' she says, on the brink of a wry smile that makes me think of Lara. 'But do you really believe it? I mean, that's some pretty crazy theory you've got there.'

'I don't know what I believe any more.'

She drags long and hard on the vape. 'I lost someone once. I know what it can do to your mind. I used to look everywhere for him. I would think he'd come back and then . . . poof. He was gone again.'

'Who was he?'

Her smile is full of sadness. 'My brother.'

I smile weakly, and look down at my shoes.

'I lost him that day he got hit by lightning. And you know what, Neve? When I got the call tonight to say he'd been run over, there was a tiny part of me that was *excited*. Do you know why? Because I thought there might be an outside chance his wiring had been knocked back into place, somehow, and I might just get back the Ash I'd known all my life.' She takes her phone out and swipes into it, then passes it to me.

She's opened up an album of photos, all of Ash, albeit much younger. But I don't recognise this version of him at all. Bare chested and covered head to toe in body paint, tongue out, running at the camera. Standing on top of a building, a lit flare in one hand. Mid-air, jumping from a craggy clifftop. On stage somewhere, arm in arm with a friend, singing. In handcuffs, being led away by the police, laughing over his shoulder. Passed out, with various affectionate insults scrawled all over his face in what looks to be eyeliner. Part covered by a pile of coats on a sofa, again passed out. Dancing at a festival, eyes rolling, two cigarettes hanging from his mouth. Running bare-arsed down a European street. Dancing with a traffic cone on his head.

I wonder how many of these moments Ash remembers. Is this why he brushes off any mention of his past life? Because if he *is* Jamie, he would have no recollection of any of it.

I pass the phone back to Gabi.

'That guy doesn't look at all like the Ash you know, does he?'

I am torn between acknowledging her pain and reassuring her. 'He said he just . . . grew up. No offence, I don't—'

'It wasn't a "growth" thing. The change was too sudden. Too dramatic. It literally happened overnight. One day he was dancing on top of buildings in the rain; the next, he'd decided to ditch everything – his career aspirations, his friends, his family. And the only explanation I can think of is that something came between us that we don't understand. Something . . . other-worldly. Some anomaly of science. And that's coming from a science-lover.'

I can hardly believe it. 'You think . . . I might be right?'

'That depends. Tell me what your boyfriend was like. The one who died, I mean.'

So I do. I describe all the intricacies and hallmarks of who Jamie was. His innate tenderness, his dry humour. His passion for architecture. Where he hoped to live. Who he wanted to be. I open my phone and show her the list I made of all the ways in which he was similar to Ash.

When I'm done, Gabi puts her vape away then pulls her cardigan a little tighter, her breath making mist in the air. 'See, your man was the opposite of the Ash I knew. Ash was a livewire, a joker, loved a prank, would never shut up. We all thought he was going to be famous one day. Like, a household name. We just didn't know for what.' She laughs faintly. 'I guess he sort of got there, with the lightning strike and the papers and all that. Which I actually thought was funny at first. Like, the kind of thing that could only happen to Ash.'

We say nothing more for a couple of moments, until the silence is dismantled by the wail of an ambulance siren.

'What do your parents think about what happened?' I ask her. 'Your mum didn't say much when I was talking the other night.'

Gabi smiles. 'No. I don't think she *quite* bought what you were telling her. Well done for trying, though. You delivered quite the speech, apparently.'

I shut my eyes briefly. 'I know.'

'It's okay. I'm assuming she kind of dragged it out of you? Mum has a knack for doing that. I've always thought she missed her vocation as an MI6 interrogator.'

'Kind of,' I admit. 'But it's not her fault. I didn't have to say anything.'

Gabi shrugs. 'Well, if it helps, you were only saying what I think, every day: that it doesn't make sense. That something isn't right.'

Vindication sits bolt upright in my chest. 'You really think there might be something in it?'

'Maybe. But as you know, my brother definitely doesn't.' She frowns, chews her bottom lip. 'Look, Ash has had two fairly major near-misses in his life now, and countless minor ones. Tonight, it was as if he became the brother I lost all over again. And I have to be honest . . . it doesn't feel that great. So maybe he's right. Maybe I do just need to accept that he's . . . a better version of who he was before.'

'Maybe,' I say neutrally, not wanting to derail her train of thought, because I'm desperate to see where it leads.

'And maybe you need to accept who he is, too. Whether he's really your ex, or not. Because I think you make Ash happy, and I think he does the same for you. And ultimately . . . I'd rather have a different version of him than no brother at all.'

'What are you saying?'

She sighs heavily, like she's encountering the full weight of the last decade all over again. 'I'm saying that whoever Ash is now, I have a feeling that without you by his side, I'm pretty sure all is lost. So, can you two please just sort it out? Because I'll be straight with you – I would really like him to make it to old age, and I think you can probably help with that.'

'Okay,' I tell her, my mind a hailstorm of conflicting emotions. 'Okay. I'll try.'

41.

Then

A few nights after dinner with Jamie's parents, I knew.
I came back from the bathroom in the middle of the
night and sat down on the edge of our bed. The air was still,
unruffled by breeze. Through our open window, I could
hear traffic on the ring road, the sound of people walking
home from the pub. From somewhere close by, music was
playing, the incessant gallop of a repeating bass line.

'Jamie,' I whispered.

He rolled over and groaned.

'Jamie.'

I could feel rather than see his eyes snap open in the
gloom. 'You okay?'

'I think . . . I think I'm having a miscarriage.'

The spotting had started two days before. I'd been
hoping, praying, that it was nothing to worry about. But
now the cramps had come, and the pain was lower, heavier.
The bleeding was brighter now, too. An alert, an alarm.

He snapped on the bedside light, then sat up bare-
chested, blinking into its glare. He looked disorientated
and shocked, like he'd woken midway through a burglary.

It was theft of a kind, I thought. Something was being stolen against my will.

I was already smarting with shame for not having been brave enough to tell him. For this being how he found out. For him learning about, and losing, our baby at exactly the same time.

It had been ten days since the pregnancy test. Ten days of keeping it secret. In that moment, I questioned myself. Wondered if the miscarriage was my fault, somehow. If all the lying and evading and pretending had put too much stress on my body.

'What . . . What do you mean?' His eyes and voice were thick with dismay.

'I'm pregnant.' My mouth felt dry, stale from sleep. 'I've been . . . pregnant.'

He shuffled close to me then, grabbed my hand like I was in danger of floating away on an invisible current. 'You . . . can't be, Neve. How can you be?'

'I did a test. It was positive.'

'Fuck.'

'I didn't know how to tell you.' My breath snagged in my throat, became a hot coil of pain.

'Neve,' he began, but then grew quiet, like there was no language suitable for what he wanted to say.

He was right. There were no words.

We called for advice. They told us to wait, monitor the blood loss, go to A&E if the bleeding got heavy, or if we were concerned.

I am concerned, I wanted to scream at the operator. *I am concerned that I am losing our baby, and there is apparently nothing anyone can do about it.*

I took painkillers and went back to bed, but neither of us could sleep. I felt clammy and too warm, though whether that was just because Norwich had been experiencing a minor heatwave that week, I wasn't sure. I turned my face to our primrose-yellow wall, and Jamie tucked himself behind me and stroked my hair. It was all he could do, we both knew that. My body was braced against the violence of the cramps, the dizzying pain of losing what I already loved.

I wanted Lara there, too. I wanted Jamie on one side of me, and Lara on the other. But I knew this crisis belonged to me and Jamie. I didn't want to make him feel like he wasn't everything I needed in that moment.

'Why didn't you tell me?' he asked, voice muddy with emotion. I was glad, for once, that I couldn't see his face.

'I didn't know . . . if you'd want it.'

'God, Neve.'

'What would you have said? If I had told you.'

The slightest breath of hesitation, warm against my neck, though he didn't break from stroking my hair. 'I would have said . . . "Wow, we made a baby, and I'm . . . absolutely terrified. But I'm also happy. It's the scariest kind of happiness I've ever felt." That's what I would have said.'

It was everything I'd hoped for. He would have wanted it too, and the cruelty of what was happening struck me all over again.

Though dulled by the painkillers, my back and stomach were still cramping. I tried not to think about what my body was doing, entirely without permission.

'This isn't fair,' I gasped then, emotions rip-tiding through me.

He kept stroking my hair. It was helping, that gentle, repetitive motion, like a constant whisper, *I'm here. I'm here. I'm here.*

'This felt right to me. Even though . . . it was a surprise, it felt right, Jamie.' I couldn't stop thinking about the surge of joy I had experienced when I turned that stick over.

'I love you,' he whispered then. 'We'll get through this, Neve. I promise. We'll get through it together.'

An image of his mother that night at the restaurant drifted uninvited into my mind, and in that moment, I realised I hated her. For having tried to buy my complicity. For her lack of solidarity. For having, in her darker moments – I was sure about this – wished this loss on me.

It was ironic, I thought, that I'd been so envious of Jamie's family for all the years I'd known him. Like pressing my nose up against a misty window at Christmas time, desperate to soak up some of the warmth and contentment and intimacy I'd imagined they all shared.

But I knew now that he'd been raised by a monster, and he didn't even realise. Even my own mother – a woman the police had once threatened to section – would never have done to anyone what Debra did to me that night.

For the first time in my life, I felt sorry for Jamie. For the lie he'd been sold on the loving family unit he thought he was part of, which turned out to be so fragile it had malfunctioned at the merest hint of pressure.

★   ★   ★

The next morning, I bumped into Lara in the kitchen. I was clutching a hot-water bottle. My eyes were raw from crying.

Jamie had already left the house. He'd felt bad about it, but he had a seminar on climate classification he said he couldn't afford to miss.

Lara didn't even need to ask. She just looked at me, and I nodded, then burst into tears.

She took the day off from uni and made me chocolate pudding for breakfast and we put on *Gavin & Stacey* and curled up on the sofa together. Her at one end, me at the other, our legs entwined, the pads of our feet touching.

'Do you want me to call your mum?' she asked, at one point.

I shook my head. 'She's busy.'

'With what?'

'She's in trouble with the police again. They caught her smashing Bev's car up.'

'Bloody Daniela,' was all she said.

Over the course of that day, Lara would intermittently reach out and squeeze my hand or my calf, and ask if I wanted anything. But I didn't need anything. Just to have her there, by my side, was enough.

42.

Now

When I get to work on the Monday after Ash's accident, word of what happened is all around the office.

I didn't end up seeing him at the hospital that night. Ed and Juliet were there, understandably in much distress, and then Gabi started to wonder if maybe she should sound Ash out first about me seeing him, after he came out of theatre. I felt too embarrassed to face his parents anyway, so I decided to head home. It broke my heart to leave him there, but the last thing I wanted to do was stress him out, or cause a scene.

Parveen pulls me into a meeting room on the pretext of running through proposed amendments to some plans we've received for a former watermill. Her eyes are wide with concern. 'Is Ash okay?'

'I think so,' I say blankly. 'But I haven't seen him.'

'Rumour is he was absolutely off his tits, got into a fight and then just fell into the road. God, Neve – he might have been killed.'

'How do you know all this?'

'Jemma at Crave told Ryan at Tunstalls, who told Lexie,

who told Martin, who told me.'

'Do you know who he was with?' I've been wondering this, because I can't imagine any of Ash's gentle, unassuming friends standing by as he got into a state like that.

She shakes her head. 'Nope. And no-one knows how the fight started.'

I swear softly, pressing the heels of my palms against my forehead, struggling to visualise Ash being aggressive towards anyone.

'It was proper high drama, apparently. After the car hit him. People screaming and shouting and panicking. Sirens everywhere. Jemma said everyone thought he was dead.' Parveen reaches over and gives my hand a squeeze. 'I'm really sorry, Neve.'

'Yeah,' I say, my voice by now just an echo of itself. 'Me too.'

I ring his buzzer on Wednesday night, after Gabi gives me the all-clear. The building is draped in a white-gold waterfall of Christmas lights. It makes my heart ache for the December we might have been sharing together.

I didn't know what to bring. Flowers didn't feel right. (*Congratulations on living to tell the tale!*) Grapes or chocolates seemed like something I'd take my nan. So I opted for a bottle of brandy. Medicinal, if nothing else – and it would at least give him something to swig from if he wanted to take the edge off seeing me again.

'It's me,' I say, when he answers the buzzer.

A short silence, then, 'Hello.'

'Can I come up?'

He doesn't reply, just buzzes me in.

When he opens the door, a tidal surge of feelings assaults me. He's on crutches, with a black eye and a leg in plaster. I instantly want to grab him and bury my face against his shoulder, kiss him, tell him I still love him. But I know I can't.

Instead, I swallow it all down and say, 'How are you doing?'

'Ah, okay. Mates are rallying round, and all that.' He is unshaven, with unkempt hair and dark half-moons beneath his eyes. He's wearing a crumpled T-shirt and cargo shorts, I assume because of the cast. He looks like he's just been helicoptered away from a conflict zone.

'I'm so sorry, Ash.'

He nods, then – to my immense relief – shuffles aside to let me in.

I follow him slowly through to the living area, removing the brandy bottle from my bag and placing it on the kitchen counter. 'For whenever,' I say.

'How about right now?'

I feel a lick of relief. He is calling a truce: we can share a drink, maybe talk. I follow him to the sofa with the bottle and two glasses.

Being here is bittersweet, though. I have missed this apartment – albeit it's not quite the sanctuary I remember. Everywhere smells slightly stale. Surfaces are strewn with takeaway cartons and unwashed plates, empty mugs and grubby wine glasses. A lot of his stuff is still in boxes: things he'd packed up for bringing to my house before we parted ways. He clearly hasn't touched them again in the weeks since. I have no idea how to interpret that. Is there still hope for us? Or has he just not been able to face it?

And the Edward Hopper's nowhere to be seen. I wonder if he's got rid of it – offloaded it to a mate, or chucked it in a skip.

'Sorry. Bit of a mess in here. I wasn't expecting . . . Would you mind . . .?' he says, indicating the newspapers and bowls and jumpers and socks strewn across the sofa.

'Sure,' I say gently, picking up the stuff and clearing a space for us both.

I hate to see him like this. For the first time since knowing him, I am glimpsing what I can only assume is the person he used to be – chaotic and impulsive, someone who careers from day to day, who makes poor choices and bad calls, then has to suffer the consequences.

I pour us each a double brandy, then tentatively hold my glass to his. 'To your health.'

He laughs, but like it's slipped out unintended.

Without looking at each other, we both half drain our glasses. The liquid torches my throat, fireballs its way to my stomach.

'You smell nice,' I tell him, because he does, despite the dishevelment. It's a scent I don't recognise, fresh and sweetly aquatic.

'Thought I'd take a break from the Tom Ford,' he says gruffly.

Oh God. I must have told his mum that he and Jamie smelt the same. I don't even remember saying that.

'Are you okay?' I ask him, feeling chastened. 'Physically,

I mean.'

'Ah, fine. They fixed my leg, reinflated my lung, told me off for walking into traffic. It could have been a lot worse.'

I swallow and nod. 'Apparently everyone was worried you were . . . you know. Dead.' It's hard enough to think it, let alone say it out loud.

A brittle smile. 'Ah, the good old Norwich grapevine. Can nobody get wasted and pick a fight and get hit by a car in private any more?'

I smile faintly. 'And you made the paper again.'

'I bet I did.'

'Who was the fight with?'

He rubs his face. 'No idea.'

'I came to the hospital.'

He nods. 'Gabi told me. You should have stayed for a drink. The tea in that place is pretty special.'

'Maybe next time.'

He meets my eye. 'Yeah, maybe.'

'How long till you're back on your feet?'

'A few months, they think.'

'What about work?'

'I'm going back next week. I don't want to miss too much. They've not got an awful lot of sympathy for me, if I'm honest.'

'Are you . . . managing okay?'

He looks directly at me now, eyes damp and fierce. 'No, Neve. I'm not managing okay at all.'

I reach out and take his hand, squeezing it so hard I risk adding to his list of injuries. 'Me neither.'

'This whole thing is mad. I've never felt about anyone

the way I feel about you.'

I fight tears, but I don't know what to say. I can't say, *Me neither*, because we both know it wouldn't be true. But it is true that I hate doing life without him. That I'm not sure I'll ever be the same, if we're not together.

A couple of moments pass. The flat is excruciatingly quiet. Ash usually has music playing, or the windows flung open to let in the sounds of the city. Tonight, the hush feels almost unbearable.

'Do you want to know what I was doing, when I got hit by that car?'

I take another sip of brandy. 'Gabi said you were drunk.'

'Off my face, thinking about you. About us.' He frowns. 'Don't get me wrong, I'm not blaming you, not at all. None of this is your fault, obviously. I just . . . Nothing seems to make sense any more, without you.'

I want to tell him it's all going to be okay. But how can I, when I'm not sure it will be?

'It was bad. I was the drunkest I've been in . . . maybe ever. Even back in the day.'

'Gabi told me all about your wild-child ways.'

'I bet she did. Weird that my sister feels nostalgic for a version of me that definitely wouldn't have made it to thirty.'

I think about what Gabi said to me at the hospital. *I'd rather have a different version of him than no brother at all.*

I finish my brandy, shake my head. 'I just . . . I still don't get it, Ash.'

'Get what?'

'You. Jamie. Your accident. The person you became. Any

of it.'

He mirrors me, swigging back the last of his drink before reaching over to top us both up. 'Well, whatever happened, Neve, I still don't believe I have the ghost of your ex-boyfriend living inside me. Because ghosts don't exist. They just don't.'

I'll get nowhere with convincing him. Or even discussing it. I can see that now. There is nothing left for me to do but show him, somehow, how much I still love him.

I set down my glass. Our gazes fuse. I lean in, relieved when he doesn't turn away. We kiss hesitantly for a few seconds. His lips are glazed with brandy. And then he teases my mouth apart with his tongue, and I respond. I have missed this so much, these moments of intense, volcanic wanting. He moves a hand to my chin, grasping it gently, tipping my face up to his, bettering the angle for both of us, the kiss growing deeper, hungrier. Our breathing becomes ragged. I run a hand over his leg, begin to lift his T-shirt.

And then, without warning, he pulls back. 'Ouch.'

'Oh, God. Sorry. Are you okay? Where does it hurt?'

The wince becomes a smile. He shakes his head, then looks away, takes a few deep breaths. 'Ah, Neve. Come on. Don't ask me that.'

'Well,' I whisper, smiling back at him, 'tell me. Where does it hurt?' I lean towards him again, but this time he dodges the kiss, shuffling fully away.

I stay where I am. I don't need to ask what's wrong: it's written all over his face.

'Neve, I . . . I love you so much, and this feels so . . . But this thing about Jamie . . . I can't live with that. I need to be with someone who loves me for who I am. You know that, right?'

I nod, because of course I do.

'But you know what's crazy?' he says, eyes blazing suddenly. 'It's *us* who're supposed to be together, Neve, not you and him – and it kills me that you'll never, ever see it.'

My mind flails madly for lifebelts. 'Okay, what if – just humour me for a minute – what if I could find someone who agrees with me? Who could back up what I believe? A scientist. Or a doctor. Someone who can categorially prove I'm not mad. Even your sister—'

'Even my sister what?'

'Even your sister thinks there might be something in it.'

He shakes his head. 'My sister thinks there might be something in those conspiracies about Elvis being alive.'

'But she *is* a doctor. A scientist.'

He sighs now, like even the idea of loving me again is exhausting.

And love shouldn't feel that way.

Still. I have to try. Just one more time. 'If I can find someone who can back up what I'm saying, could we at least talk about it?'

He looks at me for a long moment, then says, 'No, Neve.' His eyes are varnished with tears now. I can tell he is fighting to hold it together.

Suddenly, I know what I have to do.

'You're right, about this being wrong,' I realise, out loud.

'Of course you can't live like this. Why should you? And actually, neither can I.'

'Neve—'

I get to my feet. 'I'm going to . . . try to figure all this out.'

'Hang on, that's not good enough. Where the hell does that leave me?'

'I just need some time.'

'And I need clarity.'

I swallow. 'Look, if you . . . meet someone in the meantime, or you decide you never want to see me again, that's okay. I mean, not okay – that's not what I want – but I'd understand. I'm not asking you to wait for me, Ash, because I actually don't know if I'll be able to get past this, or work it out. But I'm going to try. I promise.'

'No. You need to answer me this – and . . . be truthful. Don't just say what you think I want to hear.'

The space between us is a snowdrift of silence.

'Do you love me? If you say yes, I'll wait for you.'

My heart cracks apart even as I answer him. 'I don't know if it's wholly you I love, or—'

'Right.' I watch him struggle to reply. 'Well, at least I know where I stand.'

My eyes fill with fresh tears. 'I'm just trying to be honest.'

'First time for everything, I guess.'

43.

'What if you just faked it?' Lara says, when we meet for Sunday lunch a few days later at a pub near her mum's house. She's just back from Rome, and we've spent the past half-hour looking through photos of her and Felix meandering around the world's most romantic city.

'What do you mean?'

'I mean, fake it till you make it. Tell Ash you've forgotten about Jamie, get back together, and then . . . over time, it gradually becomes true. Until you wake up one day and realise that what you have with Ash far surpasses what you ever had with Jamie. It's got to happen one day. It's practically science.'

I blink at her flippancy. If it was that easy, I'd have done it long ago. Thinking about Jamie all the time has been exhausting. It's not what I want. But I don't know how to stop.

She looks past me and out through the window, onto the roundabout and main road. Her face looks pinched and peaky in the wintery light. She seems on edge today. Not with me, necessarily. Just the world at large. She was brisk with the waiter earlier, which isn't at all like the Lara I once knew. She's never been into chastising people who can't argue back: we've both worked in customer service jobs, and have experienced more than our fair share of being told off by people in salmon-coloured trousers complaining about their salads being cold.

I guess taking care of her mum must be getting to her more than I thought.

I frown. 'Ash is a good person. I can't lie to him like that.'

'You really think you're going to find a scientist or doctor who can prove your theory?'

'I might.'

'Well, if you do, remember to check their alma mater isn't the University of WTF.'

I recoil slightly. 'Okay . . . I will?'

She shuts her eyes briefly. 'Sorry. I'm tired. Sorry. Look – in the nicest possible way, maybe before you try to find a doctor or a scientist, you should talk to a counsellor.'

'Yeah, maybe.' I feel faintly nauseous at the thought of being confirmed mad, instead of it merely being suspected. I set down my drink. 'Anyway, are you okay? You hardly ate.'

When we lived together, we used to have a league table of the best Sunday roasts in Norwich, pinned up on a piece of graph paper in the living room. It was Jamie's thing, really, because Lara and I were usually too hard up to buy lunch out. But he liked to treat us.

She wrinkles her nose. 'Just knackered.'

'You do look a bit translucent.'

She smiles faintly. 'And you look like a person with a broken heart.'

'I'd like to come and see your mum.' I'm not too sure how Corinne feels about me these days, given I blanked her daughter for nearly a decade, blamed her for Jamie's death and failed to be there when Billy died. I'm not sure *I'd* want to see me, if I were Corinne.

'She'd love that,' Lara says. 'She always adored you, Neve. That never changed.'

'Work's going to be a bit full on this week, but . . . next weekend?'

'Any time. Whenever. You know you're always welcome.' She reaches for my hand and squeezes it hard, in a way that feels like she is trying to tell me something.

'Lar. Is she dying?' The thought is almost unbearable, even as I'm saying it out loud. It hasn't occurred to me before now – I've been so caught up in my own problems. But now that I think about it, why else would Lara have taken extended leave from work to move back to Norwich and help out for so long?

But Lara just smiles weakly. 'Christ, let's hope not.'

That night, I head to Mum's. The house is freezing, and she's tucked up in the living room beneath a blanket, a glass of something amber-coloured in her hand. She's watching *Strictly Come Dancing*. It's one of her favourite programmes, because some guy once told her she had the rhythm to make it as a dancer. Despite this clearly being a line to get her into bed, she's never forgotten it, and enjoys behaving every year like she's judge number five.

'Oh,' she says, glancing up as I come in. 'Thought you were Ralph.'

I'm surprised to see she's sitting on a new, crushed-velvet silver sofa. 'Mum. What's this?'

'*Strictly*. It hasn't been very good this year. Aren't they supposed to be celebrities?'

'Not the TV. The sofa.'

She smiles and strokes it with one hand. 'Someone at the pub was selling it. And my old one had all those broken springs, so I thought, why not.'

'How much?'

'Couple of hundred quid.'

'Mum, I could have got you a gorgeous sofa.'

'What's wrong with this one?'

Perhaps she's seen a version of it on Bev's Instagram. When Bev got a leopard-print beach cover-up, Mum started wearing an identical one, for pottering round the house. And when Bev dropped the name of her collagen-retinol-whatever night cream, a pot of it showed up in Mum's bathroom the following week. 'It doesn't really . . . go, does it?'

She surveys the room and shrugs. 'Go with what?'

Fair point. This room is a mishmash of peeling William Morris wallpaper, a peach deep-pile carpet straight out of the 1970s and some wonky white flatpack furniture. Not for the first time, I wonder if my dream of restoring this house together will ever actually happen. Mum just doesn't view it in the same way I do. Its character and charm completely pass her by.

Perhaps, after all these years, I need to finally accept that's never going to change.

It's only three weeks till Christmas, but she hasn't got any decorations up. After Dad left, she never bothered, because Christmas is apparently only worth celebrating if you have a man by your side.

I sit reluctantly down on the sofa. The velvet grates slightly beneath me.

'Whisky?' Mum asks, nodding at the bottle on the sideboard.

I shake my head.

'How's Ash?'

'Not good.'

She lowers the volume on the TV. 'What happened?'

My instinct is to make something up and change the subject. But then I remember that nothing I can say could ever out-crazy the way she behaved over Dad. I should just tell her the truth. Lying is starting to become too exhausting. 'This is going to sound weird, but when I first met Ash, I thought . . . I thought he was Jamie. There's this thing called walk-ins, where—'

'And he didn't like that.'

I blink. 'Mum, listen. I honestly think that Ash . . . might be Jamie. I know it sounds mad, but when I met him—'

'I know. I heard you talking to Ralph about it.'

'What? When?'

'Oh, I don't know. A few months ago, maybe.'

That Saturday I came over, back in June, when Ralph was eating soup and Mum was blaming her alcohol habit on open bars. 'You heard me . . . telling Ralph I thought Jamie walked into Ash's body?'

'Yes. I heard everything. And I must admit, I did think you were talking a load of—'

'So that time Ash and I came over here, and you were drunk and you kept calling him Jamie . . .'

'I suppose,' she says, with a heavy sigh, 'I thought I could make you see sense.'

'You what?'

She shrugs, sipping her whisky. 'You were always so *obsessed* with Jamie. I wanted to make you see how ridiculous it was. I thought we might be able to . . . I don't know. Have a laugh about it, I suppose. That it might wake you up, somehow.'

My breath catches in my throat. 'Why would you—'

'Because all these years later, you still can't forget him. And for what it's worth, Neve, I never thought your relationship with Jamie was healthy.'

I deep-breathe in that way people do when they're trying not to punch someone. 'Um, in what way, exactly?'

'You were like I was, with your dad. Infatuated.'

'No. I *loved* Jamie. Massive difference.' Goose pimples have broken out across my skin. I glance at the gas fire, which is always dormant, and wonder what the risk to life would be of switching it on. Probably high. I expect we'd both explode, though hopefully Mum would go first.

'But all these years later, you're still not over him.'

'Well, that's love, isn't it?'

She shakes her head. 'No, it's obsession. I could never get over your dad, either. Not for years afterwards. So it turns out, we're not so different, you and I. They'd have given *you* a restraining order by now, if Jamie was still alive.'

My mother's said a lot of stupid stuff over the years, but I think this just about tops it.

I find my voice, though it comes out in flakes and layers. 'This is *nothing* like that.'

'Yes, it is. It's our fatal flaw, Neve. We get in too deep.'

'No. I'm nothing like you.'

'Oh, you're more like me than you think.'

'I can't believe . . . you knew I thought this, all along.'

She knocks back the last of her whisky, and I watch her gaze stray straight away to the bottle on the sideboard, eyeing up her next refill. 'Except there's nothing to know, is there? Not really. You know Ash isn't Jamie, deep down. You know that in your heart, Neve. You want him to be, but you know he's not.'

'I *don't*. And I wouldn't expect you to understand.'

'You know, I don't think Jamie ever loved you in quite the same way you loved him.'

'Mum, I'm serious now—'

'I know you lost the baby, darling.'

Ice plates my stomach. 'What?'

'Lara told me. Well, actually, she didn't *tell* me. I guessed. You hadn't been round for a while and you weren't answering your phone and so I rang Lara, and she said you'd been unwell, and I asked her what with, and she said she didn't feel it was her place to tell me. And so I guessed. Straight away.'

For once, the anger I feel isn't directed at Lara. I can hardly blame her if my mother chose that moment to demonstrate perception for the first time in her life.

'You never thought to mention this to me?' *You never thought to wrap me up in your arms and kiss me and tell me how sorry you were and that your heart was breaking along with mine?*

'It wasn't my place. You obviously didn't want me to know. Though I do wish you'd felt able to talk to me, of course.'

I think resentfully back to that summer, to the months before Jamie died. 'That was the year Bev kept calling the police on you. Remember? You were a mess. How could I talk to you?'

It had been years since my father left, and she was still so furious, the police had to officially tell her not to be.

But it's been nearly a decade now. And what am I doing? Self-destructing like she did – just breaking hearts instead of stuff.

I reach for a tissue from the box on the coffee table and dab my eyes. Being unexpectedly wrenched back to the trauma of losing the baby is hitting me hard.

Mum frowns slightly. 'I am sorry, Neve. I wish I could have been there for you more.'

'Why wish it? You could have been. Nothing was stopping you.'

Wordlessly, Mum removes the blanket from her lap and places it on mine. It feels soft, warmed by her body. The gesture brings fresh tears to my eyes. It's the kind of thing Corinne would have done.

'Did Jamie support you, when you told him about the baby? Was he there for you?'

I swallow away the memories of those last months. 'What does it matter, now?'

'It matters,' says Mum, leaning keenly forward like she does whenever she's about to dispatch some pop psychology, 'because Ash is a perfectly nice boy, who seems desperate to love you. Yet all you can think about – all these years later – is Jamie Fraser.'

'Jamie was the love of my life.'

'Jamie's gone, sweetheart.'

'No,' I say fiercely, though I can feel my resolve buckling like metal in the fierce heat of my heart. 'You don't know what you're talking about. No.'

44.

'So I suppose,' I say, looking around the counsellor's office, 'that's why I'm here. I was hoping you might be able to help me ... prove myself to Ash. I'd like to persuade him I'm not going mad.'

Meena appears unruffled, like people say this kind of thing to her all the time. 'And how would you define "mad", Neve?'

'Someone ... who no longer has a grip on reality.'

For the past half hour, I've been telling her about Ash being Jamie, barely breaking for breath, and now my head feels like fog, my mouth tacky from talking.

I survey the room we're in on the top floor of an ancient narrow building in the city centre. It's calming and quite olde worlde, with creaking floorboards, sloping walls and lattice-paned windows. But I'm sitting in a chair which bounces disconcertingly whenever I move. It inclines naturally backwards, and would, I suspect, take some effort to climb out of. So I couldn't make a quick getaway, even if I wanted to.

Still. The room is quiet, and the walls are thick, which means I don't have to worry about being overheard.

'Is there anyone else who you think believes you're "mad", Neve?'

321

Meena is slightly built, with hair pulled into a French plait. She has very large eyes that are affecting as searchlights. Somehow, they make me want to confess all my secrets.

'Well, Ash, obviously. And his parents. And my mum. And probably Lara too. But there's just no other explanation for all these coincidences. The similarities. And only I can see it.'

There is a short silence. Meena taps the edge of her notebook with her pen. 'Neve, have you ever heard of something called confirmation bias?'

I nod. My hands are folded in my lap, like I'm being interviewed. 'It's where you look for evidence to prove your theory about something.'

She nods back. 'I wonder if this may be your coping strategy, Neve. Instead of confronting your grief and working through it – which may feel too overwhelming – you're looking for ways to avoid it. For it not to be real. For Jamie to still be alive. Does that make sense?'

'It would, if you could explain all the similarities and coincidences and million ways in which Ash *is* Jamie. I haven't invented them. They're right there, in front of me.'

'But is Ash Jamie,' she says, carefully, 'or have you perhaps have fallen in love with someone who closely resembles Jamie, who's helping to ease your grief?'

'No,' I insist. 'I lost Jamie nearly ten whole years ago. I don't need to ease it, not now. Ash appeared out of nowhere. It wasn't as if I was looking for him. I'd actually stopped . . . thinking about Jamie, pretty much, before I met Ash.'

Meena shifts in her chair. The floorboards creak slightly.

'But would you say you ever came to terms with Jamie's death? Did you fully grieve him?'

I think back to the dark, cyclonic aftermath of the accident. Cutting Lara off. Jamie's family refusing to let me attend the funeral. His dad coming to the house, and taking his stuff. Thieving it, really.

It had always felt easier to blame Lara for what was happening than to focus on the pain of losing Jamie.

'Maybe not. I don't know.'

'And the miscarriage,' she says gently. 'That's grief as well. No less painful. No less valid. Did you ever talk to anyone about that?'

I talked to Jamie, of course, but then he was gone. And soon afterwards, Lara was gone, too. 'A bit. Not much.'

'Neve, what's been happening with you and Ash indicates to me that you never fully worked through all these very complicated and intense emotions.'

I feel my body bristle. 'But this is all missing the point. Why did Ash suddenly want to become an architect, after his accident? Why does he live in the *exact apartment* that Jamie was hoping to live in? Why did Ash take me to Amsterdam? Why does he kiss me just like Jamie did? Which I feel bad about saying, by the way, but it's true. Why did Ash's family tell me he was like a different person after the lightning strike? Why does he love the exact same music, artists, coffee, aftershave? Why is Ash and Jamie's handwriting *exactly* the same? If you can explain any of that, then maybe I can accept that Ash . . . isn't Jamie. But you can't. You can't explain it, because *Ash is the person Jamie was meant to become.*'

Meena waits for a long time before answering. But when she does, it's to offer up precisely none of the rationale I'm hoping for. 'Is it also worth considering that if Jamie was alive today, he might in fact be nothing at all like the man you knew nearly a decade ago?'

I stare at her. 'No. I mean, he would be. That's what I'm telling you: Ash is who Jamie was going to become.'

'Or maybe you wouldn't recognise him at all.'

'Of course I would.'

She challenges this with a suggestive shrug, a momentary pout of disagreement. 'Maybe not. People change. Maybe if you met Jamie Fraser today, and the two of you went for a drink together, you might think you had nothing in common at all any more. Maybe, for example, Jamie wouldn't have become an architect.'

'He loved architecture,' I say fiercely. 'It was all he ever wanted to do.'

She presses her lips together, sets down her notebook, steeples her fingers. 'Okay. But let's just . . . explore an alternative reality for a moment, shall we?'

Even though I really don't want to, I nod, because I suppose this is what I'm paying her for.

'Come with me on this, Neve.' Her expression is thoughtful. 'So let's say, just as an example . . . Jamie dropped out of his master's degree. Maybe he was getting fed up of studying, and all his friends had already started earning money, so he decided to get a job at . . . one of the big investment banks.'

Never would have happened, says the voice in my head, but I don't interrupt her. Defiance and curiosity are playing tug-of-war in my stomach, and right now, the latter has the edge.

'And let's say . . . he's made some new friends at this bank, and he decides he's really into what they're into, which is . . . swish bars and driving nice cars and going to the gym, for example. And perhaps European city breaks no longer really do it for him, and he's into . . . skiing holidays instead. And he doesn't read much these days, especially not books about architecture, and the Edward Hopper painting is no more significant to him than . . . a one-time gift from his grandmother. Maybe it's even gathering dust in an attic or cupboard somewhere. And he's now into . . . opera music, and coffee gives him migraines, and he can't remember the last time he cooked. In fact, he's decided he loathes cooking.' She pauses, fixing me again with those heat-seeking eyes of hers. 'I'm obviously playing with stereotypes, here, Neve – but do you get my point?'

I sit very still for a long time, staring at the rug beneath my feet. I knot my fingers as I force myself – really push myself – to at least try to see where she's coming from. 'I think so,' I say, eventually.

'You believe that Ash is who Jamie was meant to become. But the reality is, you've no way at all of knowing who Jamie would have grown up to be. If you were to meet him today, there's a chance you might not even recognise him.'

'But Ash's accident,' I say. 'It happened at exactly the same time as Jamie's, just a street away. And after that, Ash completely changed. How can that be coincidence too?'

'People can change drastically, after major life events. I would say that was entirely normal, Neve. It still doesn't mean Ash is Jamie. Remember confirmation bias?'

'So, I guess you're not going to argue my case to Ash for me?'

She shoots me a kind smile. 'I've got a suggestion that I think is even better. I want to see you next week, and I'd like you to spend the time between now and then making a list of all the ways in which Ash is *different* to Jamie. Okay?'

'That'll be a short list, but okay. I'll try.'

Our time is up. I gather my bag and coat and haul myself out of the chair to leave.

'Neve?' Meena says, as I'm heading to the door.

'Yes?'

'When the human body is struck by lightning, it takes an unbelievable hit. Did you know that a lightning strike can contain millions of volts?'

I nod, because of course I knew that. Well, not *exactly*, but everyone understands that lightning equals serious voltage.

'Many people don't survive lightning strikes. But if they do, their internal circuitry will most likely be a bit jumbled up. It makes sense that something that forceful will alter you on some level, if you get in its way. Ash is undoubtedly lucky he didn't die. But I would suggest that there's nothing mystical about that. No more than ... weather itself. In fact, it's the exact opposite of mystical. It's science. So it's worth considering there's nothing strange at all about the fact Ash was a different person before and after surviving such a huge event.'

'How do you know all this?' I ask, even though I get that you're supposed to pretend your counsellor's part robot and doesn't have a personal perspective on anything.

But Meena doesn't seem too bothered. 'Actually, I trained as a meteorologist. So I know a bit about physics and weather. But as I grew older, I decided that wasn't my calling. Not that you'd have known it, when I was eighteen. I'd always been determined to work for the Met Office. It was all I used to talk about.'

I meet her eye and smile. 'Okay.'

'Like I said. People can change, Neve.'

I nod, but say nothing further.

'Get working on that list of differences, okay?'

'All right,' I tell her. 'I'll try.'

45.

Then

It was August. In the middle of the night, one Saturday, my phone rang.

'Lara?'

She was crying. She couldn't speak.

'What's happened? Lara? Can you tell me what's happened?'

Eventually, she said, 'I told him no. I *said* no.'

'Okay.' My biggest fear was on the verge of coming to life. 'Okay. You're okay. It's going to be all right. Where are you?'

She was on the other side of the city, alone in a postcode she didn't know.

'Stay on the phone,' I said. 'I'm coming to get you.'

I slipped on a pair of trainers, grabbed my wallet, gripped the phone, and ran.

I flagged down a taxi on Earlham Road and went to find her.

We didn't speak for the whole journey home. I just held her hand, while she stared out of the window.

Back at the house, I sat her down on the sofa and made us both tea. I found a blanket and draped it over her, pressed the mug into her hands, took a seat next to her.

'Talk to me,' I said.

She drew a deep, shuddering breath. 'I can't remember his name.'

'Did he hurt you?'

She shook her head. 'But I could tell that he . . . wanted to.'

'Tell me what happened.'

She let out a breath. 'We got talking. In the club. He asked me back to his. But when we got there I realised . . .' She started crying again.

I squeezed her hand. 'It's okay. I'm here. I'm here.'

'He was *married*. There were wedding photos, and her stuff everywhere, and he said, "You don't mind, do you?" And I told him I did mind, and to call me a cab, and he . . . He lost it. He was grabbing me, shouting at me . . .'

I felt a silent tear of fury slip down my cheek. 'I'm so sorry, Lar.'

She looked at me, tear-stained. 'What the hell is wrong with me?'

'Nothing,' I said firmly. 'Nothing is wrong with you. You're allowed to say no. To change your mind. To have *principles*.'

'But I keep meeting guys and sleeping with them, and it never means anything.'

'So what? That's what your twenties are for.'

'Why haven't I settled down like you?'

'Because . . . that's not what you want. And anyway, you haven't met your person yet.'

She laughed softly, but it sounded hollow. 'Reckon he's out there, do you?'

'Yeah. I do. And you'll meet him when you're ready.'

'Yeah,' she said, eventually. 'Maybe.'

'Lar.' I swallowed. 'Can I say something?'

'Is it going to annoy me?'

'Probably.'

She smiled faintly.

'You're *so* much better than some arsehole who wants you for one night. Okay? I mean it. You . . . You deserve someone who knows your worth and who never forgets it.'

She didn't reply.

'I really want you to remember that.'

'I'm going to stop kissing deadbeats in clubs,' she said, eventually, putting her head in her hands.

I set my palm on her back, started rubbing it in slow, soothing circles. 'Only if you like. Only if you want.'

'I do, I think.'

'Okay.'

She blinked up at me. 'What would I do without you?'

'That's not something you ever have to worry about.'

The following weekend, I went to visit Jamie in London. He was interning again. Heather, apparently, had gone off to work at another firm. Jamie didn't know where, or seem particularly fussed. I was relieved to hear she'd gone.

Three months had passed since I'd lost our baby. And even though my pregnancy had been so horribly short-lived, a constant hunger had taken hold inside me. It commanded my thoughts, had burrowed into my brain, skewed my view of the world.

I saw pregnant women everywhere. On the street, buses, TV programmes. My whole body throbbed with longing whenever I encountered them. And every time I saw Jamie, too, it was all I could think about. Making another baby. My belly ballooning. Picking out newborn clothes. Debating names.

I'd come so close to having the family I'd always longed for. And I simply couldn't bring myself to let that go.

'I want to try again,' I whispered to Jamie in bed that Saturday night.

He rolled towards me. I felt the delicious comfort of his unclothed body, warm as turned earth.

He moistened his lips with his tongue. 'Try what?'

'To have another baby.'

For two weeks now, the papers had been declaring a heatwave. The whole country was brittle and brown, scorched by unrelenting sun. We had the air-con on full in the flat, but I knew that outside, the darkness smouldered.

Jamie's eyes opened fully then. He took me in, his gaze tracking mine like he was waiting for the punchline. We were lying face to face, our noses almost touching. His breath felt hot in the false cold of the room.

It must have been the very middle of the night. The world was quiet as a church.

We'd discussed it a few times. The soul-searing sadness. Whether our baby would have been a boy, or a girl. If they might have arrived early, and been born on Christmas Day.

'What do you think?' I whispered, working a finger across the dips and peaks of his chest. His physique had softened over the course of that summer. Lots of barbecues and work drinks and client dinners. I didn't mind. If anything, I liked that there was more of him. It made him seem sturdier, somehow.

He lowered his head to kiss me.

'Should we try again?' I asked, unable to wait for his reply.

I watched him taste-test the right words for a couple of moments. 'I think we should hold off till we've graduated.'

This, of course, was logical. Which made it so much harder to argue with. But to me, a ten-month wait already seemed unbearable. My body wanted back what it had had.

'It would just be less complicated,' he said. 'There'll be fewer distractions. And my parents . . .'

I could see he believed his mum and dad might be more on board if we waited until next summer. But I knew different, of course.

I'd encountered Debra the previous month, when she made a flying visit to Norwich to see Jamie's grandmother. It was the first time we'd come face to face since that night at the restaurant. She simply looked me up and down, then offered me a tight nod. I'd asked Jamie not to mention the miscarriage to his parents, so did she think I'd done as she'd asked?

I assumed she was satisfied, though it was hard to tell, since Debra was generally about as expressive as someone invigilating an exam.

Several times, I'd considered telling Jamie what Debra had done. But she'd been right about one thing: I loved him way too much to break his heart like that.

I fingered his crisp white bedlinen now, which smelt heavily of fabric conditioner. He must have washed the sheets, ready for my visit. The flat had been immaculate when I'd walked into it earlier. Every surface gleaming, the wooden floors so clean they were practically reflective. He'd even lit scented candles.

I thought of Lara, of the arsehole who'd wanted to hurt her last week. The whole thing had made me appreciate Jamie even more deeply. Why *wouldn't* I want to start a family with this man?

'Don't you think having a baby might make life more difficult?' Jamie said, shuffling a little closer. 'I won't be earning any kind of salary for another two years at least. You'll need a job, next summer. And with a child to think about—'

'I could work part-time,' I said, hopefully, naively. 'Or shifts, or something. Plenty of people do it, Jamie. We'd muddle through.'

Our plan had always been to stay in Norwich after graduating, but over the past year I had already seen that our life trajectory was changing. Jamie had been spending an increasing amount of time in London. And Lara had been talking about moving there too, because that was where all the TV contacts were, the best assistant jobs.

Earlier in the summer, she'd stayed with her cousin in Haringey while she shadowed an art director on a comedy series being shot in Finsbury Park. I'd missed her hugely. She was my oldest friend. My sister. She had every one of my best interests at heart. Any prolonged separation felt as unthinkable as running out of air. I wanted her – *needed* her – living near to me.

London was starting to feel like where we were all supposed to be.

The high peal of a fire engine penetrated the stillness then. Something set alight by the heat, maybe. Tinder-dry grass ignited by the spark of a chucked cigarette, an abandoned barbecue.

I tugged Jamie's arms more tightly around me and we lay wordlessly together for a few minutes. I was trying to remember to stay in the moment, to enjoy the press of his bare skin to mine, the cushion of his stomach against the ridge of my hip.

'You never told me you wanted to have kids so young,' he said.

'I didn't till I met you. And I was so happy when that test came back positive. So doesn't that mean it's the right thing?'

As Jamie seemed to be working out how to reply, my emotions overtook me without warning.

'I don't know how to let go,' I gasped. Panic poured into my throat. 'I don't know how to not want this, Jamie.'

'Hey, hey. It's okay to want it, Neve. It's okay.' He put a hand out to stroke my face and hair, his palm cool against my skin.

I knew by now that my longing had moved beyond the boundaries of anything rational. The need to have another baby felt physical.

I'd tried to explain it to Lara before. The overwhelm of yearning for motherhood. She said she'd never felt anything physically that way. But she didn't judge, or try to dissuade me. She was unfailingly supportive, if slightly despondent about my career, and the apparent forthcoming destruction of my vagina.

'Let's wait till we graduate. Ten months is going to fly,' Jamie whispered. And then he moved tenderly on top of me, and we made love, and it was long and intense in a way that felt like he was giving me his word.

46.

Now

I've arranged to meet Lara at her mum's house. Before I've even had a chance to ring the bell, Corinne opens the door, enveloping me in a hug. Felix is standing in the hallway behind her. From within Corinne's grasp, I raise my hand and nod. He meets my eye, smiles softly, and nods right back.

She looks even older than I'd been expecting, and she feels fragile in my arms, more bone than flesh. Exhaustion clings to her like smoke. Her cropped hair is almost white now, and her skin has the texture of cigarette paper. But she still has her trademark suntan, even though it's nearly Christmas. I smile as I recall the Corinne I knew years ago, who would dash hopefully outside in a bikini whenever the centigrade hit twenty.

'I've missed you, darling girl,' she murmurs into my hair. She smells exactly how I remember, a cloud of coal tar soap and Estée Lauder.

'I'm so sorry about Billy,' I say, my voice flimsy with emotion. I think about watching them dance in the kitchen, late at night, to 'At Last'.

I wonder if that was their song, if they played it at Billy's funeral. But I don't ask.

Corinne squeezes me harder, and after a couple of moments I realise it's because she can't speak. Behind her, Felix puts a silent hand on her shoulder.

Eventually, she pulls out of the hug and manages to say, 'How's your mum, Neve?'

'Same as ever.'

'I still think of her, sometimes.' Then she tells me Felix is taking her out for lunch. 'I'm being spoilt,' she says, smiling.

I stare at them. 'Oh, I . . .' *I thought I was here to see you.* Have there been crossed wires? Is this something to do with Felix? 'Please don't leave on my account.'

'Not at all,' he says, graciously, as Corinne puts on a coat. 'Nice to see you again, Neve.'

I must have misunderstood.

Just before Corinne shuts the door behind her, she gives me a funny look, one I can't quite interpret. 'Lara never stopped loving you, Neve, you know.'

'I never stopped loving her, either,' I say, realising the raw, unprocessed truth of it only in this moment.

As the door closes, Lara appears in the hallway. 'Hey. Come through.'

I step back in time a decade, to the last time I was here. The living room is just as cosy as I remember. It has been decorated for Christmas, draped in greenery and baubles and rivers of sparkling lights. The tree is a six-foot feast of colour. Corinne's Christmases were always the best.

But year-round too, this room was a treasure trove of fresh flowers and blankets and pairs of slippers and bowls filled with boiled sweets and thick piles of newspapers and shiny magazines, and today is no different. There is a radio playing, tuned to a succession of jangling Christmas songs.

Lara makes tea and we move to the sofa. The room is stuffy, like they've had the heating cranked up to max for days on end, but Lara still pulls a blanket over her lap. She is make-up free and looks drained, as though someone's syringed the energy right out of her.

I still haven't got to the bottom of exactly what's wrong with Corinne. I should have asked at the door. I'm sure she would have told me. But her lunch plans threw me – I'd been expecting her to be here.

'I thought . . . I wanted to have a chat with your mum,' I say.

Lara tuts fondly, like her mum and Felix are for ever cavorting around Norwich enjoying long lunches. 'I know. Sorry about that. But Felix suggested taking her out, and I think it was a good idea, actually. So you and I can talk.'

'Okay.' I try a smile, though I feel unsettled in a way I can't quite put my finger on.

'Recognise these?' Lara says, passing me a tea.

It breaks the tension perfectly. I laugh. The slogan mugs from our first night at uni, the ones we drank Jamie's mum's champagne from. A little faded, but still as ridiculous as they were back then. 'I can't believe you kept them all this time.'

'Are you kidding? These are seriously precious mementoes.'

'Lar.' Her name rushes from my mouth before I'm fully ready. 'Be straight with me. What's wrong with Corinne?'

She meets my eye. 'I'll tell you in a minute. First . . . how's it going with Ash?'

'No – never mind Ash. Tell me now.'

'No, Neve. This is important.'

'My relationship woes are not more important than your mum being ill. Tell me.'

'I will. But first . . . please just humour me.'

I shake my head, slightly bemused. 'Okay, but . . . there's not a lot to tell. Ash and I still haven't spoken.' I fill her in on my counsellor, and the slowly growing list of the ways in which Ash and Jamie do differ, and the many nights I've lain in bed wondering if it's possible that my theory has been built on false assumptions. That all these incredible coincidences could really be just that. Coincidence.

And yet, somehow, my mind always ends up tugging me back to Jamie. He is still moored to my heart. I can't bring myself to fully dismiss the idea that he might have come home, that perhaps we have been given a chance to revive the love story we never got to finish.

'Okay,' Lara says, when I'm done. She sets down her tea, folds her hands in her lap. 'Neve, I have to tell you something.'

I can hear from her voice it's the kind of something that might make a person want to run into traffic.

'It kills me to have to say this to you, especially after . . . the baby, and everything you went through with that. And . . . all the stuff that happened when Jamie died.'

In my mind, a jolt of renewed grief. Or maybe it's fear.

'It's about Jamie.'

Even after so much time, hearing someone else say his name still makes my heart lurch.

She shudders out a breath. 'God, this is so hard.'

'Lara . . .' I begin, but then something about her expression stops me.

'Neve, I haven't ever told you this because I know that what happened pretty much ruined your life. And I didn't want to add to your pain. Please know that I only withheld it because I didn't want to hurt you any more than I already had.'

'You're scaring me now.'

'Jamie . . . was cheating on you.'

Everything blurs. I feel the world tilt beneath me. I stare at her, hot astonishment behind my eyes.

'He . . . was seeing someone else. A girl called Heather. She worked at that firm he interned at.'

Heather. The name that is still, infuriatingly, branded onto my brain.

A hurricane of fragmented memories – of phone calls and excuses, times he brushed away my questions – begins to blow through me.

'Jamie told me in the car that night. Just before he died.'

The room seems to shrink suddenly, like the walls and ceiling are closing in. I struggle for a few moments to focus, form thoughts, draw breath. 'No, Lar.'

She just shakes her head, like, *I'm sorry.*

'*No.*' I cover my mouth, trying not to cry out with shock and pain. *Jamie, no. Not you. Not this. Not us.*

Lara sets a hand on her chest, like it's physically paining

her to tell me this. 'He told me everything because he was a coward and he couldn't face confessing to you. He actually asked me to tell you for him. But after he died, and I saw how broken you were . . . I couldn't bring myself to do it.'

The realisation hits me like a truck. That everything I thought about Jamie and me – and the life and future we'd lost – is turning out to have been a lie.

'He'd figured out a plan to do the last year of his course in London. He was planning to leave Norwich and move in with her, while you were out of the house.'

'Why?' I say, my voice wrenched with anguish.

But I know it is too tiny and inadequate a word for such a huge, fathomless question.

'He said you'd told him you wanted to try for another baby. But he wasn't ready. He kept saying you wanted different things from life, that he did think he was being held back by staying in Norwich. All that stuff. With the flat and London and Heather . . . his head was just turned.'

Cold, blunt devastation lands inside me. This, unequivocally, is proof she is telling the truth. I've never repeated to anyone that conversation I had with Jamie, about trying to get pregnant again.

Lara pulls her mustard-yellow cardigan more closely around her. I have no idea how she isn't sweating. 'What Jamie was saying to you and what he was doing with Heather were two completely different things. I'm so sorry, Neve.'

On the radio, the music switches to Coldplay. 'Christmas

341

Lights'. My heart aches in time to it. I swallow back wave after wave of sadness, fresh grief, the startling knife-wound of betrayal.

'All those weekends during term-time when he went back to London, claiming he was with his dad in Putney . . . he was with her. For almost a whole year.'

No. Not Jamie. No.

'Jamie was a cheater. A liar. A coward. The truth is . . . he didn't even come close to deserving you.'

I think back to what Meena said to me about Jamie, only a few days ago. *If you were to meet him today, there's a chance you might not even recognise him.*

I set down my cooling tea on the coffee table. The slogan on the mug is like a taunt: *CUP OF POSITIVI-TEA.* I feel the abrupt urge to fling it at a wall. I want to break everything.

'Did Jamie's dad know? His mum?'

Lara nods, silently.

I picture Chris, the contempt with which he used to look at me. 'But . . . why did they never say anything? They would have relished the chance to see the back of me. God, I even wrote to them a few times, afterwards.'

Lara swallows. 'Well, to be honest, it turns out we had that wrong. Jamie admitted they never disliked you, not really. *He* was the one raising doubts, saying he wasn't sure. They argued about it, sometimes. They thought he should come clean with you.'

'No. His mum . . . she offered to pay me, to get rid of the baby.'

Lara looks down at her lap. She already knows this, I

realise. 'I guess he'd made it clear things weren't going to last between you.'

I think of my own mother, the things she used to mutter to herself as she paced the house after my father left. *Idiot ... open your eyes ... right in front of you ... wake up, Daniela!*

'At the end of the day, Jamie was a coward,' Lara says. 'And after he died ... no doubt his parents wanted everyone to remember him as an angel, not a liar and a cheat. So they never said anything. I mean, that's how you've thought of him all these years, isn't it? Saint Jamie.'

I don't reply. The power of speech has left me completely. I still can't seem to square the idea of it – Jamie being in love with someone else. *Sleeping* with someone else. Lying to me, every single day for twelve months. Maybe more. And behaving the whole time like he was deeply in love with me.

Slightly dazed, I try to recall how many times Jamie and I were physically intimate during that year. A hundred, maybe? More?

How the hell could I have got it so wrong?

I feel a violent swirl of nausea, bile biting the back of my throat.

'I swear I'm not saying any of this to hurt you, Neve. But the truth is, I can't bear to see you chuck away what you have with Ash for the sake of someone who – let's face it – was not in love with you. Ash is a *good guy*. If you needed proof that he isn't Jamie, then this is it. No scientists required. And this is going to sound harsh, but if Jamie was coming back to life for anyone, then . . . it would be her, and not you.'

These words do a fresh number on my gut. I turn my face away.

'Let Heather have his ghost,' Lara whispers.

But how do I explain how mad and impossible that sounds to me, even now, because for the best part of a decade, I have been gripped by loving and grieving and revering the memory of this man? How do I make her see the agonising humiliation of realising I have compared every potential partner to someone who never actually loved me? That I have been worshipping at the altar of a cheat and a liar? How can I possibly convey how horrified I feel to have wasted so much precious time?

'Were you angry, when he told you?' My voice sounds low and lifeless now, crushed flat by the weight of our conversation.

Lara nods. 'I don't think I've ever been that angry. In fact, me raging at him would have been one of the last things he—'

'Why didn't you tell me?' A sob clambers into my mouth. 'You could have . . . messaged, or emailed. You could have just let me know, so I wouldn't have wasted the last decade of my life obsessing about someone who—'

'I did message, and email. I asked if we could meet, but you never replied.'

I swallow, and look down. This, of course, is true. Besides which, the blame for all this lies only with one person. And it is not Lara.

'Anyway. I should probably say, I didn't believe you, when you said you thought Ash was some kind of reincarnation of Jamie. For reasons that I hope are obvious now. But I desperately wanted my best friend back, and I thought if I argued with you, that might not happen.' She shuffles up straighter, taking my hand with hers. It feels oddly bony in my grip. 'You have to see that this . . . This is *good information*. It means you can finally move on from the past. Because Jamie was, unequivocally, an arsehole.'

The tears start to fall now. 'It's not as simple as that. I can't . . . ask him why. I can't get angry, because there's nowhere for it to go. I just have to accept that he did this. But how can I, when he – what we had – meant *everything* to me?'

Lara doesn't reply.

I glance over at her, and realise with surprise that her eyes have fluttered closed. She almost looks as though she's drifted off to sleep. Christ, she must be exhausted. 'Hey, are you okay?' I say, putting a hand on her arm.

She starts. 'Say again?'

I feel a strange urge to laugh. Disbelief maybe, that Lara – a person who's always had seemingly boundless energy – could have dropped off as we were talking, in the middle of the day. 'Are you okay?'

Swallowing, she shifts slightly, nods. 'Sorry. Yeah. Not sure what happened there.'

She looks strangely vulnerable suddenly, and I remember with a jolt of bitterness how privately grateful I'd felt that I had Jamie, the night a married man nearly hurt her.

'Anyway, look,' Lara says, 'there's actually another reason I wanted to get this all off my chest. And this … This does feel a bit more complicated.'

Something cold forms a ball in my stomach, and I know straight away that it is fear.

She starts to talk, and incredibly, my world turns even darker than before.

47.

'So, it turns out you were right all along. I'm stupidly stubborn. I left it too late to see a doctor. I convinced myself it was IBS. I spent a fortune on antacids. I refused to even consider the fact it might be cancer. People kept saying it to me, and I just . . . didn't listen.'

I can't look at her face. I stare instead at the heightened outline of her clavicle. She's thin, so thin. And tired, and entirely without appetite. She looks drained. Every movement is laboured.

How the hell did I miss this?

Because I was too busy thinking about Jamie to notice what was happening right in front of me.

'But . . . I thought . . . I thought it was your mum who was ill.'

'I know. I'm sorry. It was just easier to let you assume . . . until we could have this conversation. Until you were ready to hear about Jamie – and really hear it, without your mind being clouded by my news.'

I think about the diet I've been so convinced she was on. 'But you said you were detoxing . . . Were those pills—'

'Digestive enzymes.'

'But . . . Felix took them too.'

'His were vitamins. He's been doing that lately . . . if I'm not quite ready to tell people.'

'This can't be happening. It isn't fair. It isn't . . .' But I trail off, my thoughts by now a waterfall, far too fast to grip onto.

Lara lets out a shallow laugh which turns quickly into a cough. 'I think Jamie's dad might disagree with you there. He'd say this was karmic justice or something, I'm sure.'

'You know that's not how cancer works, Lar,' I whisper fiercely, squeezing the tiny mass of her hand in mine, feeling a fresh bloom of anger towards Chris for his life-long commitment to being a complete arsehole. 'Let's not mention Chris, or Jamie, or any of them, ever again, okay?'

She smiles softly. 'Sounds good to me.'

A battle plan is already taking shape in my mind. 'Okay. A second opinion. We'll get a second opinion. I've got savings – you could go private.'

'I've had three separate opinions,' she says, calmly. 'They all said the same thing.'

'But have they exhausted every option? What about alternative therapies?'

'Neve, listen,' She quietens me with a squeeze of the hand. 'It's over. Okay? I'm dying. They told me in July I'd have about a year.'

But five months have passed since then. 'July?'

She swallows. 'Yeah. Actually . . . I found out a few days before you and Ash met Felix for the first time.'

To be told she knew she was dying that night on

Tombland feels nothing short of devastating. 'Why didn't you tell me?'

'I wanted to sort everything out with you first. Because selfishly? I quite fancied spending some time being your friend again.' She laughs softly. 'The last few months have been bizarrely comforting. While I've been with you, I've been able to pretend . . . this isn't actually happening.'

'There must be something they can do.'

She shakes her head slowly. 'The cancer's too advanced. Surgery's . . . not an option.'

I can hear nothing now but the scream inside my head as I revisit all the signs I've completely failed to register during the time I've spent with her lately. The skipped meals and booze forgone, the weight loss, her permanent lack of energy. *How the hell did I miss this?*

'What about chemo?'

'I'm not having chemo.'

'What?'

'I've said no to chemo.'

'What do you mean?'

'Exactly that. I don't want chemotherapy.'

'What? Why?'

'I watched my dad go through it, and Neve . . . it was grim. Look – if there's a chance it could shrink the cancer or make it operable or save me, then it would absolutely be worth a shot. But they're only talking about it extending my life by a few months.'

'But I'm sure it would be worth—'

She shakes her head. 'You're going to have to trust me

on this one. I'm dying. I've seen a lot of doctors and had a *lot* of tests. There's nothing they can do.'

I choke back a sob. 'Lara. No.'

She squeezes my hand again. 'Listen. I'm going to California, to be with Felix.'

'When?'

'Soon. I'm going to spend my last months there with him, in the sunshine, overlooking the ocean.' She smiles bravely. 'Since I met him, it's grown to be my absolute favourite place in the world. So, if I've got to die, then that's the best way I can possibly imagine.'

'You're going . . . to California?'

She smiles. Unbelievably, there is light in her eyes. 'He has incredible care lined up for me. Everything's arranged. I love him so much, Neve. I just want to be with him, out there.'

'And is . . .? Is your mum . . .?'

Lara shakes her head. 'The trip would be too much for her. We've agreed to say our goodbyes here. In fact . . . that's what I'm doing with everyone. Out there, it's just going to be me and Felix. We've discussed it a lot, and that's what I want.'

'No, Lara, this is . . . This can't be it. This can't be happening.' I start to cry. 'I wish you'd told me. I'm so sorry. We've missed out on so much.'

'I know we have. I'm sorry too.'

Through the window, a stripe of winter sunlight falls across her face. It affords her a glow that makes her look so pristinely radiant, I want to shake her with frustration. Because she can't – she *cannot* – possibly be dying. I mean, yes – she looks very unwell, I have finally realised. But not as if she's only got a few months left to live.

'Hey, at least I'm sticking to my side of the pact.'

I frown, confused.

'Don't you remember? That holiday in Devon. We pinky-swore to never get old.' She smiles wistfully, and I feel my heart fragment.

'Yeah,' I say, softly. 'I remember.'

'So, look, Neve. Can we . . . talk about the accident? Because I've been wanting to do that ever since I came back.'

'It doesn't matter any more,' I say, through fresh tears. 'I don't care if I never think about that night again in my life.'

'Okay. But let me just say this, because I've never said it to you before: you were right, that night. You were right, and I was too stubborn to listen, and now Jamie is dead. And whatever kind of guy he turned out to be, he didn't deserve to die.'

'The accident wasn't your fault, Lar.' I should have admitted this long before now. Because of course it is the truth. It always has been. But the strength of my love for Jamie would never let me see it.

'No,' she says, 'but my attitude that night was horrible. And . . . I am sorry. Truly.'

I stare blankly at the *POSITIVI-TEA* mug, wondering how many teabags you get through if you're diagnosed with terminal cancer. Hundreds? Thousands?

'Ironic, isn't it,' she says. 'That you turned out to be just as stubborn as me. Refusing to let the idea of Jamie go, all these years. Maybe that was why we were such good friends. We were more similar than even we realised.'

Our eyes meet, and my body floods with love for her.

'Are you in pain?' I ask, even as I'm thinking, *Please say no*.

'Not right now. I'm on decent pain relief, and it's working so far. And I've got options, if it gets worse. I haven't hit the opioids yet. But, you know. My thermoregulation's shot to bits. And my stomach's a mess. I can't digest food too well, obviously, hence the enzymes.'

I want to ask if she's scared, but I don't. Because of course she is. Who wouldn't be – even someone as fearless as Lara?

'So, listen. Neve. After I die, they're going to fly me home . . . so my ashes can be buried next to Dad's. It's all arranged.'

I want to beg her to stop talking, tell her I can't handle hearing this. That it's all too crazy, too sad, too unbelievable.

But she's being so brave – and she's the one dying. The least I can do is be brave in return.

'Everything's sorted: the funeral and cremation, the whole thing. I didn't want Mum to be burdened with any of it. And next Saturday . . . I'm having a living funeral, the night before I fly. We're going to California the next day. Everyone's coming. I want you to be there. I *need* you there, Neve.'

'Next week?' I stare at her. *We've only got a week?*

She smiles, but it is frail. 'Well, everyone's always at a loose end between Christmas and New Year, aren't they? Thought my parting gift could be an extra party.'

Despite my best efforts, I start crying again. She can't be dying. She just can't be. She's still so . . . alive. She's smiling, forming sentences, ordering me about. This isn't what dying looks like.

'At my dad's funeral,' she says, 'we all agreed how happy he'd have been to see his friends and family together in one room. How much he'd actually have enjoyed the day. So that's what I'm going to do: I'm going to dose up on pain-killers and do my best to have a lovely last afternoon with all my favourite people.'

A last afternoon. How unfathomably awful to know it.

'Don't be sad for me, Neve. I'm actually . . . incredibly lucky. A lot of people don't get to die this way. With time to say goodbye. The best care at their fingertips. I'm fortunate, I really am.'

Trust Lara to find the upside of a terminal diagnosis.

'If I have any regrets,' she says, 'it's missing out on ten years of friendship with you.'

'I regret that too.' I am spilling tears now, struggling not to completely lose it. 'And I will for the rest of my life.'

'No. You need to listen to me now.' Her blue eyes begin to blaze, more fierce than I have ever seen them. 'I want you to take the years I had left and run with them, okay? Make it up with Ash. Grab love with both hands and don't let go. It's too late for me, but it isn't for you. It's your time now. Don't waste another second.'

48.

A few days after my conversation with Lara, I drop into Mum's house after work. The air on my walk over is layered with winter mist, scented by frost and woodsmoke.

Mum is on her sofa, wearing a voluminous kaftan in a geometric print that makes my eyes swim. She's damp-skinned, hair wrapped in a towelling turban. I'm guessing she's got a gig tonight, because she's painting her nails and half singing, half humming to the Michael Bublé Christmas album.

I sit down next to her, scanning the room for booze, because I could really do with something to shear away the edges of what I'm feeling right now. But unusually, I can't see anything.

'I've got something to tell you,' I say.

'Right.' She draws the brush along her thumbnail with a flourish. 'Okay.'

'Lara's dying.'

My mother rarely looks me in the eye. But she does now.

'She's got ... cancer. It's advanced. They can't ... There's nothing they can do.'

A thick globule of nail polish drips onto Mum's kaftan. We both look down at it for a couple of moments.

Without saying anything, Mum holds out a hand.

I pass her a tissue.

She attempts to dab the spilt polish, but ends up smearing it into a vast stain instead. Then, seeming to accept it's ruined, she folds it over to hide the damage and says, 'How long has she known?'

'A few months. She wanted us to . . . sort everything out before she told me.'

'There's really nothing they can do?'

'They've offered her chemo, but . . . it wouldn't save her. She's dying.'

To my surprise, she leans over and wraps her arms around me. 'I'm sorry, darling.'

'Remember the guy you saw Lara with?' I say, into her Nivea-scented neck.

'Oh yes,' she says, pulling out of the hug. 'Very suave gentleman.'

I nod. 'Felix. He lives in America. And she's . . . flying out there to be with him. That's where she wants to be when . . .' I trail off. I can't say the word again, because every time I do, it makes it seem more real.

'What's her prognosis?'

'They said she had a year, back in July.' I let Mum figure out the rest, because that's the most painful kind of maths there is.

On the stereo, Bublé starts singing 'Have Yourself a Merry Little Christmas', and everything suddenly feels too much, too cruel.

Next to me, Mum is shaking her head in apparent disbelief. 'Poor Lara.'

355

'She's having a living funeral next week.'

She brightens slightly. 'Oh, they're good, aren't they?' she says, like we've decided to switch topics to the merits of slow cookers, or that hand car wash she really rates on the Ipswich Road. 'I know someone who had one.'

'What did they have?'

She frowns. 'A string quartet, I think? And a buffet – though a lot of the guests did get food poisoning the next day. There were speeches, too. It was quite similar to a wedding, really.'

I shut my eyes briefly. 'No, Mum. What did they have, as in, what did they die of?'

'Oh, they didn't in the end. False alarm.'

I smile wearily. 'This wasn't The Duke, by any chance, was it?'

'I just call him Duke.'

'Right.'

'It wasn't, actually,' she says. And then, thoughtfully, 'Although they do share a lot of the same personality traits.'

My smile fades. 'Well, Lara's funeral . . . definitely isn't a false alarm.'

'You know, after your father stopped bothering to keep it in his trousers, I did sometimes worry about how you were faring. But I always knew you'd be okay. Do you know how?'

I shake my head, wondering what she's on about now, praying she doesn't mention Jamie, or anything else to do with my dad's trousers.

'Because you had Lara.'

I smile softly. 'Really? That's nice.' I shuffle back on the sofa so I can look at her properly, tucking my legs up beneath me. Then I take a breath. 'Jamie was cheating on me.'

It's funny how quickly the taste of his name has already altered in my mouth. It's turned into something oily and unpleasant – and especially today, given my oldest friend is currently having to organise her own death. But a part of me wants to let Mum know she was right. That maybe her maternal instincts weren't so defective back then after all.

She stares at me for a couple of moments. 'Who told you that?'

'Lara. She said he confessed, just before he died. He was going to leave me and move to London with another girl.'

'Was he indeed,' she says, murderously, as if she's already considering a midnight excursion to decant eggs and flour all over his headstone.

'Did you know?'

'Did I know what?'

'That Jamie had it in him . . . to do that?'

'Do I have a functioning cheating bastard radar, you mean?'

I think of The Duke, and The Duke's wife, and smile weakly. 'Never mind.'

She raises an eyebrow. 'For what it's worth, I'm not at all surprised.'

'I was.'

'Well, that's the way it always goes,' she says sadly. 'The first time.'

'So you did suspect?'

She rolls her eyes faintly. 'Of course. That boy was a shiny penny, Neve.'

'I don't know what that means.'

'Oh, you do – shiny, perfect, always glinting. They look like treasure, but in fact they're next to worthless.'

'Right,' I say, surprised to realise this makes a strange sort of sense.

'Yes. So very shiny. But I never quite felt that he was shining for you. Sometimes I'd watch him, and that smile would fall from his face as quickly as it appeared, once your back was turned. Like a curtain on a stage. His behaviour was very . . . performative.'

'How come you never warned me?'

'Would you have listened?'

'Probably not,' I admit.

'Some things you can be told a thousand times by other people, but you can still only ever really discover for yourself.'

'Well. You were right, anyway.'

'Gosh, it doesn't really matter who was right, does it?'

Silence spreads through the space between us. For a moment or two, we just look at each other.

'But . . . what if I'd had the baby, Mum, and Jamie had survived? I'd have his *child* now. An eight-year-old son, or daughter. And Jamie would be . . . with someone else. Not me.'

Her face draws together. 'I don't see that there's much point in thinking like that.'

'And that's exactly what happened to you. You had me, but Dad was cheating on you, and—'

'I never regretted having you, Neve. Not once. Not ever.'

'You found it hard, though.'

She smiles. 'Shall I let you into a secret?'

I consider saying no, because being appraised of my mother's secrets is usually about as fun as receiving a herpes diagnosis.

'I found parenting hard because it *is* bloody hard. But would I have swapped it, or changed it? Never. I know I wasn't like all the other mums, and I know I let you down, sometimes. But that wasn't because I didn't want you, or regretted having you.'

I'm finally wondering whether, in her position, I'd have fared much better. Whether I might have become dysfunctional in the way she so often seemed to me.

I think back to what she said a couple of weeks ago. *You're more like me than you think.*

'Anyway,' Mum says, 'I'm a better judge of character now.'

I shoot her a look. 'No offence, but are you?'

'What do you mean?'

'Er, The Duke?'

'Well. I've actually got some news for you, on that front.'

Oh God. She's having a baby with The Duke. I'm going to have a half-sibling who'll be born into endless drama and be given a name that sounds like a pub.

'I've asked Ralph to move in.'

I blink furiously. 'What?'

'I've asked Ralph to move in with me.'

'Which Ralph? Our Ralph?'

'Do you know any others?'

No, I think. *Ralph is one of a kind.*

'Remember what I said about very few people being worthy of your heart and devotion?'

'Y-es,' I say, uncertainly.

'Well, I realised . . . that maybe it was time to take my own advice.'

There is a creak on the floorboard behind me. I turn to see Ralph standing in the doorway, beaming like someone who's just been let out of prison on good behaviour.

My heart fattens with happiness. I get straight up and pull him into a hug.

'Well, what is it they say?' I can hear the smile in his voice. 'Better late than never.'

I am heartbroken for Lara and boiling with fury at Jamie and buzzing for my mother and Ralph all at once. 'Congratulations,' I manage.

'Daniela and I make a good team,' he says, which makes me smile, because Mum's team has for so long been filled with duds and last reserves. But now, finally, it seems she's picked a winner.

'Will you do me a favour?' I say, pulling back from Ralph and looking at them both.

'Of course,' says Ralph, while my mother – true to form – waits to see what the favour is first.

'*Please* do something about the state of this place. It won't take much. I know you've got the money, Mum. And I can help. Just please, please, give this beautiful house a bit of TLC . . . It hurts my heart, okay?'

Mum rolls her eyes. 'I'm sure I didn't bring you up to be this affected, but fine – if it bothers you so much.'

'Thank you,' I say, exhaling like I've just crossed some sort of finish line. '*Thank* you.'

Later, cocooned in my bedroom back at home, I search online for any shred of hope that Lara's cancer is curable. Unsurprisingly, I find plenty. Stories of miraculous recoveries, defying the odds, tumours shrinking then vanishing. I search for cancer experts living within any sort of radius of Santa Cruz. I think about contacting Felix, asking if he thinks his bank account might be big enough to save her.

But then a message pings on my phone. It's from Lara.

> Please understand I'm at peace with dying, Neve
>
> I know you haven't had much time to get used to it. But it's not up to you to save me.
>
> I'm not considering other treatments. I just want to make the most of the time I have left Xx

It takes me a long time – maybe more than an hour – to slowly shut down everything I've bookmarked. To strike thick black marks through the entries I've been making in a notebook.

Okay then, Lar.

This is not my fight, I finally realise. This is Lara's choice, Lara's life. Ruining the time she has left by refusing to accept the call she's made would be the pinnacle of selfishness.

It's mind-bendingly hard, but I know I have to respect her decision.

Before I close the laptop, I idly type in Heather's name. I found her on LinkedIn once, years ago. Maybe it's down to some strange, self-destructive impulse, or maybe I just want a distraction from thinking about Lara.

I find her on Instagram. She's married, two kids, is a paramedic now. A willowy, ash-blonde beauty, she still looks about twenty, even though she must be in her thirties. When she's not in uniform, she favours photos of herself wearing pastel colours against pastel backdrops. There are lots of shots of her standing next to flower arches. She lives in a nice part of London, judging by the many images of particularly wide and leafy sections of the Thames.

I stare at her frozen-in-time smile, astonished afresh to remember that Jamie loved her and not me. What did he promise her? What did she believe? What did she know about me? Does she ever think about him?

My fingers hover over my keypad. That tiny, electrical impulse to reconnect to a past life is still sparking somewhere inside me. I could send Heather a message, start a conversation, uncover the truth.

And then I force myself to take a breath, close my eyes, think of Lara.

Grab love with both hands and don't let go. It's too late for me, but it isn't for you. Don't waste another second.

What the hell am I doing?

I shut the laptop. It's finally time to stop looking back.

I owe that much to Lara, and to myself.

49.

Then

It was a wild storm, that night. A violent August thunderstorm brought on by days of crackling heat.

Lara had just passed her driving test, and – for reasons known only to himself – her dad had congratulated her with an old sports car he'd bought cheap from a mate instead of a card that said *Well Done*.

It was a miracle she'd even been insured – a staggering error of judgement that was for ever being affirmed by her growing tally of near-misses. The bodywork got a new dent every time she went out. One night, she accelerated too hard out of a bend and ended up in a hedge.

But she seemed to think it was amusing. I guess the more you survive, the less scary things feel. But I was afraid she would hurt herself, or worse. A fear so dark, I couldn't even voice it out loud.

Jamie was still interning in London, but he and his parents were in Norwich for the weekend. It was his grandmother's eightieth birthday, and the four of them were going out for one of those big-deal dinners at a swanky restaurant. I'd been fortunate enough to secure a second internship with

Kelley Lane that summer – but I was also working at the pub down the road again and had a shift, so I couldn't make it. Not that I was entirely sure I'd have been invited anyway.

The rain was savage that night, so forceful it made us pause for breath just watching it. A relentless, liquid whipping of the trees, pavements, rooftops. We had a leak in the flat roof of our bathroom which had already filled three buckets. The weather was so bad, the wait for a cab was nearly ninety minutes.

Jamie had been at our house all day, working on an A&L brief – concept plans for an intergenerational housing project – and had lost track of time. Already stressed, he was growing increasingly flush-cheeked and agitated, his panic always disproportionate whenever his father was involved. 'I'm so late. Dad's going to hit the *roof*. I've got four missed calls from him already.' He turned to Lara. 'I'll never get a cab. Will you give me a lift?'

'Sure,' Lara said, no breath of hesitation. Any opportunity to jump in that car.

The rain was belting the windows so hard I was half expecting the glass to give way. I could hear the rush of the leak in the bathroom, the vicious crack of thunder close by. I had a bad feeling, one I couldn't put words to.

'Wait for a cab,' I said. 'Or get the bus. You can't drive in this.'

Lara laughed. 'You are *such* a square about my car, Neve.'

'Well, you do keep crashing into things.'

'More fun that way.' She winked at me and jangled her keys. 'Come on then, posh boy.'

'Jamie,' I said, trying to make eye contact with him, to communicate my fear.

'Relax,' he replied. But he wouldn't meet my eye.

It was the first time he and Lara had ever been a team against me. 'Well, please drive slowly,' I implored.

As if on cue, lightning sliced through the sky.

Lara did something then that she'd never done before. She rolled her eyes, looked at Jamie then back at me, and said, 'All right, *Mum*. Chill out.'

She'd never mocked me before, ever. Had never tried to make me feel small.

I became suddenly speechless, hot with humiliation.

'What do you reckon, Jamie – top down?' Lara said, laughing.

I wanted to remind her the roads would be dangerously slippery after a long spell of no rain at all. I wanted to ask if she'd ever checked the tread on her tyres. But her words had stolen the voice from my throat.

The bad feeling persisted. I could feel it clinging like a creature to my back.

It was strange, when they left the house. Jamie and I kissed, and he put his arms around me. But oddly – for the first time ever – he seemed unable to say, *I love you*.

I convinced myself afterwards that, somehow, he'd known it was our last goodbye.

Which was why the call, when it came later that night, wasn't even a surprise. Lara had lost control of the car on a corner of the ring road. Jamie hadn't been wearing a seatbelt and had been flung through the windscreen, into the path of a delivery van. Lara escaped with only minor injuries.

He died that night. The love of my life, the man I thought I would live out my days with. I would never again get to hold him, share a smile with him, kiss him, make love to him. I remember the physicality of the shock I felt – or maybe it was fury. The force of my feelings reverberated through me for days afterwards. I felt like a human earthquake. I would shake uncontrollably, whenever I looked at his photo, or a pair of his jeans, or his empty side of our mattress. I spent hours over the ensuing days sitting in ill-advisedly hot baths, trying to sweat the convulsions from my body.

When Lara came to see me after the accident, I wouldn't let her in the house. We faced each other, just once, on the doorstep. She still had nicks of dried blood on her face, and the vast purple petal of a bruise around one eye. Her skin was pale as candle wax, and she seemed unsteady on her feet, kept placing a hand on the brickwork for support.

'I'm sorry, Neve.' She was saying the words, but not even looking at me.

It took everything I had not to shove her backwards with both hands. 'I asked you not to take him. I *warned* you about the weather, and you laughed at me.'

'Neve.' She was crying now. 'It was an accident. It all happened so quickly—'

'He knew,' I said, my voice cracking. 'Jamie *knew* something was going to happen, I could see it in his eyes.'

She moved out, after that. I think we both understood that we couldn't live together any more. I stopped taking her calls, and eventually, she stopped making them.

I couldn't face asking to view his body at the mortuary. The funeral was a family-only affair, and it was made clear I would not be welcome. I'd had to steal the items of his I'd wanted to keep before Chris swept through the house and cleared out all Jamie's stuff, letting himself in with Jamie's key without even asking me first.

Back then, I thought this was because they blamed me, somehow: Chris had said I was bad news all along, and now his youngest son was dead. But I realise now it must have been because they knew about Heather, and felt too ashamed to look me in the eye.

There was a police investigation, but Lara was never charged with anything. The conditions had been atrocious that night, and there was no evidence to suggest careless or dangerous driving. It was, they concluded, just a terrible accident. At the inquest, the coroner simply recorded Jamie had died from a road traffic collision.

I wasn't completely wrong about that last ever look Jamie and I shared, though. Because it *was* a final goodbye. But not because he could foresee the accident. It was because he was leaving me for someone else, and he didn't even have the guts to tell me.

I wish Lara had found a way to let me know sooner who Jamie really was. Because maybe then I'd have been able to forgive her, and we wouldn't have lost so much time.

But we can't undo the past. The world has moved on. Some people have died, others are dying.

And others have yet to really live.

And that's what I intend to do now. I'm sorry Jamie died – I'll always be sorry for that – but I refuse to waste another moment mourning him or chasing ghosts, dwelling on questions I will never have the answers to.

It turns out that – against all the odds – my mother was right. You can give your heart and soul to whoever you want, but very few people will actually be worthy of it. And now, at last, I know who that person is.

What I had with Jamie was magic while it lasted, but he never deserved me. And now – if it's not too late – I finally get to be with someone who does.

50.

Now

Christmas this year is different in a million ways to how I thought it would be. I guess in life there are never any guarantees. This time six weeks ago, would I have imagined I'd be single again? That Lara would be dying? That my mother would have found true love?

Lara invites me to spend Christmas Day at her mum's house. 'It'll be just like old times,' she says, and I can't tell if she's joking.

Because on some level, it will be. Then again, back then, there was never a Felix, or cancer, and Billy was always there to light up the room.

But when she asks, I don't hesitate. 'I'd love to,' I say.

Now I know that she's dying, it is all I can see when I look at her. The breathlessness and exhaustion. Her newly tiny frame. The drugs and the layers of clothing and her inability to take more than a few mouthfuls of food. Felix has to support her when she goes to the bathroom, and I wonder again how I managed to miss all of this for so long. Was she putting on a show of strength for my bene-fit, so I didn't guess until she was ready? Or did I really just not notice?

But for today, it is Christmas. And this year, no expense has been spared – thanks, I suspect, to Felix. There is a turkey about five times too big for the four of us, piles of gifts and boxes of chocolates and bowls overflowing with nuts and crisps and tangerines. Billy's favourite Elvis Christmas album is playing. The fire crackles sumptuously. In this moment, death and unhappiness feel so distant, I can barely believe they are real.

After lunch, Lara insists we play Monopoly.

'But you can't let me win,' she says, sternly. 'I don't want a pity-victory.'

So we play, but it's obvious Felix is letting her win. And I can't help thinking, *She meant that. She didn't want a pity-victory.*

Then again, the love of his life is dying. She might only have a matter of weeks left. We're all floundering here. None of us knows what the hell we're supposed to do.

I catch up with him in the kitchen as he's making coffee. Lara and her mum are in the living room, trying to find a good, uplifting film to watch. No James Bond for us this year. None of us wants to think about death or suffering, even in the context of a film franchise we always loved.

Felix and I are both wearing Christmas jumpers, on Lara's orders. His says, *Pull My Cracker*. Mine says, *Festive As F**k*.

Next to the kettle, I touch his arm. 'I just want you to know. I still loved her, even when I was angry with her.'

He turns to face me. His eyes are so kind. I see it fully, now. All my doubts were misplaced. Lara's discomfort was never about him. It was about the cancer taking hold inside her. Nothing to do with her gentle, loving boyfriend.

'I know,' he says. 'And she always knew it too, deep down.'

'I just didn't know how to process what had happened.'

He nods, leans back against the kitchen worktop. He looks tired, I realise. Drained of hope, even though he puts on a superhuman show each day for her.

'How are you coping?' I say, softly.

'Uh, some good days. Some bad. I'm not sure I'll ever be ready to . . . you know. Say goodbye.'

'I'm so sorry,' I whisper.

'I love her,' he says, as if he thinks I might not know.

'She loves you too. So much.'

He nods. 'Thank you.'

'I'm so glad she found you.'

'I'm so glad she found me too.'

A moment passes. I feel his eyes on me, like he's trying to think of the right way to say something else.

Eventually, he says, 'Neve, for what it's worth – I think Ash is a really good guy.'

I smile sadly. 'So do I.'

'Is it too late?'

'I can't . . . think about that right now. I can only think about Lara.'

'She'd hate you to lose what you have with him. She wants you to be happy, Neve.'

I nod, because I know. But still. I am only able to focus on getting through the next week. Saying goodbye to Lar.

'You could invite him. To the funeral.'

'No. I just need to be there one hundred per cent for Lara. No distractions. He'd understand.'

'Okay. I get that.'

'Ash and I have time, but Lara . . .'

He nods. Neither of us needs me to finish that sentence.

As he's loading the coffee cups onto a tray, Felix turns and says, 'Neve?'

'Yeah.'

'Please take this in the spirit it's intended, but . . . if there's one thing I've learnt over the past year, it's that we often have less time than we think.'

51.

I am motionless in the doorway of the large conservatory of Lara's favourite hotel on the North Norfolk coast. I just want to stand still and watch for a little while. To commit to memory the sight of my friend with all her favourite people, for the very last time.

On the drive out here with Mum, I was pensive and quiet, off-kilter with apprehension. I was baffled by the idea of this being the final time I would be in the same space as my oldest friend. How do you prepare for a goodbye like that? What's the etiquette for the last ever day? It feels so incongruous, so at odds with being human. The best thing about being alive is the illusion it will go on for ever.

But now, standing here, the storm inside me subsides a little. Mum was right before – you could easily mistake this for a wedding reception. The room is adorned with bunches of Lara's favourite white and blush roses, and the tables are dripping with white linen, sparkling with crystal. There are packets of forget-me-not placeholders. Snippets of laughter waft through the space. The mood is upbeat, no hint of mourning or discussion of impending death. No-one is crying. Not yet, anyway.

It's three days before New Year's Eve. And though it's cold outside, crisp Christmassy sunlight has overpowered the clouds, flooding the conservatory with light. The hotel gardens roll down to the salt marsh and beyond it, the sea. Gulls soar over the glass roof, the tree branches braced against a bolt of wind. Everything seems so vital and alive. Or maybe that's just how I've started to see the world, now that Lara is leaving it.

All of her immediate and extended family are here, and old friends, and friends she's made in the years since I last knew her. And there is Felix, of course, in whose arms I now know she will pass away.

He is talking to a group – TV people maybe? – and I am struck, not for the first time, by how charming he is. Six foot three of solid-gold charisma, one of those people who talks with his whole body. It comes from years, I guess, of motivational speaking and courting investors, but underneath all that, I know he is wholly and authentically good. Magic and true, all at once. A planet of a person.

Here he is, I think. She has found him. But she can't stay.

And now I see her, sitting with a couple of her cousins, laughing about something.

She's wearing the pink jumper I got her for Christmas all those years ago, to replace the one she lost, and she looks beautiful. Her hair makes gold waves around her face, and aside from the slight pallor to her skin, and her laboured movements, you wouldn't necessarily assume she was ill. She could almost be someone who's just checked out of hospital, in fact. Got the all-clear. Rung the end-of-treatment bell. Made it to the other side.

Felix is walking towards me now. I am trying not to get too emotional, because today isn't about me, my grief, my sadness.

We hug. He smells of soap powder and safety, and I am grateful for the warm wall of his body. 'Thank you for making this all so much easier,' I whisper.

He shakes his head. 'The credit's all hers. She knew what she wanted – I guess I just had the means to help make it happen.'

We draw back from the hug.

'I hope you don't think I'm taking her away,' he says, his brown eyes scanning my face.

'I'd never think that.'

'She loves it out there. But for what it's worth, I did try to persuade her to stay.'

I smile. 'Once Lara gets an idea in her head—'

'Oh, yes.' He smiles too.

'Well, your place out there looks amazing.'

'I'd like you to come out,' he says, sincerely. 'Perhaps next year, after—'

'I'd like that,' I say, quickly, because there's still a part of me that hopes I will call Lara in January and she will say Felix's doctor has prescribed her a revolutionary new drug, or that she's started ingesting some transformative herb, and the cancer has gone, she's in remission, cured.

'You should know,' Felix says, 'she always spoke very warmly of you. She always loved you, always missed you.'

'Thank you. That means a lot. I'm just . . . so broken-hearted for both of you.'

He puts a hand on my arm. 'I count myself lucky. Truly. I'd choose a few years with the best person in the world over a lifetime with someone who isn't her, a thousand times over. I'm blessed. I've known it from the first moment we met.'

The time disappears too fast. I know Lara doesn't feel up to more than a few hours. I feel the clock in my stomach tick harder with every passing minute, each time I catch her eye from across the room, and she blows me a kiss. Because I'm not ready to say goodbye. I'm just not. How could I ever be?

Lara invited Mum to sing today, even letting her pick the songs. I try not to cry as Mum, resplendent in dove-grey satin, sings 'Songbird', 'Time After Time' and 'Endless Love'. And, incredibly, she gets through it. How? I know I wouldn't have been able to.

I rarely experience pride when it comes to Mum, an emotion that would be wasted on her anyway. But I feel it roaring at gale force through me now. And not just for today. She's knocked drinking on the head, apparently, with the help of Ralph and her local AA group. It's early days – she's just over a fortnight sober. How the hell she got through Christmas, I'll never know. But so far, things look promising. I can't remember a time when she's gone more than twenty-four hours without a drink in her hand.

As evening arrives and darkness descends, Lara appears by my side and passes me my coat. 'Shall we?' She nods towards the door to the garden, and wordlessly, we walk out there together.

We sit down on a bench, facing the faint rumble of the distant sea, half illuminated by the light spilling out from the conservatory.

We don't say anything for a minute or so, letting our breath mingle and become fog in front of us. The air is rigid with cold, the sky an endless map of galaxies. We are both gazing up at it, because it's too hard to look at each other.

'You're wearing the jumper,' I say.

'Well. I used to take it out of the wardrobe from time to time and think, *One day, we'll find each other again.*'

I swallow and nod, because it's all I can do.

'Thank you,' she says. 'And I don't just mean for today. Thanks for doing life with me. It wouldn't have been the same without you.'

Her words are a lump hammer to my heart. I shake my head and put my arms around her, still unable to believe I am feeling the rush of her pulse, the warm press of her cheek to mine, for what I know will be the last time. How can she be dying, when she's right here, sitting by my side?

The tears start to stream. 'I don't know how to say goodbye to you.'

'Then let's not,' she whispers. 'Okay? Let's just say, see you later.'

I pull away and look into the fathomless blue of her eyes. Though she's crying too, she's still smiling. 'How are you so brave?' I ask her, through my tears.

'I'm not,' she says. 'I'm just very, very loved.'

★　　★　　★

In the car on the way home, I open the envelope she passed to me before we left.

Inside is a postcard of a Californian sunrise. On the reverse, she's simply scribbled, *Make the most of every one x*

Mum, who's driving, asks me what it says. But I can't answer. In fact, I can't speak at all. I just stare out of the window as the countryside becomes a motion-blur of tears.

52.

Six months later

Eight weeks after Lara's death, I fly to California, to stay with Felix. His place already feels oddly familiar to me, since Lara and I FaceTimed daily after she left Norfolk in December.

She passed away four months later, with Felix by her side, just as she'd wanted. And though I know some people questioned her choice to be on the other side of the world, it's clear to me as soon as I set eyes on the last view she ever saw – Felix's lavish green lawn with its fringe of cypress trees and decking overlooking a vast blue wilderness of ocean – that she made the right call. How could it not have been? She spent her final days on earth bathed in sunshine, with the man she loved, and all the care and attention she could ever need. Which was just so perfectly Lara. She did everything her way, right up till the end.

But after her living funeral, the actual funeral hit hard. Because although people tried to smile and be upbeat, and had dressed as she'd requested in bright colours, the day was bleak and sombre in the only way it ever could be at a crematorium, with Lara's coffin in front of us. But it was a warm spring morning, and the sun shone for the speeches at the wake. And the closure, ultimately, felt comforting. Like the gentle turning of a page. The start of a new chapter.

Felix takes me on a tour of his house, which seems to be full of people – family members, a gardener, a maid, and a couple of guys from his company who are working from one of the many office spaces.

The whole place is, by any measure, spectacular. There are bay views from the windows, and a stunning garden and infinity pool, the house itself a breathtaking fusion of concrete, glass and steel.

Felix tells me he sometimes rents it out to film and TV crews.

'For what kind of thing?'

'Well, no horror films,' he says. 'Only ever . . . feel-good stuff.'

I don't know if he's joking, but I like the sentiment.

It was always the sunrises here that Lara loved the most. When she was still able, she and Felix would head out onto the deck with a pile of blankets while the world was still dark, and hold hands as the horizon began to roar with colour. It was a daily comfort, she told me – witnessing the beauty of another dawn. She used to say it made her feel braver. That little bit more invincible.

When we reach the room where Lara spent her final few weeks and eventually passed away, Felix pauses.

I recognise every inch of it. The walnut floor and expansive windows. The vast sofa that was folded out as a bed. Coffee-coloured linen, though when she was using it, it was always smothered in a cloud of cushions and quilts.

'Would you like some time alone?' Felix asks me, kindly.

Gratefully, I nod, because I've been wondering privately if I might be able to get a sense of her in here, somehow.

He leaves me and I go inside, shut the door, then take a tentative seat. The room is quiet and still. It smells faintly of frangipani flowers.

I run a hand over the surface of the sofa, hoping to alight on a patch where her palm was once, too. Instinctively, I scan the room for the water bottle she was always sipping from, and for the fan that was constantly on, despite the air-conditioning. For her silk pyjamas, her hairbrush, her lip balm.

The last thing she ever said to me was a whispered, 'Love you, Neve,' two nights before she died. And I knew, somehow, that she was close to the end. That she was ready to go. I took some time off work as I waited for news, wide awake each night with grief. I kept my curtains open. For some reason, I didn't want to take my eyes off the sky.

At one point, I felt the atmosphere shift slightly, a loss of pressure, like I was feeling her leave. Then, several minutes later, my phone rang. Felix. She was gone.

'We had time together,' I whisper to her now, letting a few tears fall, thinking back to what she said about Billy. 'And you were right, Lar. That's all that matters, in the end.'

Her childhood teddy bear is propped sweetly up in a corner of the sofa. I bend forward and pick him up, stroking his fur, which is silky now from years of repeated touch. He is just a bear, but he reminds me of her, somehow. He has kind, bright eyes. The softest heart.

As I prepare to leave the room, I hold his paw in my hand, momentarily unable to let go.

Evening approaches. There are still people milling around the house. I think that's how it is, when you're rich. You never have to be alone. I don't blame Felix for that. Back at home, I've been working late and going on midnight walks and keeping up with a constant carousel of friends, just so I never have to feel my own solitude.

Felix opens a bottle of champagne, for us to toast Lara. We take it outside to the lounge chairs on the decking. The sunset tonight is pure cinema, the air fresh with salt and night-blooming jasmine. Beyond the garden, the sea is deep and dark as a reservoir. It shifts slightly with the tide, its surface clotted with seaweed. I get the urge to shed my clothes, run down to it and jump in, to feel myself caught in the cold squeeze of its fist.

I imagine swimming out to a point where Lara is treading water, waiting for me. I picture her waving, the smile on her face.

Felix proposes a toast. Together, we raise cold glasses in the warm air, and drink to her.

We spend two restorative weeks together, hiking and sunbathing, eating well and drinking great wine. Felix becomes a firm friend. I feel healthier, revitalised. We play tennis most days. I try yoga, which I've always assumed I would never have the patience for, and am surprised to discover I enjoy it. I regularly sleep in till ten. Felix introduces me to his friends and family. I get to see his offices in Silicon Valley. There are drinks and barbecues at the house nearly every night. The mood, if not upbeat, is determined, at least. To honour Lara's passion for living. To pay tribute to the kind of life she would – should – have been enjoying now.

I enjoy the novelty of time off work. I haven't had two weeks' annual leave since I started at Kelley Lane eight years ago. Felix points out that taking holiday is essential for maintaining perspective and a clear head, and I have to say, I am starting to agree. True, I have checked my email occasionally, but Parveen is doing a fantastic job of holding the fort, and I am beginning to enjoy the feeling of opening my eyes in the morning and my first thoughts not being about my meeting schedule, or the problems on my to-do list that need solving, or Mrs Ogilvy's bespoke library shelving.

One night, Patrick, a friend of Felix's from San Francisco, finds me standing alone at the very end of the garden, looking out over the cove.

He touches my arm, making me jump.

'Sorry,' he says. 'Didn't mean to startle you.'

We've been out a couple of times, along with Felix and his wider circle, for drinks and dinner. He is handsome in a way that's hard to ignore, and he's charming, and athletic, and is very good at making me laugh.

'Not at all,' I say. 'I was in my own little world there.'

We stare out at the water together for a few moments. Its surface is spangled with moonlight. It reminds me of the view at night from Ash's apartment. But right now, Norwich feels a world away.

'I wanted to ask,' Patrick says quietly, eventually, 'if you'd be open to having dinner, just the two of us, before you leave?'

I look over at him and smile.

'Just something relaxed,' he says. 'I'd love to get to know you better.'

I wonder what Ash is doing right now. If he's thinking of me. Or if he's in a bar with a girl somewhere. It's been six months since we last spoke. How could I blame him, if he'd moved on in that time? If there's one thing I've learnt from Lara's death it's that life is short. You have to live it while you can.

But I'm not ready to move on yet. I still have so much I need to say to him.

I look kindly at Patrick, who is very sweet, with wholesome energy. 'I'm sorry. It wouldn't be right. I have some . . . unfinished business with someone, back at home.'

'No problem. Just . . . thought I'd ask.' Then he smiles, half raising both hands in a gentle gesture of acceptance, before walking slowly away in the darkness, back towards the house.

On my last morning, I get up at dawn, making my way outside and to the water's edge via the narrow steps leading down from Felix's garden. The sky is patched with lilac clouds, the blue sea unpleated by wind. I taste salt in the air, the sweet tang of morning. Above my head, a few gulls caw and soar, riding invisible breezes. The sight of their freedom comforts me. Because I am sure that freedom is where Lara lives now.

Lara. The other love of my life. I've begun to believe her spirit still lingers somewhere here – that maybe, right now, she is watching me and smiling, willing me to do this.

Long time coming, you idiot, I'm sure she'd say.

I finger the paper bag that's filled with the remains of everything I kept related to Jamie. I tipped it all into Felix's firepit last night. Tickets from *Mamma Mia!* Birthday and anniversary cards. Champagne corks. The insert from a London Grammar CD. Beer mats from pubs we'd been to. Cinema ticket stubs from before we were even officially dating. Answer sheets from quizzes, busy with Jamie's handwriting. Even crumpled parking tickets, from days spent at the beach.

I crouch down now and upturn the ashes into the water, watch the dusty residue of my former life get swallowed up by the sea.

The last remnants of a love for someone I thought I knew, but never actually did.

I wanted to do it here, because I know she would approve. I know she would be proud of me. I know she'd want to look on as I finally say goodbye.

53.

S oon enough I am back at work, and life is rolling unim-
aginably on.

Most days, it still feels impossible, the certainty I will
never see her again. During our lost decade, there was
always the chance that we would be reunited one day.
But it's a different thing entirely to know I definitely
won't be at her wedding, or her mine. That we won't ever
meet each other's babies. Or go out for coffee in our
retirement to bitch about the price of milk. That our
friendship won't ever evolve. That it will be permanently
frozen in time.

And Felix . . . He will move on, eventually. Of course he
will: he's only in his thirties. I know he'll always love Lara,
but one day, he will meet someone else. That's just the way
life goes.

So I do what I always do when I'm struggling to make
sense of things: I throw myself into work, staying in the
office until it's ten at night and my head is pounding, my
eyes stinging from staring at a screen. I get up before dawn
each day and power-walk around the block, not wanting to
be alone with my thoughts for too long. I start drinking
soluble vitamins as a substitute for food.

But, as with all sticking plasters, this strategy eventually begins to weaken. I begin losing weight and the headaches are lingering. I know this way of coping isn't actually coping at all.

I reconnect with my counsellor, Meena. I book a session, my first since Lara told me she was dying.

Meena asks how I'm dealing with it all.

'Work. Work helps.' I don't mention the headaches.

'How does it help?'

'It takes my mind off everything. And . . . I clean.'

She nods neutrally. 'You clean.'

'I know that sounds a bit . . . you know. But I find it calming. And I like the distraction.'

'What might happen if you weren't distracted?'

'I'd . . . fall apart.'

'Why do you think you'd fall apart?'

'Because I wouldn't be able to . . . The pain would be too much.' A sob rises in my throat, and I swallow it down.

'Have you ever done that before?'

'Done what?'

'Experienced your feelings without any distractions. Focused on what you're feeling, rather than jumping onto your laptop, or cleaning, or leaving the house?'

Why would anyone do that? 'I don't think so, no.'

'You know, the benefit of really allowing yourself to feel all your emotions in the present is that you can begin to process them, rather than storing them up to dwell on, weeks, months, or maybe years down the line. There's nothing wrong with healthy coping mechanisms – we all need them, in some form or another – but not if we use them to avoid our emotions altogether.'

Touché, I think.

'You strike me as someone who ruminates a lot over the past – and the future, too. But Neve, when we spend all of our time looking backwards, or focusing relentlessly on where we're going, we risk missing out on the life we're living right now.'

'I've stopped thinking about Jamie. And I'm not bitter any more. Despite everything that happened, I think it's still possible to . . . appreciate him for who he helped me become.'

Meena looks thoughtful. 'Who did Jamie help you become, do you think?'

'Well, he encouraged me to pursue my career. He taught me a lot about ambition, and—'

I stop myself abruptly. I so nearly said *love*. Old habits die hard, I guess.

'Lara was the one who suggested you might become an interior designer, wasn't she?'

Hmm. This woman has a better memory than a teenager with a grudge.

'And didn't you say she encouraged you, too, not to make your whole life about Jamie? To think about work and being solvent and standing on your own two feet?'

I concede the point, and shortly afterwards, our session comes to a close.

As I leave, I think about what she's said. I'd always been so certain it was Jamie who gave me the fire in my belly to really focus on my future. But now, as I make my way home through throngs of summer drinkers and football match-goers and couples strolling in the soft light of evening, I realise – perhaps for the first time – that all along, it was Lara. My wing woman. My sister.

It was Lara who proposed I work in interiors. Who pushed me to pursue it, to get work experience. Who reminded me there was more to life than what I had with Jamie. Who doggedly insisted I was my own, whole, person. Who taught me how to stand up for myself. Who showed me how to love, and how to be loyal, and that you can choose your family, if the one you were given isn't up to the task. And that even if you have all the money in the world, time – and time spent well – is the only thing that truly matters, in the end.

It was Lara who encouraged me to live a life bigger than the one I had planned for myself.

When I get home, I stand in the kitchen for a few moments. Everything is shiny. Everything is clean. Everything is calm.

It takes a monumental effort, but I switch off the light and my phone, and go to sit down on the sofa. And then I allow myself to sob, really sob. Harder than I've ever sobbed before in my life. The kind of tears that get so out of control, you begin to wonder if they might never stop.

Two days later, Kelley calls me into her office.

'How are you, Neve?' she says briskly.

(The correct answer to this is only ever, *Great, thank you, how are you?*)

'Great, thank you, how are you?'

'Take a seat.'

I obey swiftly. My heart rate rockets. I can't remember the last time Kelley encouraged anyone to make themselves comfortable in her office.

She gets straight to the point, telling me she's been impressed with my recent work, in particular my contribution to the refurbishment of a Cotswolds hotel which has been widely picked up by the design and interiors press. That project was complex, and coronary-level stressful. But it's been worth it now to know Kelley's taken notice.

'I'd like to offer you the role of head designer, Neve,' she says, with characteristic detachment, as if we're discussing the bin rota, or the merits of one electrician over another. 'It will mean longer hours and more responsibility, of course. But I'm sure you're up to the task.' She shoots me a smile so short-lived I half wonder if it was some sort of spasm.

I exhale slowly, trying to prevent myself from shaking with joy and resolving not to think yet about the *longer hours* comment, because in my case, I'm not too sure they exist. But right now, none of that matters. I've done it. I've made it. This is everything I've been working towards for years.

'Thank you. Thank you so much,' I say, blinking at the chandelier hanging from the ceiling of Kelley's office. *Don't cry, don't cry, don't cry.*

'No need for thanks. You deserve it,' she says, so briskly I almost laugh, because only Kelley could promote a person with the same cool indifference as if she were issuing a P45.

*   *   *

Parveen and I head to the pub after work for a mini-celebration, where together we scrutinise every last detail of my promotion – our key agreed highlights being the pay rise, and getting to share Kelley's assistant, and accompanying Kelley on a trip to Milan next month. Not to mention receiving my first ever company credit card. (We gloss over the extra pressure, and the stopping of more bucks with me. There'll be plenty of time for me to flip out about all that further down the line.)

'So, what's next?' Parveen asks me.

'How do you mean?'

'Well, what's your next big life goal? You've got the promotion. Now what?' She says this fondly, like she particularly loves my screwed-up way of thinking.

'Actually, I'm going to bathe in the glory of this for a while.'

She looks sceptical. 'I've never known you to bathe in the glory of anything.'

Considering the past couple of nights' skipped housework, I sip my drink, a tiny toast to myself. 'Well, this time, I think I'm genuinely ready to appreciate what I have right now. Or, I'm ready to try, at least.'

She laughs. 'Yeah, okay. Until next week.'

I ask after Maz and the twins. She tells me she's dreading the summer holidays, having to juggle childcare with Maz and her parents and her in-laws. 'This is what they don't tell you about having kids,' she says darkly. 'The logistics involved in trying to take time off *with your own husband*.'

'But the twins,' I say, with a smile, because Parveen's love for her kids is nothing short of ferocious.

'Hmm. Yeah, it would be easier if they weren't quite so bloody adorable.'

I get another round in. As I set down her drink, she asks if there's any news on the house.

Last week, my mother dropped a bombshell – and for once, it was the good kind. She told me she'd decided to move into what she calls Ralph's 'snazzy little apartment' on the south side of Norwich. Then she casually asked if I fancied taking over the house.

She was packing at the time, in preparation for the move. I was biting my fist, watching her stuff hair pieces, outdoor shoes and a fish poacher into the same box.

'What?' I said, when she asked, thinking I might have misheard. I couldn't even attribute it to her being tipsy, because miraculously, she was still sober – six whole months and counting.

'Move in here. You're always lecturing me about how much you love it.'

'I could never afford to buy this place.'

'Well, you could buy part of it and pay me rent on the rest, or something. I won't be paying anything at Ralph's, so . . .'

My tear ducts geared up. 'Mum . . . are you serious?'

She shrugged, like it was no big deal. 'Yes. This place always felt like a prison to me. Full of bad memories. You know I think he used to bring her back here sometimes, while I was out gigging?'

I nodded sadly, wondering if there would ever be a day when my mother might forget about Bev, the irony of which was not lost on me.

'I can't stand it,' she continued. 'I should have left years ago, moved on.'

'Yeah.' I smiled softly. 'I know how you feel.'

'Breathe some life back into it, darling. It's what you're good at, isn't it?'

After she asked, I did have to think long and hard about swapping my place for hers. At first, the prospect sat awkwardly inside me, pressing painfully against some of my more vital organs. But eventually, I said yes. I knew in my heart that I wanted to. That here, now, was a chance for a new start, to do something brave.

Straight away, the decision felt good. It's still scary, but good-scary. Every night since, I've sat cross-legged on my living room floor, surrounded by magazines, drawings, plans and mood boards, mapping out the restoration like I'm solving a crime. Which, I guess, in many ways I am.

Lara always loved Mum's house. I have still-vivid memories of her sipping coffee next to the double-height windows in the kitchen, hair dappled with sunshine, watching the world go by outside. I've already planned a full shelf of slogan mugs in her honour.

'We're talking to the solicitor next week,' I tell Parveen now.

She smiles. 'Look at you, you're buzzing. I never actually thought you'd leave your place.'

'Mum's house will be gorgeous too, eventually. I can't wait for you to see it.'

'So, I guess you do have another big project up your sleeve, then,' she says, with a wink.

'Yeah. But this time, I'm going to enjoy the process. Not obsess over the end result. I'm going to appreciate every day.'

Parveen laughs. 'You sound like a fridge magnet.' Then she pauses for a couple of moments before touching my arm. 'Listen, I meant to tell you. I saw Ash while you were in California. We were on site quite a bit together at Millbrook.'

'Oh.' I try to keep the trepidation from my voice. 'How is he? How's his leg?'

She blinks at me a couple of times. 'How's his leg? Is that really what you want to know?'

A beat. 'No, obviously.'

She draws a breath. 'Look, rumour has it, he's started dating someone. Lexie, from Tunstalls, apparently.'

'Oh.' I feel my heart peel apart in my chest. 'Does he know you know?'

'I guess so,' she says sadly. 'I mean, it doesn't seem like it's a secret.'

I nod slowly, trying to accept it, trying to feel happy for him. I did say, after all, that I would understand if he met someone else. All he's done is take me at my word.

'Do you think it's serious?' I ask Parveen.

'I'm not sure.' She tilts her head, her usually flawless forehead crumpled with frustration. 'Why haven't you been in touch with him?'

I get her confusion. It's been six months.

But I needed that time. I had to get my head together. I owed it to myself – and to Ash. I was long overdue unjumbling the emotions inside me. Figuring out how I truly felt about Jamie and Lara and the whole last decade of my life.

'I wasn't ready,' I say. 'I wasn't ready even before I met him, Parv. I treated him badly, and . . . he deserved better than that.'

'Were you unfaithful?' she asks, face braced like she's praying I won't say yes.

I shake my head. I still haven't told her the full story. And maybe I never will, since all I want now is to bring that chapter of my life to a close. 'No. But I wasn't honest with him. And I didn't always make him feel good about himself. And I needed to work through that, and if that means I've missed the boat with him, then . . . yes, that's something I'll always regret. But I'd rather regret doing the right thing than doing the wrong one.'

'So, what now?'

'I want to go and see him. But there's a couple of other people I need to see first.'

'I'm sorry,' is the first thing I say to Ed and Juliet, once I've handed Juliet my huge apology bouquet and they've shown me, in vague bewilderment, into their living room.

'Neve—' Juliet begins.

'No, I know. I know Ash is seeing someone else. And I get that he'd probably think it was weird, me just turning up on your doorstep like this. You do too, I'm sure. But I have to apologise to you for the way I behaved on your birthday. It was completely inappropriate, and for what it's worth . . . I no longer believe those things. A lot has changed since then. I was so busy obsessing about the past that I failed to notice the amazing person who was standing right in front of me. Your son,' I add quickly, for clarity.

They exchange a glance. 'Well,' Juliet says, 'I do feel partly to blame. I did press you rather hard that night to tell me what was on your mind.'

'It wasn't your fault. I should have kept it to myself. I didn't need to burden you with all that.'

'Well, thank you, Neve. I do appreciate you coming here to say that.'

'I just want you to know, I think the world of Ash. Truly.'

'Oh, that much was already clear to us.'

'We've actually been attending therapy as a family for a few months now,' says Ed. 'The four of us.'

'Oh,' I say, surprised and pleased. 'That's great.'

'We've found it to be incredibly beneficial so far. We feel closer to Ash than we have in a long time.'

'People act out of character when they're grieving, don't they?' Juliet says to me sympathetically. 'I once climbed into my mother's wardrobe and sat inside it for three hours, just to be close to the smell of her clothes. Just sat there, and breathed her in. Ed thought I'd gone mad, didn't you?'

'Well, you had, a little bit,' he says. 'But grief is a kind of madness, isn't it?'

I nod sadly. 'I just wish I'd dealt with what happened at the time, and not tried to paper over the cracks for so long.'

'Well,' Ed says, 'that's life, at the end of the day. You have to function to survive. You don't always have the time or the headspace or the money to do otherwise.'

'You're being very kind,' I say. 'I'm not sure Ash would think I deserve it.'

'I think he would. He talks about you a lot, in therapy,' Ed says.

My heart lifts. *He does?*

Juliet elbows him. 'That's supposed to be confidential.'

Ed raises his hands. 'Fine, sorry, I know. But . . . well. It's true.'

Juliet leans forward. 'I'm sure Ash would love to see you, Neve.'

'Is he . . .? I mean, I heard he's seeing someone. And the last thing I want is to get in the way of anything. Genuinely.'

This I mean with my whole heart. If Ash is happy now with someone else, I know I have no right to re-enter his life and demand to be in it. I had my chance, and I messed it up. Sometimes, you simply don't get a second shot.

Juliet evades the question by offering me tea, and then Ed changes the subject, asking me about work. Perhaps they don't feel it's their place to discuss it, which I understand.

I want so badly to know the truth about Ash's life right now, but at the same time . . . I don't. There's a part of me that's happy to remain ignorant for a while longer at least, to convince myself I might still be able to make things right.

It's as I'm leaving that Juliet looks me in the eye and says, 'Neve. I probably shouldn't be saying this, because it's really not my place to, but . . . all those qualities of your ex-boyfriend that you admired so much . . . the things you loved about him that you saw in Ash . . .'

'Yes,' I say, tentatively, because she doesn't know, of course, who Jamie really was.

'Well, maybe you fell in love with your ex so you could one day recognise him again in Ash. What I mean is, maybe it was meant to be Ash all along.'

My eyes fill with tears.

Maybe it was never meant to be Jamie.

The idea sprouts wings inside me.

'Yes. Maybe. Maybe you're right.'

54.

It takes me a few days to muster up the courage to get in touch. Should I call him? Message? Send an email?

In the end, I opt to sit quietly on my sofa and ask Lara what she thinks I should do.

Doorstep him, she'd have said, without missing a beat. *It's the only way you'll get an authentic reaction.*

I decide she's right. Anyway, I'm reluctant to leave a trail of messages on his phone, in case this thing with Lexie is serious.

I get to his apartment at around eight o'clock on a Wednesday night. Midweek, I thought, I'll be more likely to catch him at home. But when I press the buzzer, there's no reply. I decide to wait for a bit, because I really can't bear to do this over the phone.

I sit down on the concrete step at the front of his building and watch people come and go. None of them are Ash. Traffic thrums from the road beyond the car park.

As the minutes pass, I start to think that maybe it was ill-thought-out to turn up without messaging first. Six months with no contact, and I just show up one night and expect him to be waiting for me?

And what if he suddenly arrives with Lexie? How could

I be willing to put him in that position? How could I do it to myself?

I get to my feet, sling my bag over my shoulder and prepare to make my way home. I'll email him instead, I decide. That way, he can choose whether he wants to see me, and can let me down gently if he doesn't.

But just as I am starting to walk off, a cab pulls up.

I feel my pulse in my throat as I watch him climb out from the back of it.

He is alone.

The cab turns around, and he is almost at the front door when he sees me.

He takes a single step forward.

'Hello,' is all he says.

I had a bit of a speech prepared. But it goes out of my head as soon as his eyes meet mine, and I feel the kinetic rush of just being close to him again.

'How are you?' I ask, because I'm not quite sure how to begin.

'I'm okay.' He swallows. 'Have you . . . been here long?'

'I'm sorry,' I say, the words tumbling from my mouth. 'For not seeing you for who you really were. Even though I loved you all along, I know comparing you to Jamie was really disrespectful and short-sighted and cruel and I'm so, so *sorry*, Ash.'

It takes him a long time to reply. Eventually, he just says gruffly, 'You'd better come in.'

★   ★   ★

I'd imagined, for some reason, that within seconds, we would slip straight back to how we were. That we'd share a look, or a laugh, and be away. But in the lift, we say nothing, nor do we make eye contact. You could measure the tension in voltage. I think about Lexie, and wonder if he's annoyed that I have just shown up like this.

Once we're inside, he asks me to give him a minute, then disappears towards the bedroom.

I look around as I wait, finally able to see the apartment as Ash's home, and not just a version of something Jamie once wanted. I pace a small circuit of the space, running a hand over the window frames and bricks and steelwork, taking in their textures with my fingertips, just as I did the first time I came here. I look at the lamps I picked out, and the cushions and console tables and rugs – all back in place now – and feel the open wound of my regret. Why couldn't I have come to my senses before I destroyed what we had? Before he met someone else?

I scan the room for hints of her, but there are none. I know it's not my right to care, but I do. I care so much, it's setting fire to my insides.

Pausing by the windows, I survey the star-speckled sky, the dark slither of river. The city at night is a carpet of lights. And – possibly for the first time – I am not thinking, *Jamie would have loved this*, but *I can see why Ash loves this*.

Behind me, I hear him clear his throat. I turn around. He's swapped his work clothes for a sweater and jeans. Tonight, he is clean-shaven. His dark hair looks newly trimmed.

'Okay,' he says calmly, like he's ready now to hear what I have to say.

I have thought so hard about this moment. My first instinct was that I should open by telling him Lara is dead, but I know I cannot. That has to come later. I can't risk clouding his reaction by eliciting his pity. I have to know how he really feels.

I draw a couple of tense breaths. The fear of rejection is making me shake. 'I need to tell you that . . . it turns out Jamie never really loved me. He was cheating on me – he was planning to leave me for someone else on the night he died – and I know you'll think I'm only here because Jamie was a cheat and a liar, but . . . you're wrong. I'm here because I missed what was staring me in the face all along, which was you, Ash. You, and not Jamie's ghost.'

'Neve—'

'No, don't say it. I mean, I know you're seeing Lexie from Tunstalls and I don't *at all* expect you to forgive me. I know we can't just go back to what we were. And I'm not asking you to pick me over her, or anything like that. I have zero expectations, I swear. I just . . . had to let you know. I had to tell you I'm sorry.'

He just listens, his expression calm as open water, his dark eyes patient.

'I never told Jamie about what his mum did, you know. Asking me to get an abortion. I never told him, and I convinced myself that was because I loved him too much to break his heart, but I actually think it was because I didn't feel good enough to say, *You know what? I'm better than this.* I never spoke up for myself. I was always too scared to rock the boat. But now I know – I *am* better than that. I'm better than losing the rest of my life to the memory of a man who never loved me to begin with.'

'Yes,' Ash says softly. 'You are.'

'I . . . I started seeing a counsellor. And she made me realise that everything I used to think . . . I had it the wrong way round, Ash. Yes, there are similarities between you and Jamie, but there are actually way more differences. She asked me to make a list.' I remove a piece of paper from my pocket.

'Neve . . .'

I ignore him. 'And I did start making it. But then I thought, this is all really missing the point a bit, isn't it? Because I *know* you were never Jamie. You're a million times the person he ever was.' I rip the piece of paper in two, letting its halves flutter down to the floor. 'Actually, you're beyond compare. You're your own, incredible person, and . . . I've said goodbye to Jamie now, for ever. I'm never going to think about him again.'

I draw a breath. He is just watching me, his eyes steady.

My heart flails helplessly through the seconds that follow.

'I'm not seeing Lexie from Tunstalls.'

'Oh.' A beat. 'I thought . . . Parveen said . . .'

'Well, what happened was that I went on two dates with her and realised . . . she wasn't you.' He shrugs, almost like he's powerless but glad to be. 'It's always been you, Neve.'

My blood rushes, a spring tide of hope. 'I loved you all along. I was just too caught up to see it.'

'That's . . . unbelievably good to know.'

'I really want to . . . If *you* want to, that is—'

'There's nothing I want more.'

I am giddy with relief. And now, at last, he closes the space between us, a smile on his face. In the next second, his lips are on mine. And it is the best kiss of my life, an expression of love as fierce and firm as I have ever known it, a landslide of emotions, every one of them finally real.

Acknowledgements

This novel started life in a very different form to the book you are holding now, and I owe a huge debt of gratitude to everyone who helped bring it into being. Firstly, my wonderful agent Rebecca Ritchie at AM Heath, for all your ideas, wise words and unfailing encouragement. And Kimberley Atkins, the world's most patient, passionate and astute editor. You are always so brilliant at helping me figure out what is really at the heart of an idea, so for this – and the many suggestions, and all-round editorial excellence – thank you. To my German publishers Blanvalet, and Olivia Robertshaw, for your valuable insights and feedback. Helen Parham for expert copyediting, the ever-incredible rights and sales teams, and everyone at Hodder – you are all superstars. I feel so lucky every day to have you on my side.

Thanks also to Euan Thorneycroft and Harmony Leung at AM Heath, for your guidance and support. And to all the book bloggers, bookstagrammers and reviewers, and everyone who has taken the time to read and review my books – I am so grateful, and for ever in awe at what you do.

I would like to say a huge thank you as well to Meena Kumari for bidding so generously in the Young Lives vs

Cancer Good Books auction. I was honoured to be able to name a character after you. To find out more about the vital work Young Lives vs Cancer do supporting children and young people with cancer, and their families, visit: younglivesvscancer.org.uk

Thanks too, as ever, to my husband Mark, and my friends and family.

And finally, to you, the reader. Writing novels for a living is a pleasure and a privilege, and it is because of you that I get to do it. Thank you.

Unforgettable love stories by bestselling author Holly Miller

 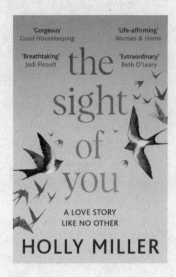

What Might Have Been and *The Sight of You* out now in paperback

'Unique and breathtaking' **Jodi Picoult**

'Clever, poignant and very special' ***Woman & Home***

'Extraordinary' **Beth O'Leary**

'A heartrending, beautifully crafted emotional rollercoaster' **Mike Gayle**

'A gorgeous, unusual love story' ***Good Housekeeping***

The Age Gap **coming Spring 2025!**